An excerpt from *Secret Heir for Christmas* by LaQuette

# Carter tipped his beer toward Stephan and offered him a playful wink.

He was trying to keep things light, even if everything about his reaction to this man was over-the-top. "Even better reason we should link up. We're the two newbies on the block."

Stephan locked gazes with him, his stare was unwavering, as if he were attempting to see if there was more to Carter's nice-guy act than just him trying to be nice.

Stephan looked up at him again and the grief was still there, but there was something else, something so intense it made Carter squeeze his beer bottle so hard, he worried he might break it in his hand.

"I don't know how much of a friend I could be right now. But I sure as hell wouldn't mind a distraction."

Stephan licked his lips and every muscle tightened in Carter's body wondering what those thick pillows would feel like pressed against his skin. Was he this hard up that he was actually standing here low-key letting a man who was obviously going through something hit on him?

"You wouldn't ___ know of any distractions I could get in ___

## "I have to deal with her. When is she due in studio?"

Mia had put it off as long as she could but it was time to face her past, present and possibly her future. The success of the show depended on Saira. She was the star, the one for whom the show was written. Mia wasn't going to let Saira ruin her big chance.

"She's been here all morning—met with the studio execs, did the rounds."

Saira hadn't come to see Mia. At least she wasn't the only one avoiding their meeting.

Gail tapped on her phone. "Speak of the devil—she's in wardrobe, and Jessica says there's a problem."

Mia took a breath. The former director had let Saira run roughshod over him. They were already behind schedule and over budget because of all the changes she'd requested. It was time to show her former lover that the new boss wasn't going to tolerate her diva-ness.

# LaQUETTE
# &
# SOPHIA SINGH SASSON

---

## SECRET HEIR FOR CHRISTMAS
## &
## TEMPTED BY THE BOLLYWOOD STAR

Recycling programs
for this product may
not exist in your area.

ISBN-13: 978-1-335-45786-8

Secret Heir for Christmas & Tempted by the Bollywood Star

Copyright © 2023 by Harlequin Enterprises ULC

Secret Heir for Christmas
Copyright © 2023 by Laquette R. Holmes

Tempted by the Bollywood Star
Copyright © 2023 by Sophia Singh Sasson

For questions and comments about the quality of this book,
please contact us at CustomerService@Harlequin.com.

Harlequin Enterprises ULC
22 Adelaide St. West, 41st Floor
Toronto, Ontario M5H 4E3, Canada
www.Harlequin.com

**Printed in U.S.A.**

# CONTENTS

**LaQuette** writes sexy, stylish and sensational romance. That means she writes sentimental and steamy stories (like Hallmark movies, but with a lot of sex) featuring at least one main character who always keeps it cute.

This Brooklyn native writes unapologetically bold, character-driven stories. Her novels feature diverse ensemble casts who are confident in their right to appear on the page. If she's not writing, she's probably trying on or looking for her next great makeup find. Contact her at dot.cards/laquette.

### Books by LaQuette

### Harlequin Desire

### *Texas Cattleman's Club*

*Cinderella Masquerade*
*Designs on a Rancher*

### *Devereaux Inc.*

*A Very Intimate Takeover*
*Backstage Benefits*
*One Night Expectations*
*Secret Heir for Christmas*

Visit the Author Profile page
at Harlequin.com for more titles.

You can also find LaQuette on Facebook,
along with other Harlequin Desire authors,
at Facebook.com/HarlequinDesireAuthors!

Dear Reader,

Welcome back to Brooklyn in the fourth installment of the Devereaux Inc. saga, *Secret Heir for Christmas*.

Stephan and Carter are each dedicated to the protection of their families. Unfortunately, both have taken their mutual need to protect to an extreme that's left little time for anything but family and work. However, when the broody Stephan returns home to Brooklyn to spend time with his dying uncle, Ace, and give his patriarch one last family Christmas, he finds Carter, his annoyingly sexy new neighbor living next door. Their chemistry is instant, and it doesn't take long before they give in to their shared attraction.

It's just supposed to be a holiday fling. So, keeping his identity hidden as an heir to the Devereaux throne shouldn't be that big of a deal, right? While Ace's life draws to an end, Stephan finds himself falling for not just Carter, but his precocious six-year-old daughter, Nevaeh, too. Though neither of them can admit it, Stephan and Carter are forced to realize that their connection is so much more than fun. As their heated bond grows, they'll have to ask themselves one question: Can they reveal the truth of who they are behind their shield of secrets, guilt and lies to find their Christmas miracle—a forever love neither of them knew they wanted?

Keep it sexy!

*LaQuette*

# SECRET HEIR
# FOR CHRISTMAS

## LaQuette

To my late grandfather, James Davidson.
I still feel your guiding hand on my shoulder
and your dedication and love surrounding me.
You were my Ace Devereaux in the flesh,
and I will never forget just how much
you meant and still mean to me.

# One

"There you are?"

Stephan looked up to find his uncle, David Devereaux, taking the last step on the staircase on the opposite side of the foyer door. Although younger than Ace by just shy of a decade, he and Ace were almost identical. So much so, there used to be a time where Stephan had difficulty telling the two men apart when he was a child.

But now, without the shroud of sickness and pallor around him, the distinction between the two men was sharply emphasized.

"Hi, Uncle David" Stephan stepped in, closing the foyer door and trying to leave the November chill outside. He quickly hung up his coat in a nearby closet and then stepped into the waiting hug David had for him.

He was grown. Thirty-eight years grown to be exact, and he had not a shred of shame in the absolute comfort he felt in being embraced so lovingly by his uncle. With the exception of his mother—whose normal disposition was icy, if he were being nice, and downright mean if he was telling the truth—most everyone in his family was down for a good hug whenever, wherever they could share one.

And right now, in the midst of all they were dealing with, it was almost impossible not to pass each other without doling a handful out.

"How you doing, Unc?"

David's eyes brightened and he cupped each side of Stephan's face with a warm hand.

"My baby nephew is standing before me instead of being more than three thousand miles away on another continent, and my only brother is still here for me to hold and tell him I love him. Add to the fact that Amara and Lennox are about to give me my first great-grand, and there's not much to complain about. Even if I wanted to."

Stephan marveled at how a man who'd lived to see his late sixties could carry the "I won't complain" motto around with such grace and humility. But even while losing his only brother, he still found a reason to hold on to joy.

Stephan closed his eyes, trying to soak up the love and warmth radiating from his uncle's hands, permeating his skin, and filling him with the strength he needed, that they all needed at this moment in life.

"Uncle David, you trying to make me feel guilty about being in Paris. You know I was over there working, right?"

"I know, nephew." David's smile grew. "But I still missed seeing your face every day while you were there. If nothing else comes of Ace's decline in health, at least it brought you home to us. I hope you're considering staying for good now that you're back."

Stephan's gut twisted into knots and the skin on his arms prickled with anxiety. Return for good? He hadn't even intended to be here for this long. He didn't regret coming home for Ace. There was no way he could've given up this time to spend Ace's last days with him. But being home wasn't a good thing for Stephan. Not when his mother's bitterness dogged him, and not when his presence threatened the well-being of his sister-in-love, Lyric.

David stood there, hope lightening his deep brown eyes, and Stephan had no idea what to say. It wasn't that he had a problem with being honest with his family members or telling them no. But David wasn't a stupid man. He was thorough, methodical, and analytical. It's why, until recently, he'd held the position of lead counsel for Devereaux Incorporated since the company's inception. Whatever Stephan said, he had no doubts his uncle would turn his answer over in his head, that eventually, he'd figure out why Stephan had left in the first place.

*Because my lies broke the family.*

"Is that my brother-in-love?" The boulder of guilt lodged in Stephan's gut shifted slightly.

Lyric Devereaux-Smith was his late brother Randall's widow. While Randall had been twenty years Lyric's senior, she was only a few years older than Stephan. This meant she'd fallen easily into their cousin group more than two decades ago.

"Come here, girl, and let me love on you."

Lyric squealed the same way she did every time she saw him after any time apart. Whether it was two days or two years, she always delighted in his presence. It was just one of the multitude of reasons staying away from his family hurt so much. Yet, he knew the alternative would bear even greater pain. Not just for him, but especially for the gentle soul who had her arms wrapped around him as she peppered his face with kisses the way only a sister could.

"You staying long? Josiah and I were gonna leave to go get something to eat. But if you're gonna be here for a bit, we can order in and hang with you"

He looked over Lyric's shoulder to find her man sitting in the living room off to the side of the foyer. Josiah gave him a quick nod to acknowledge Stephan's presence, followed by a light thumping of his fist over his heart.

Admittedly, he and Josiah didn't know each other that well. But as long as his beloved Lyric kept that ridiculous smile on her face, Stephan had no objections to Josiah whatsoever.

Stephan loved Lyric.

She'd been more than Randall's wife for two decades. She'd been his sister from the moment Randall had brought her home. He'd adored his big brother, but the love he had for Lyric and the way she'd made him feel wanted, cherished, and not a nuisance, as his mother and brother had, it meant there wasn't much in this world Stephan wouldn't do to keep her happy and safe. Something his brother and mother hadn't been so concerned with.

"Nah," Stephan replied. "I'm running behind for something I have to do anyway."

He lied. There wasn't a damn thing he had to do later. He just couldn't stay in her presence. Not knowing what he'd done. Not knowing the harm he could still do if the truth ever crossed his lips.

"I just came to sit with Uncle Ace for a bit before I head out."

He hugged her again, and by the time he released her, Josiah was behind her, extending one hand to Stephan as he wrapped the other around Lyric's shoulder.

"Good to see you again, Stephan."

"You make sure to take good care of my sister."

"I always do, my man. I always do."

Satisfied, he left his three family members standing in the foyer and made his way upstairs to Ace's room. The door was large, sitting at the top of the stairs, looming, making it impossible for him to forget what lay on the other side of it.

He took a breath, as he always did since he'd returned home to find his uncle slowly succumbing to cancer's hold. It was time to put on the mask. Time to find the joy and love he needed to impart to Ace.

The love part was easy. Ace had showered him with so much love growing up, he'd been a decidedly neutralizing effect on Martha's acrid and detached demeanor.

But finding the joy right now, when he knew how Ace was suffering, when he knew how much it hurt to think of not having his uncle in his life anymore, that was the hard part.

One last breath in, then Stephan squared his shoulders and knocked lightly on the door before twisting the knob and slowly opening it.

There, in the center of the room was his uncle, Jordan Dylan Devereaux, I, aka Ace. His thin frame was covered with his signature silk pajamas. Today's were a royal purple, a stark contrast to Ace's pale brown skin. Regardless of how sickness dogged him, he sat in the middle of his bed, the perfect statesman, waiting for his next visitor to enter.

"There's my favorite nephew."

Stephan shook his head. "I win that prize because I'm your only one?"

Ace shook his head. "Not the only, just the only one…" Ace stopped as if he couldn't bring himself to say the words. Stephan didn't blame him. Thinking of Randall in the past tense was still difficult for him too.

Ace looked to the large clock sitting on a far-off wall and brought a reprimanding gaze back to Stephan.

"It is well after dinnertime on a Friday night. Why are you not out and about doing what young people do?"

"Thirty-eight ain't all that young, Uncle Ace. After work there are only two places I want to be—here with you, or in my bed asleep."

The amount of pity in the old man's eyes told Stephan exactly what he was thinking.

"You have life. Take it from an old fool who wasted too much of his, go out and live. Go meet new people. Go find love. And if you can't find love, have a whole lot of fun practicing. Don't waste any time on me."

Stephan stepped closer to Ace's bed, sitting slowly next to the spot the man had patted with his hand.

"There's no place in this world I would rather be than here with you, old man. Why are you trying to run me off when I just got here?"

"Because I've lived my life, baby boy. I want you to do the same. I won't be here for much longer."

Stephan bristled at the truth in Ace's words. "Uncle Ace, the last time I checked, God wasn't one of your names. You've beat this thing longer than the six months the doctors originally gave you. Who's to say you won't continue to put cancer on its ass?"

Ace pointed a finger at himself as a weary smile hung on his mouth.

"I wouldn't exactly call this beating cancer's ass. I'm still here and I'm grateful for that. But I'm tired,

Stephan, and the only reason I'm still here is because I haven't yet fulfilled my promise to my dearest Alva. When I know in my heart that all our babies are all right, then, and only then will I take my leave. As it stands, you're the only one left I need to look out for."

Stephan snickered. Not that he found anything remotely funny about this situation. But he knew if he didn't laugh, the ball of grief growing at the base of his throat would be too large to breathe around soon if he didn't disrupt it.

"I don't want to talk about this, Uncle Ace. It's morbid. And if death wants you, he's gotta go through me. And for the record, I'on think death's really ready to catch these hands."

Ace's eyes lit up with amusement until laughter shook his frail frame. Stephan was sure it was the absurdity of the image of him literally coming to fisticuffs with the Grim Reaper that had Ace's infirm voice sounding the slightest bit fuller and lighter, and he didn't care. The joy illuminating Ace's face was enough to fill Stephan's heart with a lifetime of contentment.

Ace wiped the sides of his damp eyes while finally exacting some control over his amusement.

"While I would definitely pay money to see that brawl, I don't think it's one you will win."

Ace reached for Stephan's hand, giving it a squeeze.

"A foolish man wastes his time trying to run from death. A wise man embraces it and spends his time enjoying and appreciating every moment he's granted."

Stephan could definitely see the truth in Ace's words. It didn't mean it made his heart hurt any less, though.

"Stephan, I know that if I tell you not to worry yourself trying to take care of the rest of the Devereaux cousins, you'll just ignore me. You're very much like me in that respect. Taking care of those we love is instinctual. It's encoded in our DNA."

There was no need for Stephan to deny the veracity of Ace's claim. The fact was, he'd hightailed it on the first thing smoking back to the States as soon as he'd heard Ace's condition wasn't as stable as the old man had led him to believe. If that wasn't proof that he had helicopter parent written in his future, Stephan didn't know what was.

"You can't stop loving your people, Stephan. But if you're going to pour so much into them, suffer so much for them, you must have someone to pour into you so that beautiful light of yours doesn't go dim."

Ace's words were precise, cleaving his heart in two like a heated scalpel cutting clean through his flesh.

"All of the Devereaux cousins will have a role to play in this family once I'm gone. You're all gonna try to give your all to cover up your broken hearts. Which means all of you will need a rudder to help you navigate. Your cousins have that, Stephan. If you don't find something or someone to hold you together soon, I'm afraid you will destroy that big beautiful heart of yours. And we both know that if you fall, you have secrets that could tear this family apart."

Stephan stood up, walking to the window. It was almost winter, so the sun had disappeared into the horizon long ago leaving behind a midnight blue sky, whose inky hue felt like a replica of the darkness floating around in his soul.

"Are you asking me to keep those secrets to the detriment of myself?"

"No." Ace's response was clear, even in his frail state. "I would never ask that of you. I've begged you to let me set you free of these secrets for a long time. I never agreed with you having to swallow all of this down. You were so busy protecting everyone else, you wouldn't even take time to mourn the brother you'd lost."

Stephan shoved his hands into his slacks, his heart beating in his chest and his emotions welling up so fast that he was afraid he'd shatter into pieces right there.

He'd mourned his brother.

Every day of the last two years. Even more so when he was away from his family in Paris, paying penance for the secrets he held to protect those he loved the most. He hadn't stopped grieving as far as he was concerned.

"I don't know what you want from me, Uncle Ace."

"I want you to give yourself permission to be free so you can open your heart up again and let love in."

"There's no room for anything but this weight that my brother forced me to carry. You know that, Uncle Ace."

"Come here, baby boy."

There was nothing like the elders in your life reminding you that no matter how grown you got, you'd never be more of an adult than them.

He'd like to say he hated it. Well, he certainly hated it whenever his mother tried to pull rank like that. But when Ace did it, it always seemed so loving that Stephan could never find even a sliver of anger to toss at Ace.

He returned to Ace's bedside, lowering himself on the mattress and waiting for his uncle to speak again.

"Let me take this burden to the grave with me, Stephan. I should never have allowed you to take it up in the first place. You were hurting so much, and you insisted this was the only way. But if I'd known it would take you from me, I never would've gone along with it. Please, let me take this from you."

Stephan could feel the fire of pain filling him. His entire body tensed, trying to cage it all in.

"I can't do that, uncle."

Ace's smile was sad, his mouth slightly drooping as he took in the picture of Stephan.

"I somehow knew that would be your answer. So, here's my counter."

Ace held up two fingers as he looked Stephan directly in the eye. "I have two conditions." Even in his current state with his body appearing so thin and feeble, a light breeze could probably topple him over, Ace was still the ultimate businessman. He'd wheeled and dealed, until he'd made his company a household brand and his name a bright star in the sky. Stephan should've known that dying of cancer wouldn't be the thing to deter the man's command and spirit.

"I cannot have you sitting here waiting for me to die. If you won't let me lift this from your shoulders, then I want to see you spend a little time every day finding joy outside of this family, outside of our business, and outside of me."

Stephan tilted his head, watching Ace, trying to suss out exactly what Ace was playing at.

"So, you're saying I can't come visit you?"

"No." Ace chuckled and shook his head as if to say, *this simple boy.* "I'm saying that when you do, I want you to share verifiable proof that you are out there living and experiencing life."

"What the hell does that mean, Uncle Ace. How am I supposed to prove that I'm living life?"

Much like when Stephan was a child and Ace had given him a directive, the man simply sat back, raised a brow, and dared Stephan to say another word. In Ace's generation, grown folks didn't explain themselves to the younger generations. Apparently that dynamic hadn't changed even now when Stephan was nearing forty.

He took a deep breath, realizing being ticked off

with a dying man probably wasn't going to gain him any brownie points in the karma department.

"What's the next condition?"

Satisfied with Stephan's acceptance of the situation, Ace continued.

"I want to experience joy myself. And as time slips away from me, my mind keeps drifting back to those wonderful Christmas parties we used to have. You remember them, don't you?"

He certainly did. Every year, Ace would go all out hiring the party planner de jour to turn Borough Hall into a Christmas delight. Devereauxs from all over the globe would gather and literally eat, drink, and be merry throughout the night until the wee hours of the morning.

Those parties, more like galas, were the high point of the year, and Stephan had always looked forward to them. Until two years ago. Randall's passing, and Stephan's departure immediately after the funeral, had seemed to erase Ace's drive to put it all together.

"Your Aunt Alva began the tradition when we married. I kept it going after she died to keep her close to my heart. I want to experience one last Devereaux Christmas and I want you to plan it for me. This way, you'll know how to carry on the torch when I'm gone."

"Uncle Ace. I don't think anyone in the family is up for a party right now, least of all you."

"I am still the patriarch of our family, and my word is still law as far as our bloodline is concerned. You will do these things I have asked, or I will set you free of your burden whether you want to be free or not. What say you, young man?"

Ace squared his shoulders as best he could, daring Stephan to challenge him again. The old man's ability to control the room, even from his deathbed, was unmatched and Stephan knew he was outranked immediately.

He scratched his hand lightly against his beard pretending consideration of his imaginary options. They both knew he was caught and there wasn't a thing he could do about it. Not if he wanted to protect his sister-in-love, and even though she deserved it least of all, his mother.

"I guess it's a good thing mistletoe is in season. Seems I'm going to need a lot of it."

# Two

Stephan walked Gates Avenue, to get to his Grand Avenue home. Walking through Brooklyn had always been a way to clear his head when he needed it, and right now, after dealing with his difficult uncle, the crisp air and the concrete sidewalks were exactly what he needed.

He'd just crossed Washington Avenue when his gaze landed on Brown Memorial Baptist Church. The bright red brick building had been standing since 1958. The purplish-blue sky of the evening already settled over the large structure, but even in the coming night, it stood as a beacon to the community.

It reminded him of Ace, strong, vivid, and able to weather the test of time. But now where slightly visible wear on the building stood as a proud reminder of what it had endured, Ace's frail shell showed anyone at a glance that he'd soon leave this world. And as much as the old man aggravated him tonight with talks of Stephan settling down and planning a blasted Christmas party, knowing he was leaving soon plagued Stephan like an ulcer eating away at his insides.

"Well—" he leaned his head upward as he looked at the church "—if the sight of you can't bring me comfort, then I know what will."

He opened the Lyft app on his phone and typed in his destination. Walking to Fulton Street and Franklin Avenue wasn't that long of a trek, but he just couldn't spare the energy to take the first step on his journey.

Brooklyn neighborhoods were densely populated with attached homes and buildings lining each street. Like many places in New York City, real estate was built up not out. That meant fitting more people into homes while minimizing how much land was needed. That translated into a large amount of people in the area, but also meant there was less space for things like parking and driveways.

His cars were stored in a private parking facility nearby. He didn't really need them. He never traveled more than walking distances in any direction from his house. If he needed to, there were always rideshares or buses and subways to get where he needed to go.

When his ride was confirmed to be a few moments away, Stephan shoved the phone in to his pocket, knowing his refusal to chart another path was just the reason Ace was strong-arming him into this proof-of-joy nonsense. He understood that completely. He also understood that Ace was trying to help, not harm him, as a means for Stephan to open up and not keep everything so bottled up inside.

But sharing who he was had only ever brought pain, and so there wasn't a chance in hell he was going to willingly cut himself open for all to see his flaws and failings, not even for Ace.

The world thought it was so easy being a Devereaux.

That was a whole lie.

Nothing had ever come easy to Stephan, not the things that mattered anyway.

People only wanted to be around him for what he could do for them, in both the professional and the personal. And after the last time he'd dared let someone inside, they'd repaid him by blackmailing him in his darkest hour.

That had been the case with Dexter. The last man Stephan had ever let get close to him. Dexter and Stephan had met in Jamaica six months after Randall's death. Stephan had gone there on official Devereaux Inc. business, but the real reason he'd volunteered for the trip was one, he needed to make sure the secrets the beautiful island held for his brother would never come to light. But most of all, he'd gone there hoping to find some kind of closure.

He'd met Dexter in a club for the elite and they'd instantly been on fire. Finding that sort of happiness when you'd suffered a tragic loss turned out to be dangerous. A month later, Dexter was living with him in Paris. And when he caught Dexter with another man in Stephan's bed four months after that, the nightmare he'd have to endure to rid himself of Dexter, began.

Dexter had apparently figured he'd need an insurance policy just in case shit went sideways between them and he lost his meal ticket. To find what he needed, Dexter had bypassed Stephan's security on his personal laptop and discovered enough information about Randall's death to blackmail Stephan.

Evicting that man out of his life had cost Stephan his already compromised ability to trust, the trouble of having his legal team put together an ironclad NDA, and a five-million-dollar payoff.

After that debacle, people in hell had a greater chance of getting ice water than Ace had of getting Stephan to let anyone else inside.

Just as he'd come to that conclusion, his ride arrived, and within minutes he was standing in front of Crown Fried Chicken on Fulton Street and Franklin Avenue. He was certain his salvation couldn't be found in this place. But his momentary comfort, yeah, it had that in spades.

Stephan stepped inside of the storefront that

barely held enough room to house more than a few customers at a time. The entire food counter was shielded behind a wall of plexiglass, so he had to bend down from his six-two height to speak into the order window.

No, it wasn't the most ideal dining experience, but the salty, fried goodness of the dirty wings would more than make up for that.

Stephan ordered from memory, even two years of fine dining in Paris couldn't dim his recollection of everything he liked at chain stores like this. Dirty wings were fried crispy, seasoned well enough to give a mythical giant high blood pressure, and best of all, cheap. He was a billionaire, that didn't mean he didn't enjoy a good bargain too.

As he pulled out his debit card to pay for his food, he wished decisions regarding his real life—especially where matters of family, trust, and love were concerned—were as sure and uncomplicated.

He stepped outside, watching the hustle of Fulton Street rush hour traffic, filled with cars and B25 MTA buses and bicyclists and pedestrians weaving their way through the smallest of openings to get to their destination.

The chaos of it all calmed him, made his brain stop thinking and the unsettled anxious feeling that had shrouded him since he left Ace's house, quiet. But soon enough his order was up and he was walking the remaining five blocks to his home. All he wanted to do was get inside his house, strip out of his suit, and plop down on his living room floor as he ate his dirty wings and watched trash TV.

After the shitty day he'd had, that shouldn't be too much to ask, right?

"Hey, mister!"

Stephan couldn't focus on the small distant voice. He ignored it, allowing it to fade into the background noise of a Brooklyn street.

He stood at his door, balancing his key in one hand and a large red slushy and a bag with a twelve-piece of fried wings, fries, and a sweet potato pie.

After spending two years in Paris with all its fine dining, being a car ride away from one of his old Brooklyn haunts was a familiar joy that he'd desperately needed at this moment.

He'd been home for four months now, but spending nearly every day at Devereaux Inc.'s Brooklyn headquarters and every night at his Uncle Ace's bedside, there had been few opportunities to venture off to hit up the hole-in-the wall spots like Crown Fried Chicken that only born and bred Brooklynites could appreciate.

Sure, he could've used a food delivery app to get it. However, he figured if he wasn't going to employ any restraint when it came to indulging this way, if he wanted it bad enough, he should at least go get it himself.

Between the sodium, fat, sugar, and carbs in the bag, he was certain he could put himself into a food coma so he wouldn't have to deal with the pain of impending grief trying to swallow him whole from the inside out or the frustration that Ace had forced on him.

He'd just gotten the door open when he heard the small voice again, closer this time, three seconds too late.

Just as he looked around, he saw a little girl with wild brown curls in every direction that fell all around her shoulders. She was waving her hand, trying to get Stephan's attention, and by the time she did, he felt something small and furry bump across his ankle.

He jerked back, losing his balance as a blur of black fur ran in circles around his ankles before darting inside of Stephan's half-opened door.

Stephan felt himself falling backward as wet cold spread across his pecs when his cup tipped over and the red slushy bled all over his Armani shirt and suit jacket, and his wool peacoat.

Stephan expected to hit the hard concrete steps in front of his door, but instead, he hit a wall of hard flesh instead.

The only voice he'd heard he assumed belonged to the brown-skin sprite that had been calling him before. She couldn't have been any more than five, maybe six. There was no way she had the strength or the muscles to hold up his six-foot-two-inch frame.

"I gotcha."

The voice was deep and smooth, like a fine bourbon that you sipped to savor its rich flavor.

When Stephan could feel the ground beneath his feet again, he turned to finally lay eyes on the owner of the voice, the person who'd saved him.

Deep brown eyes, tan skin, and high cheekbones filled his gaze. Of their own volition, his eyes continued to take in his apparent savior. Jet-black hair combed back off his face. It was tapered on the sides, and Stephan could see just the tiniest hint of gray teasing at his hero's temples, and a few more sprinkled into his neat, close-cropped beard.

*Damn, he's pretty.*

*Pretty* was an understatement. Now that Stephan was standing mostly on his own, he could see the man was an inch shorter than him, but matched him in the same lean but muscular build.

"Mister—" Stephan could hear that little insistent voice again "—can I go get Ebony?"

Tugging on the hemline of his coat broke through the mesmerizing hold the stranger's gaze had on Stephan, finally making him look down to see a smaller version of the same gaze staring up at him.

"E-ebony?" Stephan stammered. "Who's Ebony?"

"My puppy," the little girl said.

Stephan blinked, trying to figure out what the child was talking about. If he wasn't so busy staring at the beautiful man standing in front of him, he might be able to make some sense of what was going on.

"Nevaeh." That molten voice spoke and Stephan was forced to look into those hypnotic eyes again.

"I think we've disturbed this man enough. Go and ask your grannie to fix you a snack. I'll get Ebony."

The little girl nodded, nearly skipping down the stairs and walking to an older woman waving from the stoop three to four doors down the block.

"I'm sorry. This is a hell of a way to introduce myself to my new neighbor."

A crooked smile tilted his tempting mouth, dragging Stephan's eyes directly to it.

"I'm Carter Jiménez." Carter held out his hand. "That little busybody tugging on your jacket was my daughter Nevaeh, and the little menace that escaped into your house is our new black lab, Ebony."

Stephan instinctively went to shake Carter's hand until he saw the red sticky remnants of his slushy all over his palm.

"Are you new on the block?" Carter's voice pulled Stephan's attention away from his very messy state. "I don't recall seeing you around much."

Stephan's personal alarm went off. As a Devereaux, he was always suspicious when random folks asked questions about him. Not that he believed himself to be so interesting, but when folks knew you came from a wealthy and powerful family, sometimes, they did strange things like sell information. The next thing he knew, he could end up on the Shade Room, being dragged for some filth he hadn't even had the pleasure of curating himself.

"I travel overseas a lot for work, so that's probably why we haven't run into each other before." He pulled a small pack of wet wipes out of his coat and cleaned his hands, then shrugged. "Or, just because it's Brooklyn and nowadays folks quietly mind each other's business without actually physically getting in each other's mix."

That comment garnered Stephan a wide grin from his neighbor that put him somewhat at ease.

"This is true." Carter's huff of laughter felt like sunlight poured directly into his soul. Stephan had the unrecognizable urge to cut loose and join in. "I remember growing up on the block in Bed-Stuy. You couldn't get away with anything, because at least one nosy adult was gonna rat you out to your moms, and all hell would break loose when you walked in at the end of the day."

At that, Stephan did laugh. He'd had quite a few of those experiences when he was a kid too. But as he aged, those informants went from being the caring residents on his block to newshounds and business competitors trying to use Stephan for one thing or another.

Suddenly aware that they'd been standing outside for more than a handful of minutes, Stephan placed his hands back in his pockets. He didn't hang, he didn't dawdle, and as alluring as his neighbor's smile was, standing outside long enough for prying eyes to catch a glimpse just wasn't his thing.

Carter must've managed to understand Stephan's unspoken desire to wrap this up, because he stepped up another step, bringing him closer to Stephan, making him more aware of just how good-looking Carter was. Hell, the man's edge-up game was so nice, Stephan was damn near mesmerized by how crisp those lines were around his forehead and his beard, and how badly they made him want to trace his fingers across them.

"I'm sorry about this little accident. Those wings look like they were good as hell."

The mention of his wings cleared his head. Looking down, Stephan saw his delicious wings spread out on his stoop, taunting him.

"Dammit," the expletive slipped from his lips. "I really wanted those, too."

"Again, I'm sorry…"

"Stephan." He took another longing glance at his wings before lifting his gaze to find remorse written all over Carter's face. "I guess my Friday night buffet isn't going to happen after all."

"Hey." Carter gave him a wary smile. If his remorse wasn't so cute, Stephan might be mad as hell. He really did want those wings in the worst way. "Your evening doesn't have to be tanked. I own The Vault."

"The VIP lounge?"

"Yeah," Carter replied. "Why don't you stop by tonight? I'll comp you all the wings you can eat. We don't sell red slushies, but I have a delicious, imported beer on tap that all my regulars seem to love. What do you say?"

Stephan had come home to wallow in his grief

and fear, and somehow, he found himself covered in red slushy, his comfort food all over the ground, and a fine as sin man standing on his steps trying to give him all-he-could-eat wings and beer. Grief was the furthest thing from his mind right now, and at the moment, Stephan wasn't exactly put out by that.

"That…um…that sounds like a plan."

Stephan gave Carter one last smile, determined to get away from this man's unprecedented magnetism and out of his very sticky and essentially ruined clothes.

"See you later, Carter."

Stephan turned around to walk away.

"Stephan?"

He turned back around to find Carter pointing toward Stephan's door. "My dog?"

*What the absolute hell is wrong with me?*

"Sure." Stephan opened the door. "Let me get her. It's been a while since I've been home. I'm not sure what condition I left the place in."

Stephan left Carter standing on the stoop and went inside. He found his uninvited guest chewing on the edge of his very expensive silk rug like it was her favorite chew toy.

He should be mad. This little ball of fur had ruined his dinner and his rug. But when Stephan bent down and picked the little menace up, she instantly snuggled into his arms, licking the side of his face.

"All right, Ms. Ebony, you should know Black folks don't believe in kissing their dogs in the mouth."

The dog ignored him and went right back to licking his jaw.

He chuckled. "Just like so many of the women in my family, you're just gonna do what you wanna do anyway, huh?"

The dog proceeded as if she hadn't heard anything. Stephan scratched behind her little floppy ears, smiling as the little thing showered him with affection.

"You're lucky you're cute and your daddy's even cuter, otherwise I'd have an attitude."

Stephan stepped outside and was greeted by Carter's megawatt smile, and once again he was transfixed and his reaction to this man was beginning to piss him off. He was Stephan Devereaux-Smith, a member of the most powerful Brooklyn family there was. People were caught up with him, not the other way around.

But when Carter took the small creature out of his hand and their fingers touched for the briefest moments, Stephan was open all over again.

"Thanks, Stephan. I'll be looking out for you tonight at the lounge. I'll see you soon."

Stephan watched as Carter's long legs carried him down one set of stairs and up another. It was only when his neighbor disappeared down the block that Stephan smiled, shoving his still slightly sticky hands in his slacks. Life was hell right now and Carter had presented Stephan with a distraction. Things would still be terrible in the morning. Ace would still be dying all the same. But maybe, just maybe, the pretty man with the cute kid and dog could make Stephan forget for just a little while.

"You certainly will."

# Three

Stephan stood in front of his floor-to-ceiling mirror in his closet, trying to settle on the final touches of his outfit.

On his worst day, Stephan could always throw a look together without much effort. But tonight, even though he'd been dressed in Armani when Carter's dog assaulted him, he wanted to make sure his outfit said "in control, yet chill." He wanted Carter to see him as an everyday brotha just dropping in to enjoy some wings.

He shook his head, unable to believe the story he was trying to sell himself. He knew this was about something more than his "fit" being together. This was about making a good impression on Carter. He didn't know why he cared what Carter thought of him. He hadn't known the man for more than five minutes. But in that short amount of time, Carter had definitely made an impression on him.

He was friendly, outgoing, and Stephan could tell he had a great sense of humor. When you grew up with everything you did being scrutinized because of your family's social position, sometimes humor was all you had to help you keep your sanity.

He moved to his jewelry display case, going back and forth between the Rolex and the Cartier, before the sleek yet bold platinum link bracelet from Tiffany and Co. caught his eye. Satisfied with his choice, he quickly put it on and then grabbed the matching chain and secured it around his neck.

Deciding he'd fiddled enough with his clothes and accessories, it was time go. Better that than sitting around trying to analyze which demon he would attempt to ignore at present.

Besides, it's not like he was going to allow his interest in Carter to go beyond the superficial. He'd learned long ago that allowing anything deeper, meant inviting hurt into life. And right now, dealing with Ace's illness and Stephan's long-suffering entanglement with guilt was all the hurt he had tolerance for.

He grabbed his jacket, took a deep breath, and then headed out the door. Happy that he didn't have to care why he wanted to impress Carter. No, he didn't have to care, not one bit at all.

* * *

"Carter, you expecting somebody?"

Carter barely glanced at his best friend Lennox Carlisle as he vigorously wiped the bar top while looking at the main entrance.

"Why do you ask?" Carter managed to answer Lennox's question with a question, which he knew would annoy his friend.

Serves him right. Lennox was actively distracting Carter's ability to watch the door like a hawk in anticipation of seeing a certain tall, dark, and sexy man walk into his lounge.

"Because you've been shining the same spot on the bar like you're trying to take the paint off it. S'up?"

What was up, indeed. Damn if Carter knew. He'd been walking with his daughter and their puppy when his little princess had ignored his warning about holding on to the puppy's leash. The next thing he knew, he was taking two steps at a time to keep an innocent bystander on the porch a few houses down from Carter's from hitting the concrete.

"Nevaeh lost control of Ebony's leash and the little miscreant nearly tripped one of my neighbors, causing him to lose the bag full of dirty wings and his red slushy all over his shirt front and porch."

"You worried he's gonna cause a fuss?"

Carter shook his head. "Nah. Most of all, he just really looked sad. At first, I thought it was over his lost food. But when I looked at him, it seemed to run deeper than that. Like he was going through something. So, I told him to come down here and I would comp him all the wings he could eat."

Lennox leaned against the bar, his pointed eyebrow acting as a bullshit detector.

"And so, you thought the wings you serve here would somehow magically make this stranger happy?"

Lennox tilted his head, looking Carter up and down with suspicion until he had a wide grin settled on his face, and he asked. "What's he look like?"

Carter immediately went back to wiping down his bar. It wasn't just an action to keep up with the city health code, it also calmed his mood when his best friend was getting on his last nerve.

"Carter," Lennox sang, placing a hand on top of Carter's, stilling his repetitive motion.

Carter huffed. "He was a walking wet dream, okay. An inch or so taller than me, lanky build with broad shoulders, and rich, dark skin. But no matter how attractive he was, that wasn't the reason I invited him."

He waited for Lennox to crack a joke, but true to form, his friend could tell there was something more happening here. And just like always, Lennox was there for him with no judgment at all.

"I looked in his eyes and I saw something familiar reflected in them, something I've seen in my own whenever I looked in a mirror."

"What's that?" Lennox asked, waiting patiently for an answer.

"Grief." Carter met his friend's eyes and watched them soften at the utterance of the word.

After tragically losing his wife, Michelle, in an accident five years ago, grief had become an unwanted guest that had barged into his life uninvited.

"And so, you just want to give him a little bit of grief therapy?"

Carter shrugged, not really knowing how to answer Lennox.

"I just know that some days, the grief was so powerful I could hardly breathe. But whenever I wanted to crumble under it, you or my mom or Gracie came through to throw me a lifeline."

Carter threw the cloth over his shoulder as he looked his friend in the eye.

"I just know what it is to need a little kindness when life has its foot on your neck. I'm just trying to pay it forward, man, you know?"

"Yeah," Lennox agreed before taking the last swig of his beer. "But don't be so disappointed if he doesn't take you up on your offer. If you remember, you weren't the easiest person to help either, and we had a lifetime of friendship under our belt when you went through that hell. Maybe he's just not there yet, and that's okay."

Lennox stood up, taking a few bills from his pocket and laying them on the bar.

"You leaving already?"

"Yeah," Lennox replied with a little more excitement than was necessary. "Amara's at that point in her pregnancy where she can't get enough of me, and as much as I love you, ain't no way I'm missing what she's offering to sit at your bar."

"God, you're a pig," Carter replied.

"A well-satisfied pig. Can you say the same?"

Carter certainly could not and they both knew it. He'd dated here and there over the last two years, but when you were a single dad and a business owner, dating, even hookups that required no dating at all were a luxury Carter didn't always have the time or the energy for.

Lennox winked at him, chuckling as he headed out the door. Carter spread his hands flat on the bar, enjoying the slow pace of his lounge. The Friday night rush hadn't come in yet, and there were just a few members scattered throughout the front room.

The Vault was a members-only VIP lounge. There were three floors open to the patrons. On the main floor, a bar, a dining area, and a private dining room for private parties. Carter's office was also on the main floor down a private corridor off to the side of bar. The upper level was for gaming tables and TVs, which were flanked by another bar and lounge area. The third floor held a dance floor, a DJ booth, and yes, another bar. They served brunch, lunch, and dinner, or for those patrons that just wanted a drink and some apps, they were more than welcome to eat at any of the bars.

Although the food and drinks were top-tier, that's not why his clientele came. At The Vault, the Brooklyn elite came to get away from the public world.

Here, other than the house security cameras, which no one had access to other than Carter and his head of security, no cameras, electronic devices, or audio equipment were allowed. Each member had to deposit those things into an assigned locker in the coatroom that was always staffed with two attendants.

There was a zero-tolerance policy for breaking the rules. Carter was that protective of his members' privacy. You couldn't even enter through the street level. While there were emergency exits that let out to the street, allowing for safe evacuation if necessary, you had to actually drive or walk down a ramp and be cleared to enter the building by a host and a security team.

Membership was a rigorous and expensive vetting process that included background checks, personal recommendations from other established members, and an okay from Carter's gut as the last checkpoint. So if you could get past all those hurdles, The Vault was a place for you to let go and be a normal person for the time you were here.

It was born out of Carter's inability to get away from the eyes of the world when he was at his lowest and the world just wouldn't let him be human for one damn minute.

Five years ago, thirty-two-year-old Carter had been living a completely different life. He was married to his beautiful wife, Michelle, and they were new parents. He was on top of his career as one of the most sought-after actors in mainstream Hollywood. A feat doubly impressive for a bisexual Puerto Rican boy from Brooklyn.

But as quickly as his star rose, it came crashing back down, shattering into a billion tiny pieces when his wife was ripped from his life.

Refusing to revisit the pain that came with allowing his mind to venture back to that very dark time, he went about setting up for the crowd he knew would be coming soon.

Glancing up from the glass he was drying, Carter's gaze came to an abrupt halt when Stephan seemed to just appear. His presence quickly filled the room like thick smoke.

There, his neighbor with the sad eyes and beautiful lips stood still, his gaze combing the room until he found Carter.

Carter knew the exact moment Stephan spotted him. It wasn't just because of the flicker of fire in Stephan's dark eyes. No, it was because he felt it, like a jolt of electricity sizzling through him, burning each layer of his skin as it dissipated throughout his system.

Slowly, he moved across the room and Carter took a moment to really soak up this vision of a man.

Stephan had traded his Armani, slushy stained suit for a red Billionaire Boys Club helmet varsity jacket paired with a black Henley and black straight-cut jeans.

Carter let his eyes drift to the floor to get a glimpse

of the wheat nubuck Jimmy Choo X Timberland boots that brought the entire outfit together, and he smiled.

Outside of his brownstone, Stephan had seemed a little stiff if Carter was to be honest. But if this was relaxed Stephan, Carter wasn't mad at all. Brothas in a pair of Timbs had been his weakness when he was in his teens and early twenties.

He'd thought he'd outgrown that particular quirk, possibly because, once he'd met Michelle, he'd fallen so hard for her, no one caught his notice but her. But there was something about the confident way that jacket hung on Stephan's broad shoulders, and the rhythmic swag in his walk that woke up something Carter hadn't felt in a long time…lust.

He was still processing that when Stephan sat down on the stool directly in front of him.

"Well," Stephan began slowly as he took a moment to look around. "I'm here. Where are these amazing wings and beer you promised me?"

"I'll put in an order for you now. It's should take a few minutes. But while you wait, here's the beer."

Carter filled a glass from the tap and handed it to Stephan, an innocent action he'd performed countless times in the five years he'd owned this lounge. But tonight, Stephan's fingers grazed Carter's and fire burned where their flesh met.

The heat made him want to draw his hand back, but somewhere between Stephan's touch and Carter's brain, the message was lost.

"Thank you, man."

The deep timbre of Stephan's voice rattled through Carter, drawing him in, making him lean onto the bar to get closer.

It was only so he could hear Stephan better. It had nothing to do with the fact that the sight of this man made his pulse jump or that being this close, the spicy sweetness of his cologne was more intoxicating than any of the alcoholic beverages lining the mirrored wall behind the bar. No, it had nothing to do with any of that.

"What are you thanking me for? You haven't even tasted the wings yet."

Carter tried to make his tone light and fun, but his words seemed breathier, and he wondered where the hell had his hardcore Brooklynness gone? He was a real one. No matter that his face used to be plastered on big screens all over the world, he'd never lost his down-to-earth "carismático" persona.

"You did me a solid I didn't even know I needed."

Carter watched Stephan's eyes fill with an ache that rang so familiar in his chest. Carter wanted to press to ask what he had lost, but remembered Lennox's warning.

He didn't know this man and he had no right to push into his life, even if his intentions were good and he just wanted to help.

He filled a glass for himself, stepping back, trying to put space between them and give Stephan room to breathe.

"I know I'm probably gonna sound so pathetic.

Like a stereotypical bar patron crying over their beer."

"This is a no judgment zone. I've needed to cry over my beer a time or two in my life, and my friends always let me do it, so I'm paying it forward."

"So…" Stephan raised a brow as he peeled away the label on his now-empty beer bottle. "We're friends now?"

"We're neighbors," Carter said between sips, trying his hardest to keep things cool and unbothered. "I don't see why we can't be friends too. I'm new on our street, after all. I could use someone to give me the rundown on the haps on the block."

"I don't know how much good I would be on that score. I've been in Paris working for the last two years. I bought my brownstone a year before I left, so I haven't exactly bonded with any of the neighbors either."

Carter tipped his beer toward Stephan and offered him a playful wink, again trying to keep things light, even if everything about his reaction to this man was over-the-top.

"Even better reason we should link up. We're the two newbies on the block."

Stephan locked gazes with him, his stare unwavering, as if he were attempting to see if there was more to Carter's nice guy act than just him trying to be, well…nice.

Stephan looked up at him again and the grief was still there, but there was something else, something more intense and it made Carter squeeze his beer tumbler so hard, he worried he might break the thing in his hand.

"I don't know how much of a friend I could be right now. But I sure as hell wouldn't mind a distraction."

Stephan licked his lips and every muscle tightened in Carter's body, wondering what those thick pillows would feel like pressed against his skin. Was he this hard up that he was actually standing here low-key, letting a man who was obviously going through something hit on him?

"You wouldn't happen to know of any distractions I could get into around here, would you?"

If Carter were a better man, he'd turn down the innuendo etched in the sharp lines of Stephan's face, that burned so deeply in his soulful eyes. But he wasn't a better man, apparently, because when he opened his mouth, instead of saying no. He said, "Yes, I certainly do."

# Four

"This is certainly not the distraction I was expecting."

Stephan watched the corners of Carter's mouth curl into a devious grin. It was at that moment Stephan understood that Carter was extremely aware of what Stephan had been expecting and was enjoying Stephan's enlightenment. Obviously, Stephan was the only person in the room who'd assumed they'd be partially disrobed by now.

"Oh, I know exactly what you were expecting." Carter leaned down, aligning his shot on the ebony pool table with the bloodred velvet top. "And don't get me wrong, I wouldn't mind it. In fact, I very much want it."

"Then why not take what I'm offering?"

Carter stood up, holding his cue stick at his side. Stephan could tell the man was choosing his words carefully, thinking before he spoke. It showed a thoughtfulness and awareness the businessman in him appreciated. But the flawed man in him and his half-hard cock weren't as appreciative of this quality.

"Are you married?"

While Stephan's question may have appeared cynical, it wasn't. He didn't believe every devastatingly hot man he encountered was a devoted husband by day and trolling for hookups by night. Unfortunately, that didn't mean he didn't have to always be cautious. There were too many wealthy, powerful men who presented one face to the world so they could enjoy the privilege their apparent heterosexuality brought them.

But when they thought no one could see them, they would forget about the wives they had at home and slake their desires with men behind closed doors.

Stephan wasn't about that life. Being on the DL, more formally known as the "Down Low", didn't appeal to him one bit.

Yes, he was a wealthy man. But what little he did expose to the public about himself, hiding who he was wasn't part of that. He also wasn't for knowingly or unknowingly hurting someone else's spouse. He had enough dirty little secrets to carry. Knowing about someone else's deception regarding their sexuality wasn't a confidence he had any desire to hold. His life was complicated enough being part of the Devereaux family. Upholding the public image of perfection—an image needed to keep the family name and the business profitable—while knowing how flawed they all were was sometimes more weight than he could bear. He didn't need to add being someone's side piece to the mix as well.

"No, I'm not married." Carter paused for a second before he continued. "I've been a widower for the last five years."

Stephan's back straightened at the word *widower* and his stomach tightened with remorse. When death was stalking someone you loved, the knowledge that very soon you would walk the same painful path others had rang loud, like the knell of a bell filling a cathedral.

"I'm sorry."

Carter took a deep breath, allowing what looked akin to peace to soothe his features.

"Thank you," Carter replied. "But please don't feel sorry for me. I had the love of my life for ten years and she gave me a beautiful daughter. That's more than most people get."

Stephan saw a twinkle of heartwarming nostalgia mixed with the ache of loss, and the fact that Carter could still smile and grasp even a sliver of happiness from his memories made envy hang in Stephan's belly.

*You have to first accept Ace's fate before you can move on to that sort of peace.*

The thought caught Stephan off guard. Sure, in

his head he knew that Ace was dying. That very soon he'd lose someone so precious to him, he wondered if he'd survive. But knowing, and experiencing the finality of it in real time were two different things.

"My late wife has nothing to do with the reason I put the brakes on the very clear subliminals you were throwing."

Carter's voice broke through Stephan's grim musings, pulling a chuckle from him. "Was I that obvious?"

"I'm a fan of obvious honesty." Carter turned away from the pool table in his office, walking to a mini fridge in the corner and returning with two beers in his hand. "We live on the same street. I just don't want to make things awkward. It can get a little weird running into a one-night stand when you're pulling up on the block. I've only lived there for a year. My daughter and I are just feeling settled. I don't want to rock the boat for her."

Stephan took a sip of his beer, nodding briefly. He could respect Carter's perspective. But he'd certainly be an outright liar if he said the thought of peeling every stitch of the fine silk shirt and fitted black slacks Carter wore away from his skin didn't have the lick of desire still burning through his veins.

"Well, since you're not interested in sleeping with me, why did you invite me back to your office?" Stephan stepped in a circle around the large room with its slate gray walls and black furniture that made the room both stylish and inviting. "I mean, the office is great and the pool table is top-tier, but if you didn't plan on letting me have my way with you on top of it, why bother?

Carter hung his head as his muscled form shook in laughter.

"There's that honesty again."

When Carter brought his head up again, Stephan's gaze caught the gleam of Carter's wide grin and his chest tightened.

Since when had he ever been into a man's smile? Never, in the history of ever, as far as he could remember. Not even as a besotted teenager who'd fallen hard for the upperclassmen in high school who hadn't known his young freshman self was alive had his stomach fluttered over a man. And when Carter's deep brown eyes sparkled with the right mix of mischief and "I'm sexy and I know it" mojo, Stephan's stomach definitely felt like it was on the high spin cycle of a washing machine.

"For the record, I never said anything about being uninterested."

Carter's heated gaze slid down the length of Stephan and back up again, taking him in as if Stephan were a tasty treat locked behind a display glass.

"I brought you here because you looked like you were going through something and I know what that feels like. And I can tell you, when life was kicking my ass, sex wouldn't have fixed anything, even if I could've ignored the pain long enough to get lost in someone else."

Carter put down his beer on a nearby table and walked across the room until he was standing so close to Stephan, he could smell the subtle spice in Carter's cologne.

Stephan's skin felt tight with need and his muscles ached with desperation as he tried to keep himself still so he didn't do something stupid like pull this man into a kiss and do his damnedest to discover what that beautiful bow in Carter's upper lip tasted like.

"If sex didn't work," Stephan ground out, his voice like sand over rough gravel, causing his throat to burn as he spoke. "What did?"

"Having friends who checked in on me even when I didn't want them to. But most of all, having someone to talk to without judgment. And for some reason, I get the sense you don't have that readily available to you."

Stephan pulled in a ragged breath, placing his hands on his lean hips to pull his rib cage up so he could force more air into his lungs.

"I live in a world where opening yourself up can mean your literal destruction. Sharing anything other than what people need to know isn't something I can readily do."

"I can't believe there's no one, Stephan."

Carter's words forced Stephan to go through his mental Rolodex. Friends and acquaintances were out. He couldn't chance what he'd done being leaked to the authorities or the press. It would ruin the family, and Devereaux Inc. would take a hit he wasn't sure it could recover from.

Yes, his cousins loved him and would do anything for him. But if they found out he'd lied and run like a coward for the last two years to cover it up, they might not want anything to do with him again.

*Especially* Lyric.

Lyric could never know the truth he was hiding.

He could never trade freedom from his own guilt if inflicting pain on her would be the result.

Uncle David would bear the secret if he knew. As the family lawyer, that would be his job. But he wouldn't use legalities to bind that man to a secret that would break his heart.

And his mother, she was so filled with anger and the desire for vengeance since his brother's death, there was no way he could tell her the truth. He couldn't trust that she wouldn't use the information to harm Ace. Hell, she'd already tried to enact a hostile takeover of Devereaux Inc., If Stephan opened his mouth, looking for someone to lighten his load, he just couldn't be sure Martha wouldn't use it to her own ends, even if that meant cutting her one remaining son down at the knees.

No, there was only Ace. Ace, who had been by his side. Ace, who had helped him protect the secret all these years. Ace, who was dying, and Stephan didn't have the heart to ask the man to bear another thing for him.

"You don't know anything about me, Carter. Why do you care whether I have someone to talk to or not?"

"Because I was you, and now I'm not. I'm proof that you can survive loss, however significant that loss is. I'm proof you can live again."

Carter's words hit Stephan in the middle of his chest, and if he hadn't had his hands on his hips, the sheer impact of them would've folded him over like a soggy French fry.

Living? What the hell was that? He hadn't lived since he received the news that his brother had died. All he did was exist. He existed to bear the secret that could destroy his family and their business. He existed to protect his sister-in-love's heart and peace of mind. He existed to do whatever was needed to calm Ace's fears as he transitioned from this life unto the next. Living? No, that wasn't part of the equation at all.

Carter kept staring at him, his warm brown eyes offering Stephan a soft, warm place to let down his armor and rest.

He was tired. So tired of bearing this weight. Every moment he held on to all this sadness, pain, and secrecy, Stephan felt like the walls were closing in on him.

*Maybe it can't hurt to share just a little of your woes?* His mind whispered that to him like a pusher seeking to hook a new user. Stephan was strong and smart, though. Surely he could share a tiny bit—just enough to release just a little of the pressure—without baring his complete soul, right?

*You don't need what this man is offering, Stephan.* The timing was all wrong. Somehow that did nothing to slake Stephan's desire for him. But more importantly, it did not extinguish this unnatural urge in him to share his burden with Carter. Someone who knew exactly how corrosive loss was.

"My uncle is dying."

Stephan fought every lesson he'd ever been taught about keeping the family's business private.

*Keep our business out of the street. Never break the cipher.*

He closed his eyes to quiet the clanging alarms sounding off in his head. It wasn't his sheer will that made them stop, however. It was the sliver of relief that was beginning to weave its way through every sinew of his body.

"I'm so sorry, Stephan."

Carter's reply was just the push he needed to make him continue, even though it went against all Stephan's instincts.

"My uncle raised me, loved me through some pretty rough times. And he's never asked a single thing from me in return, until today."

Carter folded his arms, waiting for Stephan to continue. His attentive but soft gaze letting Stephan know if he wanted to end the conversation, he was okay with that too.

"He asked me to throw him a Christmas party, a nod to happier days in my family."

"That doesn't seem like such a strange request."

"It's not." Stephan rubbed a hand down his face, pursing his lips as he figured out how to say what he needed without exposing Ace to this perfect, albeit hot, stranger. "It's just, there's a very real possibility he won't make it till Christmas and celebrating right now feels wrong."

A flash of a Christmas past at Borough Hall with he and his cousin Amara fiddling underneath the tree with the other Devereaux kids while the adults drank eggnog cocktails and laughed about old times that Stephan and Amara hadn't been old enough to understand. And now that he was in fact old enough to understand, that wonderful warmth that surrounded him was disappearing forever.

"To you," Carter replied. "But have you considered that this may be the last time for him to see all of his loved ones before he goes?"

"My uncle practically said as much when he asked me to throw him the party. I just can't see myself celebrating the fact that he's leaving us."

Carter shook his head and shared a comforting smile as he laid a gentle hand on Stephan's shoulder.

"Not happy that he's leaving, happy that he's still here for another holiday with you and the rest of your family."

Stephan's mind took in Carter's words, planting

them somewhere in his consciousness, where things began to take root.

Carter was right. Ace did want a final memory of all his family together. He knew this would make the old man happy. But an event for the family included his mother too. He knew Ace had probably already considered this, but in his nostalgic and sickly haze, Stephan wasn't sure the man really accounted for how bad things were between Ace and Martha. Knowing how much tension there was between the two, could Stephan really give Ace the loving Devereaux Christmas he longed for?

"My family's complicated, Carter." Stephan shrugged, trying to shake the tension building across his shoulders.

"All families are complicated, Stephan. That shouldn't stop you from doing this for your uncle, if this is what he wants."

"Trust me," Stephan huffed. "My family's built different. The standard rules don't always apply."

Carter's unrelenting optimism was painted across his mouth in a comforting smile, letting Stephan know whatever excuse he came up with, Carter had an answer for it. That, however, didn't mean Stephan wasn't going to try to find a suitable justification anyway.

"This sounds good in theory, but the truth is, I don't know if my uncle will make it until Christmas. With Thanksgiving being three weeks away, I don't really see getting this thing done as quickly as it would need to happen."

Stephan took another swig of his beer, hoping this would quiet the mild throbbing in his head and loosen the ache in his back.

"Listen. It doesn't matter if it were August at the height of a sweltering New York summer. If your uncle wants this and you're able to do it for him, I don't see the harm in giving him what he wants. And if you need any help, you can always call me. Party planning is part of the job of owning this place."

Stephan released a long huff, relieved that some of the tension in his neck was starting to fade away.

"I think I'd like that." Stephan tried to find the strength to offer a warm smile. "Thanks for the offer." It was probably just out of pity. Who would want to get involved with planning something like this, especially when there wasn't any history between the two of them? Knowing that didn't stop Stephan from appreciating Carter's gesture nonetheless.

"Are you free tomorrow night?" Stephan's eyes widened at Carter's question. This man couldn't be serious, could he?

Stephan nodded and waited for Carter to continue.

"You have any food allergies? I make a mean paella, along with a few other dishes I could bring for you to sample for the menu that will make you forget about everything that ails you."

Stephan seriously doubted Carter's claim. But the warmth radiating in the middle of his chest told him to give it a try anyway.

"No allergies. Paella and whatever else you want to bring sounds great."

"Good. I'll bring the food, and while we eat we can brainstorm about this party."

More warmth spread through Stephan as he listened to Carter. No romantic interest had ever touched Stephan like this. And since he hadn't actually had the opportunity to act on his attraction to Carter, he couldn't truly call him a romantic interest—which only baffled him further.

"You're bringing me food and helping me get this last-minute Christmas party for the ages together. The least I can do is have some wine for you to drink and a dessert for you to enjoy. I make a delightful lemon sorbet, and unless the cleaning service I've used to keep the place together while I was away has hit my wine cellar, I think I should have the perfect wine to go with it. Is eight too late. I've got work and then a family thing immediately following."

"Eight is perfect," Carter replied. "See you then."

This man had set aside Stephan's advances, and instead of telling Stephan to kick rocks with open-toed shoes on, as he deserved for acting like a creep, Carter was offering to help him heal his family.

This was all very strange to Stephan. Strange, but enjoyable.

Carter's mouth curved into a bright and wide grin that nearly stopped Stephan's ability to breathe.

*What the hell?*

This wasn't a date. This was a nice guy doing him

a favor. So the excitement fluttering in his stomach shouldn't have been there.

But it was.

Stephan took a swig of his beer, wondering when he'd reverted into a teenager with no impulse control instead of the grown, disciplined man he was.

He put his half-finished beer on a nearby tabletop, gave Carter a brief nod because he couldn't trust himself not to stay, and not to touch Carter. When he was arm's length away from escape, Carter stopped him.

"Oh, and Stephan," The way that Carter's rich baritone enveloped his name made him bite down on his bottom lip to keep a satisfied moan from escaping his mouth. "If anyone was going to be having their way tonight, it would've been me having my way with you."

Every muscle in Stephan's body tightened as the rumble of Carter's voice trembled through him. That wasn't an empty threat or just one Brooklynite joking with another. Game recognized game. Stephan had thrown that tone around a time or two. It was a voice so deep it was as if it were bathed in whiskey. Stephan had used it only when he'd needed to take control of a rudderless ship and give clear guidance on what the next step on the journey was. This, however, was the first time he'd been on the receiving end of it.

Control and organization kept things running smoothly and kept the people he loved from getting hurt. Ace had taught him that and Stephan had held tightly to that lesson. But standing at the edge of this room, held in place by the sheer will delivered in Carter's voice, for once, everything in him ached to let someone else control him and his situation.

# Five

November in Brooklyn meant the night encroached upon the day before five. Streetlights and stars lit Clinton Hill in a soft amber light that always comforted Stephan. Yes, he'd traveled all over the world and seen iconic places that were praised in lofty circles. But to him, the rhythmic hum of a concrete Brooklyn street would always, always be a thing of beauty.

He took one last gaze outside of his office window at Devereaux Inc., comforted by the familiarity of the Dekalb and Clinton Avenues intersection. This was home. And even though his family situation weighed on him, he would always be happy to let his gaze linger over these streets.

"And what about the preliminary numbers for the

upcoming quarter?" Stephan rejoined his conversation with the second-in-command of the Paris office.

"Are already in your inbox."

Stephan smiled as he looked down at the computer screen, finding the lifted brow his assistant Henrí offered. Henrí was just as much of a perfectionist as Stephan. He triple- and quadruple-checked everything before he let it grace Stephan's inbox or desk.

Leaving Paris as abruptly as he had upon getting the news of Ace's decline, Stephan had only had enough time to pack a bag and get on the first flight he could book back to the States. Once notified of the situation, as Stephan's second-in-command, Henrí seamlessly took over the operations of the Paris office of Devereaux Inc.

Both knew Henrí could do both their jobs in his sleep, so the fact that Stephan was nitpicking over quarterly reports was a glaring sign that he was still feeling unmoored after last night's encounter with Carter.

"Thanks, Henrí," Stephan managed. "I'm slightly concerned that I'm obsolete with how well you've been running things these last five months. When I left, I never imagined working remotely for so long."

"I know you didn't. But honestly, knowing how much you love Mr. Devereaux, there was no way I could imagine you not going home to spend his remaining time with him. You made the right choice, Stephan. And the blessing of technology is that you can still do your job while being so far away."

Devereaux Inc. allowed for flexible schedules and remote options for its employees. Unless your work required you to be in-house, it wasn't mandated that you be bound to a Devereaux Inc. desk. Stephan had never imagined when that policy had been enacted, he himself would need to take advantage of it. But here he was.

Stephan shook his head. "No, the blessing is having you as my second. I couldn't leave the office in anyone else's hands."

Henrí gave Stephan a brief nod before the tentative furrow of his brow signaled there was something more he wanted to say.

"How is Ace?"

Stephan leaned back in his chair, one elbow bracing his tired torso up against one of the arms. He hated this question. Especially when he was at work.

Devereaux Inc. was the one place he could pretend his world wasn't ending. But as loyal as Henrí had been to both Stephan and Ace, he knew the man's concerns deserved to be addressed.

"His prognosis is the same. He's dying. When he ended up in the hospital this summer, we thought he was leaving us then. But he just seems to be holding on for something. I think he's fighting to see Amara and Lennox's baby be born. That's the only loose end I can think of."

A sad, but loving smile curved Henrí's lips. "I'm sure Ace would love to meet a new Devereaux. But the only thing I've ever heard him talk about fighting for was his 'babies,' and if I remember, that's pretty much all of the cousins in your generation."

Stephan narrowed his gaze. He and Henrí weren't the closest of friends, so if he knew that, it was because he'd heard it come from Ace's mouth. That man was worse than any grandparent with pictures of their new grand. Ace had doted on Amara, Lyric, Jeremiah, and himself forever and always. Now that Ace's estranged granddaughter, Trey, had returned, falling in love with Jeremiah and marrying him, she too was included in that overarching "babies" that Ace always lovingly spoke of.

"You're right, he does love us. But everyone is boo'd up and Amara is even cooking a human. As far as all his old-fashioned markers go, Ace's 'babies' are doing just fine."

"Maybe in your eyes, Stephan. But maybe Ace sees something that you're blind to. Something only the love of an elder can recognize."

The crack in Stephan's heart spread just a millimeter more every time he thought about Ace leaving him. He'd like to say it was just his specific connection to Ace he was grieving, but Stephan knew that wasn't the case.

For all the Devereaux cousins, he'd been a rock, a pillar, a cheerleader, and if you went left when you should've gone right, he'd been the correction they'd needed too. Having someone who just knew—without you having to say a word—that something was going wrong, it was a gift Stephan was ashamed to say he hadn't truly appreciated until it was slowly being taken from him.

Stephan placed a finger at his temple as he leaned into the cushions of his chair, trying hard not to crumble under the wall of sadness that seemed to get higher—brick by brick—with every day.

"God—" Stephan cleared his throat "—you're over three thousand miles away and you're sounding like him, Henrí."

"For the most part, I've never known the old man to be wrong, so I'll take that as a compliment. Anyway, you have all the documents you need. If there's nothing else, I have a bottle of wine chilling and a beautiful young woman on her way to help me drink it. I'll see you next week, Stephan. Give my best wishes to Ace and the rest of the Devereauxs. Call if you need me for anything."

Stephan gave him a mock salute before the screen went black.

He was just about to exhale all the tension Henrí's gentle demeanor had helped soothe when he could hear a slight disturbance on the other side of his door.

"He's on a conference call right now and not taking visitors. If you would kindly make an appointment, I'll see that you get on his calendar immediately."

Stephan sat up quickly and he could feel the tension his body had tried to release, bunching the muscles of his neck into a hard knot.

His executive assistant, Andre, had on his professional but defensive voice. He only used it when people were crossing the boundaries he'd asked Andre to enforce.

And since no one in the office had an issue with those boundaries, Stephan knew he could only be talking to one person.

"Five, four, three, two, one." He counted slowly, and exactly on cue, the cold but familiar voice spoke.

"I am not some business associate to be handled, my dear. I am his mother, and I will see him right now."

Within seconds, his door flew open and the very last person he needed in his presence right now entered with a frantic Andre running behind her.

He silently waved Andre off, letting him know he'd deal with his mother from here.

Martha Devereaux-Smith stood in the middle of his office, wearing a wide-leg black pantsuit covered by a fashionable white wool coat. Her use of color against her rich, tawny brown skin, coupled with her gray hair pulled into her signature bun gave her an elegant, aristocratic appearance that made most people fearful to cross her.

But he'd been raised by this woman and was immune to her toxicity. And more than anything, that was the reason he was never her favored son. That honor went to one man only, his late brother, Randall.

"Your brother would never have had me wait in the waiting room like some commoner."

He snorted. Martha never missed a beat to bring the drama.

"Mother, contrary to your delusions, you are not royal or noble, so I think that means you are in fact in a commoner."

"You were always too rude and ungrateful for your own good, boy. A lingering effect of my poor choice in allowing you to spend so much time with that wretched Ace."

"Don't"

His voice was intentionally sharp, slicing through the air and hitting his target dead center. To most, his mother still seemed cold, unfazed by his command. But he knew Martha Devereaux-Smith better than anyone else. He'd grown up in her house and seen how she maneuvered and manipulated people to get exactly what she wanted. Though he wasn't skilled enough to master her as a child and use her powers against her, he had learned to stay out of her way, keep her eyes off him so he could hold on to some semblance of peace. And the best way to do that was by disappearing to his uncle Ace's house, where he was cared for instead of weaponized or trained to dominate the world like the heir apparent, Randall, had been.

The narrowing of her gaze, the sharp jut of her jaw, those were her tells. The instinctive tells she couldn't keep in check that revealed when her control was disturbed by something she either hadn't seen coming or didn't know how to restrain.

"If you want to spew your ugliness about Ace, do it somewhere else. But what you're not going to do is disrespect him in his own company, Mother. Not while I sit here."

That man she'd referred to as *wretched* was one of the only adults in his life who didn't see him as a nuisance. He was an "oops" baby. Conceived just as his mother was embarking on menopause when she'd thought she'd be free to focus solely on making Randall Ace's heir. The universe had another plan, and here he was, born more than twenty years after her first child with none of the insatiable need for power Randall seemed to inherit in doubles from her.

She'd had no use for him because she'd had her precious. When his father died just a few years before Stephan's first double digit, Martha had had no idea how to deal with a sensitive boy who didn't want to bend the world to his will. But Ace had.

Ace... Ace had taken every moment he could to let the lonely little boy in the family know that he was loved, wanted, and appreciated.

It was punishment enough that there were only a finite number of moments he had with Ace left. He wouldn't let Martha sully even one of them with her long-held hatred of her brother. Especially...when he knew the reasons for her hate were his fault, and not Ace's.

Stephan took a breath, trying to find some compassion for his mother, but it was so hard when she worked so diligently at erasing even the smallest crumb of empathy in his heart.

"You defend him so profoundly." Her words were

strong, but appropriately reserved. She was a diva of the highest order, and never would she allow anyone to see her act out of character in public. "What a joy it would be if you could find that kind of love and vigor for me, the woman who gave *you* life."

"Mother, I'm sure you didn't come all the way down here for this. Did you want something?"

"I want my son to act like he can stand to be in a room with me for more than five minutes. You've been home over four months, and yet, I've only seen you a few times. When am I going to rank on your list of priorities, Stephan?"

"Mother, Ace is dying. Can't you find the slightest bit of grace. He's your brother, for God's sake. The patriarch of this family, and this entire family is hurting from the fear of his loss. Do you understand that, Mother? He's dying. Can't you find it in your heart to put your differences aside to work things out before it's too late? Can't you have the slightest bit of concern for those of us who love him?"

She straightened her shoulders, pulling them back as she arranged her coat around them.

"That man cut my heart out when he killed my son. And even though you didn't hold your brother in high enough regard to stop following behind Ace like a little puppy, I will either find a way to avenge my son or I will dance on Ace's grave. At this point, I'm just as partial to one as the other."

Stephan had to squeeze his hands into tight firsts to keep himself from speaking the words that had lingered in his heart and mind for the last two years. But as Martha turned on her designer heels and exited the door, Stephan knew he'd have to watch her. Whatever scheme she was up to, he knew it would not be good for Ace, Devereaux Inc. or anyone else in the Devereaux clan.

# Six

Carter stood in his large master bedroom, standing in front of the mirror that stood in the corner.

The room was decorated in warm browns, burgundies, and creams. Being raised by a mother who was born in the Caribbean, Carter had always been surrounded by bright, exciting colors. But when he'd lost Michelle, he could never seem to bear that brightness again. When they moved into this place, Carter had instructed the interior decorator to create a space that was warm and nurturing but had just a splash of the masculine. As the only man living in this house, sometimes he needed something that was distinctive and something all his own that didn't appear in any of the other rooms of the house.

"So, this boy you're going on a date with?" His mother continued through his speakerphone with a tone that told him whatever it was she was about to ask, she had a stockpile of information on the topic already. "Is he nice?"

"Mommy, I told you, this isn't a date. I'm helping someone plan a Christmas party for a sick relative. There's no dating involved."

"Carter, mijo?"

He shook his head. Anytime she started with his name, followed by the loving endearment for *my son* in Spanish, he was looking at a serious guilt trip session.

"Mommy, I'm serious. I know you want to see me happy and married off again. But the truth is, Michelle was it for me. And I'm raising your granddaughter. I don't have time to devote my attention to a relationship."

"Carter," she huffed, and if she were here with him, he knew she'd be looking up at the ceiling as she mouthed *Dios mio* to the heavens. That was always how she dealt with him when his exasperating obtuseness was on display.

"You know I'm not telling you to marry if that's not what you want. But you gotta stop hiding. You have to engage with the outside world."

"I do," he added.

"No, you don't. You work and you take care of Nevaeh, and now you have this dog… What on earth possessed you to get that dog anyway. Don't you have enough on your plate?"

He most certainly did, and adding a puppy to it really made him question his own sanity most days.

"Nevaeh asked me for a sibling. I knew I couldn't give her that, so a puppy was the next best thing."

"Carter—"

"Mommy, I'm not there. Losing Michelle, the way I did, I just don't know if I can open up myself enough to let someone in."

He could hear compassion softening the breath she released through the phone.

"I know, mijo. I loved her too. We all did. But Michelle would want you to live fully. To love again. You know that, don't you?"

"I know, Mommy. I just…being in the world without her, sometimes it hurts so bad. And I don't know if I have enough strength left to give my little girl all she needs and love someone else too. So, until that passes, I'll just keep doing what I'm doing. Because the last time I let the world in, it took my wife. I couldn't survive another loss like that."

"Daddy, are you upstairs?"

Joy blossomed in his chest at the sound of his daughter's voice. She was his reason for living, and knowing she was happy and thriving would always bring him joy.

"Ven, mija." He called over his shoulder then walked over to where his phone rested on a nearby dresser.

"Mommy, I gotta go. Nevaeh and Gracie just came back from walking the dog, and I don't want them to walk in on this conversation."

"Okay," she agreed. "Just kiss my little nieta and tell Gracie to take care of my babies while I'm gone."

He lovingly agreed and ended the call just before little footsteps thumped into his room.

"Oh, Daddy, I like that color on you."

Carter turned around to find the light and center of his life, Nevaeh. Her deep brown skin and her wild curls proudly displayed both her African American and Puerto Rican heritages. His pretty, brown-eyed girl, who was so full of life and joy it made his heart burst with love for her, leaned into the doorjamb, giving him a grin so big he was sure it brightened the room.

"You like the blue on me, mija?"

She squinted her eyes as if she were really taking him in, and knowing just how perceptive the mind was behind those deep brown orbs, he knew she really was taking in every inch of the electric blue Brett Johnson cashmere turtleneck, his black slacks, and black ankle boots. She allowed her gaze to scan him from top to bottom and back again before she nodded her approval.

"It looks good on your skin. I bet your date's gonna like it too."

Carter turned and lifted his gaze to meet his daughter's, trying to see if she was joking or not.

"Little girl—" he tilted his head and lifted his brow to let her know she'd gotten his attention "—just because I put on a nice outfit doesn't mean I'm going out on a date. I wear dressier things than these when I go to work."

"Yeah," she agreed. "But you never fuss so much with your clothes when you're just going to work. So this has to be a date, right?"

*Out of the mouths of babes.*

Every time his little one opened her mouth nowadays, Carter found himself wondering if this kind of awareness was usual, or was he just lucky, and by lucky, he meant not so much in this instance, to have a kid who managed his personal business better than he did.

"I'm not going on a date, date, mija. I'm going to see if I can offer our new neighbor some help."

"What kinda help?"

Carter walked over to the foot bench at the bottom of his bed and motioned for his daughter to meet him there. When they were both seated, he covered her fingers with his, giving them a playful squeeze to get her to look up at him.

"Mr. Smith needs help planning an event for one of his family members who is very sick. Since party planning is a big part of my work, I offered to help him."

She tilted her head back and forth as if she were tossing his words around in her head until the motion made meaning.

"So it's not a date?"

"Not in the traditional sense, no."

She looked up at him, the way only a six-year-old could, calling his bullshit with pursed lips in one mo-

ment and then tiring of the adult game of vocabulary keep-away he seemed to be playing in the next.

"Well, I hope his family member feels better. And
even if it's not a *date* date, use your manners and
smile a lot. That always makes you happy when I
do those things. Maybe it will make Mr. Smith feel
better if you do 'em too."

God, her innocence twisted something deep in
his soul. This, this was the reason he'd walked away
from everything in Hollywood after his wife's death.
Michelle, more lovingly referred to as Mish by all
her friends…losing her had nearly broken him. But
being responsible for this little cherub of his made
Carter hypervigilant when it came to her protection.

There was no way he could've kept a mind as curious as hers innocent out in LA. Even worse, there
was no way he could protect her privacy there either.
Out there, she was always going to be the daughter
of superstar Carter Simon, the man who'd tragically
lost his wife to the perils of fame.

By its nature, New York was a town where folks
were nosy but tried hard not to get involved in other
folks' business. That, and New Yorkers, especially
Brooklynites, never thought anyone was special
enough to hold up traffic or get special favors. Dammit, they had places to be and not a whole lot of time
to get there. Because of that, here, his little girl was
just Nevaeh Jiménez, a beautiful brown girl with big
curls and an even bigger smile. And that was exactly
the way he wanted her to remain. After losing her

mother before she had a chance to even know Mish, Nevaeh deserved at least that much.

Carter turned back to his mirror, trying hard to keep it together. Thinking about his late wife, especially when it came to their daughter, always made him feel like his skin was tight and itchy and uncomfortable. Not because he didn't want to think about Mish; he'd loved her with every beat of his heart. But loving someone so wonderful and having her snatched away in one unforgettable moment, it sometimes made it hard for him to walk that fine line of happy father and grieving widower.

There was no end to grief. It came in waves. For years you could be fine, and then a memory crosses your mind and you're right back in the thick of it, feeling like you're being pulled beneath the undertow of dark, icy waters.

He was fortunate that he hadn't experienced one of those lows in over two years, and he didn't want to find himself adrift now. Tonight, he wanted to focus on the twinge of excitement that meeting his new neighbor had sparked in him. Yes, this wasn't a *date* date, but he didn't want to show up to Stephan's place with red swollen eyes. Considering everything Stephan was going through, Carter was sure Stephan wouldn't allow Carter to be of any help to him if he worried about Carter's emotional well-being.

"I promise to use good manners and smile, baby girl." He pointed toward his door and motioned for her to walk through it. "Now, go get ready for bed, and don't give Grannie Gracie any problems tonight."

"Daddy," she admonished him with just the flourish of her voice and the slightly disrespectful roll of her eyes. "I never give Grannie Gracie problems. We're besties."

He chuckled. His daughter was right—she and his former mother-in-law were besties, and Nevaeh never gave her problems because Grace affectionately called Gracie, always spoiled the little girl rotten. Carter knew it came from that soft place where loss and love dwelled, commingling to make you cherish every moment with your loved ones. Hell, before his own mother had taken her annual sabbatical to ride out most of the New York cold weather in Puerto Rico a few weeks ago, she'd worked just as hard as Gracie to prove Nevaeh was the most loved little girl in the world.

"I know. But I'm your dad. I still gotta state the rules so you can remember them.

He could see the laughter light up her eyes as if she were calculating all the mischief she and her grandmother were going to get up to tonight. Figuring it was easier to pretend either of them was going to listen to his so-called rules, he fiddled with his clothes again.

*You just told your daughter this isn't a date, date. Why are you still primping?*

*Why indeed?*

This wasn't the first time he'd met someone that

sparked his interest. He'd been on quite a few dates in the last two years. But those were just one-offs. A means to a satisfying end. None of those dates, however, had him hyper focused on making sure his mousse worked to secure his naturally curly hair into coiffed perfection.

"Daddy?"

Nevaeh's voice pulled him from his thoughts of hair products and casual but cute attire.

"Yes, mija?"

"Try to have some fun too. I like it when you smile."

He scrunched his brow, walking toward her and then squatting down so he was closer to her eye level.

"You talk like I don't smile. I smile all the time."

"Yeah, but sometimes I can tell you're smiling 'cause you don't want me to know you're sad…" Her words drifted off, leaving the *about mom* part floating on the wind.

His throat tightened. He dropped his gaze for just a moment, trying to pull himself together. He was supposed to be the one looking out for her happiness. Not the other way around.

"Hey, it's okay to be sad sometimes, especially when we're missing the people we love. But that doesn't mean I'm sad *all* the time. Because I'm not. You wanna know why?"

She nodded, her curls bopping eagerly as she awaited his answer.

"Because I have you. Getting to be your dad makes

me the happiest man in the world, even if I get sad sometimes because I miss mom."

"You sure?"

"Never more sure of anything in the world."

She launched herself at him, giving him just enough time to brace for the impact of an excited six-year-old, wrapping her arms around his neck while he was still squatting.

After she'd squeezed her little arms as tightly as she could around him, she gave him a quick kiss on the cheek and a, "Love you, daddy," as he put her down and she bounced out of his room.

He turned to the mirror, taking one last look at himself. Satisfied with his reflection and deciding that sans a full glam squad, his appearance wouldn't get much better by his own hands, he headed out of the bedroom, down the stairs, and through the front door.

"Ready or not, Stephan, here I come."

# Seven

"Hey, you made it."

A snap of excitement crackled inside Carter's chest as a flash of delight sparked in Stephan's eyes and wide grin.

"Yeah, the commute was a beast, but I'm here."

Stephan's cheeks turned a deep mauve under his espresso brown skin, and Carter had to fight the urge to swipe his thumb against one cheek to see if the skin there was as warm and supple as his mind imagined.

The only thing stopping him was the nagging voice in the back of his head telling him how repugnant he'd be if he went through with that desire.

Oh, he knew this wasn't supposed to be about

his attraction to Stephan, but his helping the man do something nice for his dying uncle and providing a bit of friendship for someone who was going through something difficult. But that didn't seem to stop the want curling in his stomach.

It was all so unsettling for him. Not twenty minutes ago he'd told his mother he wasn't ready for any romantic entanglements. But then he was here, in front of Stephan, and now he had to remind himself that Stephan was off-limits.

Carter had been around plenty of attractive people. Between being an actor and being the owner of a very successful VIP lounge for the elite, it meant good-looking people weren't an oddity to him. But his reaction to Stephan was something altogether different.

Because it wasn't about finding him attractive. And boy, did Carter find everything about Stephan's tight broad body appealing. But it was his haunted eyes that called to Carter, that made him want to dig deeper and provide support wherever he could.

He felt compassion for the guy. That's all it was. That's all it could be. Because, like he'd told his mother, he wasn't ready. He might not ever be ready to invest his heart in someone else again.

Carter focused on Stephan once more, loving the flush under the man's skin despite the fact that he'd just chastised himself for his poorly timed, foul thoughts.

"Oh, let me get that." Carter could tell the moment Stephan realized he was grinning like a child in a toy aisle because the man cleared his throat, down-playing his zeal by swiftly taking the insulated food bag out of Carter's hand.

"Thanks for agreeing to do this, Carter." He stepped aside and politely ushered Carter in. "I know we don't know each other well, and I can't figure out for the life of me why you'd want to spend your time doing this, but I appreciate it."

Carter stepped into the foyer and followed Stephan into the back of the house and into his modern kitchen. Everything from the cabinets to the appliances and countertops were white, giving a crisp, showroom look to the space that Carter envied. There was no way he could indulge in an all-white anything with the hurricane that was his daughter constantly exploding all over everything.

He motioned for Carter to take a seat in the breakfast nook in the corner by the large window that looked into the well-kept backyard.

"The mudroom's behind that door if you wanna wash the commute off you before I serve the meal."

Carter smiled, liking the fact that Stephan could take and make a joke, then made quick work of getting up to wash his hands.

When he returned to the kitchen proper, Stephan was bringing two heaping plates to the table.

"Carter, this smells amazing by the way."

"My mother's recipe." He used his fork to shift around the food on his plate before answering. "According to her, good food lifts the spirits. And since eating her food always makes me feel good, I'm inclined to agree with her."

"Well, if the menu you have in mind smells anything like this, I might actually believe we can pull this off. My uncle isn't much for fancy food. He likes food that speaks to a people's culture. Soul food, Asian, Mediterranean, hell, even American classics like a good cheeseburger—he loves it. But if he can't pronounce it, chances are he won't eat it, so keep it elegant but simple."

Stephan sat down, looking over his plate before lifting his eyes up to Carter.

"Do you get to do that often—eating your mother's food, I mean?"

Carter relaxed at the mention of his mother. Although she knew how to ride his nerves like any good mother did, she was his greatest supporter. No matter the challenge, she always had him, and he adored her for it. "Yes. She lives further up on Bedford. But right now, she's snowbirding in Puerto Rico for the next few months. When she's home, Nevaeh, Gracie, and I spend as much time with her as all our schedules allow. The four of us are pretty close"

Still feeling too raw after the conversation he just had with his mother, Carter pointed his fork at Stephan's plate.

"Eat up before it gets cold. You look like you need a good, hot meal."

"Is your superpower as a VIP lounge owner that you can always anticipate the needs of your patrons?"

Stephan took a bite and waited for Carter to respond.

"It's more likely something I pulled in from my old life."

"Old life?" Stephan snorted. "You make it sound like you were part of the mafia."

"In a way," Carter replied, "I guess you can say that's true. I used to work in Hollywood. To succeed there, you have to sell your devotion and obedience to the machine. Any act of defiance or disloyalty can ruin, if not take, your life."

Stephan's fork stopped midway between his plate and his mouth, as he stared at Carter.

He recognized the look blooming across Stephan's face. He'd seen it plenty of times when people realized who he was and what he had been.

His stomach tightened, tension stiffening his limbs as he waited for the expectant excitement and over-the-top fanfare that usually made him feel like he was being put on display.

It always made him uncomfortable. And when Stephan hadn't seemed to make a big deal about him, he'd figured either Stephan didn't care, or he simply didn't know who Carter was. Either way, it suited him just the same.

But this rapport the two men seemed to be building from their very first interaction was now threatened. Because the last thing Carter needed in his life was a fanboy looking for access into Hollywood.

But just as quickly as recognition flared in

Stephan's eyes, it passed, and he focused on his fork-ful of food.

He took the bite, wiping his mouth with a napkin before reaching for a nearby glass of water.

"You don't have to hold back on my account. I'd rather get this out in the open if it's gonna make things weird."

"If you're asking if I've always known you were actor Carter Simon, Hollywood heartthrob, the answer is no. I didn't until you just mentioned your work in Hollywood. The beard makes you look totally different."

Carter blinked, wondering if this was a facade, or if Stephan was really this at ease with Carter's past.

"That was the whole point. I wanted a normal life again. I didn't want Carter Simon to intrude on the life I was trying to build for us here. The beard, the new profession, it all was the exact opposite of who I was when I was him."

"Except, your lounge is literally an exclusive hot spot for the who's who in New York. Celebrities, politicians, business powerbrokers, they all come to The Vault for a good time away from the cameras."

Carter leaned forward, raising a brow.

"So you did look me up?"

Stephan shook his head. "No, I looked up the lounge when you invited me for wings. I live by 'the who all gon' be there' query. So I checked it out before I showed up. The search fails to mention anything about you being a renowned actor, though."

Carter nodded at Stephan. "Carter Simon and Carter Jiménez are two different people. Simon has nothing to do with Jiménez. With the exception of my late wife, my daughter, and my best friend who works in politics, I hate everything about Hollywood and the celebrity lifestyle. Notoriety is a cancer that destroys, and I have no intention of ever inviting it back into our lives."

Now that Stephan knew who he was, he assumed the man knew how he'd lost his wife. Carter Simon's life put her in the path of the paparazzi who chased her to her death. There was no way he could remain associated with that world and protect his daughter and his sanity.

"It's why I came back here. I needed to be around real people and protect my daughter from the vile truths of living in that world. It's also why I'll never go back."

"So owning a club that the rich and elite patronize is…"

It was a fair question. But the truth was, it had nothing to do with keeping a foothold in that life.

"Membership to the club isn't offered to the who's who because of who they are. It's offered to them because I understand what it is to live in a fishbowl. My place offers them a safe space to be normal without fear of having their normalcy exploited or broadcast around the world."

"So, this really isn't an act, I take it?"

Carter grimaced as he tried to figure out what Stephan was talking about.

"This pay it forward thing you have going on?" He took another bite of food and continued. "I thought it was a ploy to get into my pants at first. But now, knowing who you were, I can honestly understand why you do what you do."

Stephan's statement struck Carter in the middle of his chest with as much force as a sledgehammer on a tiny nail tack. Somehow, he got who and why Carter was, and as unnerving as that should've been, it drew Carter in.

When your career was becoming everyone's fantasy, the reality of who you are didn't often matter. As an actor, he was always on. As a Puerto Rican actor who also happened to be bisexual, that meant he was never allowed to do something as simple as look like he'd rolled straight out of bed and out on the street. He had to be perfectly coiffed at all times for fear the tabloids would paint him as having some kind of breakdown that would put his employability in harm's way.

He knew it sounded far-fetched, but the reality was, just because he could pass for white in the right lighting didn't mean that Hollywood execs ever forgot for one moment that he wasn't. And from the moment he'd landed his first big role, he knew the deck was stacked against him, and he had to play by a different set of rules to win. It was fucked up. That was for certain. But it was fact, nonetheless.

Sitting here with this man, who didn't seem to care about his past fame, it felt good. It felt good enough that he kept himself from asking a bunch of questions to dig into Stephan's past. He would learn him—so he could help him, of course. But he would learn what would made the handsome man with the soulful eyes tick.

"Now I'm curious." Carter put his fork down, giving Stephan his complete attention and making it decidedly harder to keep his hand-mouth-eye coordination in check while he was eating. "When most folks find out who I used to be, they're never this chill about it. Not even New Yorkers."

Stephan understood why. There was a time you couldn't go to the movies and not see a promo poster with Carter's clean-shaven face staring back at you.

Stephan opened his mouth to speak but hesitated. He too had his own issues with fame and notoriety. And right now, he wasn't really sure if Carter was someone he should share that with.

First, he seemed cool enough, but Stephan had to protect Ace and his family at all costs. Trust was a precious commodity in his world. Sharing it with the wrong person could destroy you.

However, it was the next reason that weighed on him more heavily. Would Carter be able to disassociate Stephan from the world he lived in?

If Stephan remembered the headlines correctly, tabloid reporters had surrounded his wife while she was on the street and chased her when she found a break in their human wall. She ran blindly into the street, putting her into the path of oncoming traffic. Fame literally cost her her life.

After experiencing something like that, and given Carter's disclosed hatred of Hollywood, Stephan worried that Carter wouldn't be able to discern the difference between who Stephan was and the world he was forced to live in by virtue of his last name.

"My work often puts me in contact with people from all walks of life."

"What exactly do you do?"

Stephan could feel a slight twitch in his sharp jawline. He struggled to control it, hoping it would look like more of an involuntary muscle movement than a reaction to Carter's question.

"I run the Paris branch of an American-based venture capitalist company."

*That's it. Make it sound as boring as you can so Carter drops the subject.*

"So you're on leave now to be with your uncle?"

"I'm back in the States to be with uncle. Fortunately, my job allows for remote working when necessary. If I need to go back, I will. But with the advent of video chats, I don't have to go back at all, if I don't want to."

Stephan's conscience howled at the colorful version of the truth he was presenting. Yes, he was telling the truth. But the fact that he was keeping Carter in the dark about who he really was nicked at him for reasons he didn't understand.

It wasn't like Stephan wasn't justified in this behavior. Time had taught him over and over again that people would screw him over in a second if it benefited them. Or that he was only valuable as long as he was doing something for them.

Dexter had never made that point clearer. Six months after his brother died in Jamaica, Stephan had gone back there partly for Devereaux Inc. business and partly looking for some sort of peace. It wasn't that he hadn't accepted Randall's untimely death; he had. It was that Stephan's soul was so full of hurt, anguish, and guilt about shoving family secrets so far down his throat, he felt like he was choking.

He'd run into Dexter over the course of his business, and they'd hit it off. Laughing, playing, and relaxing, the time he spent with Dexter had healed something in him. Until he'd discovered it was all a ploy to cash in on the bank of Stephan Devereaux-Smith.

Dexter was just one in a long line of people who had proven to Stephan he couldn't let his guard down or let people in.

As a result, Stephan stuck to his "no new friends" policy, and after assholes like Dexter, he never felt the slightest bit bad about being vague about his life, work, and background. That's why the sliver of guilt tugging at the back of his brain didn't make any sense.

This was standard operating procedure. Don't let anyone in, and you don't have to worry about them using you.

What the hell was wrong with him? What the hell was Carter doing to him?

"Well…" Carter beamed as he picked up his glass of water and held it up for a toast. The momentary darkness talking about his past cast over him disappearing quickly. "I know being home must be hard for you right now. But I'm glad the universe saw fit for our paths to cross. I can never have too many real folks around me."

Stephan picked up his glass, clinking it to Carter's. Real? Stephan couldn't remember the last time he'd been allowed to be his real self. But sitting here with Carter, Stephan desperately wanted to be the real him again.

"Now," Carter said with a bit of exuberance in his voice. Let's finish this good food, and get to planning the best Christmas party that ever was. I know someone that can make the walls look like snow-capped mountains if you're into that kind of thing."

The idea of gaudy fake mountains in Borough Hall should've made Stephan choke on his food. But seeing the outright joy beaming on Carter's face as he said it, Stephan was pretty certain he'd suffer that level of tackiness any day of the week if it meant he got to watch Carter smile like that.

Because more than anything, Stephan was realizing that every time Carter smiled, he did feel more and more like the real Stephan Devereaux-Smith. It was just too bad being the real him would mean he'd have to push Carter away. And that, even though it galled him to admit it, wasn't what he wanted.

# Eight

"Are you gonna share why you have us in this early as hell meeting, or are we supposed to guess?"

Stephan looked to his side to find his cousin Amara squirming around in her chair trying to find the perfect spot to support her back. From what he'd heard, with only two more months to go in her pregnancy, there wasn't really a comfortable spot to be had.

Make no mistake, Amara wasn't a bowl of sunshine before her pregnancy. But this baby was raising her hackles in such a way, everyone who crossed her path was on notice.

He laughed off her grumpy response. Hell, if he had to do the work of cooking a human, he'd be pissy all the time too.

"Because, cousin…" he replied with as much compassion as he could muster, which was saying something, because Stephan didn't coddle most people he encountered. "We're the cousin crew and I wanted to let y'all in on a few things."

"Everything okay, *cousin*?" Stephan watched as Trey, the newest edition to both the Devereaux family and Devereaux Incorporated, walked into the room and sat at the head of the conference table. Her taking that seat was a reminder to everyone in that room she might be new to the crew, but she was definitely in charge.

She was Ace's estranged granddaughter, someone who managed the impossible by bringing Ace and her father, Deuce, back into each other's lives again.

A miracle worker like that, Stephan understood without question why Ace had chosen her as his direct successor as owner and CEO of the family's billion-dollar company.

She'd married, Jeremiah, Ace's ward from the time he was sixteen years old, and an honorary Devereaux cousin, around the time Stephan had returned home for Ace. She was smart, headstrong, ambitious, and her Brooklyn glam girl fashion sense was on fire. But the thing that made him embrace her openly was the fact that she was just as loyal to Ace as he was. Up until Ace's mandate that he go out and find a life, Stephan had seen Trey and Jeremiah at Ace's bedside or downstairs in the family room of Devereaux manor almost every night.

And when they were all huddled in that big bedroom of Ace's, she loved on that old man the way only a devoted granddaughter who thought her granddaddy hung the moon could.

I'll admit," Trey continued, "I get a little worried when my branch directors call for an unexpected meeting like this."

"Everything's fine, Trey." Stephan tried to assure her, although he wasn't exactly sure any of them would find what he had to say agreeable. "I was just waiting for you and Jeremiah to get here so I could begin."

"Where's Lyric?" Amara interjected. "If I gotta be here, so does she."

"Lyric is filming this morning. She couldn't make it, but I plan to call her later to fill her in."

"Then let's get to it so we can start the rest of our workday. Is something going on with the Paris branch you need us to know about?" Jeremiah gave him a nod. He was co-CEO with his wife, so he would have just as much of an interest in this meeting as Trey did.

"Everything's more than fine with the Paris branch. This isn't about the business. This is about the family, specifically Ace."

He could see worry literally etch into their faces. Every one of them was aware of Ace's poor prognosis. Mentioning Ace nowadays created an immediate call to attention. He meant that much to every one of them.

"Ace wants me to throw him a Devereaux family Christmas party."

"I'm sorry," Trey replied. "A Devereaux what now?"

"A Devereaux family Christmas party," Jeremiah, Amara, and Stephan said in unison.

"It was a tradition long before any of us was born," Amara continued.

"It was still a thing even when I came to the family at sixteen," Jeremiah added by way of answering his wife. "It was this grand Christmas party where all the branches of the Devereaux family came together to celebrate Christmas under one roof. It was the biggest event in the family until two years ago."

Amara looked up at the ceiling as if she were looking back into Devereaux Christmases past and Jeremiah was beaming too. There was a distant smile on both their faces that Stephan couldn't help but match.

Just the mention of those Christmases past made him think about some of the loud boisterous times they'd had with their family, where the kids played with their toys while the adults talked. Where Ace would lead the family in a solemn prayer they said before they sat down to a feast. And the best part, the best part was when they'd get to the call and answer portion of the evening where Ace would use his rich baritone to lead them all in spiritual or devotional songs that had been sung through the generations of the Brooklyn Devereauxs since time began.

It was love, plain and simple. And it had all stopped because of him, because of what he'd done, the secret he still carried to this day.

"Sounds like a wonderful time. What happened two years ago to make it stop?"

Stephan watched his two cousins as their smiles faded and their gazes fell on him. They were looking to him. His stomach roiled and his neck tightened. Two years and speaking these words still hollowed out his soul.

"My brother died two months before Christmas, and I left home and refused to return. To Ace, having Christmas without his only living nephew wasn't going to happen. So, he refused to have another one until I was ready to come home."

Silence in the room was overpowering. Not because he thought his family was judging him. No, because he was judging himself. If he'd only known Ace's time was nearly up, he probably would've made another decision. But being so overrun by the guilt of secrets and lies, Stephan ran, leaving Ace to deal with the family so Stephan could keep the ticking time bomb of truth locked down far away where it couldn't do any damage.

"It's my fault this family has been fractured for the last two years. I owe Ace this." After everything Ace had done for him, after taking all the blame Stephan should've shouldered himself, he owed this debt.

His words hung in the air as they all stared at each other, trying to figure who would say what next.

"Stephan." Trey stood as she called his name, making her way to his side of the conference table and placing a comforting hand on his shoulder. "I think my dad broke the family when he married my mom thirty-some-odd years ago. You don't have to take that burden on all by yourself. Not the blame for the family nor the load of planning this party on your own."

The tension that made his neck ache was joined by pain that lanced through the center of his chest like a sharp knife. If she knew, if they all knew, none of them would be so eager to help him appease his conscience.

"I appreciate it, cousin. I do. But if you don't mind, if none of you mind, I'd like to do this myself. He asked me to do it, and it's the least I can do after all he's done for me."

"I'm surprised you agreed to anything that would take you away from Ace's bed." Amara's voice broke through the heavy emotions weighing down his rib cage, making it hard to breathe. "Let me guess, you're planning the whole thing from the chair at his bed-side?"

"No, smart-ass," he countered. "I've actually connected with a friend who has experience in party planning. He's agreed to help me get this thing together." He stopped to look at his watch as a reminder of how little time he had left between now and when the party would take place.

"We sketched out some plans the last time we met up and he's agreed to help me get this thing together quickly."

Jeremiah sighed heavily, drawing the attention in the room to himself. "He might not have that long, cousin."

The words were heavy, somber, and quiet, yet they all heard them as if they were spoken through a megaphone.

"I know," Stephan answered quietly. "That's why I'm gonna make this happen quickly. The date's set for two weeks from this Saturday."

"Two days after Thanksgiving?" Trey asked the question, but Jeremiah and Amara were nodding in unison while she did.

"Yeah. It's the earliest I can make it happen. It seems even Devereaux money can't move mountains for the holidays."

"Well," Trey continued. "We're here for you, cousin. Whether it's to plan this party, or talk whenever something's wearing you down, we're here for you."

Jeremiah joined her, stopping to give Stephan a warm hug before he and his wife left the room. Realizing Amara was still there, he reached out to help her out of her chair.

"You are such a good man, Stephan. Regardless of whether Ace makes it to see this party or not, you are the best there is."

She kissed him on his cheek and left him in the large conference room by himself. As always, the familiar darkness that dogged him for the last two years closed its cold fingers around his throat and squeezed tightly and he struggled to breathe.

But somewhere through the anxiety building in his head, he could hear the chiming of his cellphone in his pocket. With shaking hands he turned it over, and when he saw Carter's name flashing, his airway opened up again, and sweet air traveled freely into his lungs.

"Hello." Stephan's voice was raw, and he knew Carter would probably sense something was wrong.

"You were on my mind, so I decided to call and see if you were up for lunch today. It's pretty quiet this time of day at The Vault, so I could hang out a bit. You free?"

Stephan's shoulders relaxed and he managed a weary, grateful smile. He had a ton of work to do and his emotions were all over the place. But for some reason, the idea of spending more time with Carter made every anxious thought in his head go silent.

Carter was fine and then some with his dark hair and eyes, and a body that wouldn't quit. Stephan could definitely see why he'd been such a sought-after actor in the past. Yes, his looks had attracted Stephan in the beginning, but between spending time with him at his club and having dinner at Stephan's place, Stephan had been way more interested in just talking to Carter.

He was funny, a typical doting dad who adored his daughter, and even though Stephan had only met the girl once in passing, he never tired of the flash of joy that streaked across Carter's eyes when he spoke about her. However, above all else, the thing that

Stephan cherished most about Carter was his compassion. His need to check in and make sure someone was all right.

Stephan assumed this was something Carter did for all the people around him. He hadn't really known him long enough to determine otherwise. But if he were honest, he liked knowing Carter cared enough about him to make sure Stephan was okay.

He hadn't felt cared for like that in a long time.

That had to be the reason, right?

"What other reason could there be? Stephan wasn't built for anything else.

Sure, it wasn't like he made their visits and calls all about him. In fact, he was way more interested in listening to Carter go on and on about garland versus tinsel. Stephan didn't remember which he'd chosen, because he'd been so busy watching the animated delight on the man's face as he talked. It was all perfectly natural and harmless.

At least, he could pretend it was all harmless until Carter was near him, like bending over a catalog to show Stephan a new option for the winter wonderland Carter was helping him build—that's when things went straight to hell in a handbasket. That's when he had to fight his base need to touch Carter, to smell and taste him, and have him do the same to Stephan.

The need to smell him was almost an uncontrollable urge at this point. Stephan's dick had never been hard over the way a man smelled. But every time Carter wore whatever the hell that sweet and woodsy scent was, Stephan had to damn near sit on his hands like some uncontrollable child who couldn't be trusted not to touch the new shiny thing in front of him.

His conscience chose that moment to wag its metaphorical finger in Stephan's face. He was wrong for this. He was essentially using Carter as if he were human Valium at best and spank bank material at worst. Carter deserved better than that. But no matter how terrible Stephan knew he was, he couldn't resist the euphoric high he knew he'd experience being in the man's presence. If that made him an asshole, he'd accept it. He'd certainly called himself worse.

He took a breath, trying to temper his excitement. "For you," he said calmly. "And your club's wings, I'm always free."

# Nine

"Hey, boss. Where'd you want these?"

Carter smoothed out the linen on the table he'd had set up in the corner.

"Just bring the rolling cart over here. I'll set the food out when I'm ready."

Ian, his bartender/server/jack-of-all trades when Carter was in a staffing crunch, pushed a small cart filled with a few platters.

"You entertaining a potential big client? Because this is an extensive menu list."

From the variety of foods Carter had brought to Stephan's house, Carter figured the best way to tackle the menu for this event was the same way he handled the menu here at The Vault.

Brooklyn was made up of many little neighborhoods with strong ties to ethnic communities. He had everything from soul food, Asian, Latin American, and Caribbean cuisine, to Italian at The Vault. So, coming up with a diverse menu wouldn't be the problem. The problem was they didn't have a great deal of time, so everything they added would have to be locally sourced and available in abundant quantities.

Carter decided to put a heavy emphasis on soul food because of the time-constraint issue, but also because Stephan said it was his uncle's favorite. He'd use Latin and Caribbean cuisine to round out everything nicely.

Ian made a show of shaking the order list out before reading it aloud. "First up is your bread service. Honey corn bread and buttermilk biscuits. You've got your starters—lime-pepper wings, crab cakes, mini Jamaican beef patties, plantains, and pasteles. You've got your entrées—blackened catfish, braised oxtails, pernil, smothered pork chops, and short ribs. Next are your sides—Jamaican rice & peas, collard greens garnished with smoked turkey, baked macaroni and cheese, candied yams, potato salad, and Spanish rice. The dessert should arrive before you get to the entrées. The sweet potato pie and peach cobbler were just coming out of the oven when I was leaving the kitchen."

Carter began checking the lids to make sure everything was to his specifications when he felt Ian's heavy gaze on him. As Carter met it, he could see

Ian's eyes processing every detail of Carter's behavior. Five minutes in his presence, and he could read anyone. That particular superpower along with his unmatched skill at mixology made him one of the most popular and well-tipped bartenders in his employ.

"I don't have a big client. Just a friend I'm helping plan an unexpected party. We're on a time crunch, so I needed to come up with a sample menu he could taste in one setting so we can get the ball rolling on things."

That's all Carter could say by way of explanation. It's all he would say to Ian, and more importantly to himself.

Carter would not admit that he never took this much care with setting a table for a client. Hell, he wouldn't even do this for his best friend Lennox.

*Then why are you doing this?*

*Nope, not going there. Not even for a little bit.*

He lifted his gaze from the table to Ian and caught his employee offering him his signature slick smile that he usually reserved for patrons who made a habit of lying to themselves as they made themselves the victors or the victims of their tales. That grin screamed, *You see this fool right here? He actually believes the crap he's spewing.*

It was always hilarious before, an inside joke that he'd found entertaining so many times in the past. But now that Carter suspected he was playing the role of the fool in today's scenario, he wasn't amused at all.

Ian didn't wait for further explanation. He just gave

Carter a knowing wink, then left as quietly as he'd entered.

Carter didn't want to think about what was going on here. For one, Stephan had a lot of emotional upheaval going on right now and people made really bad decisions when they were hurting.

Not that Carter was looking for forever, but he'd meant what he'd said the last time he and Stephan were in this room. They were neighbors, and getting close could become problematic if things went left. He didn't want his daughter impacted by that. She was safe here. The world of the rich and famous wasn't coming to Brooklyn to find her, not like they had her mother in L.A. And above all else, Carter had to protect the sanctity of the fortress he'd built for them here.

He rubbed the back of his neck, trying to self-soothe the nervous energy that was coursing through him.

There was no harm in being attracted to Stephan. He was the walking depiction of tall, dark, and handsome. Add to that his deep soulful eyes and his big heart, and Carter would be a fool not to be attracted to him.

He wasn't afraid of being attracted to Stephan physically. He'd be grateful if that's all it was.

But that wasn't all there was to it and therein lay the problem.

He wanted to connect with Stephan. He'd felt this intense need to check on him, make sure he was all right from that first moment on Stephan's stoop. He wanted to make it better, whatever *it* was.

Carter had blamed it on the brokenhearted recognizing a heart currently breaking, but now that he was helping Stephan, now that he'd had a little tiny glimpse into who the man might be, Carter wanted to keep digging until he'd uncovered it all.

He realized how trifling it was to want to be firmly planted into someone else's business when he'd literally moved across the country to keep people out of his. But the more time he spent with Stephan, the more he hoped he'd open up to Carter, give him a little more insight than he had. Because from the tiny bit he could see, Stephan, by all accounts, was a good man. And good men going through hard times deserved a break.

That was it. That's all it could be. He wanted to connect because he wanted to give this gorgeous man, who loved his uncle enough to come home and spend the man's last days with him, a break. Anyone that selfless deserved all the fucking breaks in the world as far as Carter was concerned.

Nice guy or no, Carter still had to pay close attention to himself and his motives. Codependence was a real thing, and just because Carter was on an even keel now with his grief, didn't mean he couldn't subconsciously be looking for a literal partner in grief.

He couldn't do that to Stephan when his heartache and loss was so present. And he couldn't upend his own healing process either. Not just for him, but the beautiful little girl who depended on him. He needed to be whole.

Then why was he standing here setting the perfect mood for an afternoon delight?

The answer was simple. He wanted Stephan Smith. He wanted to know him. Listening to him talk the other night about his work and then brainstorming the initial planning stages of the Christmas party had made Carter feel at ease with the man. So at ease in fact that he'd revealed his past to Stephan.

He never let people in that far. But part of him had wanted to know if Stephan could be trusted or not, and so he'd shared his truth. The man had come through with flying colors, understanding Carter's reticence around fame and his absolute hatred of the business that had stolen his wife from him.

The relief he'd felt at Stephan's reaction had broken something free in him. The hesitance and trepidation he always felt around new people drifted away.

And now, much to his dismay, all that remained was this want, this desire to just be in the man's presence. Hence this impromptu lunch—he still couldn't bring himself to call it a *date* date, though.

That would mean he was looking for something more, and he wasn't actually sure if either of them was ready for more than food and a little emotional support at present.

"I hope whatever's under those covered silver platters tastes as good as its packaging looks."

The trepidation of his reasonable mind vanished and Carter's entire being buzzed with excitement at the sound of Stephan's voice.

"Please prepare to be impressed, sir." Carter lifted the cover for the small center dish. "These are our famous wings for starters." He placed the covering on the rolling cart and then pointed to the larger covered dishes still remaining on the cart. "And these," Carter uncovered the remaining dishes, pausing to give Stephan a chance to take the presented bounty all in. "are everything else."

"Damn, Carter." Stephan beamed as he stepped into the room, closing the door behind and making his way to the table in the corner where Carter stood. "All this is for me? To what do I owe the pleasure?"

What indeed?

It was a fair question. And he didn't really have an answer except for the fact that he just really wanted to pamper Stephan, take care of him.

"Well, for one, I appreciated how you treated me after finding out about my past. Usually when someone discovers who I was, things immediately get weird. You treated me like a normal person, and I appreciate that."

Stephan gave a slow nod, raising a brow to bid Carter permission to continue.

"And second?"

His voice was somewhere in his lower register, as if his words were meant for Carter alone. Of course, that intent should be obvious because they were the only two people in the room. But the way the richness of his deeper notes teased Carter's ears and ghosted over his skin, leaving goose bumps behind, he knew Stephan was speaking this way solely for his benefit.

A small smile curved his lips in appreciation for this constant volley that seemed to pass between them.

One moment, Carter was the one being forward with all the double entendres, and the next, Stephan was turning the tables on him. They didn't just shift dominance, this space they were creating between them allowed for either of them to be vulnerable when they wanted or needed to be.

Carter liked it. He liked it too much. So much so he kept his hands clasped behind his back for fear that he would cross a line that neither of them could afford to ignore right now.

"I pulled some strings and I was able to get a venue for this Christmas gala."

"Oh yeah? Where?"

"I know you didn't think we'd be able to get it at such late notice, but if you want it, Borough Hall is available," Carter answered. "That is, if you're not too worried about budget. And even if you are, I'm sure my people can get us a steep discount."

Stephan stepped closer until he was on the same side of the food cart as Carter. He was so close, the mix of spice and soap, with a slight twinge of sweetness filled Carter's senses, making it hard to focus on anything but those full lips that were so close to him, all he'd have to do is lean forward just so, and he'd know what they tasted like.

"I'm not worried about the budget. There are

enough of us Smiths that if we need to chip in to cover the costs, I'm sure it won't be a problem."

"Good." Carter swallowed. "I gave the contact your number, so you should be getting a call either later today or tomorrow."

Stephan gave Carter a slow nod, his gaze drifting to Carter's mouth as he stepped so close that Carter had no choice but to step back until he felt his desk pressing into the backs of his thighs.

Stephan picked up his hand, cupping Carter's cheek, caressing the line of his jaw with his thumb. Every inch of his skin the man's thumb slid across burned, aching for Stephan's soothing touch.

"You are a godsend, Carter, and I find myself wanting to show my appreciation to you right now."

"You don't owe me anything, Stephan." Carter tried to keep his eyes open, but being this close to Stephan with his hands touching Carter's bare skin was making him dizzy with need.

"Oh, you misunderstand me. I want to show you my appreciation because I want you. Not because I feel obligated to you. Will you let me?"

Carter knew the correct answer to Stephan's question should've been no. He knew allowing this was going to cause trouble down the line that he would more than likely regret. But with this fine-ass-man all in his face, taking up all his good air and replacing it with the most enticing aroma Carter had ever encountered, he knew damn well he wasn't going to turn this man's request down.

"Yes."

A small, simple world. But damn, did it hold so much power. Just that small utterance was enough to unleash all the repressed desire they'd both haphazardly juggled since they'd met.

Stephan's first press of his lips was soft and tentative. Seeking, as he tried to learn what Carter liked. But the fire that burned between them elicited such a deep moan that within seconds, Stephan had skipped passed tentative and his lips pressed firmly against Carter's, teasing, tasting, tempting him until the only thing his body could do was burn and quiver.

Stephan's hand slipped from Carter's jaw, to the back of his head, raking the scalp beneath his buzzed fade, and the heat that had been coursing through him turned into a full-on blaze, making his cock twitch as it ached for some personal attention of its own.

His hands were on Stephan because he wanted to touch him, but also because he needed something to brace against, since this kiss had snatched his innate ability to remain balanced on his own two feet.

Carter wasn't sure who ended the kiss, although the desperation raging inside of him made him believe it had to be Stephan who'd had strength enough to step away. Because everything in Carter, and he did in fact mean everything, wanted that kiss to continue and move on to the point where they were stripping each other's clothes off and humping on Carter's desk.

It's not like it would be the first time. Lennox and

Amara had conceived their soon-to-be-born baby on this very desk. A little more action wouldn't hurt the obviously sturdy piece of furniture.

"Now…" Stephan stepped away, a sexy twinkle in his eye beckoning Carter to follow him as he sat down at the perfectly set table. "Who exactly's going to have their way with whom?"

The smirk on his lips should've pissed Carter off. The sheer arrogance of the statement, and he knew he had a lot of audacity to see it as such, considering he'd said much the same to Stephan a week ago. But mad was the furthest thing from Carter's mind at this moment.

No, he wasn't mad, he was turned on beyond all recognition and had not the slightest bit of shame in admitting he wholeheartedly wanted Stephan to have his way with him as often and in whichever way he deemed fit.

Because that kiss had him reciting the rosary in his head to get his cock to relent and his blood to stop boiling him from the inside out.

*Oh, Mr. Smith, it is most definitely on.*

# Ten

Stephan stood in front of the white double brown-stone mansion that seemed to have stood on Clinton Ave from the beginning of time.

Devereaux Manor, the place where Ace had created a legacy and a home for his family. Even though Stephan had never technically lived here, he'd spent so much of his life within its walls that it was hard to find very many memories of his childhood that hadn't started there.

He hesitated slightly as he took the first step across the threshold and into its hallowed halls filled with family portraits of those who came before and those still here. And every time he stood before them, gratitude and pride filled him that he was granted access to such a legacy.

Even in the depths of his guilt for the lies he'd told and the secrets he'd kept, he knew he'd done it to protect his family. The people he loved more than himself. The people who deserved happiness, even if it was at Stephan's expense.

He didn't see anyone lingering around when he came in, so he quickly headed directly for Ace's room, taking the steps two at a time. When he reached the landing, he gave himself a shake, trying to douse the good mood flowing through him. He'd kissed Carter last night, and even the weight of his sins couldn't stop Stephan from feeling like he was on top of the world.

Before he could let go of the memory of how good Carter tasted, he took a settling breath and stepped toward the door. Laughter greeted him, so Stephan tapped quickly on the door and walked inside.

*Remember, be chill and don't act different.*

"Heyyyy, family! What we got going on here?"

Both Ace and Trey stopped laughing to look at Stephan and then each other. Their searching gazes told him his greeting was just a tad bit over the top.

"Hey, nephew," Ace greeted him, waving him into the room that held a light energy Stephan knew came from the laughter he'd heard through the door. "Trey was just telling me about how upset she made some of the more seasoned board members at the last quarterly meeting."

"My day isn't made if I'm not making one of them

mad." Trey stood next to the small wet bar in the corner, pouring herself a healthy glass of water from the Svalbarði bottle Stephan recognized. When she was done, she came over and wrapped an arm around him. They were still getting to know each other, but the bond, that thing that forced the Devereaux family to stand against the world together, that was strong and present. "How you doin', cuz? You looking good. Got a little sparkle in your eye and pep in your step. Anything new you wanna share with the class?"

He stilled his features, trying hard to lock everything down. He was a grown man—a kiss shouldn't be enough to make him lose all his chill like this.

*Don't be that goofy dude, Stephan.*

He cleared his throat and tried again to make his face impassive so he wouldn't give anything away. There was no way Trey could've known anything about the kiss Stephan and Carter shared. But he'd seen this cunning woman in the boardroom. If she sensed the slightest bit of blood in the water, she would pounce like the apex predator she was.

"Nothing's happening, cousin. It's just a beautiful day outside and I'm happy to spend a little time with my family."

Trey stepped around him as she watched him with a lifted brow, then stopped to take a sip of water from her glass. When she was done, she sat back down in her chair with a suspicious gleam in her eye and broad grin on her face.

"If you say so." She crossed one thick leg over another as she settled back into her seat.

"So, anything to report, nephew."

"Can I take my coat off first, Uncle Ace?"

The old man waved a pointed finger in the air. "No you may not. As per our last conversation, you're only supposed to come here if you've got proof of joy."

Stephan faked a shiver, rubbing his hands up and down his arms to drive his point home. "Damn, you're talking to me in professional clap-back now? Uncle Ace, that ain't right."

"If I were you, cousin," Trey interjected. "I'd give the old man what he wants. He's got a nasty way of gathering us when we don't cooperate."

She wasn't wrong, but Stephan couldn't let that comment fly without a response. With a fake scowl on his face, he removed his jacket and sat down in a nearby chair before he spoke again.

"You know minding your business and drinking your water is free, right?"

Trey took a long sip and then lifted her glass in Stephan's direction.

"You's a damn lie," Trey replied. "A month's supply of this Svalbarði Limited Edition water cost more than some people's rent.

Stephan held his laughter for as long as he could, but the moment he snickered, Trey and Ace followed suit.

Once they recovered, Trey excused herself, leaving Ace and Stephan to face each other with no barriers.

"My granddaughter is right," Ace began slowly as his gaze took Stephan in much the same way Trey had. "You do seem to have little spark about you."

Kissing a sexy man who had great conversation, a compassionate heart, and a sweetheart of an ass would do that for you. But seeing as he couldn't share that or rather he wouldn't. What would be the point? He already knew that nothing serious could come of a liaison between him and Carter. Getting Ace all excited about something that would amount to nothing in the end seemed cruel to Ace, to Carter, and Stephan.

His decision further cemented, Stephan found something else to talk about.

"A friend of mine has agreed to help me plan this party of yours, and he's been sharing some great ideas I think you're gonna like."

"Such as?"

The old man's smile looked as innocent as the sky was blue, but knowing what a mental ninja Ace was, Stephan didn't fall for the sweet old man act Ace was playing right now. If Carter could see Ace, he'd probably nominate this performance to the Academy. Yeah, *could* being the operative word here.

Enjoying his good mood too much to let the realities of his situation bring him down, he decided the best thing he could do in this situation was play along.

"I told him you're pretty much royalty in our circles, so he found some tablecloths that were owned by an Ethiopian empress he's going to see if we can rent. It's going to cost a mint if he can come through, but from what I could tell from the photos, they'll be more than worth it."

"And that's all you're excited about?" Ace asked again. "These royal linens?"

"Of course," Stephan answered quickly. "What other reason could there be?"

Ace narrowed his gaze, his cheeks rising with a slightly sinister gleam in his eyes.

"Okay, nephew," Ace said. "Tell me about these party plans you and your *friend*—" Ace put emphasis on the word, letting Stephan know he wasn't fooled by his bullshit "—have come up with for this event."

Stephan stepped out into the cold air, bundled into his North Face and a beanie as he left Devereaux Manor and walked the seven blocks up Gates Avenue to his home. He was just about to turn right onto Grand Avenue when a jolt of restlessness hit him. It was still Saturday morning and since he didn't have any plans, he figured he might as well stop into his favorite local café and get some pastry and a coffee. CUP aka Coffee Uplifts People, was located just five blocks away from his brownstone at the intersection of Gates and Bedford Avenues. It was a Black-owned coffee shop with a mission to source from Black and Brown growers around the world.

Even though he was part of the notorious 2 percent of the superwealthy in America, he wholeheartedly believed in supporting the businesses and people the world often forgot about. And being one of the few Black-owned billion-dollar businesses, not only in the United States but the world, Stephan, his family, and Devereaux Inc. felt an unshakable commitment to giving back in meaningful ways to their community. The only time that promise had ever been in jeopardy was when his cousin Amara had made a fast deal for the wrong reasons. But his uncle David had gathered her quickly, and she'd gotten herself, and the company's focus back on track. As a bonus, she ended up with a husband, a baby on the way, and was about to become the First Lady of New York City in the new year.

Feeling it might be a tad early for him to get so hopped up on his urban renewal stance, Stephan hurried into the coffee shop, sighing his relief when the warmth enveloped him. He waved at the owner, delighted that his usual table in the corner was available.

"Stephan? Is that you?"

He followed the voice until he found Carter sitting at a table with a tiny person who was currently wearing an oversized white sweater that in conjunction with the fuzzy cap on her head, looked like a human plushie.

Stephan waved, not sure if he should walk over to their table.

To be clear, he wanted to walk over to their table and kiss Carter hello. But the man was sitting with his young daughter; now might not be the best time to act on his desire to tongue the man down.

Not to mention, there were Carter's hang-ups about drawing attention to himself in public, all of it making his usual confidence when it came to matters of attraction seem ill-fitting at present.

"We're having cocoa, Mr. Smith."

Once those big eyes found his and that wide grin spread across the little girl's face, there wasn't a chance Stephan was walking away.

"Thank you for the invitation, Nevaeh." Stephan sat down, reciprocating her grin, then lifting his gaze up to find the same wide eyes looking at him, just in a bigger, sexier form. But the effect was still the same. Both father and daughter had Stephan Devereaux-Smith, the smoothest talking brotha in the world, wrapped up in endless lashes that shielded dark brown eyes deep enough to drown in.

If he didn't get control of this situation, he'd have to return his player's card.

"What are the two of you doing here today?"

"Having breakfast after washday."

"Is that so?" Stephan replied, trying his best to give his finest attentive face to the little girl.

"Yeah. My mother-in-law and I take turns doing washday. Today was my turn and I was too tired to think about cooking after that."

Stephan didn't blame him. He'd kept his hair long until his teens and braiding that much fabulously coily hair was a whole job, even when a salon professional was doing it.

"I can imagine. My cousin and I used to take turns doing each other's hair when we didn't want to sit in a salon all day. It was a lot of work, but our hair was always styled to perfection, especially when we wore matching cornrows and beads."

Carter's jaw dropped, making something in Stephan's chest swell with delight.

"You wore cornrows and beads?"

"I did. My joints were always on point too." Stephan was speaking absolute fact. He and Amara really did slay back in the day. A sad ache tried to horn its way in on Stephan's mind when he had to resist the urge to grab his phone and show Carter.

That was the problem with secrets. They wound their sneaky tentacles into even the most innocuous and innocent aspects of a person's life.

"Mr. Smith." Stephan's ears perked up at the small voice using such formal language, and he smiled.

"If it's okay with your dad, you can call me Stephan too, Nevaeh."

When she turned to him, Carter met her with a nod, and she hurriedly brought her gaze back to Stephan's.

"Stephan," she continued. "Do you still know how to do cornrows. I asked Daddy, but all he knows how to do are boring ponytails."

Stephan hissed at that body shot Nevaeh had thrown at Carter.

He waved off Stephan's sympathy. "Kids don't

care nothing about your feelings. I'm used to it by now."

Without pausing, Nevaeh jumped right back into her line of questioning. "Do you think you could do some for me today?"

Stephan blinked, unsure of how to respond. Yes, he knew how to cornrow hair, but this was Carter's daughter, and doing hair was such a personal and intimate thing in the Black community, Stephan didn't think he had the right to cross such a line. Not when he knew he couldn't allow either of them the same kind of access to his own life.

Stephan's eyes caught Carter's and he could see a slight tenseness growing there. Had he wanted Stephan to say yes?

"Nevaeh, I'm sure Stephan has a bunch of things to do today. Cornrows can take a long time. If Grannie Gracie is too tired to do them after spending the weekend with her cousin, maybe we can find an African Hair Braider to do them for us."

"It's fine." Stephan watched as Carter's brows rose. Yeah, he'd surprised himself with that one too. He should not be doing anything that was going to further entangle their lives. But when Carter's surprise turned into the corner of his mouth lifting, Stephan couldn't remember all the reasons he was supposed to be staying away. "I can do it."

"I warn you," Carter fake-whispered. "She's tender-headed."

Stephan gave Nevaeh a conspiratorial wink. "No

one is tender-headed if the folks doing the combing would learn how to properly detangle the hair attached to sensitive scalps."

"Yeah, Daddy," Nevaeh chimed in. "You gotta be gentle."

Carter was chuckling and Stephan's heart felt like it stopped as he watched this dedicated father with his child. And that's when he realized he was definitely in danger of allowing Carter to get too close. But for some unexplained reason, he couldn't seem to find the panic that should've come along with that realization.

"Now that we've settled that," Stephan continued, "let's go around the corner to the beauty supply store and you can pick out some pretty beads, then we'll catch a Lyft and go down to Targét so we can pick up a bunch of Pattern Beauty products to keep the ouchies away."

"Targét?" The confusion on Carter's face was so adorable Stephan had to fight to keep from laughing.

"Target is for basic—" Stephan caught sight of Nevaeh's gaze locked on him and bit his lip to keep the explicative from leaving his mouth "—folks," Stephan continued. "We're too fabulous for all that, so when we walk in it's Targét."

Nevaeh was excitedly bouncing on her feet as she stood and started putting her coat on. Carter took that moment to lay his hand across Stephan's on the table, forcing him to laser in on the warm pressure his hand provided.

"I'm sorry you got roped into this. You really don't have to do it."

Carter attempted to pull away and Stephan caught his hand, lacing their hands together. "I want to do this," he murmured."

It was the truest statement he'd ever made.

There was something so special about this man and his daughter, Stephan just wanted to experience their magic for a little while. That wasn't so wrong, was it?

He knew it was, but if they were willing to share their joy with Stephan for just a little while, he'd soak it up the way dry hair sopped up cheap hair products."

"Look at how pretty I am, Daddy!"

Carter couldn't help how a wide smile bloomed on his face when his baby girl stood up from the bar chair Stephan had her seated on, with an intricate pattern of braids that were adorned with red and clear beads at each end.

"You are the prettiest girl in the world. Did you thank Stephan for taking such good care of your hair?"

She nodded.

"Good, then go upstairs and get your tablet and FaceTime abuela so she can see how pretty you look."

His daughter left the two men alone, and Carter still couldn't tamp down the excitement and joy he'd been experiencing since he'd spotted Stephan at CUP.

"You have to let me repay you for this, Stephan."

Standing tall and lanky in Carter's living room, he folded his arms and shook his head.

"Nope. Beauty days are always a gift whether I'm on the receiving end of them or not. Not to mention, doing Nevaeh's hair gave me a reason to flex my skills, so I'm calling it a win."

It had taken them more than an hour to get all the supplies Stephan insisted they needed, and then it had taken more than two hours with built-in snack and bathroom breaks, for Stephan to finish.

And that little traitor of his, who started bawling the moment Carter came near her head with a brush or a comb, had sat so sweetly for Stephan, Carter could hardly recognize her.

"That was labor. Also, you've gotta show me how you keep her from crying. That girl can burst an eardrum with her crying when it's time to get her hair done."

"No secret, just have to know what products to use to really detangle without traumatizing the girl. Those products I brought in will work wonders. Just follow the directions on them and take your time."

The moment stretched out between them. It was so full with unspoken words. No man gave up his entire Saturday to braid a child's hair when that child wasn't his. And yet here Stephan was.

Stephan was being a perplexing enigma to Carter, and more and more his curiosity wanted to explore, seek as much information as he could to have the man make sense to him, or more importantly, help

Carter understand why he wanted to know so much about him.

"I really enjoyed myself today, Carter."

"Did you?" When Stephan nodded Carter asked, "But why?"

"Because spending time with you and your daughter made me forget about everything else in the world at the moment. It helped me remember just how fun it was to be with family and friends before life added so much pressure, I couldn't breathe."

He stepped closer to Carter, leaning in slowly until all Carter could do was shiver in anticipation of a repeat of their kiss.

"But most all, because you have a great kid and she has a great father, and I'd be out of my mind not to want to spend as much time as I possibly could in your collective presence."

Before Carter could respond, Stephan pressed his lips to Carter's in such a sweet and gentle kiss, Carter had to actually wonder if it had happened at all.

By the time he found his bearings again, Stephan had stepped away from him, grabbing his coat and yelling his goodbyes up to Nevaeh. And just like before he let himself out of Carter's door he said, "Can't wait to do it again."

# Eleven

"Hey there."

Carter bit his lip to fight the moan that was circling the bottom of his throat. Dammit, in the week since he'd seen Stephan last, since he knew what that man's lips felt like against his, just the thought of Stephan Smith turned Carter into a puddle. Hearing the rumble of Stephan's voice tickle his ear was somehow signaling to his dick that this was the appropriate time to stand at attention.

*God, how hard up must you be, Jiménez?*
*Very, apparently.*

"Hi, Stephan," Carter replied softly. It was Saturday morning and his nosy daughter always seemed to find her way to him when he was on the phone. Usually, he didn't mind so much. Considering his current state of partial arousal, he figured it was probably best he stayed off her radar.

"Did I wake you?"

"No," Carter replied. "I've been up for a bit. Did you need something? Aren't you supposed to go meet with my connect at Borough Hall today? Is that still happening?"

Stephan's gentle laughter put Carter at ease, forcing him to take a breath and pull himself together.

"Everything's fine, Carter."

He was still chuckling as he replied and although Carter knew that laughter was at his own expense, hearing it somehow eased something in him, as if knowing Stephan was all right soothed him somehow.

"I'm actually on my way inside Borough Hall now to secure the venue. But, after I take care of that and a few other errands I need to run today, I was hoping you'd be available to have dinner with me tonight."

"Dinner? Have we forgotten anything off the party list? We finalized vendors last week for everything."

The sultry chuckle slipped through the phone lines again, forcing Carter's micromanaging tendencies to relax.

"No, everything for the party is set. Once I pay for the venue, the stationery company has the go-ahead to hand deliver all of the invitations to my uncle's family, friends, etc. I wasn't asking for more of your help with planning the party. I was asking you out on a date."

"A date?"

"Yeah," Stephan replied. "You know, when people who are interested in getting to know each other romantically, so they go out to eat and maybe entertain themselves to sort of help that process along?"

Carter sat up, unable to stop the smile from bending the corners of his mouth.

"And you want to get to know me, romantically?"

"Well, I certainly don't go around sharing fantastic kisses like ours with just any random on the street."

"So, I'm special?"

Stephan let a moan of his own escape, and Carter had to admit he liked knowing Stephan was just as affected by him.

"Baby, you're so much more than special. And the truth is, I have no idea why. Everything about you has called to me from the moment I met you. And I thought it was just because I wanted a distraction from my family issues. But that's not it. There's something about you, Carter, something I'd probably leave alone if I knew what was good for me. But after knowing how that mouth of yours tastes, I just can't get you out of my head. So, since you don't necessarily seem like the type of guy who's into hookups—"

"Hey," Carter interrupted. "You don't know me like that. I could very well be into all of the hookups. Would that turn you off if I were?"

"Your unruly dog ruined my damn dirty chicken wings and I still wanted to be around you, touch you. Your hookup history wouldn't even faze me. Besides,

I've never been a saint, so I definitely can't point fingers when it comes to someone having a healthy sexual appetite."

Carter's insides churned into a hot sour mix of jealousy. He didn't have to even think about it. From its first lick inside his belly, he wanted to lay waste to anyone who'd ever had the audacity to touch Stephan.

Was that response rational? Not the tiniest bit. They weren't even an item. They hadn't even gone on their first official date, date. Did that make the fire and tension growing inside Carter any less real? Not in the least.

Carter had held back from pursuing anything physical with Stephan because he firmly believed sex would've only complicated whatever his issues were. And even though Carter had no doubt those issues were nowhere near resolved, after the kiss they'd shared in Carter's office, there was no way in hell Carter could deny how much he wanted Stephan.

God, he was such a hot mess of contradiction.

"If it's a nonissue, why did you say I don't seem like I'm into hookups?"

Stephan chuckled, and Carter could tell by the rich tones of his voice he wasn't just BS-ing. He was absolutely enjoying himself.

"Because, that first time I came down to The Vault, the only thing I had in mind when I walked into that place was finding a sturdy enough surface with enough privacy that I could tease and taste as much of you as I wanted for as long as I wanted. But you put the kibosh on that ASAP. Those are not the moves of a player who's just looking for the next available body."

Why was this man so good at reading him so well. If he was this good at it out of bed, Carter hoped like hell it was an indicator he'd be just as good when there was nothing between their bodies but air.

Heat burned across Carter's skin. Just the thought of being naked with Stephan was searing him, burning through each layer of skin, leaving Carter exposed in a way that should make him so uncomfortable.

But he wasn't.

To the contrary, he was excited by the idea. So excited in fact, he knew there was no chance in hell he wouldn't let Stephan strip him naked if he had the opportunity.

He pinched the bridge of his nose. As he gave in to the realization that this was probably going to happen, and soon, Carter thought they had better set some ground rules first.

He'd fought like hell and given up his career to protect his daughter from all the messiness Hollywood peddled in. He'd be damned if he upset the happy, healthy peace she had here in Brooklyn just for a chance to satisfy this damn itch he had where Stephan Smith was concerned.

"Okay, you've convinced me."

"Great," his reply was smooth and even. "I'll make reservations for us at Negril BK, it you're okay with it."

"Well, I love Negril BK, but after working most nights in the service industry myself, I'd really prefer just sort of Netflix-and-chilling when I'm off."

"You don't want to be seen in public with me?" Stephan's voice was strong, but quiet, as if he were trying hard to put his strength on display, bracing himself for unwanted revelations Carter's reticence had obviously prompted. It clawed at that part of Carter that had wanted to be a lifeline for Stephan from the first day they met.

Knowing that his hang-ups with public life would hurt or disappoint Stephan even a tiny bit made him wish that he was much further along on his healing journey. Because if he could ever get past what the celebrity press had cost him, he knew he'd parade Stephan around for the world to see. Carter shook his head, trying to figure out how to say everything rolling around in his head without sounding weird or offensive.

"It's not that, Stephan—I just, I need to keep my life private. I know that may not make sense to you, but for me, whatever happens between us, I need to be able to trust that this stays our business and no one else's."

"Carter, you don't have to say it. I get it. You don't want to draw attention to yourself. Brooklyn is your safe space and being out and about drawing attention to yourself isn't in your best interest. No worries. I think I can do this first-date thing justice and keep prying eyes away. Trust me to take care of you."

For some strange reason, Carter instinctively knew he could trust Stephan.

Maybe it was the way he worried over the uncle who'd raised him. Maybe it was because he just seemed to read Carter and anticipate his needs.

Whatever it was. He wholeheartedly believed Stephan would protect him. And no matter how foolish it was to espouse that belief, Carter was all in.

*"Whatever happens between us, I need to be able to trust that this stays our business and no one else's."*

Stephan bristled as a cold gust of air passed through him. He attributed it to the usual Brooklyn chill that came with living where there was so much stone, concrete, metal, and glass. Deep down, however, he knew the weather had nothing to do with why he felt so off.

Stephan should be happy Carter didn't want to make a big spectacle of whatever this thing was that kept pulling them together.

*Should be* was the operative phrase.

When this ended—and it would certainly end—there would be no messy split if Stephan agreed to what Carter wanted, a clandestine affair that only they were aware of. They'd simply say their goodbyes and go their separate ways.

But somewhere deep inside Stephan could sense disappointment spreading through him, tainting the delight he always experienced when he was in Carter's orbit or simply thinking about him.

*This isn't about you. It's about Carter and what he needs. So just swallow whatever this is that has you feeling on edge. It's not like it's the first time you've had to ignore discomfort for the greater good.*

"You really can't walk two blocks in Brooklyn without running into a Devereaux."

Stephan turned around to the familiar voice to find Lennox standing in the corner of the Starbucks, presumably waiting for his order to be called up. Stephan shrugged and tilted his head toward the man.

"That should be an obvious truth for someone who's married to one of us."

Lennox shared a good-natured laugh as he grabbed Stephan into a big hug.

"S'up, man. I meant to call and congratulate you on your win. My cousin-in-love, the next mayor of the Big Apple. I'm surprised you're even allowed to walk around by yourself anymore. Shouldn't you have secret service surrounding you at all times."

"Bruh, you've only been in Paris two years." He held his hands out in a WTF manner. "That shouldn't be long enough for you to forget how our government works, and what agencies work together within that government. Secret Service is the president, dude. NYPD protects the NYC mayor."

"If it ain't about money, or making money, it doesn't really cross my mind."

Lennox pursed his lips. "You're a Devereaux, so that tracks."

Both their names were called at the same time.

They each grabbed their coffees and moved in a corner to get out of the way of the door.

"Listen, man." Lennox took a sip of his coffee before he continued. "I've got a million and one meetings today. I only came down to make sure a favor I needed done for my best friend was taken care of."

"You're not even mayor yet and you're out here doing political favors for friends?"

Lennox lifted his brow, managing to scold Stephan better than his mother used to as a kid.

"Don't even play like that, man. My best friend has a client who was looking to rent out Borough Hall for a private event. I just put him in touch with the person he needed to deal with."

Stephan's mind stumbled over Lennox's words as he repeated them in his head and then spoke them again.

"Your best friend?"

Lennox nodded. "That's right, you've never met Carter. I know you've been holding it down where Ace is concerned, so you haven't had a lot of time to hang out with us."

"You two are newlyweds, Lennox. You don't need me underfoot."

"You're family, Stephan, and you're always welcome. But seriously, our little one is gonna be here before you know it. You gotta come check us out before then. Let me know when you're ready and I'll make sure Carter is there."

Stephan stiffened. What would be the odds that

his cousin's, husband's best friend is the same man he'd been fantasizing about doing dirty things to?

Could fate really take that kind of sick pleasure in dicking him around like this?

"We could have dinner at our place, or if you're up for going out, we could probably eat at The Vault. Carter owns it."

The few sips of coffee Stephan had ingested left a sour taste in his mouth that made him feel like retching in the middle of Starbucks on Court Street.

"I think you'd like him." Lennox continued as if he needed to drive the imaginary dagger deeper into his chest.

*Like him? I want to strip him naked and run my tongue against every inch of skin he has. I'd say that goes well beyond liking him.*

He was sure Lennox would agree if he was aware of all the moving pieces to this particular puzzle.

"I'm sure I would." Stephan barely maintained his composure, even if alarms were sounding off every two seconds in his head.

"Look, man—" Lennox hooked a thumb over his shoulder in the direction of the door "—I've got another appointment to get to. But don't be scarce. Your cousin's thrilled to have you back home. Drop in soon."

Lennox went out of the building, and a half dozen people who seemed to come out of nowhere encircled him before they stepped out of the door.

Stephan looked at his watch and saw he had another twenty minutes before he had to make it across the street and secure the venue for Ace's Christmas gala.

That was more than enough time for him to have a controlled freak-out about this mess.

He was attracted to Carter, a man who hated the elite and worked his best to stay out of the limelight. He was certain that's why he hadn't seen Carter anywhere near Lennox's campaign trail.

Realizing he and Carter had barely a degree of separation between them, let alone six, the game was changing.

Next to Lyric, Amara was the closest thing he had to a sister and Lennox was her husband. If he handled this poorly, this thing had the potential to blow up in all their faces.

Yes, Stephan had exiled himself away from his people for two years. But he'd always known they would be waiting for him with open arms when he was ready to return home. But Carter's connection to his cousin, it was too close for Stephan's comfort. It threatened the delicate peace his loved ones enjoyed as long as Stephan guarded the ugly truth like a hardened warden.

They'd never see that he was protecting them. They'd only know Stephan had lied. And no matter how much he loved them and they him, he wasn't sure they'd ever be able to forgive him. How could he be certain when the truth was he couldn't forgive himself.

He tightened his fists, wondering who in heaven decided Stephan was the person who should bear all the volatile shit that had—and could again—blow up the family. Because right now, Stephan sure as hell felt like asking for a meeting with the manager, because this for damn sure didn't make the slightest bit of sense.

He took a breath, calming himself. He couldn't make rash decisions under this type of duress. When he felt he was calm enough to think about this chaos with a clear mind, there was only one conclusion he could draw.

He had to tell Carter who he really was. Which meant, he'd also have to face the very unpleasant reality that Carter wouldn't want to have anything else to do with him.

And didn't that just suck large donkey balls.

# Twelve

"You rented a yacht?"

Stephan couldn't help the slip of laughter that escaped his lips. Although Carter moved and once resided in a world of luxury, having access to a yacht in Brooklyn wasn't exactly commonplace.

Just one of the perks of being a Devereaux. *Common* wasn't part of their vocabulary, so things like asking your cousin if you could borrow his yacht so you could spend some quality time with your date was just as normal as asking to hang out in their furnished basement.

He was about to share that thought with Carter when he realized the man wouldn't find it the least bit funny. It was the reason he'd walked around with a boulder sitting in the pit of his stomach since he'd run into Lennox that morning. Carter hated where Stephan came from and who he was.

Notoriety was a birthright of every Devereaux. The only reason Stephan didn't receive as much fanfare as the rest was that he'd spent most of his life working behind the scenes. But if he'd stood at Ace's side the way the rest of his cousins had, the world would know his face as well as the others.

"It's a work perk. I thought our first official *date* date was a perfect reason to splurge a little. Don't you?"

Carter's grin radiated, its gleam reaching the depths of his dark eyes.

"Now, let's get below deck," Stephan said, eager to have Carter all to himself. "Being on a yacht might be cool, but since it's November and this water is brick-as-a-mug, I'on wanna spend too much time admiring the vessel up here.

"Man, you have no idea how much it warms my heart to hear terms of measurements like 'Than/as-a-mug'.

"I think I do," Stephan replied. "I've lived in Paris for two years, remember?"

Stephan led him below deck, taking his wool coat and scarf.

Carter continued their conversation. "My best friend, who's a Black man born and raised in Brooklyn, came to visit me on set out in LA once and he used it while we were talking to this Beverly Hills type. Blond slick hair, crystal blue eyes, polished from head to toe, and the luxury watch and sports car as the perfect accessories.

"He looked at my boy like he had two heads, then turned to me, because I'm the white-passing Puerto Rican, to ask what the hell he meant, like I was his walking 'hood-to-standardized-English translator.'"

"Did you explain it?"

Carter shook his head. "No, I was inclined to tell him to google it. But my best friend took pity on him and told him 'a mug' represented the most extreme condition/state of something. When using it as a comparative, you're saying that whatever your subject is, it's in a more extreme state than 'a mug', i.e. , it's extremely cold outside, so it's colder than, or cold as-a-mug.'"

"Let me guess," Stephan replied. "Even once he got the explanation, he still tried to act like he was confused. Like AAVE isn't a whole language?"

"You know it. But being back home in Brooklyn, where phrases like that are common, it just feels so good. I don't care where I go in the world, there's just no place like Brooklyn"

Stephan could definitely relate. He was well-traveled the world over. But his heart was right here in Brooklyn, and as he looked at the happy spark in Carter's eyes, he realized that phrase might literally be the case if he didn't curb things with this man soon.

"Did you get a whole lot of that in Paris?"

"A lot of what?" Stephan thought on Carter's question, realizing what the man was talking about.

"People dismissing the significance of Black American culture?" When Carter nodded, Stephan continued. "Everyone loves to consume Black American culture, but when Black Americans put their own culture into practice, it's often not received well.

"My job gives me access to money and power the way very few Black Americans are expected to possess. It means wherever I go in this world, I have to navigate people's expectations in the boardroom, in the bedroom, and everywhere in between."

Paris had allowed him to build an emotional fortress around himself so he could heal. But as a Black gay man who could access money and power, it meant men who were drawn to both wanted him not only for his money and power, but because he was the object of their "Black guys have big dicks" fantasies, and they wanted to see if the rumors were true.

So, after Dexter, Stephan had stayed protected in his fortress, because trying to deal with his brother's death and Dexter's deception, Stephan understood that the only person he could trust was himself.

Feeling the twinge of discomfort from old wounds being abraded, he shoved them back down and turned to his guest.

"Listen Car—"

Carter inhaled once they reached the cabin. "Is that oxtail I smell?"

"Yes, oxtail pizza to be exact from Cuts and Slices."

Carter moaned and the rich sound did more for Stephan's libido than his appetite.

"The spot on Howard and Halsey Avenues?" Stephan nodded, pointing toward the two large pie boxes settled on the bolted coffee table. "That smells divine. I've always wanted to try their offerings, but they usually have a line around the corner."

"Well," Stephan continued as he sat down and motioned for Carter to sit down next to him. "I had time to kill, so I figured why not."

"You are really trying to impress your way into my pants, aren't you?"

"Is it working?"

Stephan was master of the quiet flex. Oh, he could definitely do flash with the best of them. But when it came to the people he cared about, subtle was always the best way to show he cared.

"Yes, but the truth is, good food is a bonus. I came here with every intention of giving you what we both want."

"Straight and to the point, huh?"

Carter grabbed his hand. "I'm a single father and a business owner with very little time to myself. I don't plan to spend one moment tonight playing coy. I don't need the buildup, I just need you. Can you give me that, at least for tonight?"

"Carter, I do want to give you that, give us both that."

He really did want to satisfy them both. But if he

crossed that threshold with Carter, he wasn't so sure he'd be able to easily walk away. Every moment with Carter made Stephan feel like a new person, like he didn't have to hide in his lonely old fortress. Being with him gave Stephan the tiniest hope that maybe, just maybe, he could let someone else in. Which was exactly why he needed to slow things down and tell Carter the truth about his identity and his life as a member of the Devereaux family.

As surely as he recognized his own name, Stephan knew that the moment Carter's body touched his, he'd be too far gone to walk away, to do the right thing, to accept that Carter wouldn't want anything else to do with him.

"Then what's the holdup? Are you having second thoughts? I'm not looking for forever. I just want to enjoy the here and now."

"I get that," Stephan replied. His voice was rough, scraping against the inside of his throat. Stephan knew he couldn't say with such clarity that he just wanted to have fun with Carter. Because fun had gone out the window for him once he pressed his lips to Carter's and tasted him for the first time. "But I feel like there are important things we need to discuss."

*Like the fact that I am part of the very world you despise, the world that took everything from you.*

Life was so damn cruel. Here was this beautiful man with eyes only for him. Carter's skin was flushed with desire, body trembling in anticipation of his touch. It should've been so simple. Have fun, enjoy what he hoped was going to be phenomenal sex, and go back home in the morning.

Carter was helping him plan a Christmas gala. In addition, him having no expectations beyond this night, and Stephan could see the proverbial cherry on top of this scenario.

Stephan rarely saw that kind of selflessness. Its display was complicating things, making him ache for more when he should detach himself and move on. His feelings for Carter were deepening. The truth was he didn't want to ruin their chance at something real by deceiving Carter one moment longer.

"Carter, I—"

He never got the chance to finish his sentence. Carter pressed his lips against Stephan's. The urgency and strength demanded Stephan's submission, his compliance, and his reciprocation.

Carter teased until Stephan's lips were open and he dipped his tongue inside of Stephan's mouth, eagerly tasting every inch his tongue met.

Stephan had never been at a true loss for words, but having Carter's mouth, and now his hands which were currently reaching under the hem of Stephan's turtleneck and touching the sensitive skin there, had him dizzy, unable to determine which way was up.

Soon, Carter was pressing Stephan's back into the sofa, straddling his thighs and lowering himself over Stephan's clothed cock. He shifted his hips, driving a needy moan from Stephan that tested the limits of his restraint. And when Carter moved his hips again and Stephan's cock went from half-hard to fully erect in two and a half seconds, those restraints that he'd been struggling so hard to maintain, snapped.

Stephan placed a firm grip on Carter's neck, pulling him flush against him and loving the sweet moan he gifted Stephan with. He locked his remaining arm around Carter's waist, making certain he stayed right where he wanted him, pressed firmly against his cock, making Stephan ache, and hopefully feeling just as achy himself.

Stephan growled as he turned them sideways, flipping Carter beneath him and thrusting his hips forward so Carter was aware of what he was doing to him. He needn't have bothered, though. Because the sweet smirk placed firmly on Carter's lips told Stephan the eager man beneath him knew exactly what he was doing.

"Ah," Carter mewled. "There he is. There's the man I've been waiting to show up and show out."

"That mouth of yours is going to get you in so much trouble." Stephan knew Carter was egging him on, but the bait was too inviting not to take.

"Promise?"

The man was playing with fire. Lying beneath him with his brow arched and his bottom lip tugged between his teeth, Stephan knew he didn't have a shred of control left in him.

"Fuck it."

He leaned up long enough to remove his shirt,

and when Carter lay back on the couch still clothed, Stephan gritted through his clenched teeth, "Are you waiting for an invitation."

"No." Carter beamed. Just enjoying watching you lose the blessed control you fight so hard to keep."

Carter was right. He did have a need to control all the emotion, fire, the secrets that dwelled within him. If he lost control for even a second, the fallout would be chaos.

But tonight, he didn't have to hold on so tightly. Tonight, he would give Carter what he was asking for, what they both so desperately wanted, and enjoy the pure bliss of letting go in this silent space where only the two of them existed.

He leaned back on his haunches, unbuttoning his pants, then stood so he could finally free himself of the rest of his clothes. When Carter wasn't moving fast enough for his liking, he growled, "Strip."

A spark of something hungry flashed in Carter's eyes and a lightbulb went off in Stephan's head. Carter said he was waiting for this take-charge man to show up. He said he wanted Stephan to lose control, but from the way he scurried off the sofa and began removing his clothing, Stephan wondered if what Carter was looking for was someone who knew how to manage *him* in the bedroom.

The outside world often thought that when someone asked to be dominated when it came to sex, it meant they were weak, that somehow they weren't real men. But it was the furthest thing from the truth.

To submit meant you allowed someone to have control over you in the ways in which you deemed appropriate.

Carter managed every part of his life: his family, his business. It would make sense to Stephan that Carter possibly needed to let his guard down. Could he need something, or perhaps, someone, to take control so he could enjoy being cared for?

Was Carter here because he trusted Stephan enough to take care of him, to give him what he needed and keep him safe?"

Stephan didn't get off on needing to control others. Yet, the idea of Carter submitting to him had him hard enough to cut glass. As someone who didn't find it easy to trust, he knew what kind of sacrifice it was to allow yourself to be this vulnerable when you had so much to lose.

It had ruffled his sense of well-being when Carter had said he only wanted tonight. But realizing how much trust Carter was putting in him, Stephan knew one night would never be enough.

He was an asshole for allowing that realization to stroke his ego. Especially when he was aware that they might be walking their separate ways by the end of the night. But everything in him wanted to please Carter right now and if this man needed to stop taking care of everyone in his life for this brief moment they shared, Stephan would make this so sweet for him, Carter would never be able to forget it or re-create it with someone else.

Carter went to lower himself to the sofa, and Stephan pulled him into his arms, placing his hand at the front of Carter's neck, allowing his thumb to barely touch his Adam's apple and basking in the beautiful tremor Carter gave him in response.

"You don't want this to be gentle, do you?"

"What gave it away?"

"That smart-ass mouth of yours, for one. I think if you have this much air and brain power to talk slick, you might need something to fill it."

Carter closed his eyes and shivered and Stephan wanted nothing more than to bury himself as deeply as he could in Carter's body. But he was a man living on borrowed time as far as Carter was concerned, so he would savor this for as long as humanly possible.

"So, all that strong talk about having your way with me, that was just for show?"

Carter swallowed, licking his lips as if they were dry from the heavy breathing he was doing.

"Maybe." Carter's voice was gravel over concrete, rough, scraping over every nerve Stephan possessed. "Or maybe—" he breathed deeply, opening his eyes and looking into Stephan's "—maybe this is exactly the way I wanted to have you all along, and I needed to know if you could handle it. If you could handle me."

That was the proverbial straw that broke the camel's back. Stephan pulled Carter's body into his, loving the sensation of hard flesh against hard flesh. With one hand, Stephan held Carter's head where he wanted it as he devoured the tender flesh of his partner's mouth.

He used his other hand to stroke Carter's cock from root to tip, letting his thumb glide over the domed cap. The pearl of pre-cum there set him aflame, making him ache to taste it. But tonight was about giving Carter what he needed.

Carter thrust into Stephan's hand, the smooth silk of his flesh in Stephan's palm made him want to spill his pleasure right where they stood. He was already addicted to the way Carter's skin felt pressed against his. He'd have this every night and twice on Sundays for the rest of his life if he could. But he knew the likelihood of that was nil, and if by chance tonight was all they had, Stephan was going to give Carter everything he'd asked for.

He pulled his mouth from Carter's, leaving the man chasing his mouth as if it were a lifeline.

"I need to get you to one of the staterooms before I lose it right here on this damn sofa."

"I've…" Carter stopped to catch his breath, "I've got whatever you need in my inside coat pocket."

"Keep us busy then, while I grab it."

Stephan sat down on the sofa, taking Carter by the hand so he would follow, straddling Stephan's legs. He took Carter's hand and wrapped it around both their cocks, showing him the slow rhythm Stephan wanted him to keep while he grabbed the hem of Carter's coat to bring it closer.

Stephan's head lolled against the back of the couch

at the delicious and distracting friction Carter was creating. Fortunately, he was able to find the exact pocket Carter had mentioned easily, otherwise, his next move was to rip the thing to shreds and shake it until its contents fell on the sofa cushion next to them. Because there was no damn way in hell Stephan was moving away from Carter.

His fingertips could make out the square foil and a small plastic tube he knew had to be lube. He lifted the foil, opening his eyes to glance at it and then placed it into Carter's hand.

"Get me ready."

Carter made such quick work of getting the condom on Stephan, he'd almost had to laugh. But since he was just as needy as Carter, he knew he couldn't.

He opened the lubricant, applying it to his fingers and gently rubbing at the puckered skin of Carter's entrance, trying to hold on to what little restraint he had, because as eager as he was to bury himself inside of Carter, he didn't want to make this uncomfortable for him.

"Are you sure you're up for this tonight?"

"I told you I don't want gentle."

"Carter, look at me." The deep rumble of his voice cleared up any misunderstanding Carter might have about how serious Stephan was right now.

"Not being gentle isn't the same thing as hurting you. So, I'm asking are you sure you're up for this. Because it isn't a requirement for either of us to be satisfied tonight."

Carter's eyes morphed from a deep brown to a bottomless inky black. Stephan might've been alarmed until he saw the corner of Carter's mouth lift into a sly grin.

"I prepped myself before I got here."

Stephan's lungs seized as his brain processed what Carter was saying. "How?" he wheezed out. "With your fingers?"

Carter leaned in, licking and then nipping Stephan's earlobe before he whispered, "I had to take the edge off for fear I'd explode when you touched me. So just before I jumped into the shower, I reached into my toy drawer and pulled out old faithful." Carter gave Stephan's cock a squeeze before continuing. "He's a lifelike dildo with all the ridges, girth, and length I need to get myself ready for fun with a partner."

"God, Carter," he hissed through clenched teeth. "You're trying to kill me with that image."

Carter's smile broadened, and since Stephan was the master of one-upmanship, he sank two fingers into Carter's entrance, and reveled in the pleasure-filled moan that Carter let loose into the air.

Satisfied that he wouldn't hurt Carter, he removed his fingers and lined his cock up pressing slowly into Carter's body.

Blinding heat enveloped him as Carter lowered himself gradually.

Carter's body tightened just before they were completely joined.

"That's it, baby," Stephan crooned in his ear, wrapping his arms around Carter, giving him something to brace against as Stephan pressed further into his body. "Take all of me. Take me like you took your toy."

Carter swirled his hips, giving Stephan the go-ahead to move. The next time Carter moved his hips again, Stephan thrust up to meet him, and Carter moaned so pretty, Stephan slid his hands down to Carter's hips and dragged him forward again.

"Ride me like you rode that fake cock."

Carter picked up the tempo, meeting Stephan's powerful thrusts with just as much vigor. They were already slick with sweat and tense with pleasure, and if Stephan could stay like this for the rest of his life, he'd die a happy man.

Carter's cock was hard and dripping against Stephan's stomach, trapped between both of them. He was so blissed out, so overwhelmed with the dual sensation, his eyes were closed and his mouth hung open as if he couldn't figure out how to breathe through it.

Stephan wasn't far behind. He would be falling soon too, but not until he wrung ever drop of pleasure from Carter that he could.

"Did you come with that toy deep inside you?"

Carter's body shook.

"Did you clamp down on it like a damn vice?"

"Stephan…please… I"

"I know what you need, baby."

Stephan tightened his grip on Carter's hips, pistoning into his body until Carter keened in ecstasy, his body milking Stephan for his essence, his strength, his ability to focus on anything other than the point where their bodies were joined and how damn good Carter felt clasping him. And when he couldn't hold his release back any longer, he buried himself so deeply inside Carter, hoping to erase the memory of every toy, be they plastic or of the human variety, he'd ever let enter his body. Because the only cock, the only name he wanted this man to ever remember was his.

Once they cleaned up, Stephan pulled Carter into his arms, needing to hold on to this moment longer. Because now that he knew what they were like together, Stephan didn't think there was any way he could willingly walk away from this man now.

# Thirteen

"Not only does he avoid me when he's away from me, but he ignores me when I'm in his presence too. A girl could catch a complex dealing with you."

Stephan blinked the thick fog in his head clear just in time to bring Lyric, who was now sitting in front of his desk, into focus. He'd spent most of his morning replaying the time he and Carter had spent since their first night together a week ago.

Every touch, every smile, every whispered plea or outburst of laughter had taken up every working brain cell in his head. That's exactly how he'd forgotten to call Lyric and update her on this gala. Being with Carter made Stephan forget everything, especially the really bad things that made his heart ache.

"Sis, you know it's not even like that."

"Do I?"

Stephan knew Lyric's tone was supposed to be light and amusing, fun between two siblings-in-love getting at each other. But Stephan knew Lyric, and she didn't play like that. So although that "Do I?" was posed as if it were a joke, for damn sure, Stephan knew she was dead serious.

"You call a cousins' meeting and tell everyone you're going to update me, but then you don't actually update me. You've been home for months, and we've barely spent any time together. My husband dies, and the little brother I think I'm going to grieve with just ups and leaves no sooner than his brother's in the ground and doesn't come home for two years. Exactly what am I supposed to think other than you don't want to be around me."

Stephan stood up, walking around the desk and kneeling down in front of her.

"I know I've been a shitty little brother, Lyric, and I'm so sorry about that."

"Why, Stephan?" she whispered. "Is it because I moved on, because I'm with Josiah?"

He shook his head. "Sis, this has nothing to do with you, and everything to do with me. I'd like to say this has all been part of my grieving process, but I won't even insult you by telling you that lie."

"Then what?" She leaned forward, taking his hand between hers, doing the Lyric thing and finding a way to comfort him even when he'd been the one to cause her pain. "Is everything okay?"

"Am I safe? Yeah. But, I've just been going through a lot of emotional ups and downs and returning home just brought it all to bear. Add to that everything that's going on with Ace, and sometimes my feelings are just too big to force anyone else to be around me and them."

"Is that what's going on right now," she asked. "When I came in, you seemed like you were in another world."

His sister-in-love was always so good at reading him. It was one of the things he adored about her, but also the main reason why he couldn't stay after Randall died. If he'd stayed around her, there was no way he could've protected her from the truth.

"I've… I've been seeing someone and it's sort of messing with my head. I'm just trying to figure out how best to handle it."

Her smile was soft and supportive. "I don't think I've ever heard you say out loud that you're seeing someone before. This must be serious."

"The only thing serious about it is the sex."

"I'm sure it is, Steph, but the fact that you're actually sitting in your office brooding over a man tells me it's much more than sex."

Again, she knew him too well, and if he wasn't careful, she'd have all his secrets out on Front Street if he didn't bring this impromptu "let's talk about our feelings" session she was trying to have to a close.

"When Ace leaves, so will I, Lyric. So, there's no way for this to be more than it is. His entire life is here in Brooklyn and he has no intention of ever leaving. It can't work."

She leaned forward, squeezing his hands lightly.

"What was that old saying Ace used to always say to us?" She fake-scratched her head as if she was looking for the answer in the air. "Oh, I remember. 'Old man Can't been dead a long time.' So, by my calculation, that means you literally can."

"Please don't quote that old man to me. You know he refuses to see me unless I have some proof of joy to share with him."

Stephan waited to see her astonishment at such an unreasonable request, but all she did was smile.

"Can you blame him? With the exception of Trey and Jeremiah's wedding, all you've done since you returned home was work and sit by his side."

"Lyric, not you too."

He threw up his hands in exasperation, sitting on his desk as his shoulders slumped in familiar despair.

"Stephan, he's leaving us. As scary as that is for us, think about what that might feel like for him."

*Fear? Ace?* Those two words never took up the same space in his head.

"Ace is afraid, Stephan. Ace loves two things in life, Devereaux Inc. and the Devereaux family. He has put so much into the business, but it's cost him his sister, his nephew, and for a long while, his son and his granddaughter. He's using what time he has left to try to make sure the current generation will always look to love and not a bottom line for the answers."

Stephan's brow furrowed as he tried to make sense of Lyric's words. She was the empath in the family, the one who always sensed what was happening with everyone else. Was she once again seeing through another Devereaux man in this family who looked like polished gold on the outside, but was drowning silently in all his unspoken pain?

This conversation was beginning to hit too close to home for his taste.

"Sis, I think you're making more of this than necessary."

"No, I don't think you're paying close enough attention."

She shifted in her seat, leaning forward a bit, as if she were making sure he heard what she was saying.

"He wants us to be better than those that came before us. And you're the last holdout."

"Are you really standing here telling me you ended up with Josiah because Ace told you to?"

She smiled at the mention of her lover's name and part of him braced, not because he was against love and all its supposed splendor, but because part of him knew that he'd never be worthy of a man smiling at the mention of his name the way Lyric did at the mere whisper of Josiah's.

How could he be when there was just so much to atone for?

Outside of Lyric, Carter was the closest thing to a

saint Stephan had ever seen. He was loyal, friendly, so compassionate that he reached out to Stephan simply because he looked like life was kicking his ass. Who does that? No one. That alone made Carter special. When you added in his dedication to his daughter and his mother and mother-in-law, his near sainthood was pretty much solidified.

Carter deserved someone better than Stephan, a man who'd lied to his family to protect them. A man who'd sold his own soul just to keep a very ugly truth from destroying the people he loved. Did he do it because he was selfless? Not likely. And now, knowing that he'd eventually have to give Carter up at some point, he didn't want to tell them because he didn't want to lose them. He didn't want them to hate him and abandon him.

That wasn't selfless. That was as selfish as it came and Carter deserved better.

"I didn't fall in love with Josiah because Ace wanted me to. But I was open to him being part of my life because Ace made me realize I had so much love left to give, that I didn't die with my husband."

She stood, then placed a gentle kiss on his cheek. "I don't know what burdens you bear that keeps you so closed off from love, Stephan. But whatever it is, Ace is trying to tell you that you don't have to carry it alone, that you're worthy of love despite whatever thing in your heart and head is telling you otherwise. Just do like the rest of the cousins did, and listen to him. Maybe if you do, things between you and this secret lover of yours won't seem so bad."

There was so much hope in her smile that Stephan wanted desperately to hold on to. If Lyric said it, then maybe it really could be true. Then…then there might be a way to keep this thing that warmed him from the inside out whenever he was near Carter.

"When you've got a better handle on what you're feeling for this mysterious man, come tell me about him."

She was halfway out the door when he called to her. "Wait, I really do have to update you on the cousins' meeting."

"You know doggone well the cousins crew can't hold water. Two minutes after y'all completed that meeting I had two different sets of voice mails relaying what happened. I've already marked the day on our calendar. Josiah and I will be there to support you in whatever way you need."

She dashed out of the room, leaving him with a big grin on his face and his heart feeling a tad bit lighter. How his brother had treated her so poorly, Stephan would never know. But he'd always known what a gem his sister-in-love was, and that's why he'd go to his grave to protect her. No matter the cost.

Now he just needed to figure out how to keep Carter from falling victim to a Devereaux-Smith man too. The only problem was Carter made the perpetual ache he'd carried around for two years go away. And Stephan knew no matter how much he didn't want to hurt Carter, he was also selfish enough to keep him in his life to stop the slow hemorrhaging of the blood his family unknowingly demanded.

*Well, that should be no big deal, right? All I have to do is figure it all out and everything will be just perfect.*

He laughed at his nonsensical response to this impossible situation he'd placed himself in. And as the panic and ache began to spread, pushing against his chest, making it difficult to breathe, he knew exactly what, or more aptly who, he needed to make everything all right.

"Dammit!"

Carter grabbed a nearby bar cloth and wiped furiously to stop the coffee he'd just prepared from spilling all over the bar rim and possibly scalding the patron seated on the opposite side.

"I'm sorry," Carter apologized. "I'll get you another coffee as soon as I get this cleaned up."

The patron nodded and Carter continued to rub the cloth back and forth until all the liquid was absorbed.

He turned around to find Ian with a hip leaned casually against the shelves, watching Carter as if he was trying to figure out some kind of puzzle.

"You okay, boss?"

Carter had to think a minute on how to answer that. He wasn't slow to respond because he was searching for the answer. No, he paused because he had to decide which of the varied answers to that question he was going to share.

"It's been a rough week and I haven't been getting as much sleep as I obviously need."

"If you need to head out early, I can hold it down for you."

Ian's offer was so tempting. To put it mildly, Stephan had spent the last week wearing him out. Between finalizing the details of the party including finding a Christmas tree large enough to rival the one at Rockefeller, and having some of the best sex he'd had in the last few years, Carter was exhausted. Not just physically, but the emotional high he'd been on had him wired, and Carter was afraid of the crash that would inevitably happen when he came down.

This was supposed to be fun. But fun was quickly turning into an addiction, and Carter couldn't afford to let anyone, especially someone as closed off as Stephan get underneath his skin like this.

Oh, he was fun, and selfless in his acts. But there were moments Carter could tell he was manic with desire because he didn't want to face whatever it was that was happening in his family life.

Carter understood needing that distraction. He'd been there himself when Michelle died. But this connection Carter had with him, how vulnerable he felt when Stephan held him in his arms. This was dangerous territory.

If he were smart, he'd work his shift and then take

his ass home and get some sleep. That's exactly what he needed to do.

But, God, the sex was everything Carter needed it to be.

Energetic, passionate, fun, and so damn hot, Carter didn't understand how they hadn't burned through every surface they'd slammed each other against in an effort to get naked and connect to some part of each of their bodies.

"Thanks, man. But I've got a bunch of invoices to go through this afternoon. I need to dig into them."

"Okay," Ian replied. "But the lunch crowd won't be in for about an hour. At least try to catch a few winks in your office before then."

"Will do."

Carter finished making the fresh coffee and handed it off to the eager patron. He was about to make his way to the back when the bell over the door chimed, and Stephan, walking in big and bold, sucking all the oxygen up in the room with his unbelievable sex appeal, entered Carter's establishment.

Every muscle in Carter's body tensed in delicious anticipation, as if he was supposed to be ready to give or receive pleasure on sight of the beautiful man walking toward him.

Carter wanted to wring his own neck for lacking self-control where Stephan Smith was concerned.

How did this man's mere appearance still render this visceral reaction from Carter, where his body, that was two seconds ago asking for a catnap, was now craving Stephan's touch like he'd never seen the man nor spent nearly every night this week making love to him.

Like clockwork, he'd leave Stephan's bed in time to wake Nevaeh up for school, feed her breakfast and get her out the door for school. Then, he'd catch a few hours of sleep and then run errands for The Vault or for Stephan's Christmas gala. Next, he'd pick Nevaeh up from school, help her with her homework, and spend quality time with her. And once he'd tucked her into bed, he'd go to work, then tell her grandmother he was staying late because they'd been swamped.

As soon as he closed, he'd make a beeline for Stephan's house, where the man would systematically dismantle every part of Carter simply to put him back together and send him on his way in the morning.

It was so exhausting and exhilarating, and even though he walked away satisfied every time, Carter still craved something more.

More time, more tenderness, more intimacy where they opened up and let each other in. But he'd been the one to tell Stephan he only wanted it to be about the sex, so he couldn't very well be the one to change his mind now. Could he?

Did he?

Did he want to change his mind and reach for something deeper, stronger with Stephan?"

He was a father and he always had to consider his daughter first. He was sure she'd be thrilled if Carter pursued something more significant with Stephan.

After the way he braided her hair in cornrows, she was happy to be his best friend. But after he came back the next weekend with some beads and other hair accessories to add to the latest style he'd given her, he was sure Nevaeh loved Stephan more than him.

Too bad relationships couldn't be based on something as simple as one's ability to cornrow and style a little girl's hair. No, they were based on things like being open with each other. And he still didn't know enough about Stephan to leap headfirst into a relationship with him.

He was a good man, Carter was sure of that. The way he talked about his uncle, the fact that he was giving his time, and several pretty pennies to boot, to make his dying uncle happy, that definitely said something about the man's character. But outside of knowing that his brother passed away a couple of years ago and that he grew up with a cousin whose hair he used to braid, he had no idea about Stephan's past.

*Why have you let it get this far without asking him about his family and his background?*

Because having his privacy violated on almost a daily basis when he was an actor had taught Carter to be protective of not just his, but everyone else's too. When Michelle had died, the press had been relentless. They'd even paid one of the funeral home employees to sneak a picture of him kneeling at Michelle's opened casket when he'd gone in to approve her final appearance. Before he could put her in the ground, that picture was all over the news cycle.

It wasn't enough that they'd chased her into traffic and taken her life, they needed to exploit her death too.

He knew how deep betrayal like that went, and as a result, he'd never barge his way into someone else's life, even if that man seemed to be taking up so much space in Carter's.

And no matter how much Carter's curiosity wanted to know everything about Stephan Smith, there was one last reason he would never push for more: he wanted Stephan to offer that information freely. Because if he did, Carter wouldn't have to stand behind his bar wondering if he should try to deepen his relationship with Stephan. Carter would know beyond a shadow of doubt that Stephan Smith was the man for him.

"Hey," Stephan said, pulling Carter out of his rambling thoughts. His voice was pleasant, respectable, and no one in the room, including Carter, would assume he'd had Carter bent over the back of his sofa, calling for every deity his addled brain could remember in both English and Spanish.

"Hey, yourself," Carter replied. "Did you need something?"

"Actually, I did. I have a question about some of the details for the gala." Stephan pointed his chin toward Carter's office in the back. "You got a minute?"

Carter signaled to Ian he was going to the back

and he led Stephan into his office. The second he closed the door, he found his back pushed against the nearby wall with Stephan's body flush against his and Stephan's mouth devouring his.

Carter should put his foot down—this was his place of business and he didn't make a habit of taking sex breaks in his office. But when Stephan's tongue licked into his mouth, Carter thought sex in his office in the middle of the day with the hot guy who sexes you stupid might be the best work perk he'd ever heard of.

"Mmmm," Stephan moaned as he gentled the kiss.

"You said…" Carter cleared his throat, "You said you had a question about the gala."

With his head tilted and his gaze locked on Carter's, he tucked his bottom lip between his teeth and nodded. "Yes," he began. "I needed to know, how can I be expected to focus on finalizing the details we've set up for this gala when I miss you so damn much?"

Before Carter could utter a word, Stephan buried his face in his neck, nibbling the sensitive spot just beneath Carter's ear as he palmed Carter's instantly hard cock through his pants.

"Fuck, Stephan. You better plan on doing something about that."

"So damn bossy." Stephan squeezed again and Carter flattened his hands against the wall trying to find purchase.

"Stephan, please."

"Ssshhhh," he whispered, tickling the same spot

underneath his earlobe. "I promise to take care of you. You just have to do one thing for me first."

This son of a bitch literally had Carter by the balls and had the audacity to try to strike up negotiations right now. If that wasn't the coldest, yet sexiest thing he'd ever heard, Carter didn't know what was.

"Anything, please."

"You know I love it when you beg so pretty, baby."

"Stephan, I swear I'm gonna resort to violence if you don't stop playing games and get me off."

He could feel Stephan's smile against his cheek. This damn man was enjoying ruining him and Carter was helpless to stop him.

"Promise me that after you put Nevaeh to bed that you'll come spend the night with me again."

Carter hissed. "I need to go home and sleep, Stephan."

"You can sleep at my place."

Stephan pushed Carter's hands above his head, gripping his wrists in one hand and using his free hand to undo Carter's belt and zipper and pull his cock free, stroking him from root to tip.

"Stephan, please."

"All you have to do is give me what I want, and I'll make it so good for you. Don't you want that?"

Damn if he didn't. Not just because Stephan's hand felt like silk against his skin. It certainly did. But really, it was because at that moment, Stephan found his gaze and Carter saw need and hunger that exceeded his own. It flashed like lightning in those deep brown eyes, and Carter, for the briefest moment, could swear that Stephan's hunger wasn't all about the sex.

"Yes," Carter moaned, and Stephan set his hands free, taking a step away from him.

Before Carter could speak, Stephan was on his knees, pulling Carter's pants down, shoving his nose where thigh met pelvis. He took a satisfying breath, stroking Carter's cock with one hand and letting his fingertips graze Carter's balls.

"What the hell are you doing to me, Stephan. What would you do to me if I let you?"

Stephan gazed up at him, then took one ridiculously long lick of his cock and smiled.

"Anything and everything, you want me to."

And with that, he took Carter so deep into his mouth Carter was convinced in that moment, he'd lost his soul to this man.

# Fourteen

"Oh, look who the wind done blew in?"

Stephen narrowed his eyes to throw just enough shade at the supposedly frail old man sitting in the middle of the huge bed.

"Uncle Ace, weren't you the one who told me not to come around?"

"See?" he grumbled. "That's the problem with you young'uns right there. You think you know so much and don't know a thing. I told you not to come back unless you had something to share. Have you at least tried to find some joy since you were last here?"

"Uncle Ace, I check in with you every day on the phone. You know exactly what's going on with me."

"Don't sass me, boy."

If Ace wanted to know where Stephan had found his smart mouth, all he'd have to do was look in the mirror. He got that sass from Ace, and watching the man serve him up a heaping helping of it was just the kind of thing he needed to keep his earlier good mood in place.

"Is that a smile I see on your face, nephew?"

"If it is, it's because I'm happy to hang out with my uncle again. I've missed our daily meetings."

Ace pursed his lips, silently conveying an entire conversation, the way only an elderly Black man could, with such a small gesture.

"You must think I got Boo-boo the Fool written across my forehead. You ain't ever been that happy to see me. Is this about my gala? Did you get those linens you told me about the last time you were here. The ones you said were used by an Ethiopian Empress?"

Stephan inwardly laughed. He didn't know who Boo-boo the Fool was, but he'd heard about him repeatedly from almost every Black parent he'd encountered throughout his lifetime.

Trying to get his thoughts back on track, his shook his head to clear his mind. Carter had managed to get those royal linens for him, and the memory of how they'd celebrated that victory burned through him like molten lava slipping into the sea.

Stephan opened his mouth to reply as Lyric's words about Ace wanting to make sure he was bound in love and not the business crossed his mind. As Ace sat there staring at him, his eyes bright and eager with anticipation of even the smallest sliver of personal happiness for Stephan, he realized she was right.

And that's when it hit him.

The only sliver of happiness Stephan had in his life *was* Carter.

"I met someone, Uncle Ace."

He moved closer to Ace's bedside, sitting just on the edge.

"Do you remember when I told you a friend of mine was helping me put your Christmas gala together? Well, we sort of hit it off and started seeing each other." His uncle didn't say anything. He simply nodded and Stephan continued. "He's a really a good man, Unc."

"He'd better be if he's managed to catch your eye."

Ace's protective streak warmed him. "I like him a lot, Uncle Ace."

Ace's eyes softened and the tense lines of illness receded ever so briefly.

"Just how much is a lot, nephew?"

Stephan paused to consider Ace's question. There was just so much about Carter that pleased Stephan, they'd be here all day if he tried to explain in detail what "a lot" meant.

The way Carter always looked after him when they were together, whether it was bringing him something to eat or drink, or checking in with Stephan to make sure his day was going well, for example. He could even talk about the way Carter was with his daughter and why seeing him with the little girl made

Stephan happy, especially when he tried to be strict even though it was obvious that little one knew just how to play her daddy. Or his favorite thing about Carter, the way he sought Stephan out in his sleep, curling his body into Stephan's and humming a sleepy sigh of relief when he unconsciously found him.

And then there were the things he liked that he wouldn't share with Ace. Not that he couldn't find a way to be both truthful and respectful about the sex while speaking to his uncle, but being with Carter in that way was so special, he just didn't want to share it with another soul. Not even Ace.

*Fam, that don't sound like, like. That sounds like love.*

His head snapped up, looking at Ace to see if those words had come from his uncle, but the way Ace stared at him, Stephan could tell he was still waiting for him to answer Ace's previous question.

Those were *his* thoughts not Ace's words.

Too afraid to face his realization he tried to remember what Ace had asked him.

"How much do I like him?" He ran his hand down his face, pursing his lips as he tried to find the words. "I like him enough that sometimes, I want to be able to tell him the things I can't say to the rest of the world."

Ace tilted his head and Stephan could see understanding settling on the older man's face.

"So why don't you tell him…everything."

"If I do, he'll hate me."

The bright glimmer of hope was dashed as a cloud of sadness seemed to fill the edges of Ace's eyes.

"That's not possible. How could he hate my nephew when my nephew is one of the best men I've ever known?"

"You're supposed to say that. You're my uncle."

Ace waved a dismissive hand around between them. "I'm old and I'm dying. I say what I want. Not what I have to. Now what's this nonsense about him hating you?"

Ace leaned back into his pillows as Stephan told him the entire story of how he and Carter had met and what fame had cost him and his young daughter.

"Well, I don't blame him for wanting to stay out of the limelight. And I see how that might make being with someone in this family a bit trying."

Ace lifted a shaky hand and placed it on Stephan's cheek and smiled. "But I think you have to give him the choice of whether what he feels for you is stronger than his fear. You can't make that decision for him, Stephan."

"Uncle Ace—"

His uncle placed a finger across his lips to silence Stephan. It was something Ace had done many times over when Stephan would get too excited or afraid to hear beyond his own thoughts.

"You didn't think Lyric could deal with the truth, and because of that decision, you took on a burden that wasn't yours to bear. Why is it you believe everyone's feelings are more important than your own?

You deserve to be happy too. And this young man deserves to know all of you. Not just the tiny pieces you think he can handle."

Stephan kicked off his shoes and crawled into the bed, laying his head in his uncle's lap and wanting so desperately to go back to a time when things were so simple that comfort from Ace made all his worries slip away.

"Eventually I have to go back to Paris. What sense does blowing up his world with the truth make when I won't be here to help him deal with it?"

"Running won't make it hurt any less, Stephan. It will only make it bigger."

"Uncle Ace."

"You made a choice because you were afraid that Lyric wouldn't choose you. That your word wouldn't have been enough and that she would've hated the messenger. You're doing the same thing now. You're keeping this young man in the dark for all these selfless reasons you've concocted in your head. But the truth is, you're just afraid you're not enough for him to choose you."

Ace rubbed his head, soothing away so much of the pain he'd lugged around like permanent luggage.

"You're worth choosing, Stephan. And from all that you've told me about your Carter, I think he'll come to that conclusion too if you let him."

God did he want Ace to be right.

"If you want this Carter of yours to accept this very complicated truth, then you've got to accept it yourself and begin your own journey of healing. But until you're ready to face some of the events and people linked to that truth, it will always haunt you, and you will never be free to love your family, Carter, or yourself.

Stephan lay still until Ace eventually fell asleep, then he slipped from the bed and exited the room.

Ace had given him so much to think about, his head was spinning. But as always, the old man's words felt like a weighted, heated blanket swaddled around Stephan, comforting him, while keeping him safe.

He walked a few doors down until he found the guest room he used whenever visits to Ace turned into sleepovers. When the door was closed, he pulled out his phone, scrolled through his contacts, and pressed the one he was looking for.

Ace was right; he needed to be free. He wouldn't offer himself up to Carter any other way. If that meant facing his past, then he would start right here.

"Well, to what do I owe the pleasure of a call from my only living son?"

God, his mother was dramatic for no damn reason. He looked up to the ceiling, suppressing a chuckle. As much as her melodrama plucked his nerves, Stephan had to admit it kept things interesting, to say the least.

"Mother, I don't want to fight. I just want to talk. I want to be able to reach out to my mother and ask her to do something for me without us having to go through military-grade strategies before we do so.

I want things to be different between us. Mother. I
need them to be different. I need to be free, and that
can't happen until we can talk without our usual de-
fenses being engaged."

He let it all out, not stopping to give her a chance
to interrupt him. It was the only way he could get
all those words to cross the threshold of his lips and
travel across the air and through the phone lines.
And when he was done, his breathing ragged as if
he'd just climbed a mountain, he called to her again.

"Mother, are you still there?"

She cleared her throat and Stephan thought she
was gearing up to deliver her usual cold and still ca-
dence. But then she said, "Son," so quietly he almost
didn't hear her. Her voice was devoid of any of her
usual venom. Instead, for the first time in as long as
he could remember, her voice was thick and inviting. "Tell me what you need, and I promise I will
make it happen."

He'd made the first step, and some of the weight
he'd carried all these years slid off the planes of his
shoulders like a rockslide. It was scary, and exciting, but most of all, it gave him hope that he could
actually share his thoughts, his wants and desires,
with Carter too.


Stephan turned onto his block and nearly crashed
into a small body wrapped in every insulated layer
of winter wear there was. It wasn't until he looked up
and realized who was under all those layers.

"Hi, Stephan."

Nevaeh waved an uncovered hand and Stephan wondered how she managed to maintain that level of freedom. Back in his day, the old folks would've never let him leave the front door without gloves to go with the hat, scarf, face mask, and feather-lined coat.

"Hi, Nevaeh."

"Goodness, mija, where are your gloves?"

Stephan couldn't help the bark of laughter that escaped his throat.

"I was just wondering how she managed to sneak out without full winter armor."

"I left them on the couch."

"Your fingers are gonna freeze off by the time we finish walking the dog."

Stephan looked around to see the dog at the other end of the leash in the child's hand.

Carter shared a pleading look with him.

"Would you mind waiting with her while I run inside and get her gloves?"

Stephan nodded and they all stepped inside Carter's front yard. Stephan and Nevaeh took a seat on the bottom step of the front stoop while Carter took the stairs two at a time and headed inside.

"My daddy smiles a lot when your name comes up. Do you smile when you hear his?"

*Straight to the point, huh, kid?*

"I do."

"My *abuelita* and Grannie Gracie say that's because my daddy probably likes you...a lot." She didn't even blink before the next questions spilled out of her mouth. "Do you like my daddy…a lot?"

Stephan lifted both brows as he tried to figure out what to say next. He didn't think he'd get far BSing this kid, so he decided to be as age-appropriately truthful as possible.

"Yes, I do like your daddy…a lot. Is that okay with you?"

She leaned her head up to look at him, tucking her tiny fingers into her pockets. At that moment, Carter stepped out of the front door and onto the stoop, smiling down at the two of them as if he were taking in something precious.

Nevaeh returned her gaze back to Stephan and gave him a sure nod.

"Yeah, it's okay with me."

Carter handed the little girl her gloves and motioned for Stephan to follow him to the other end of the yard away from little ears.

"Everything okay?" Carter asked as Stephan turned around and glanced at the carefree little brown girl and her dog having fun on a cold night.

"Yeah," Stephan replied, feeling like he'd answered that question truthfully for the first time in years. "Everything seems to be just how it's supposed to be. And as long as you keep up your end of the bargain tonight. I think that'll remain the case. Can you still get away?"

"Ian is closing up tonight, so as soon as we get rid of the last customer, I'm on my way to you."

"You want me to pick you up?"

"We go through this every night. The place is like three blocks away. I will call when I'm leaving, and you can watch me walk up the block from your living room window like you always do."

Carter looked over his shoulder to see if Nevaeh was paying attention to them. Satisfied she only had eyes for the dog, without warning, he leaned in to sneak a quick peck from Stephan, then strode to where his daughter was standing

"Ven, mija. Let's hurry. Daddy's got to put in a lot of work tonight."

Stephan's gazed was fixed on the trio's retreating frames. As they turned the corner, Stephan couldn't help inserting himself into the wholesome vision father, daughter, and their dog made. What he wouldn't give for his fantasy to become truth.

"What's all this?"

Carter stood in the middle of Stephan's en suite bathroom, taking in all of the hard work Stephan had managed in the few hours since he'd shoved Carter against a wall in his office and sucked his cock until Carter melted into a satisfied puddle and Stephan's jaw had a pleasant ache.

It had definitely been the mood lifter he'd needed after talking to both Lyric and Ace about his emotions. But now, as he welcomed the man into the room, handing him a champagne flute to help get the night started, all Stephan could think about was taking care of Carter.

"You don't like it?"

"Like it?" Carter's eyes widened as he focused on Stephan's. I love it. But I'm a New Yorker, and we're naturally suspicious of people doing nice things for us for no apparent reason."

Stephan reached down and pulled his own flute to his lips, taking a sip before he replied.

"Maybe I just want to do something nice for you?"

"Getting me pizza from Cuts and Slices was nice—which I thoroughly enjoyed by the way."

Stephan could tell by the sexy, sated smirk on Carter's face that he was fondly remembering all that happened before and after the pizza too.

"But a rose petal trail from your front door to your bathtub, dimmed lights, flickering candles, a Jacuzzi filled with what smells like a sort of lavender bath scent, and damn good champagne?" Carter took an exaggerated gulp, emptying his glass. "I mean, it's not my birthday, is it?"

"Unless you lied to me during that whole 'what's your name, what's your sign' part of our hookup, I'd say we're a few months too early for that, Carter."

"Okay, then what's this all about? I came here for the express purpose of letting you inside my pants. This level of romance isn't necessary to get what you want."

Stephan's body tensed. Everything in him rejected the idea that Carter shouldn't have this kind of treatment just because it was a day ending in *y*. Yes, Stephan had tried to keep things light because he knew he couldn't do a long-term relationship with Carter. As he stood here, he realized it wasn't solely because he didn't want that kind of attachment to the man.

Carter was attentive, fun, caring, and sexy as all hell. Not to mention, the few times he'd seen the man with his daughter, Stephan's heart melted in his chest at how sweet and patient he was with her.

Who wouldn't want all of that in a partner?

Yet, knowing all those incredible things about the man, the one thing that kept Stephan from reaching for more is that he knew beyond a shadow of a doubt that Carter would not live in his world.

Once they left the protectorate of Brooklyn and stepped out on the global stage together, between Carter's former celebrity and Stephan's current position as a member of the global elite, there was no way their relationship would stay secret for long.

After everything Carter had lost, he could never ask Carter to risk it, even though everything in him wanted to.

"You presume the only thing I wanted tonight was to sex you." Before Carter could answer, he placed a finger over his lips to stop him from speaking. "It's a given that whenever you're near me, I want you, Carter. But I'm also concerned about you burning the candle at both ends. So, I wanted to just take care of you tonight."

He put his glass down, then took Carter's. He

stepped into Carter's space, placing a gentle, yet teasing kiss that held so much promise. He'd meant it as a gentle introduction, but he could tell by the way desire burned in Carter's eyes and the way his chest heaved, he was ready to forgo this pampering session Stephan had in mind and get straight to the point where they were naked, panting, and sweaty with need, and later, satisfaction.

Carter tried to deepen the kiss, get them to that frenzied place faster, but Stephan refused.

"Carter, just let me take my time, please. I promise I'll make it good for you."

He always did. Stephan would never leave Carter unsatisfied. But the end of their time together was drawing nigh. Learning who Lennox was to Carter, there was no way he could continue their relation and risk hurting so many people he cared for, including Carter.

He wanted to savor Carter, let him know how treasured he was, even if only for one more night.

Stephan stepped into the Jacuzzi and held Carter's hand as he followed, sitting down and pulling Carter's back into his chest before completely surrounding Carter, trying desperately to show he was safe here. That his needs would always be met if Stephan had a say.

"You are a wonderful man, Carter Jiménez."

He kissed Carter's jaw as he stroked slow circles with his hands on Carter's chest. He tweaked one nipple and then the other, loving how Carter pressed his back and ass against him in response.

"And if you'd let me, I'd show you off to the world."

"Hmm," Carter sighed. "Would you?"

Stephan slid one hand beneath the water, motioning for Carter to widen his thighs. When he did, Stephan's hand cupped Carter's heavy sac, gently kneading his balls with deft fingertips that had committed Carter's reactions to memory.

The soft sigh Carter shared in response meant he was aroused, ready for whatever pleasure Stephan decided to gift him with.

When Stephan slid his hand up and closed his palm around Carter's thick cock, the indecent moan Carter released was a garbled, "fuck yeah" meant to encourage Stephan in his current course of action.

And when Stephan's hand picked up a sensual tempo, lovingly caressing Carter's beautiful cock from root to tip while his tongue plundered Carter's mouth, and the man's body shuddered, that meant he was ready to splinter, and Stephan wanted so desperately to watch him fall apart.

"If you'd let me, I'd show you off to the world. I would take you downtown to Brooklyn Bridge at night and show the world that you were the real jewel of Brooklyn."

Carter moaned, his face tightened in impending pleasure.

"I'd take you back to Paris with me, take you to

the height of the Eiffel Tower so everyone could see how it pales in comparison to your beauty."

Carter's hips lifted, meeting each one of Stephan's firm strokes, his muscles fluttering from the spasms racking his body.

"And if you'd let me, I'd have you on my arm at the gala so everyone in my family knew just how lucky I was to be with you."

Stephan worried that he'd gone too far with that last wish. Was he baring too much of his soul by letting Carter this far in? Especially when he knew he couldn't stay in this little haven Carter had created for himself.

He didn't have the chance to ponder it further, because Carter's body arched in the water, his cock pulsing in Stephan's hand as his release erupted into the air and slapped against the water on its descent.

And when Carter's body went limp against him again, Stephan took a few moments to take his own pleasure, holding Carter against him because he needed him near. He always needed him near.

And as they sat for a moment, catching their breath, and trying to find the strength to pull themselves from the tub, Carter turned in his arms and nuzzled his neck and whispered, "If that was your way of asking me to attend the gala with you, the answer is yes."

# Fifteen

Stephan sat in the limousine currently parked in front of Carter's brownstone. He hadn't needed to arrive so early. After all, his date lived a few houses down from him. But knowing how this evening would unfold once he and Carter stepped out of this car and into Borough Hall, he was antsy.

He was a coward for waiting this long to tell Carter everything. He knew that. At first, he'd lied to himself, citing the fact that his stay in the States was temporary. He would leave, and it didn't really make sense to cause Carter all that unnecessary grief. But then he'd talked with Ace about Carter and then talked to his mother to start opening the lines of communication and then it became clear to him that, even if he did leave, he owed Carter the truth.

Why? First, because Carter deserved to know the truth. But also, Stephan needed to work his way free of all these secrets and lies so he could find peace again. Knowing that didn't make things easier for Stephan, especially since it was likely he would lose everyone he loved by the end of this evening, including Carter.

That was a hard pill to swallow, and Stephan had to admit he was terrified to face that reality. That fear had led him to putting this off until now, the very last possible moment.

"Grow a set, Devereaux-Smith. Tell this man the truth before you hurt too many people to count."

The privacy window dropped and Darren, his driver, spoke. "Did you say something, Mr. Devereaux-Smith?"

Stephan shook his head at the sound of his driver's voice, realizing he'd spoken those words aloud.

"No, Darren. I was just making a list of the things I need to do tonight."

"Yes, sir."

Darren turned around and raised the privacy glass again. Stephan took a breath, cherishing the silence until he saw Carter step out onto the top step, looking good enough to eat.

His fit form was covered in the clean lines of a dark gray A. Sauvage tuxedo whose subtle but clean lines accented every inch of Carter's delicious physique.

It should've been impossible for that man to be finer than he already was, and yet, him wearing that tuxedo made Stephan take deep slow breaths in an effort to control his response to him.

Stephan stepped out of the car and walked up to the steps to meet Carter.

"Everything about the way you look in the tux is making me want to skip this shindig and take you back to my place."

"Oh no, buddy." Carter shook his head. "I put in absolutely too much work to look this good. You are taking me out as promised."

"I'll make it worth your while." Stephan stepped closer and Carter put up a hand on his chest to stop his forward momentum.

"I'm sure you would. But this is the first time I've been to something like this in a while. I'd forgotten how much fun they can be. I'm actually looking forward to it, so, rain check on the fun and sexy times, okay?"

Stephan swallowed and stepped aside as he watched Carter retreat down the steps. How was it possible that he felt like even more of an asshole now than when all of this deception began. Carter was looking forward to this. Ripping this chance away from him would be so wrong.

As the driver held the door open for the two of them and Stephan slid in behind Carter, his conscience checked him.

It might be wrong to rob Carter of his excitement

tonight. But it would be outright cruel to let him walk into this clusterfuck unknowingly.

"Hey, is everything all right?"

No, it wasn't. Not by a long shot.

"Carter," Stephan took his hand, bringing it to his lips and placing a soft kiss there. "We can't go to this gala together. At least, not until I tell you the truth about who I am and what being with me will mean for you."

"My name is Stephan Devereaux-Smith. I am the nephew of the renowned Ace Devereaux. And if you step out of this limousine and into Borough Hall tonight, this sheltered life you've built yourself in Brooklyn will be over before they serve eggnog cocktails and start playing the Temptations' 'Silent Night.'"

Cold, frigid cold spread through Carter as he listened to Stephan Smith,—correction, Stephan Devereaux-Smith of the Brooklyn Devereauxs come clean about all the lies of omission he'd let Carter soak up over the last three weeks.

*Three* damn weeks.

Carter was numb, and the only thing that broke through the pinpricks sticking every inch of skin he possessed was the heat of Stephan's thumb gliding over his hand.

"You lied to me " Carter spat as he snatched his hand from Stephan's. "Why?"

Stephan flinched when Carter took his hand back,

as if someone had thrown some scalding hot liquid at him.

"For many of the same reasons you keep your identity on the low. I come from a very powerful and wealthy family. There are people who would use the opportunity to get close to me to access what I have and what I can offer them."

"I've never wanted a damn thing from you, Stephan."

"I know that. But by the time I was sure of that, you'd told me about what happened to your wife and Hollywood, and I knew you wouldn't have anything to do with me if you knew who I was. We'd planned to keep it light and fun. It was never supposed to be…"

"What wasn't it supposed to be? Tender, caring, powerful? Because that's what it was to me Stephan. I let you in and you lied to me."

Carter spoke through clenched teeth. He wanted to yell, to break the glass of the limousine with his bare hands. But years of training in Hollywood had taught him to always keep his cool when he was in public.

"Fine, you didn't think this was going to be anything but fun at first. I'll give you that, because I felt the same. But why let it continue. Because the last time we were together, that wasn't just random fucking, Stephan. You made love to me like I was the most precious thing in the world to you. Why would you lie to me, keep me bound to you when you knew I would never risk being with you if I was aware of the truth?"

"Because I realized I was falling for you. Because I didn't want to lose you."

A single tear slid down Stephan's cheek, breaking the smooth calm of his expression. It was enough to thaw Carter's insides the tiniest bit so that he wanted to reach out and comfort Stephan.

But he couldn't. This man had lied to him. And worse yet, he'd been willing to put Carter and his daughter at risk just to have what he wanted.

Carter sat with his back stiff against the seat cushions, giving a slow nod to encourage Stephan to continue.

"I ran into Lennox the day I went to Borough Hall to secure the venue. He mentioned you, and I realized the connection you had to him and my cousin Amara then. I knew then I couldn't keep lying to you."

"If that were true, why would you ask me to this gala? Why would you try to set me up like that?"

Stephan wiped his open palm down the length of his face and huffed. "I didn't mean to invite you. In the heat of passion I told you everything I would do if you were mine. I never dreamed you would see it as an invite and accept it."

"So you let me buy into this fantasy, Stephan?"

"I wanted it to be real. I wanted us to be real."

Stephan leaned in closer, and his nearness made Carter dizzy with want. He was mad enough to crush rocks in his fists, but he still couldn't fight the fire that Stephan always lit in him.

"I want to show you to the world, Carter. I wanted to have this night with you to prove to you we could survive this, and that I would never let anything happen to you. I wanted you to see that if we could do this here, then maybe I'd be able to convince you to come back to Paris with me."

Carter's brain short-circuited as he tried to follow Stephan's logic. "I have a child. I can't just uproot her entire life for good dick, Stephan. Parenting doesn't work that way."

Stephan swallowed, returning to an upright position. "That's the thing, Carter. I was hoping for once, I'd found someone who saw me for more than my name and more than my dick. I wanted you to want me…for me. I'm so sorry I lied. And I know I don't deserve your forgiveness, but I'm gonna ask for it anyway. Because to me, you are more than your name, and you're certainly worth more than your dick, even though I'd categorize it more as superb than just good."

"Are you really trying to be fucking funny right now?"

Carter wished they were standing outside of the car because then he'd be able to pace as he tried to wrap his mind around what was happening. But Carter didn't make public scenes. He didn't do anything to draw attention to himself, and Stephan knew that. That's why he'd told him this news inside the car. So Carter would have to remain calm and listen to him.

Too bad for him Carter was a master at relaying his anger while keeping his face, features and body language neutral from prying eyes. Thank you, Juilliard.

"Did you actually just sit here and have the nerve to tell me what you want?"

"Carter—"

"Shut it," Carter spat and held up his finger. "Don't say one more word. All this time, I've been handling you with kid gloves and bending over backward to respect your privacy, never once pushing you to share beyond what you were ready, because I cared about you, and because I understood what it felt like to be violated in such a way. All this time I just wanted to give you whatever it was you needed, even if I ached so much to know more about you that it tied my head in knots. All of this effort I'm putting out there to take care of this beautiful sad man my kid's dog nearly assaulted, and this whole time you're a damn Devereaux?"

Carter banged his hand against the panel of the door, too angry to notice the throbbing sting that remained afterward.

"You must've been laughing your ass off at me. I mean, it's obvious you had me dick whipped, I bet that was a laugh and a half for you too."

Carter's words felt like acid, bitter and corrosive, as he hurled them at Stephan.

"I never laughed at you. I loved you. Everything about you made me want to be better and tell you who I was. But I knew if I did…"

"You knew I'd leave. You knew I would never put my family's safety at risk to be with you. So you said to hell with my wishes, you'd just do what you wanted anyway."

"Carter…" Stephan leaned over, planting his forearms on his thighs. "I never would've allowed anything to happen to you or Nevaeh. I wasn't disregarding your safety, Carter. I was trying my best to navigate your fear. Fear has kept me away from my family for two years and it almost cost me this beautiful thing that we share. But I can't run anymore, Carter. And I'm begging you to stop running too. Please, just give us a chance."

"I would've given you anything!"

Carter's voice rose, banging off the interior of the limo, shaking the tenuous control until the mask fell and tears burned as they slid down his face.

"I'd have given you anything you asked for if you'd just trusted me and respected my boundaries. Because that's what love does, Stephan. It doesn't manipulate, it respects, it honors. But if you could lie about this, if you could touch me like—"

Carter couldn't finish that sentence. If he did, the memories of just how often and deeply Stephan had touched him both physically and emotionally would overwhelm him.

"I can't trust you, Stephan. After everything I've

lost, everything I've been through, I need to be able to trust that you will always have my and by extension my daughter's best interest at heart." He waved his finger between the two of them. "The way you've handled this tells me I can't trust you with my heart, and I for damn sure wouldn't trust you with her safety. So, whatever you thought we had, however you saw this ending, I'm done. I will not be taken for a fool. I will not be willingly gullible for you ever again."

And then Carter did the second hardest thing he'd ever had to do. He pulled away from Stephan when he reached out to grab him, and he stepped out of the car, taking the stairs two at a time and rushing inside his front door. When the door was closed, and he was certain he was safe from the magnetism that always pulled him toward Stephan, he let his head rest against the cold wood and wondered how the hell he'd ended up here.

# Sixteen

Breaking up with someone that was never his boyfriend was a real bitch.

"If you wake that baby up after I had to nearly tie her to the bed after she was so excited from watching you get runway ready, I promise you're not gonna like me very much."

Carter hadn't even realized he'd been making that much noise as he reached for a decanter full of liquor with one hand and tumbler with the other.

"Gracie…" His voice was sharp and raw, and he could see her flinch from the way his harsh tone wrapped around her name.

He cleared his throat, trying to keep his anger at

bay. "I don't want to be disrespectful, but I need to be alone right now."

Gracie had loved him like a son and moved her life all the way from California to New York for him because her daughter had loved him. Repaying all that kindness with a short temper and a slick mouth because Stephan had pissed him off wouldn't do.

"What are you even doing here? Shouldn't you be at the Christmas party you were helping to plan?"

Carter carelessly poured liquor into his glass, not even caring what variety it was. As long as it burned going down, that's all he required of it at this moment. He took a large gulp, hissing at the sting traveled down his throat and to his gut.

He went to pour another, but before he could tip the bottle, Gracie grabbed it and held it out of his reach.

"Can't a man drink in peace in his own damn house?"

Gracie looked over her shoulder at the empty space behind her, then turned calmly back to him.

"I don't know who the hell you think you're talking to, but it ain't me. And since I know your mama would take a slipper to your head if she heard you talking to me that way, I have no doubt you know better."

She was right. His mama's *chancleta* never missed, and if she heard him carrying on like some ogre stomping all over his house and taking this disrespectful tone with Gracie, he had no doubt he'd have caught a flip-flop to the head by now.

"I'm sorry, Gracie. Stephan and I had a fight in the limo and I refused to go to the gala tonight."

He walked over to his recliner near the fireplace, needing to be surrounded in something familiar, something he knew would never betray him. Up until a few minutes ago, he was beginning to feel like Stephan had become like his recliner, a sure thing he never had to worry over.

God, how quickly did things change?

"What happened? You seemed so excited about the night."

"I was." He leaned over, bracing his elbow on his thigh and letting his hand slide down his face. "But then…"

"Then what?"

"I found out Stephan has been lying to me about who he is."

She sat quietly, waiting for him to get it all out in one angry rush, and he was grateful for that, because he wouldn't have been able to relay the whole tale otherwise.

"He knew how Michelle died. He knew what celebrity, fame, and notoriety cost me. He knew what my selfish need to be part of that world stole from all of us. Why would he do that?"

"Carter?"

Gracie's voice was soft and soothing. Such a gentle sound that was meant to soothe him, but it nearly broke him instead.

"Carter," she said again. "Come here, baby."

His gaze met hers, and he saw the warmth of a mother, and his rage and anger morphed into guilt that hung over him like a thick cloud, nearly suffocating him.

He tried to resist her request. He'd taken enough from her. He didn't deserve her sympathy too. But when she nodded her head, he couldn't resist. He took the few steps to close the distance between them and sat on the floor, his head resting at her knee.

The first stroke of her hand in his hair cracked the last bastion of his resistance. With it, the unshed tears he'd been fighting to hold back fell too.

"I remember the day my daughter met you. You were brought down to the CT to get a scan to help diagnose your appendicitis. She was the tech that night and she had a little boy in the waiting area who was terrified and wouldn't let her come near him. But he saw you and realized you were his favorite action hero, and you used your celebrity to make that child feel brave, safe, and calm so he could get his scan done."

"I can't believe Michelle told you that. I was just trying to help."

"No." Gracie continued as she smoothed her hand through his hair. "You were being kind. You didn't want to see that boy suffer, and even though you were in pain yourself, you wanted him to be all right. Michelle knew then that you were the type of man she could love."

He remembered that night well. He'd been in so

much pain, but calming that little man had seemed way more important than his own situation. And when Michelle had finally been ready to tend to Carter, she'd been so tender with him, he'd known then he never wanted to be without that feeling in his life.

"She was such a beautiful soul, Gracie, and I took her away."

"No." Gracie scratched lightly at his scalp. "You loved her for as long as God allowed you to. What happened to my daughter was a tragic accident. It wasn't your fault, Carter. The paparazzi who chased her into the street were at fault. Not you, and not your celebrity.

"Now that we've gotten that out of the way, let's move on to your young man. A Devereaux, huh?"

Carter nodded, taking in a slow breath to try to stop the tremble in his voice.

"Yeah. One of the wealthiest and most famous families on the planet. How did I not know this?"

"Because maybe Stephan didn't want you to see his fame and his money? Maybe the only thing he wanted you to see was his heart? Is that really any different than why you moved back to Brooklyn? So you and your daughter wouldn't have a spotlight and a microphone shoved in your face at all times?"

"You don't even know the man well. How can you take up for him?" Carter knew he sounded like a petulant child, but he wanted to wallow in his self-righteousness just a bit longer, and Gracie calling him on his shit wasn't really helping him do that.

"I know the man that my daughter loved. I know she would've done anything to love you for the rest of her life. And if my angel loved you that much, then a man like Stephan Devereaux-Smith, someone who's been raised to recognize quality and luxury, there's no way he couldn't do everything in his power to keep you near. That includes omitting who he is because he's afraid to be marked as guilty by association in your eyes."

Carter groaned. "I really hate it when you do that."

"Do what?" He could hear the smile in her voice even though he couldn't see her face from this position.

"Make sense, he muttered, groaning again when she chuckled."

"Carter, you can't hide from the world forever. You were blessed enough to have my daughter, and the universe is offering you another chance to have something beautiful again with another special person."

"How do you know Stephan is special? You've barely met the man?"

She rubbed his head again and he nestled deeper into her knee, still unable to move. In the first few days after Michelle's death when he was overwrought with grief, he'd sit at her knee and it would make all the noise stop for just a few seconds. Being this close to someone who loved his wife as much as he did, it helped him endure an unbearable load.

"Because you loved a woman who had the biggest, brightest heart in the world. There's no way you could settle for someone whose spirit wasn't equally as loving, brilliant, and kind."

God, this woman. All these years later, she was doing it again. Making him feel like a son instead of a broken man. Putting him back together when the outside world tore him apart. Carter didn't know how he'd gotten so lucky to have both the best mother and mother-in-law in the world, but he knew he wouldn't let either of them go for anything in the world.

"So, I'm gonna need you to go wash your face, brush your hair, and get the Visine out of the fridge, because love is waiting, and it wouldn't do to find you looking like who did it and ran."

He barked in laughter until Gracie shushed him. When he recovered, he stood up and kissed her on her cheek and gave her a big hug. Now, all he had to do was go to this party and get his man. Fame had stolen so much from him. He'd be damned if his fear of it caused him to lose another thing.

Stephan waited outside as long as he could, looking for Carter. He'd known Carter was angry. He couldn't blame him after keeping the man in the dark like that. But still…somewhere deep down he'd hoped…

Too riddled with guilt to even continue that line of thought, he looked down at his watch and realized he had to get inside if he was going to do what he planned to do before the extended branches of the Devereaux family arrived. This was a Brooklyn

Devereaux issue and it needed to be dealt with internally before anyone else added their two cents.

He was about to turn around when he heard a familiar voice. "Were you waiting for me?"

"Hello, Mother." Stephan's heart lurched in disappointment. It wasn't his mother's appearance that disappointed him. He was actually happy about that, considering what he had planned. His mother needed to be here, and given the amount of acrimony she held for her brother, Stephan hadn't known for certain that she would show up.

She needed this.

They all needed this, and after losing the man he loved because of his role as the secret bearer, Stephan needed this too. Not because he was looking for absolution. He wasn't. But he loved Carter, and he had every intention of fighting for him. He couldn't do that until he'd buried all of his past.

Holding on to it had made him come to Carter with only half-truths. But after tonight, he would be free to be honest with Carter because he could finally be honest with his family, and most of all himself.

"Mother, I'm pleased you're here."

He leaned in, kissed her cheek, and offered her his arm to hold as they entered the building.

"I almost believe you mean that, son."

"I do. I know that you've been hurting for a really long time and I wasn't here to help you deal with that. I just hope after tonight you can understand why I haven't been here, why I needed to be away, and how sorry I am for leaving you all alone."

Her eyes widened, softening her features. Her mouth was slightly ajar, and if he weren't seeing this for himself, he wouldn't believe the sincere surprise written all over her face.

"Thank you for that, Stephan. But you weren't the cause of my pain. Ace was."

He patted her hand. "A discussion for another time. Right now, we need to meet up with the rest of the family before this party officially begins. And Mother?"

She arched a brow, waiting for him to continue.

"No matter what happens tonight, know that I love you."

She stared at him for a long moment. He couldn't blame her for her silence. Martha was a lot of things, but gushy and emotional wasn't one of them. He'd spent his life modeling the same behavior because he thought it would make her more comfortable around him. But he hadn't counted on how much it would eat at his soul not being truthful about what he felt.

"I… I love you too, son." She whispered those words to him, patting his arm softly to reinforce them, making them more real.

When they stepped inside of the main hall, Stephan stopped, looking around the room, top to bottom, side to side, taking in all the individual touches that he'd worked on with Carter.

The white silk curtains that covered each wall and

the sparkling gold shimmer woven into the canvas made the room look like it was bathed in snow. The matching linen tablecloths and gold flatware, goblets, and napkins were the perfect accents. Decorative white lights hung on artificial white branches through the room, creating a soft, warm glow throughout.

It was more than he ever could've done on his own in the short amount of time they'd known each other. Three weeks shouldn't have been enough time to pull this off, but with Carter's help, he had. Three weeks shouldn't have been enough time to fall in love, lose his heart, and lose the man he loved at once either, but apparently Stephan was an overachiever, so he'd managed that too.

Once his eyes reached the dais, they settled upon all of the members of the Brooklyn Devereauxs.

Ace sat in the middle of the dais with his brother David sitting to his right. There was an empty chair to Ace's left, and when he heard the small gasp escape his mother's mouth, he knew she understood that chair had been held for her.

Ace's son Deuce, his daughter-in-law Destiny, and his granddaughter Trey and her husband, and Ace's ward, Jeremiah, were standing in front of the center of the dais. Amara's mother, Ja'Net and her father Angel were standing with Amara and Lennox directly in front of David, and Lyric stood to the left with her beau, Josiah, directly in front of the empty chair where Martha was intended to sit.

All three children of Si and Alice Devereaux were still present in the world, and all their living offspring were here too.

It was the most heartbreakingly beautiful sight he'd ever witnessed. He stood there, quietly taking it in, committing every smile, every feature to memory just in case he never had the opportunity to see them again.

"Mother, please—"

"Stephan, I don't understand. What's happening here? Are you all right?"

He shook his head. "No, I'm not. And I haven't been for a long time. But hopefully, after I say my piece, I will be."

He swept his hand in the direction of her seat, asking once more if she would acquiesce. With cautious steps, she moved toward the dais and gracefully took her seat next to Ace.

The room was crackling with anticipation. They all knew the history, the battles that had been forged between these siblings and their offspring, but only Stephan knew why the war began in the first place.

"Thank you for coming here early tonight. The rest of our large clan will be here soon, so I should probably get on with this."

He shoved his hands in his pockets, fiddling with his billfold to help him find the words he needed. Words that he'd buried for so long.

"We have not functioned like a family for a very long time. We've functioned as a business. We've even functioned as competitors. But we have not been a family in recent times. And we need to fix that now."

He looked at Ace, who sat with a weary smile on his face and unshed tears in his eyes, closing his eyes and signaling his permission for Stephan to proceed.

"Time is not on our side, and we may never be in one place again once we leave this room."

The proof of their understanding shone in their shimmering eyes and their tense faces.

"As I'm sure you're all aware, two years ago Uncle Ace received a call from Jamaica Defense Force's Coast Guard, informing him that my brother Randall had died and someone would need to come collect his body.

"What you don't know however is the reason they called Ace, is because the details of Randall's death weren't as you've been led to believe."

He felt rather than saw Lyric's eyes on him, and his hands wanted to immediately reach for her, comfort her from the blow he was about to throw at her. But he couldn't; she as well as everyone in this room needed to hear this.

"Wait," Lyric began. "You said they'd called Ace because Randall had been operating a Devereaux Inc. vessel that was titled to Ace. If that wasn't the case, I was his wife and next of kin, Stephan. If something was amiss why didn't they call me?"

"Because they thought you'd died with him?"

"What the hell?" Her jaw tightened and her nostrils flared, and Stephan couldn't tell if it was disbelief or anger contorting her calm and tender features into something unrecognizable to him.

Questions were still dancing in Lyric's eyes, but the dark steel of Josiah's held acknowledgment as Stephan watched him step closer to Lyric, wrapping a protective arm around her.

"They thought you died with him because he was listed at the resort as Mr. and Mrs. Randall Devereaux-Smith. Believing you were both dead, the authorities contacted Ace because the vessel was his."

Stephan tore his gaze away from Lyric and found his mother's "The woman was an employee of Devereaux Inc. When we contacted her sister, she said Randall had taken her sister on the trip because they wanted to spend her birthday weekend together without prying eyes."

Stephan stepped closer to his mother and Lyric, the two women he'd tried his best to protect, silently asking for their forgiveness as he continued.

"I asked Ace to use his power and influence to cover things up so the two of you would never know what happened. You were both devastated already. Randall was everything to the both of you, and I didn't want the circumstances of his death to steal the joy his memory brought you."

"And that's why you left?"

Lyric slowly took his hand, tightening her grip on it before she spoke. But instead of anger, it was as if she was trying to give him something, someone to hold on to.

"My lie, it pit my mother against her brother because Randall told her Ace sent him on an unexpected business errand. It blackened me with guilt. I knew if I stayed, Lyric, my guilt would've forced me to tell the truth. You weren't ready for that. Neither of you were.

"My mother held Randall on a pedestal—he could do no wrong, and you loved him to distraction. I just... I couldn't take that away from either of you. So I asked Ace to lie instead.

"But because of my lie, my mother hated her brother..."

"And you got to be exiled away from the people you love?"

His sister-in-love was always so perceptive.

"Stephan, he was your brother." Lyric's voice held so much love and compassion for him, he wanted to wrap himself up in it. But he wasn't the victim here, or at least, he wasn't the only one.

Lyric held on tighter. "You were grieving too. All this time you were trying to protect us, who was there to protect you?"

"Ace," his mother said as she turned her head toward her brother. "You covered my dead son and gave the one who remained the resources and support to protect me and his brother's wife."

It wasn't a question. Martha spoke, even without any sort of confirmation, as if she knew this to be truth. From her erect posture to the stern, clear sound of her voice, she knew that Stephan wasn't lying.

"All these years you let me hate you because my son asked you to help him protect me."

"You are my little, sister, Martha. I would've borne any pain I had to soften the loss of your son."

And that's when it happened, a tear slid down her face, and Stephan could see the wall his mother had built between herself and her older brother crumbling with each tear that followed.

"I'm so sorry, Ace. All this time I've wasted hating you."

"It was better for you to hate me—" his voice was shaking with a mix of relief and love "—than to break your heart all over again after losing your boy."

Ace's words triggered something in the room: parents found children, hugging them just a bit tighter. And when Martha and Lyric each held one of Ace's hands, Stephan knew he'd accomplished what he'd come here to do. Set the record straight, unload all the guilt and trauma of the last two years, and find a way to sanctify his soul.

Unfortunately, the irony was that the moment he set himself loose from one lie, he was shackled by the heartache of revealing the truth to the man he loved. Feeling overwhelmed, unburdened, but not yet free, he stepped out into the hall.

This was the first step. He'd told the truth to his family, hopefully opening up a path of healing across generations. Now he just needed to figure out how to fix things with Carter. Because more than ever, his soul ached to be both unburdened and whole, and only Carter held the missing piece.

# Seventeen

"Carter, is that you?"

Carter turned around to see his best friend Lennox exit the main hall. Carter had arrived a few moments earlier, but when he'd heard Stephan's heavy and somber voice confessing to his family, Carter had stepped away, not wanting to intrude.

"Yeah, man, it's me."

Lennox looked him up and down, paying close attention to Carter's outfit. "What are you—"

Carter lifted his hand. "Man, it's a really long story, one I don't have to time to tell right now."

"You need something?"

"Yeah, to fight for my heart." At that moment, Stephan stepped into the hall. He pointed at Stephan.

"And right now, my heart is standing in the middle of the floor, looking like he's about to collapse."

Lennox looked at Stephan and then back at Carter with bewilderment in his eyes.

" Do you remember what I told you about love when you and Amara were going through it."

Lennox answered in the affirmative. "That no matter the risk of pain, love is always worth it."

"Yeah, well," Carter continued. "let's just say I had a huge reminder of that tonight. So, as much as I would love to stand here and break things down for you. I need you to step aside and let me talk to Stephan Devereaux-Smith because he's the man I love."

Lennox's gaping mouth was proof that after all these decades of friendship, Carter still had the power to shock his friend. A fact he would lord over Lennox's head if he wasn't so eager to make things right with Stephan.

Carter stepped in Stephan's direction, and Lennox grabbed his arm to stop his momentum. "Once this is settled," Lennox mock whispered, "I better get all the damn details or it's gonna be me and you and Amara, and trust me, you don't want that smoke."

Carter laughed because the little he knew of Amara, he was certain of that fact. She was persistent, bold, confident, beautiful, and the best damn corporate lawyer he'd ever met. And considering the way she'd owned Lennox and twisted his emotions into a pretzel, he figured the safest bet was to never get on her bad side.

\* \* \*

"I'm so damn mad with you."

Stephan watched as Carter walked closer to him and the rest of the world melted away.

"Just when I was beginning to open back up to another person, feel safe with another person, you lied to me and made me question whether I could trust you. Made me think that you loved me and I could love you."

"I did lie to you about who I was, Carter, and I was wrong for that. But never…never did I lie about loving you, about wanting to make a home with you. My feelings were always real."

Carter stepped closer, and with every inch he gained, Stephan's heart thudded against his chest in anticipation.

It was just like their first meeting all over again—his brain was fuzzy, and his heart was pounding, and it was hard to think and breathe. But standing in Carter's presence was worth all of the discomfort, because to bask in his glow transcended any pain.

"I know your feelings are real." Carter laced his fingers into Stephan's, anchoring him where they stood. "That's the only reason I'm here now. I know what it's like to lose love, Stephan. I know what it is to have to live with the finality of goodbye. I'm mad as hell that you lied to me, even by omission. But knowing how much I love you and that you're still alive, there's no way I could waste this gift between us."

Carter looked up at him, leaning in slowly, letting his forehead touch Stephan's briefly before Carter lifted his chin with a finger, and placed a sweet, delicate press of his lips to Stephan's, nearly rendering him incapable of a verbal response.

"You're gonna be in the doghouse for a long ass time." Carter eagerly shared that detail. Stephan was so afraid this was all a dream and interrupting Carter would mean he disappeared like a puff of smoke, he simply nodded.

"But no matter how long it takes for us to get right again, I need you to know that as much as I fuss at you, I'm gonna love you just as hard. And that will be a good thing. Because it means we'll have to take our time and really get to know each other and each other's families. Because if the tail end of that conversation I heard you having with your people was any indication, your family is just as messy as mine.

"That's for damn sure." Stephan nodded. "Does this mean you're going to forgive me?"

"It means I'm willing to do the work so that I can forgive you and we can get past this. You're my person, Stephan. I can't let you get away just because I'm angry with you.

"I promise, I will do everything to keep you and Nevaeh safe."

"You'd better." Carter stole another kiss. "Because, between Gracie and my mother, those two women could make a body disappear and no one would be the wiser."

"I'll be on my best behavior." Stephan pulled him into his arms, needing to feel the weight of Carter's body against his. The heft, it meant this was real, that Carter was really here, that he hadn't lost the most important thing in his life due to his own stupidity and fear.

"Good," Carter replied. "Now that that's settled, I think it's time you made some introductions. Because if I don't give Lennox the deets, he's already threatened to sick his lawyer wife on me."

Stephan clucked his tongue. "Take it from someone who grew up with that woman. She will ruin you, and then go back to eating her favorite snack while scrolling on the internet like nothing ever happened. Trust me, you don't want no parts of that."

"But I do want every part of you."

Such simple words, but their meaning held their weight in gold inside Stephan's heart. Carter Jiménez had given Stephan a reason to walk out of the dark and find the light in his lover's arms.

"Damn, baby." He tightened his hold on Carter, so grateful to have him here like this in the open where the world could see. "You really do know how to make a brotha feel loved."

**YOU** pick your books –
**WE** pay for everything.
You get up to FOUR new books and a Mystery Gift…
absolutely FREE!
**Total retail value: Over $20!**

Dear Reader,

Your opinions are important to us. So if you'll participate in our fast and free "One Minute" Survey, YOU can pick up to four wonderful books that WE pay for when you try the Harlequin Reader Service!

As a leading publisher of women's fiction, we'd love to hear from you. That's why we promise to reward you for completing our survey.

IMPORTANT: Please complete the survey and return it. We'll send your Free Books and a Free Mystery Gift right away. And we pay for shipping and handling too! *We pay for* ← *EVERYTHING!*

Try **Harlequin® Desire** and get 2 books featuring the worlds of the American elite with juicy plot twists, delicious sensuality and intriguing scandal.

Try **Harlequin Presents® Larger-Print** and get 2 books featuring the glamourous lives of royals and billionaires in a world of exotic locations, where passion knows no bounds.

**Or TRY BOTH!**

Thank you again for participating in our "One Minute" Survey. It really takes just a minute (or less) to complete the survey… and your free books and gift will be well worth it!

If you continue with your subscription, you can look forward to curated monthly shipments of brand-new books from your selected series, always at a discount off the cover price! Plus you can cancel any time. So don't miss out, return your One Minute Survey today to get your Free books.

*Pam Powers*

# Epilogue

*Nine months later...*

They'd dated for six months, getting to know each other's families, and Stephan had taken that time to fall deeper in love with Carter, and to have his heart stolen again, this time by Nevaeh. She'd taken to Stephan so easily, and it just reinforced for him that he'd found the perfect love for him.

After six months of dating, they'd gotten engaged. Stephan throwing himself a birthday dinner and using it as on opportunity to ask Carter to marry him. Since the Devereauxs didn't have a history of long engage-ments, they'd married two months after their engagement at a small ceremony in the family room of Devereaux Manor.

Ace demanded he would sit by Stephan's side as one of his best men, just like he did Jeremiah's on his wedding day. There was no way Stephan would refuse his decree. And so, on the happiest day of his life, Stephan was surrounded by all the people he loved, including his mother and his beloved Ace, who had found their way to reconciliation since Stephan had finally told the truth about Randall's death.

Since things happened so quickly, he and Carter had decided it was too soon to broach the subject of adopting Nevaeh, but Stephan knew deep in his heart, that's what he wanted, if Carter and his beautiful stepdaughter would allow it. Until then, he'd just use this time to love on them both, show them both he was ready to make the necessary sacrifices to love and be loved by this family. The one he was born into, including the newest member of his family, Amara and Lennox's baby girl, Omari Devereaux-Carlisle. And the one he'd married into with two more mothers, a precocious little princess, and his husband.

Now, here they were, together again with all the people they loved, one month after saying their vows and nine months after declaring their love for one another at Ace's Christmas Gala. Here they sat, hand in hand, watching as thousands gathered to pay their respects to Jordan Dylan "Ace" Devereaux, I, as he lay in state at Brooklyn Borough Hall. It was an honor rarely reserved for civilians. But his contributions were so great, his beloved city wanted to send him off with the pomp and circumstance of a king.

Stephan looked at his family seated in somber reverence before the ebony casket with its gold bearings. In the first row, his uncle David and Stephan's mother, Martha, Deuce and Destiny, Jeremiah and Trey, sat together. Lyric and Josiah, Amara, Lennox, and their baby, Omari, Stephan, Carter, and Nevaeh were seated in the second row. Right behind them was his older cousin Ja'Net and her husband Angel.

As he glanced around, he could see all of them holding tight to one another, bearing the great weight of such a significant loss. They were hurting, but the love that shone between each of them was going to keep them safe and bound together through ache of grief.

He knew this, not just because he knew these people, because that's what he had, what he felt so strongly as Carter and their little girl surrounded him, making the hurt just that much more bearable.

He ran his hand over the intricate braiding pattern he'd done in Nevaeh's hair last night. His little angel had climbed up next to him on the couch, bringing him the hair tools, asking him if he'd braid her hair so she could be pretty for Uncle Ace.

The sweetness of that gesture had nearly broken him. But as he parted and greased each section before cornrowing each braid, the love Ace had begged him to seek, surrounded him, holding him together when his heart threatened to break apart for Ace.

And while he'd braided her hair to perfection, Carter had sat next to him, touching him, kissing him, letting him know he was loved.

"Hey, you doing okay, baby?"

Carter squeezed his hand, lending Stephan his strength. It was then that he realized how right Ace was when he told him he needed to find someone who would replenish his joy when it was waning.

That's who Carter was. From the very first he'd taken care of Stephan when he'd needed it. And every chance Stephan had, he'd repaid Carter's kindness. Because, yes, he needed someone to pour into him. But he also needed to care for the person that cared for him too. It's the only way it would work. It's the only way Stephan would allow it to work.

He cupped Carter's cheek, tracing a gentle thumb across the skin there, and he smiled, leaning over to softly press his lips against his husband's.

"I love you Carter Devereaux-Smith. Thank you for loving me."

Carter touched his forehead to Stephan's and said, "Thank you for letting me."

\* \* \* \* \*

**Sophia Singh Sasson** puts her childhood habit of daydreaming to good use by writing stories she wishes will give you hope and make you laugh, cry and possibly snort tea from your nose. She was born in Mumbai, India, has lived in Spain and Canada, and currently resides in Washington, DC. She loves to read, travel, bake, scuba dive, make candles and hear from readers. Visit her at www.SophiaSasson.com.

### Books by Sophia Singh Sasson

### Harlequin Desire

*Boyfriend Lessons*
*Tempted by the Bollywood Star*

### Nights at the Mahal

*Marriage by Arrangement*
*Running Away with the Bride*
*Last Chance Reunion*
*Making a Marriage Deal*

### Harlequin Heartwarming

### State of the Union

*The Senator's Daughter*
*Mending the Doctor's Heart*

Visit the Author Profile page
at Harlequin.com for more titles.

You can also find Sophia Singh Sasson on Facebook,
along with other Harlequin Desire authors,
at Facebook.com/HarlequinDesireAuthors!

Dear Reader,

I wouldn't be writing if it weren't for you. Thank you for reading my books. I'm excited to share Mia and Saira's love story with you.

What would you give up for love? We would all like to believe that love conquers all but that doesn't really happen in real life. Both Mia and Saira have to figure out what they're willing to give up for love, and whether love is really worth the sacrifices they need to make. While this book alludes to the social issues faced by the LGBTQ+ community, this is not the focus of the book and I'm not the right author to write about those issues. While social issues are part of the context of the novel, it is not what Mia and Saira's journey is about. Their path to love is about the internal struggles we all face in modern love: choosing between career and love, figuring out whether we can trust someone who has hurt us in the past and realizing what is truly important.

I hope you enjoy their story. Hearing from readers makes my day so please email me at Sophia@SophiaSasson.com, tag me on Twitter @SophiaSasson, Instagram @Sophia_Singh_Sasson, Facebook/AuthorSophiaSasson or find me on BookBub @SophiaSinghSasson, Goodreads or my website www.SophiaSasson.com.

Love,

Sophia

# TEMPTED BY THE BOLLYWOOD STAR

Sophia Singh Sasson

This book is dedicated to all those who feel that love will never happen for them.
It will.
Keep your heart open.

Thank you to the awesome Harlequin Desire Editorial team, in particular Stephanie Doig.

It's lonely being an author but the amazing community of South Asian romance writers always keeps me going.

Last and most important, I wouldn't be an author without the love and support of my family.

# One

"If you tell me there are more script changes from the Bollywood prima donna, I'm going to scream."

Gail dropped a bulging manila folder on Mia's pristine desk and sank into a chair. She was wearing her standard outfit of dark cargo pants, a black tank top and silver hoop earrings that were too large for her delicate face. Her jet-black hair was scraped into a ponytail.

"She couldn't even send them electronically?" Mia picked up the envelope, weighing its heft.

"Saira worked on them during the eighteen-hour flight from Mumbai. Using a laptop on the plane gives her a headache."

"How are you able to say that with a straight face?"

Mia rolled her eyes at Gail and tore open the envelope. She fanned the pages, the sight of the familiar, perfectly formed, handwritten letters making her stomach flutter. *I had this tutor in India who made me practice my cursive for hours until I got it right.* It had been ten years since she and Saira had spent that month in Fiji. Ten years in which she'd finally moved on with her life. Mia almost hadn't taken this dream job because of Saira, but then she'd reminded herself that she had a reputation for being able to work with the angriest producers and the most narcissistic actors and actresses. Surely, she could handle Saira Sethi.

Mia threw the packet of papers on the desk, rattling the keyboard and mouse. "Shooting for *Life with Meera* begins in two days. The entire writers' room is ready to go on strike if I give them any more changes."

"We're not required to take her suggestions. Her contract gives her very limited powers, which she's grossly overstepping," Gail said carefully.

*That's Saira. You give her an inch and she takes a mile.*

"Want me to take the hit this round?"

Mia smiled gratefully at Gail. They'd met at the studio on the first day of their internship and compared notes on how many decaf soy lattes and no foam cappuccinos they'd fetched. In a city where relationships only lasted until the next job, they'd somehow managed to be friends for fifteen years. But even Gail didn't know about her history with Saira.

She stood and paced in her ten-by-ten office. The walls were covered with pictures and awards belonging to the previous director, Peter Denton. The carpet reeked of the cigarettes that he wasn't supposed to smoke inside. Mia stared at a picture of Peter holding an armful of Emmy awards. He held the record for the most Emmy nominations for outstanding producer and the most wins. In film school, Mia thought the key ingredient to success was talent, but she was wrong. It was opportunity. Shows succeeded when they had the budget to hire the best writers, stars and staff. Once a studio invested in producing the show, they spent money on marketing. Show popularity attracted better talent, and the cycle repeated. *Life with Meera* was Mia's opportunity.

Peter Denton had had to leave the show suddenly after his wife got sick. Mia had met Peter's wife at a party once; she was a kind woman and Mia sincerely hoped she recovered. But it was Peter's departure that had created this opportunity for Mia. The studio execs had finally noticed her and had given her a chance. It was her first big-budget show, and if the first ten episodes were a success, it would launch Mia's career.

Mia turned to face Gail. "I have to deal with Saira. When is she due in studio?" Mia had put it off as long as she could, but it was time to face her past, present and possibly her future. *Life with Meera* centered on a South Asian female lead, and the success of the show hinged on Saira's performance. She was the star. That gave Saira a lot of power, but Mia wasn't going to let Saira ruin her big chance.

"She's been here all morning—met with the studio execs, did the rounds."

Saira hadn't come to see Mia. At least she wasn't the only one avoiding their meeting.

Gail tapped on her phone. "Speak of the devil. She's in wardrobe, and Jessica says there's a problem."

Mia took a breath. Peter had let Saira run roughshod over him. They were already behind schedule and over budget because of all the changes she'd requested. It was time to show her former lover that the new boss wasn't going to tolerate her diva behavior.

"There's really no reason to call the producer." Saira's stomach flipped at the thought of seeing Mia. She'd been mentally preparing all day, but she wasn't ready yet.

The costume designer, Jasmine, was frantically tapping on her iPad.

"Listen, it's not a big deal. We can choose a neutral color like black." Saira began to unravel the fuchsia pink saree she'd been trying on but was intercepted by a wispy man with a pincushion in his mouth.

"I need to mark the hemlines," he muttered.

Jasmine shook her head. She was tall, broad shouldered with salt-and-pepper hair and lips that disappeared when she scrunched her face, as she was doing now. "Mia said no changes without her approval. The set designer planned around these wardrobe colors."

Saira stared at the full-length mirror. The costume room was much smaller than she was used to and felt claustrophobic, with racks of clothes and bolts of fabric cluttering the space. She had no idea what pincushion man was doing, marking hemlines on a saree. Didn't he know that she could just tuck the excess fabric and adjust it any way they needed?

"I'm not asking to change the whole saree, just the blouse." She pointed to the crop top, hating the sudden high pitch in her voice. She didn't want to sound difficult on her first day, but everything had to be right. A lot was riding on this project, her one shot at transferring her Mumbai stardom to LA. It had taken her five years to find the right show; she'd been patient, waited for the project that would give her the wide visibility she needed. But she'd made a mistake. Once she saw the final script, she realized that the network was making the same tired, clichéd show American networks had made countless times before. The script had the same stereotypical nonsense that previous shows proliferated, the kind of stuff that had ruined her sister's life. Saira wasn't going to let that happen. Even if it meant going to war with everyone on the show, including Mia.

The mere thought of Mia sent a jumble of emotions twisting and churning inside her chest. Could she handle working with Mia? Being in such close proximity to the one person who had once meant everything to her? They hadn't spoken in ten long years. Did Mia remember any of the passion that had consumed them both, or was Saira a distant memory for her?

*It doesn't matter how Mia feels.* Saira steeled herself. She couldn't afford to be distracted by thoughts of Mia. All of her focus and energy had to be on making the show a success. The past was just that, and she needed to bury it once and for all if she had any hope of unlocking the future she wanted. It didn't matter that her heart had been racing all day at the thought of seeing Mia. Saira had to keep things professional and not let her feelings for Mia affect the show. Could she hide her feelings from Mia? She lifted her chin in the mirror. Saira had been acting all her life. Her first memory from childhood was hiding under the couch from her parents. It hadn't been until a few years ago that she realized the memory was from one of her movies. Putting on an act for Mia shouldn't be too difficult.

Mia's image filled the mirror and Saira froze. Their eyes met in the reflection. Saira followed all of Mia's social media accounts using an alias. She'd seen pictures of Mia, had been prepared for the sight of her. Or at least she'd thought so.

"How is it possible that you haven't aged in all this time?" Saira turned, keeping her voice light. Mia was wearing skinny jeans and an untucked T-shirt with the name of the studio emblazoned across her chest. Her blondish brown hair was loosely tied into a messy bun. She'd never worn much makeup, but Saira didn't miss the fresh touch of pale pink gloss on her lips and the swipe of brown mascara that brought out the green tones of her hazel eyes.

Mia turned to the costume designer. "Jessica, are you finished with Saira?"

Saira's back was turned to Jessica but she was pretty sure that the woman was making faces. There was a slight twitch in the very corner of Mia's lips; she was trying to keep a straight face. Saira could almost feel the softness of that corner beneath her own lips.

"We need to discuss Saira's request on this outfit. It's for the first day of shooting, I don't have time to make these changes." Jessica stepped toward Mia, iPad in hand, her fingers dancing on the screen.

Mia cut her eyes to Saira. "What's the problem with the saree?"

Mia's tone was cold and all business. Saira's heart shrank. What did she expect after all this time? For Mia to throw everyone out of the room, embrace her and tell her how much she missed her? This wasn't a scene out of some romantic movie, and they weren't exactly long-lost lovers reuniting.

She took a steadying breath. "The blouse is the same fabric as the saree. It's too matchy-matchy. My character, Meera, is a stylish, young, Indian woman. No one like that would be caught dead in this old-fashioned style. You can replace it with a plain black blouse that won't take much time to make." If her tailor from India was here, he could do it in less than an hour.

Mia's mouth set into a straight line. "It's a fair

point, but Jessica is on a tight schedule. We need to
let it go for this episode, but she can go over the rest
of the costume designs with you and we'll try to in-
corporate your suggestions in any of the outfits that
haven't been completed yet." Without waiting for a
response, Mia turned toward Jessica, issuing her directions.

Just like that, Saira had been dismissed. She gathered the silky material of the saree into her fists. *Deep
breaths.* Arguing with Mia in front of her staff would
just make her more confrontational. She needed to
get Mia alone.

As Mia huddled with Jessica, pincushion man
turned toward her. "Could you take this off now?
I need to finish ironing it before I go for the day."

She gave him a tight smile. *This sure isn't Mumbai.* She was used to an army of assistants itching
to please her. If anything, she longed for an empty
dressing room, a break from the enthusiastic smiles
and eager offers of assistance. One of the first things
Mia had done as producer was cut her budget to bring
staff from India. Saira hadn't argued because she
wanted a break from the constant army that hovered
over her. But now, as she watched pincushion man
try to unwrap the five yards of saree fabric, she re-
gretted her decision.

Saira was used to being scantily dressed in front
of people. It was a necessity on set, but she suddenly
felt conscious of Mia in the room. After taking off
the petticoat, the long skirt worn underneath a saree,

and the crop top blouse, she was left in a lacy black bra and matching panties. Pincushion man yelled for a robe. Feeling awkward, she pretended to study her forehead. Her agent had been encouraging her to get Botox before the wrinkles deepened but Saira had resisted. She'd seen too many of her fellow actresses get seduced by the promise of procedures and injections only to end up looking like puffed-up versions of their former selves. Five more years, that's all she needed her body and skin to give her; less if those years were in Hollywood and she earned in US dollars. Then she could finally be free to live the life she wanted.

She caught Mia's eyes in the mirror and held her gaze. Her pulse kicked at the unmistakable appreciation that was written all over Mia's face. Black lace used to be Mia's favorite. Mia walked to one of the racks, grabbed a blue silk robe and threw it at Saira.

Saira shrugged on the robe, watching with satisfaction as Mia's eyes darkened before she looked away. Turning around slowly, Saira smiled. "Is this a good time for us to talk? In private?" She looked pointedly at Jessica. Pincushion man was already walking out, nearly tripping over the trailing length of saree he hadn't managed to fold.

Mia shook her head, but Jessica was already making her way to the door with ill-disguised relief.

"Please close the door," Saira yelled, her eyes never leaving Mia.

She stepped toward Mia. "Listen, while we are alone, I want to clear the air." She swallowed. "About us…"

Mia stepped back, her eyes flashing. "There is nothing to clear. What happened between us was a long time ago. I've moved on with my life, and I know you have too."

*Moved on?* Saira had scoured Mia's social media accounts. There were plenty of pictures with friends, but none that looked like a girlfriend.

"I tried to call, email, text, even tried to reach you on social media after Fiji."

"You made your feelings very clear when you said goodbye."

Mia turned away, clearly bolting for the door. Saira's chest tightened. She was used to a laughing, carefree Mia, who could warm her heart just by looking at her. Had ten years changed her so much, or was it that Mia hated Saira? "I want to explain what happened that day in Fiji…"

Mia whirled, facing Saira. Her eyes blazed an emerald green. "You don't need to explain. Either you were lying to me when we were together, or you were lying when you broke up with me. The distinction doesn't matter to me."

The ice in Mia's voice made Saira go cold. They had to make peace, the tension between them wasn't good for the show. Saira had to make it right.

"It does matter." She stepped close to Mia and placed a hand on her arm. The warmth of Mia's soft skin, the shine in her eyes made Saira's heart flutter uncontrollably. She'd waited ten years to say these words. "I hate the way I left things between us in Fiji. The things I said…"

Mia moved Saira's hand away with such gentleness that her chest tightened.

"I don't care about the past. There's only one thing that matters, and that's making this show a success. Other than that, we don't have anything to discuss."

The words stung. But what really hurt was the pity in Mia's voice. Saira hadn't really expected Mia to welcome her with open arms. She'd been ready for anger, even hatred—but not the look of sympathy that was in Mia's eyes.

Saira stepped back, her throat so tight she wasn't sure she'd be able to speak. "I am sorry, Mia," she managed to choke out.

Mia took a deep breath. "If you're sorry, then forget what happened ten years ago and work with me on making this show a success." Mia gave her a steely look. "I received the script edits that you sent. I know there's some leeway in your contract to provide input, but the read-through is tomorrow and shooting starts the day after. It's simply too late to…"

Saira interrupted her, her voice cracking with emotion. "Mia, please, this show is important to me and—"

Mia cut her off, her tone icy. "Great. Then stop sabotaging it. Every time you want to change something, the script, the costume, the set, it costs us time and money."

Saira crossed her arms. She didn't know what was harder to take, the accusation that she was some-how purposely making things difficult, or the fact that Mia believed Saira would behave this way. Mia might be angry with her, but surely she had reviewed Saira's changes and could see what she was trying to accomplish.

"Have you looked at the changes I'm requesting? I've studied every South Asian show Hollywood has produced and they're mediocre at best. This show has to be different, and the way we do that is to…"

"Oh, of course you know better than all of us what's best for the show."

Saira's nails dug into her clenched fists as she struggled to keep her emotions in check. She could handle anger, even pain; what she couldn't quite reconcile was that the once warm and supportive woman she knew was now acting like every other know-it-all producer she'd ever worked with.

"I've been in the film industry for thirty years. I've done nine TV shows, thirty-seven movies, and I don't know how many guest appearances. Show me someone on your team who has more experience than I do."

"No one disputes that you're a great actress. That's why you're here. But acting is not the same as…."

Saira put her hand, palm out, toward Mia. If Mia was going to treat her like any other actress, then

Saira was going to treat her like just another producer. "There's no reason to debate here. I believe my contract allows for final approval on all dialogue and mannerisms that relate to Indian culture."

Mia crossed her arms. "It's too late to make the changes."

"Then I suggest you consult your lawyer. I don't believe the contract specifies a timeline. You know as well as I do that scripts, costumes, sets…everything can be changed." She gave Mia a thin-lipped smile. Her bitch smile. If Mia wanted their relationship to be professional, then that's what she would get.

Mia narrowed her eyes "You're right. Everything can be changed. Including the heroine." She turned and opened the door. Just as she stepped out, Mia turned. "By the way, your husband called. He said he'll be here to support you on the first day of shooting."

# Two

Mia slammed her door and stood against it, breathing deeply. Her heart thundered in her chest and she wiped her damp hands on her pants. Damn Saira! Mia thought she'd been prepared to see her, to deal with her, to stand up to her, but one look at that woman and Mia's stomach had turned to Jell-O. All she'd been able to think about was the feel of Saira's silky skin against hers, the way her mouth felt on her lips, the warmth of her breath on her core.

She slid to the floor, hugged her knees to her chest and buried her face in her arms. *What is wrong with me?* It's not as if Mia had been alone all this time. She'd been with several partners. Beautiful women, available women, women who were comfortable being openly lesbian. She had no problem meeting people. The TV and film industry was a constant churn of writers, artists, interns, set workers and on and on. There wasn't a day that went by where she didn't have the opportunity to ask someone out, or get asked out. There was no reason to want Saira.

Twelve weeks. She just had to get through the filming. Peter would be back before the next season, and if the show was a success, Mia could have her pick of producer jobs. She'd make sure she never had to work with Saira again.

A sudden knock on the door made her jump up. Before she could even take a step, the knob turned and the door began to open. Mia quickly sidestepped to avoid being hit.

"What is it?" she snapped, still a bit rattled by the unexpected interruption.

"Sorry!" Gail stuck her head around the door. "You're supposed to be meeting with Chris to go over the budget. You can't be late—you only have fifteen minutes with him."

Mia looked at her wristwatch and cursed. She hurried to the desk and picked up her laptop. Chris was an insufferable network executive who controlled the purse strings on the TV series. He kept sending Mia red envelope emails regarding show expenses, then ignored her reply questions. It had taken Gail begging, coercing, then finally bribing his assistant to get this meeting.

Mia nearly ran to the elevators, stabbing the buttons in frustration. There were eight elevators in the bank, and the electronic dashboard showed that none of them was close to her floor. Chris's office was thirty stories up. Even if Mia raced up, she'd never get there in time. At last a door dinged open and she exited onto the sixty-sixth floor. Mia had never been to this floor before, but she wasn't surprised to see that, unlike the commercial white square tile and gray carpet on her floor, the executive floor had hardwood floors with marble inlays, modern area rugs and polished leather couches and chairs in the waiting areas. The receptionist checked her ID and then pointedly looked at her watch. "You're two minutes late. You will have twelve minutes with him."

"Thirteen." Mia said through gritted teeth.

"It'll take you a minute to get to his office."

Mia tightened her grip on the laptop. "Can you let me in so I don't lose any more time?"

The receptionist took her time buzzing Mia into the inner chamber, which was separated from the outer waiting room by a glass wall. Another assistant greeted her with thin lips and pointed her to a slightly ajar door.

Mia hurried to the door, then froze. She'd recognize Saira's fake laugh anywhere. The first time Mia had heard it was when a fan had recognized Saira in Fiji. Saira had pretended that she was *oh so happy* that the fan wanted an autograph and not at all concerned when she asked to take a selfie with Saira and Mia. *This is my childhood friend. She's just like a sister to me.* That was the first time alarm bells had gone off in Mia's head. *And those alarm bells are still clanking.*

"You must be Mia."

Chris O'Toole was the stereotypical network executive. Average height, expensive suit that couldn't hide the middle-age bulge in his waistline, male pattern baldness that he clearly thought he had covered with a state of the art hair plug transplant. His voice was slightly nasal and immediately grated on Mia.

She stuck out her hand and mustered a friendly smile. "It's nice to finally meet you in person."

"Do you need a few more minutes before our budget meeting?" Mia looked pointedly at Saira and immediately wished she hadn't. Saira had changed out of the robe that she'd seen her in less than an hour ago. She was wearing a silky pearl white blouse with several top buttons open. Mia could practically see the drool from Chris's chin in the tantalizing dip of her cleavage.

Chris waved his hand dismissively. "The budget crisis is solved." He gestured for Mia to sit on the couch across from Saira. Chris's office was a spacious and stylishly designed room, big enough to fit most of Mia's apartment without much trouble. An L-shaped desk dominated one corner, with two sleek white monitors sitting atop it. The wall opposite the desk was made entirely of floor-to-ceiling windows, offering a breathtaking view of the distant mountain landscape. In another area of the room, a large conference table was surrounded by leather chairs that were far more comfortable than Mia's own desk chair. Currently, they were all seated in the living room portion of the office, a carafe of coffee and mugs bearing the network logo resting on the table between them. The air was filled with the invigorating scent of coffee and the warm aroma of whiskey.

"Saira has saved the day."

*What has she done now?*

Mia didn't dare look at Saira. She knew her gaze would wander down her blouse and she needed to keep her focus on the meeting. Instead, she locked eyes with Chris and asked, "What did I miss?" Her tone was friendly and composed, but inside, she seethed. How dare Saira go behind her back?

"Saira has agreed to reduce her fee by 32 percent."

*Yeah, right. How many arms and legs did she ask for in return?*

"That's quite generous." She looked at Saira, who gave her one of her dazzling fake smiles. It was the one she gave the cameras, the adoring fans—a toothy grin that left people basking in her glow.

"I'm just as invested in the success of this show as the network is," Saira said, setting the coffee mug on the table. "This way, there is room in the budget to make the changes that'll make the show better."

*And there it is.*

"Exactly what changes are we talking?" Mia shot Chris a look but his gaze was plastered on Saira. Or more accurately, the curve of Saira's breast that peeked through the V opening of her blouse every time she moved.

"Little things here and there." Saira's voice was sugar sweet. She met Mia's gaze. "Like the color of the saree blouse and the dialogue changes I requested."

"All those little things add up to personnel time and production delays." Mia couldn't keep the irritation out of her voice.

Saira narrowed her eyes. "Those little things can make the difference between the show trending in the top ten in online streaming or barely hitting six figures in viewership."

"Right you are," Chris said. "It is the little things that determine whether a show is good, or if it's great."

Mia bit the inside of her cheek to keep from reminding Chris that he was a financial weenie who probably couldn't tell the difference between a producer and a director.

"Well, thank you, Saira. I'm sure you have a lot still to do, so we won't keep you here any longer."

Chris shook his head. "Oh, no rush, I can cancel my next meeting, and I don't think there's anything more I need to discuss with Mia that we can't take care of over email."

Mia clenched her jaw to keep from saying something she'd regret.

Saira stood. "Actually, I am still a little jet-lagged. I should get some rest before the big read-through tomorrow. I'll let you get on with your meeting." She shot Mia a smile, one of her genuine ones. *Is it my imagination or is there an apology in her eyes?*

Chris made a show of walking Saira to the door. When he leaned in for a hug or a kiss, Mia wasn't sure which, Saira deftly sidestepped and held out her hand for a shake. Not to be deterred, Chris took her hand and kissed it, holding it to his lips longer than comfortable for anyone. Mia nearly laughed when Saira wiped her hand on her skintight jeans.

Chris walked to his desk, completely ignoring Mia. Not to be discouraged, she took a seat in the guest chair and placed her laptop loudly on the desk. As Chris swiveled in his chair, tapping on his keyboard to wake up his computer, he asked in a distracted tone, "Do we have anything else to talk about?"

Mia took a deep breath before responding, "Are you changing Saira's contract?"

Chris nodded, a determined look on his face. "Of course. I want to lock down her fee reduction before she changes her mind."

Mia pressed further. "Did she request any other changes?"

"Just some minor wording changes," Chris replied nonchalantly.

Mia sighed. "Her changes are not that minor. We can't give her more control over the show."

Chris turned toward her, his expression hardening. "The show is already 21 percent over budget, and we both know unexpected expenses will come up during filming. Whatever Saira needs, find a way to make it work."

Mia opened her mouth to lay out all the ways in which Saira's salary discount would end up costing them in the long run, but the door opened and his assistant walked in.

"Good work, Mia, keep it up," Chris said dismissively.

"Can I at least review the contract changes?"

"Ms. Strome, you're already five minutes over your meeting time and his next meeting is waiting," the assistant said, her tone brusque. Mia felt a hand on her arm, but she shrugged it off and walked out. She didn't see the point in causing a scene. As a producer with little clout and even less experience handling people like Chris, she had to pick her battles. What she needed was to get a handle on Saira—that was a problem she knew how to solve.

She was looking up Saira's cell number on the call sheet to see if it was the same number she had stored in her phone—the number she hadn't quite brought herself to delete—but she needn't have bothered. Saira was in the waiting room chatting with Jason Brossart, one of the senior vice presidents. *Dammit.* That was the guy in charge of entertainment content. *What is Saira up to now?*

She stepped up to them.

"Speak of the devil," Saira said as Mia approached, and she braced herself. Had Saira complained to Jason? Unlike Chris, Jason had the power to remove her as producer. *Hell, he has the power to cancel the show and send us all home.*

Jason turned and put out his hand. "I don't think we've actually met, Mia. Saira was just telling me how wonderful you are to work with. Thank you for pinch-hitting for Peter." Mia shook his hand and she found herself liking him. His grip was firm but not hard. Unlike Chris, who exuded a smarmy quality, Jason had warmth.

"It was a pleasure meeting you both. I wish I could stay and chat, but I'm late for a meeting."

As he walked away, Mia turned to Saira. "Thanks for putting in a good word." She meant it. Jason had the power to make her career, and even if Saira considered it a throwaway comment, he'd remember her name when it came across his desk in the future.

Saira gave her a small smile. "Whatever differences we have regarding the show, I want the very best for you, and if I can do anything to make it happen, I will."

Mia's breath caught. Saira's eyes shone and a lump formed in Mia's throat. This was the side of Saira that Mia had fallen in love with—the Saira who instinctively understood her wants and needs, who took genuine pleasure in doing something for someone else. It was easy to forget that Saira was like a kaleidoscope with constantly changing facets and reflections, depending on which way Mia was looking. The overwhelming, disconcerting feeling of being in Saira's orbit came rushing back to her.

"I was wondering…"

"Do you think we could…"

They both spoke at once, but Saira gestured for Mia to continue. "We should talk," Mia said.

Saira nodded. "How about dinner tonight?"

Mia agreed. "That sounds great. Do you want to go to the hotel and freshen up first?"

Saira glanced at her wristwatch. "If I go back to my room, I'll flop onto the bed and fall asleep for the rest of the night. How about we order room service and catch up over dinner?"

Mia's cheeks flushed as the image of room service dinners in Fiji flooded her mind. At the time, Mia had thought all the room service orders were because they couldn't stop having sex long enough to go out. She later realized Saira didn't want to be seen in public with her. Still, the memory of those dinners had tormented her for years. Especially the way they had chosen to eat dessert.

*Tempting, oh so tempting.*

# Three

Despite it only being five o clock, the Thai restaurant was full, and they ended up at a bar table, which was noisy and packed with people. Not a great ambience for a heart-to-heart but it would have to do. If this were Mumbai, Saira would've gotten the best table in the house. *There will come a time when a crowd of fans will greet me in LA too. As long as I keep my focus on this show.*

Saira had thought she was ready to face Mia, but the day had been far more excruciating than she'd anticipated. The last few hours had been a roller coaster of emotions, memories and regrets flooding her mind with a dizzying intensity. The anger in Mia's eyes was palpable, and it cut through Saira's heart like a knife. It was clear that Mia was so focused on maintaining a wall between them that she wasn't being reasonable about the script and costume changes. Saira had to make it right; she couldn't let the weight of her past mistakes ruin her future. She had to make Mia understand why she'd left the way she had.

They ordered drinks—a Diet Coke for Mia and a mojito for Saira. Mia was staring at the menu as if it was a legal contract she was about to sign.

"Don't even pretend you're not getting the pad-see-ew."

Mia looked up at her defiantly. "Actually, I was thinking of the shrimp pad thai."

"Since when do you eat seafood?"

"A lot of things have changed in the last ten years, including my tastes."

*You haven't changed in the slightest bit. You just want me to think you have.* "So tell me what's new with you. What have you been up to since we last saw each other."

Mia took a long sip from her supersized Diet Coke, the sound of the straw sucking up ice and soda amplifying the silent tension between them. "Ten years is a long time. There have been a lot of milestones in my life:—my first show as producer, one Emmy nomination for assistant producer…many, many, girlfriends."

Saira bit her tongue to keep from asking exactly how many.

"Anyone serious?"

"You know how it is, Saira—it's so easy to think

you're in love in the moment but it's really not much more than relationship excitement."

Her chest tightened as Mia flung her own words back at her. Words she had carelessly chucked at Mia in Fiji. They were the words of a young woman who hadn't yet understood what love was.

"I didn't mean what I said back then," she said quietly.

"You meant it when you said it."

Saira shifted under Mia's unrelenting stare. *She's still so angry at me. How do I make her understand?*

"I was scared and confused. You were my first girl-friend…my parents didn't know I'm a lesbian. *I* didn't fully understand my sexuality.…"

"And you're just as confused now as you were back then. You're married to a man, for goodness' sake. You married him, what, two days after you broke up with me?"

"It's not a real marriage!" As she caught a few people turning around to look at her, Saira lowered her voice. "Rahul and I are good friends. He did me a favor—after the pictures of you and me in Fiji, there was an uproar in India. There were death threats against me, against my family. People aren't very tol-erant in India, and it was even worse ten years ago. *Six months* after I returned from Fiji, I needed to do something drastic to save my career, to protect my family. Marrying Rahul was the only way to calm the public outcry against me."

"Do you think it was easy for me to come out as a

teenager? Do you think things weren't difficult here? I know it's not quite the same, but there is plenty of stigma and hate crimes here as well. I'm not saying it's easy, but it is a choice—no one is forcing you to live a lie."

Mia would never understand. She'd grown up in America, where the streets were safe and girls whose parents disowned them had choices other than prostitution or begging. If Mia was the one getting death threats, the police would protect her, not help the perpetrators. She would never understand what it was like to be in Saira's shoes. To live in a country where she could go from being a loved icon to a symbol of hate-filled protests. Just one social media post with a picture from Fiji and a question as to whether she was "unnatural," and she'd spent weeks dealing with spray-painted doors and windows, being shunned by her friends and family and losing two lucrative movie contracts. She'd been physically attacked twice, only surviving thanks to some very expensive bodyguards. Had it not been for Rahul and their wedding announcement, she would've been killed for sure. There was no point in telling Mia all this. Saira had sent her countless emails explaining, pleading, begging for understanding. All unanswered.

Saira took a sip of her mojito, then pushed the glass away. It was too sweet and not minty enough. She locked eyes with Mia. "It was so easy for you to ask me to give up my life. But what if I'd asked you to do the same? What if I'd asked you to leave your Hollywood life and come to Bollywood with me?"

"It's not the same." Mia's expression was inscrutable. "You can have a career, a life here. I don't speak any of the Indian languages. I wouldn't be able to get a job and I'd stick out like a sore thumb being a white woman."

"None of that affects me because America is so welcoming of brown people," Saira said, bitterness creeping into her voice. No matter how much she romanticized their past, there was a reason it hadn't worked out. Saira had to deal with obstacles and expectations that Mia couldn't even begin to understand, yet Mia had expected her to give up everything without being willing to do the same in return.

Mia was back to studying the menu and Saira did the same. *What was I thinking?* Until this morning, she'd thought she could handle seeing Mia. She'd almost convinced herself that she'd idealized their month in Fiji, and that the years had dampened the intensity of her emotions. But now, sitting with Mia, Saira's heart pounded uncontrollably. Ten years ago they'd both been young and carefree, unencumbered by the grind of daily life and lost in the magic of their romance. Sometimes she pretended it had all been a beautiful dream. But now, in Mia's presence, it felt all too real.

Saira hoped that apologizing to Mia, explaining why she'd broken up with her in such a heartless way would ease the restlessness in her heart. That closure on their relationship would finally let her move on, focus on what was really important, securing her future. But Mia still got under her skin. Mia with her irritating habit of sucking down ice-cold drinks, Mia with her half smiles and hazel eyes that looked green in the light and brown in the dark. It wasn't closure that she needed. It was Mia.

The waitress finally made her way to their table, placing a fresh glass of Diet Coke in front of Mia.

"I'll have the pork pad-see-ew," Mia said, then gave her a small smile. "I still order that every time."

Saira's heart fluttered. The waitress looked at her expectantly, and she couldn't remember what she wanted to order. "I'll have the same, thank you." She handed the menu to the waitress.

Mia took a long draw from her drink. "Look, I know working together is going to be complicated, but I want to bury the hatchet. I don't want to talk about Fiji. I've worked very hard to forget about it. What do you need me to say so we can move on from that?"

*I want you to tell me that you haven't stopped thinking about me in the last ten years, just as I haven't stopped thinking about you. I want you to tell me that seeing me again is messing with your head, just as it is mine. I want you to tell me that you forgive me.*

"You're right. We should put the past behind us and focus on the show." If Mia wanted to leave the past behind, Saira would do her best to follow suit. *It's for the best.* She couldn't spend the next twelve weeks pining for what could have been. She needed to focus on what should be—her work, her future.

Maybe, just maybe, if she threw herself into her work, she could forget about Mia and move on with her life.

# Four

Mia hated table reads. The one for *Life with Meera* promised to be an extra level of torture. Normally a read through this late in the production stage was designed to sharpen or fine-tune the dialogue. Peter had said they'd had one several weeks ago with Saira on Zoom. She hadn't been able to fly over because of her filming schedule in India. This read through was just to get Saira comfortable with the rest of the actors—a formality.

They were set up in a conference room, eight tables organized in a hollow square. There were sixteen actors for the show, with only five that had major roles. Mia began rearranging the tent cards that Gail had placed just moments earlier.

"Now I'm going to have to move the scripts," Gail moaned.

"Saira needs to be in the middle of the crowd, not at the head of the table."

"You do know she's the star?" Gail said. "And that this is a hollow square. There isn't really a head of table."

Mia picked up Saira's tent card and put her in an off-center seat near the corner. "Trust me—no one will need reminding that she's the star."

It was the first time everyone on the show would get to see Mia in action. How she dealt with Saira would determine their on-set dynamic for the next twelve weeks.

"What is your history with her?"

Mia avoided Gail's gaze. Her friend had a way of being able to tell when Mia was lying. "It's not important. We ran into each other ten years ago, and let's just say that she didn't leave the best impression on me."

Mia felt a twinge of guilt not telling Gail the full story. It wasn't as if they didn't talk about their love lives.

"Is working with her going to be a problem?"

Mia lifted her eyes and met Gail's look of worry. "There will be no problem. I know how to handle Saira."

"What if she knows how to handle you?"

Mia turned away. How well did Saira know her? *About as well as you know her.* She finished moving the name cards and stepped back to survey the table. Saira knew the old Mia. The one whose heart was open, the one who used to believe in peace and love and happily ever after. That Mia was long gone.

"Did you hear about George Valencia?" Gail chatted as they rearranged the scripts.

Mia shook her head. There was too much la-la land gossip to keep up with. She could count on Gail to keep her posted with whatever was relevant.

Gail stopped what she was doing and faced Mia dramatically. "His wife outed him last night at the Netflix party."

"Excuse me?"

"Yeah, they've been married for like ten years, and Tracey said they're getting a divorce because he's gay."

Mia shook her head. Relationships were messy but she'd worked with George. He was a nice guy. He didn't deserve to be publicly humiliated.

"That's not really nice of her to out him."

"It's not an amicable divorce, and she says he's been a hypocrite. He outwardly supports LGBTQ rights but won't come out because he's afraid it'll affect his career."

"There's always an excuse. There are plenty of LGBTQ actors and actresses in LA. It's not even news when someone comes out anymore. Why do people want to live a lie? Sneaking around, not able to openly be in a relationship, hiding who you are. It's no way to live." Mia stopped before she said anything more. She wasn't just talking about George Valencia.

Mia had opened up to her parents about being lesbian in her last year of high school. She came from a religiously conservative Southern family and it hadn't gone well. Her father had raged, her mother cried. They tried to talk, cajole and threaten her into changing her mind about being gay. Finally, they kicked her out of the house. A friend's family took her in so she could finish high school, and as soon as she'd turned eighteen, she'd headed to LA and film school on financial aid.

"Well, this time George being outed is big news. It's all over social media. People are saying he's a hypocrite. He should have come out."

Mia slapped the last script on the table. "Why did he have to *come out*? Being sexually fluid is normal. What if we made everyone who is cis hetero come out and announce their sexuality?"

Gail stepped to her and put a hand on Mia's shoulder. "I didn't know you felt this strongly about it. I was just sharing news."

Mia softened. Who was she to judge anyway? She was a check writer where gay rights were concerned. She donated to organizations who worked on the ground level, but she didn't march, parade or attend protests.

"George Valencia being gay shouldn't have been a story. His wife shouldn't have been able to hold that over him and embarrass him by making an announcement."

Gail shrugged. "It's not a story because he's gay. It's a story because his show is on season ten, and his role is a seventies era mansplaining playboy. It's hard enough to renew a show once it gets to the double digits, but he's going to have a hard time convincing an audience that he's a lady killer."

Mia shook her head. "He's a talented actor who has convinced audiences for ten years that he can seduce women. The fact that his sexuality will affect his career is wrong. If the network doesn't renew, I hope he sues their asses."

"Have you ever been with a partner who was in the closet?"

Mia stiffened. Was Gail purposely asking about Saira? She shook the thought away. No one knew about her and Saira. It was too painful to talk about, so she didn't discuss it with anyone.

"Just once. That's why I don't date people who don't live their lives openly. The lying, the hiding, it all makes you feel like you're doing something wrong. The way we live our lives is not wrong. It shouldn't even be considered different."

"You know, you should join this group that the network…."

Mia held up a hand. "Please don't tell me to join a committee, working group or organization. That's another thing I disagree with. We shouldn't have separate committees to promote our rights. When we don't like the options from food services, we form a committee to tell them what they should serve. The more separate committees we have, the more we get othered. We should be part of every committee there is, we should be part of that stupid food services committee, telling them to serve rainbow sherbet. Instead, we're set aside in a committee of our own, made to feel like we should be grateful for any concession we get."

Gail held up her hands. "Rainbow sherbet?"

Mia smiled. "Bad example. But you know what I mean."

"Sorry I brought it up. I didn't know you felt so angry about this. Actually, I don't even know what you're angry about, exactly."

Neither did Mia. This was Saira's fault. It was Saira who was reminding her of all the reasons why she didn't date women who were in the closet. It was Saira whose ability to set her body on fire with just a look was making her do bizarre things like rearrange seating so she didn't have to look directly at her. She wasn't angry with LGBTQ committees, and she didn't even care about George Valencia and his life. She was angry with Saira, the woman she had loved, the woman she had wanted to spend her life with, who had chosen to live a fake life with a real husband.

They heard noise outside the room; others were starting to arrive. Gail leaned over and spoke softly. "If it makes you feel any better, you know who won by the announcement? Ned Hawkins. Apparently he and George have been lovers for years.

Mia shook her head. "I'll bet you money that Ned didn't win anything. He's spent years being alone, unable to take his lover to parties or dinner openly. Now that George is finally out, there'll be such a spotlight on them that they won't even be able to enjoy it. Everyone loses."

Mia walked away to greet the first actors that started to file in. Some gave her a hug, others an elbow bump, and a few air kisses. They had a catering table set with fruit, bagels, avocado toast and little flutes filled with muesli. Some people grabbed coffee, a few nibbled at the table. Saira hadn't shown up and Mia was definitely not watching the door for her.

After their dinner the night before, Mia had spent the night thinking about whether she'd been too harsh on Saira about her fake marriage. She didn't know what it was like to be a celebrity, or to live in India, but Mia had sacrificed a lot to live her life openly. To this day, she was estranged from her parents.

Where was Saira anyway? Mia scanned the room and startled when she landed on Saira, in her assigned seat and studying the sheets in front of her. She was wearing a see-through white shirt with a flaming red bra-like undershirt that showed off her figure in that casually sexy way that sent heat waves coursing through Mia. *Damn that woman.*

Saira looked up suddenly and Mia instinctively looked away, realizing a second too late how childish the gesture was.

"Mia!"

She turned toward Gail. "Sorry, what were you saying?"

"Do you want to start?"

Mia nodded distractedly. The faster they were done with the read through, the sooner Saira with her red bra and see-through top would be out of her line of sight.

Gail called the meeting to order and explained the process. Mia began with a welcome speech, talking about how she was honored to have the job, big shoes to fill and the most talented staff on network television. It was the speech every producer gave, and everyone nodded politely. Then the director, David, had to say his piece. Finally, they began.

The read through started off well. Everyone was perfectly timed, effortlessly dialoguing like a team of champion synchronized swimmers. Saira was brilliant, her tone and accent pitch-perfect.

They got through the opening scene and took a break. Mia began to relax and walked over to the catering table to grab a muffin.

"I see lemon poppyseed is still your go-to."

Mia closed her eyes for a second before turning to face Saira. "Nice job in the read through. You've got the accent down."

"About that. I don't think Meera should have an American accent."

*I knew things were going too well.*

"Why not?"

"She was born in Mumbai and moved here as a teenager. She's going to have an Indian accent."

"The TV show is airing here. Strong accents don't

do well with audiences. They want to understand the characters, see themselves in them."

"Then what differentiates this show from all the others? Why not cast some American actress?"

Mia blew out a breath. "There are plenty of American actresses that we can cast if you'd rather not play the role."

Saira narrowed her eyes. "You need me for this role. The network is banking on selling the show in foreign markets, and I am an international star. I want this show to be authentic, not the same bullshit this network usually puts out."

Mia crossed her arms, hugging herself to keep her temper in check.

"If you hate the network so much, why did you sign with us?"

"Because I was promised a different show, and I intend to make it happen."

She walked away, and Mia nearly shouted at her but stopped just in time. The other actors and crew were clearly pretending not to listen while straining for every word. Gossip on a set was like happy meals at McDonald's. Everyone wanted the special toy.

Mia pasted a smile on her face and made small talk with the other people milling around the coffeepot.

As soon as the second scene began, Mia knew it was going to be bad. Saira was saying her lines in her normal accent. Mia loved the sound of Saira's usual inflections. She had that upper-crust Indian accent that clearly enunciated each word. If Saira's co-actors were thrown off by the sudden accent change, they recovered quickly.

Mia waited until the end of the scene before speaking up. "That was good, but I don't think the accent is working, Saira. Let's go back to the one you used for scene 1." Mia congratulated herself on how calm and matter-of-fact her voice sounded. No trace of rage, frustration, or annoyance.

"I'd like to hear what the others think about the two accents," Saira said just as matter-of-factly. She gave Mia a thin smile and a hard look.

Gail spoke up first. "I think the American accent is more relatable."

"I like the Indian one—it fits better with the character." The actress playing Meera's boss spoke up. Mia dug her nails into her hands to keep from saying something she'd regret.

"Not saying that you don't do the American accent well, but it sounds fake, y'know, I think the Indian one sounds better too," the actor playing Meera's best friend chimed in.

"I think we should consider it," David, the director, said.

*Et tu, David?* If there was one person Mia could count on to veto last-minute changes, it was David. He was a meticulous planner. If he thought this was a good idea, was Mia shooting it down just because it came from Saira? Mia mentally shook her head. She had considered the accent issue days ago, and after researching it and talking with the marketing people, she had agreed with Peter's original decision.

"Thanks for the input, everyone. Let's take an early lunch break while I listen to the recording." Mia dismissed the group. The lunch catering hadn't been set up so most of the group dispersed. Mia caught Saira just as she was about to leave.

"Can I have a word in my office, please."

They rode the elevators in silence. Once in her office, Mia shut the door.

"What's your plan, exactly?" Mia stood with her hands on her hips. She and Saira were nearly the same height when Saira wore her stiletto heels.

Saira met her gaze with a maddeningly serene expression on her face. "My plan is to make the best series possible. We have ten episodes to convince the audience that this show is worth additional seasons."

"Then why are you hell-bent on questioning every single thing. Yesterday it was wardrobe, today it's the accent. I already have the writers working overtime because of all the script changes you keep requesting."

"I am not going to make a show that embarrasses me, and my culture. I don't want to be one more Indian actress who fakes an American accent and makes fun of the traditions I hold dear to my heart." Her lips quivered and Mia's heart stopped. There was something else going on with Saira. This was about more than just the show.

Mia relaxed her posture. "I admit that there are stereotypes in the script. Had I been involved from the beginning, I would've done some things differently. But we have to make the show palatable to American audiences. This isn't the BBC or a cultural documentary. It's a dramedy, and we need to make things extreme and funny for it to work."

"I get that. What you don't understand is that the show crosses lines I'm not willing to cross."

Mia sighed. She was tired, out of words to reason with Saira and too distracted by the way her jeans hugged her legs. Not to mention that damn red bra.

"Then quit," she said wearily.

"Is that really what you want me to do?"

*No! I want you to behave.* If Saira really did quit the show, it would be a disaster. They couldn't replace her quickly, the filming would have to be delayed and there was a good chance the network would just scrap the show. Then Mia would be back to making low-budget, limited series that nobody watched.

Saira stepped toward her. "What's really the matter Mia? Are you having trouble working with me."

*Yes. You're driving me crazy—reminding me of our time in Fiji, making me lose sleep because I spent all night thinking about you.*

Meeting Saira's gaze, Mia lifted her chin. "The only problem I have working with you is that you think your way is always the right way."

Saira scoffed. "Excuse me? You're the one who's so fixated on maintaining control over our relationship that you're not even willing to consider my suggestions. Do you know how hard it was for me to get you on this show? My agent called in every favor he had just to make it happen."

Mia's heart sank as she took in Saira's's words. She had assumed that the network had chosen her based on merit. "What do you mean your agent called in favors to get me this show?" Mia's voice trembled as she spoke.

Saira moved closer to her. "I thought you knew. When I heard Peter was leaving, I had my agent call everyone he knew at the network to get you the job."

"Why would you do that?" Even as disappointment sank in, Mia's heart perked up. Had Saira orchestrated their working together because she wanted to rekindle their relationship?

"Because I thought you'd understand my point of view. That you and I could make a good show."

Mia pressed her lips. "You thought you could manipulate me, that you could walk all over me and I'd let you."

Saira's eyes flashed, then she stepped close and lowered her voice. "When have you ever let me have my way with you? If I remember correctly, you were always the one in charge."

Mia's face went hot. She had always been the one to take charge in bed, mostly because Saira had been inexperienced and tentative. But that didn't mean Saira was passive by any means. Heat spread through her as she remembered the way Saira would brush her lips against Mia's earlobes, kiss the crook of her neck, cup her breasts and pinch her nipples with just enough pressure to make Mia growl with need. "As I recall, you knew exactly what to do to get what you wanted."

Saira's lips twitched. "I had an excellent teacher, who was quite a seductress herself."

Mia's body tensed as Saira stepped even closer to her. She smelled the same, of roses and patchouli, her lips still glossed with the faintest shade of pink. As Saira's lips parted, all rational thought left Mia's brain. All she wanted was to once again feel the heat of Saira's mouth on hers, to feel the crush of her soft breasts against her own.

It was Saira who closed the distance between them, putting a hand on the back of Mia's head to pull their bodies closer together. As Saira's lips tugged and teased her mouth, Mia ran her hand up Saira's shirt. The feel of her soft, silky skin sent waves of heat coursing through her body. She ran her hand underneath the red top. As she'd suspected, Saira wasn't wearing a bra underneath that thing. Mia ran her thumb over Saira's hardened nipples and her own core pulsed with excitement as Saira moaned sinfully and deepened their kiss.

It was the sound of her office phone ringing that brought Mia back to her senses. No one ever used the landline, and Mia was unaccustomed to its shrill tone. *What am I doing?* Even as her brain kicked in, her hand lingered for another second on Saira's breast before she extracted her hand and disconnected her mouth.

She couldn't even look at Saira. If she did, there was no way any of her neurons would work. How could she have given in to the temptation to kiss her? As if their relationship wasn't complicated enough. Why had they even come to her office?

She answered the phone. It was Gail calling. Mia had left her cell phone in the conference room. She glanced at Saira, who was adjusting her shirt, putting her breasts back into the red top. Mia looked away before the urge to rip the damn thing overtook all rational thought.

She needn't have worried. What Gail had to say worked better than a cold shower. She hung up the phone and turned to Saira.

"Mia, we still…"

"Your husband is here. He wants to see you."

# Five

As usual Rahul had the worst timing. The look on Mia's face had been clear as day. She was equal parts disgusted and furious. Whether it was with herself or with Saira, she didn't know. Saira could still feel the pressure of Mia's hands on her breasts, the touch of her lips and the heat of her skin. Mia had been so cold, Saira had wondered how she didn't feel the attraction that had been consuming Saira from the second she'd seen her in the dressing room. She had no doubts now. Part of what they had in Fiji was still alive.

Rahul had a crowd around him in the white marble lobby of the studio building. Of course he did. He was a better known star than her. He'd even acted in several North American streaming TV series. It had been his contacts that had helped her land *Life with Meera.* He wore an untucked Nehru collar printed shirt in cream and gray with straight jeans that made him look like he had legs for days. Every hair on his head was styled and sprayed perfectly to look like he'd just gotten out of bed. As soon as he saw her, he broke through his fan girls and enveloped her in a bear hug, lifting her up. She returned his hug with equal gusto. It wasn't for show. They were truly the best of friends, and despite his timing, she was glad to see him. It would be good to have someone to talk to about Mia.

"What are you doing here?" she breathed. Rahul was the extreme opposite of a homebody. He hated being at home, so whenever he had a free moment, he used his private jet subscription to be someplace else. Saira would have a hard time coming up with a corner of the world where he didn't have an Instagram post.

"I missed you, *yaar.*"

"I've only been gone two days."

"Too much for me." He pressed a kiss to her mouth, making sure it was long enough for cell phone pictures to capture the moment and share live on social media. Saira smiled dreamily at him, her acting skills in full use. She took him by the hand. "We have a small break—my hotel is nearby." She made sure her words were soft enough to seem secret but loud enough to be heard.

They walked out of the studio and she hailed a pedicab. The hotel was only two blocks away but she didn't feel like walking in heels. Plus, the driver wouldn't be able to hear what they were saying over the exertion of towing them on a bicycle and the noise of the city.

As soon as they were seated, Rahul waved to the fans as if they were in a royal carriage.

"Who did they catch you with this time?"

He sighed. "Hosiang. I thought we had equal reason to keep it quiet, but he had a crisis of conscience and told an elder. It spiraled from there."

Saira shook her head. "When will you learn?" It was the one thing she and Rahul constantly argued about. Rahul fell in love with the frequency of a tweet, and every time he did, he got careless.

"C'mon, *yaar*, he's a monk and we've been seeing each other for months. How was I to know…"

"To know what? That he may eventually question whether he wanted to continue down a spiritual path or a hedonistic one? To think for a minute that any normal human being might go talk to a friend when faced with a major life choice, and that friend might knowingly or unknowingly betray them?"

His tanned skin paled. Rahul had been her best friend since they were four years old. They had grown up in the same apartment building in the Bandra section of Mumbai, a complex with high gates, strong security and easy access to the Bollywood studios. They were not allowed to leave the complex so they played in the hallways and at each other's homes. Saira knew before Rahul did that he was gay, just as he likely knew before her that she was. He'd been the one she'd called from Fiji, torn about Mia, panicked when their time together was ending. He'd meant well and thought he knew what was best for her, so he'd involved her parents. She had long forgiven him and hadn't brought it up in years, but seeing Mia had reopened old wounds. If only Rahul hadn't been so impetuous, she and Mia would have had a proper goodbye. Things would have ended differently. And maybe there was a small chance they would've found a way to be together all these years.

"Okay, fine. I should have known better. Thank you, once again, for saving my ass. You know my new movie opens next week. The financiers have put a lot of money into making it a blockbuster hit and we can't afford a scandal right now."

"You know what would make the movie a guaranteed hit? You coming out as being gay. Think of the free publicity."

"Yeah, that's why you've come out, *nah*? The free publicity that'll result in boycotts of the movie, social media roasting, hate mail, death threats, protests at the theaters so even those who support LGBTQ rights will be afraid to go see it."

"If this TV series is a success, then I am coming out."

He looked at her skeptically as their pedicab pulled up to the hotel. They made it to her room without being accosted, and in silence. Both had learned the hard way that hallway and elevator conversations were recorded on CCTV, which the paparazzi always managed to get hold of.

As soon as the door closed behind them, Rahul rounded on her. "You said you would come out if your last movie was a hit. As I recall, it was a block-buster. So what happened?"

She stuck out her tongue. He looked around the small living room space of the suite, then made his way to the bedroom, plopped onto the bed and grabbed the TV remote. "My publicist says I just need to hang with you for the next couple of days. He's sending some local fans to put out posts. It'll be good for your show too."

He flipped through the TV channels. "This is a real third-rate hotel—no international sports chan-nel. India is playing Sri Lanka in cricket."

Saira sat on the bed next to him and grabbed the remote, turning off the TV. "Your timing is really bad. Things with Mia have been tense."

He sat up. "Did you tell her about our marriage?"

"Yes. But I didn't tell her about you."

He took her hand and kissed it. "We'll figure it out. One day, we will find a way to live the way we want."

She squeezed his hand. "What did Hosiang de-cide?"

"He picked spirituality over hedonism. We broke up."

He put his head on her shoulder and she touched his cheek. Rahul sighed. "I can't even blame him. What can I offer him? A life of stolen kisses and hidden apartments. He has a life of enlightenment ahead of him."

"He has a life of dreaming about you ahead of him. In the beginning he will miss you and wonder whether he made the right decision. Then he'll get back into the routine of daily life and think all is fine. But every few days, something will happen to remind him of you. A scent, a song, a place. Each time that happens, it will tear his heart just a little. Bit by bit, those little tears are going to create a hole so deep in his heart that he won't even know how to fix it."

Rahul lifted his head and enveloped her in his arms. "Babe, you need to tell Mia how you feel."

"What do I tell her? That I've been pining for her for the last ten years? That all the other women I've been with paled in comparison to her? That I was hoping seeing her again would magically cure me of my obsession, but it's only made it worse?"

"That's exactly what you tell her."

"Then her next question will be, 'what do you want from me?'. What will I tell her? I don't know. If the show is a hit, maybe I'll move to LA and make a career in Hollywood. Then I'll come out to the world and hope that I can make a living here. Then she'll ask what happens if the show tanks."

"What do you plan to do if the show tanks?"

Saira sighed. If she knew the answer to that question, she would have Mia in her bed right now instead of Rahul.

"I kissed her today."

Rahul raised his brows. "I thought the plan was to focus on the show and slowly rekindle things with Mia."

"That was the plan. But…" Saira buried her face in her hands. "I didn't realize how hard it would be to…"

"To keep your hands off her? To be so close and yet not touch her?"

Rahul put his arm around her and squeezed her tight against his chest. "I know. Can I give you some advice?"

"As if I could stop you."

"The more you withhold, the harder it will get. Give in to temptation. Be with Mia, see what happens. The last time you guys were together, it was ten years ago. You were on vacation. See if what you had there can exist in the real world."

That's what she was afraid of. "What if it is real? Then what? I can't leave her again. What will I do if the show tanks?"

"Worst-case scenario. You come out and ruin your Bollywood career, and you have no working options in Mumbai. You can live off your savings for years until you figure out something else. But the more likely scenario is that you'll still get some work. There are plenty of streaming channels that'll give you a chance— it might not be the lead, and you may have to reduce the number of Hermes scarves you buy on a weekly basis, but it's not like you'll starve."

Saira shook her head. "It's not about having nice things. You know I pay for Kayra's care. She likes the place in Switzerland but that costs a bucketload. If I come out, I'll have to pay for security for my parents. They are never leaving India."

"What happened to your savings? Your last few movies did really well."

"The rupee is really weak, paying for Kayra's surgeries and rehabilitation, then Jai's MBA at Harvard, and Ma's therapies have sucked up most of what I've made."

Rahul shook his head. "Your family is taking advantage of you. Kayra can move someplace cheaper, Jai should pay you back now that he has a job, and your Ma does not need her army of astrologers, pandits, yogis, and she definitely does not need those month-long ashram visits in Rishikesh."

Rahul was right. Saira recognized her family's excesses, but it also gave her joy to be able to provide those for them. Her mother's Bollywood career had ended early, and her father hadn't really been able to hold down a job. The family had only kept their home because of Saira's acting career. Saira wasn't just risking her own life, but that of her entire family.

"It's my fault Kayra is in that center. I'm not going to make her move someplace cheaper."

Rahul shook his head. "When will you stop blaming yourself? There was no way for you to have known what would happen."

"She never wanted to do it. I put her up to it. And you know why? Because I wanted more time for fun. I was tired of working and thought if Kayra had a career like mine, then it would take the pressure off me."

Rahul sighed. "You were a child!" He sat up suddenly. "You know, we don't have a prenup. If we divorce, you can take me for all I'm worth."

She shook her head. "I will not take money from you. I'll accept a guest room in one of your apartments when I'm homeless though." She bit her lip. "If I come out, what'll happen to you?"

He shrugged. "I'll have to find a hot model to have an affair with to drown my sorrows. I'm sure my publicist will spin it into something that makes me look like a hero or a raunchy horndog doing threesomes. I'll be fine. You've done more than enough for me. I should not be part of your calculation."

She gave him a hug. Rahul was the one person who not only understood her but actually cared for her.

"Saira, you're stressing over things you have no control over. Whether the show does well or not is not something you can control right now. But, finding out whether you and Mia can make it work is in your power. So stop sitting around playing what-if scenarios in your head. Go get your girl."

# Six

Mia paced the floor of her office. *What is wrong with me?!* She had asked to speak to Saira in her office to address the accent issue. Instead, she'd ended up kissing her, and now Saira was off for a nooner with her husband and she was left to figure out how she was going to get their read through back on track. Lunch was ready, Gail had sent out a text message to everyone and the only person missing was Saira. Gail had dispatched an intern to Saira's hotel.

What bothered Mia most was that she wasn't sure whether she was more upset about Saira's behavior at the read through or her running off to her hotel room with her husband. Mia had always known that Saira's sexuality was more fluid than her own. She didn't for one second believe that her relationship with Rahul was completely platonic. They might be friends, they might even have an open marriage but Rahul was too sexy and Saira was too hot-blooded. How could she have run off with Rahul seconds after kissing Mia with such passion?

Mia took some deep breaths and rubbed her temples. *Focus on work.* It was the only thing that made sense right now. The only part of the whole mess with Saira that she could control, or at least try to.

She shook her shoulders, then made her way to the conference room. Most people were sitting down with their lunches. Food services had set up an extravagant spread, including ten different types of sandwiches ranging from vegan to double meat, smoothies and green juices in little cups, pasta salad (vegan and regular), three different types of green salads, a quinoa salad, a couscous salad, and two meats and cheeses charcuterie boards. Mia heaped her plate. She knew how much the food cost. If she had her way, they would have leftovers for the afternoon snack and dinner.

"Loading up for dinner?"

She nearly jumped out of her skin as Saira's breath caressed her ear.

"Where were you?" Mia cringed at the nagging inflection of her voice. *This is my show. Saira works for me.*

"Sorry for not seeing the text messages. My phone was on silent."

"You're here now. Had a good time with Rahul?"

Saira's lips twitched. She leaned forward, her lips brushing Mia's as she whispered. "Are you jealous we didn't finish what we started in your office?"

Mia's face heated. *How dare she!* She cleared her throat. "Actually I wanted a second with you to discuss the issue of the accent you'll be using." At least her voice had returned to normal.

Saira straightened. "Look, I understand your and the network's concerns about accents. You want to cater to an American audience and make sure that people won't lose interest in the show because they're having a hard time understanding the main character. Also, you want them to be able to relate to me, and it's hard to do that with someone who has an accent."

Mia stared at her. *Where is this rational side coming from?* The Saira she knew in Fiji was intractably stubborn. Once, they had planned to take a hike to see a waterfall. The locals had waved them away when they'd gotten near the top of the viewing hill, saying the rains the night before had made the trek too muddy. Saira had literally dug her heels in and made them trudge forward anyway.

Saira placed a hand on her arm. Mia ignored the warmth of her touch. "How about if we go halfway. I won't talk like I normally do, but I won't go all American either. That way the character authentically has an Indian accent but it won't be so strong that the audience won't like it."

Mia sighed.

"Let's try it out with the next scene and see how you like it." Saira's tone was so reasonable that Mia found herself nodding.

They started the read through of the next scene, and Mia marveled at Saira's ability to effortlessly change her accent once again. They took a short break, then started the next scene.

"Saira, I want to you to read this scene in your normal accent," Mia said.

Saira raised her brows but didn't say anything. Mia hated to admit it, but Saira had been right. The dialogue worked better with her precise pronunciation and slightly musical way of stringing words together. It was charming.

Gail slid a note to her that said "good call." Mia gave her a sideways look.

It was evening by the time they finished. Mia had set an early morning call for taping. The first season wouldn't be filmed in front of a live audience so they had the flexibility of being able to start early. The filming schedule was aggressive—they were taping ten episodes in sixty working days for an average of three days per episode. It was one of the hardest schedules that Mia had worked with. Mia finished the day with a pep talk to the actors and crew, promising an amazing wrap-up party when they got through the next three months. Fighting for as much time as possible was one of the many things she'd had to negotiate with the network. The brutal schedule was necessary to make sure the series could air in February, and her ability to deliver would make her career. On the other hand, if there were significant delays, no one would remember what an impossible schedule she'd had. She would simply be blamed for not being able to cut it.

Most of the actors escaped as soon as Mia was done with her instructions and wrap-up. Some lingered and socialized with each other and the crew. Mia checked in with key crew members, making sure they were ready for the next day. TV series always made it seem as though actors messing up their lines was what took so long on set but the truth was that a lot of time was spent in scene transitions, changing camera positions and a myriad of other back-end tasks. Mia had tried to minimize those as much as possible so they could transition more easily between scenes. Tomorrow would be a test of whether all her planning would work. A lot depended on Saira. If she kept requesting changes, they would fall behind, and with a schedule so tight, they had no wiggle room.

"You hate chitchat." Mia closed her eyes. How did Saira manage to sneak up to her?

"I'm not socializing. I'm making sure we're ready for tomorrow."

Saira gave her a smile. "This is the most organized set I've ever been on. I'm sure everything will go smoothly."

The compliment warmed Mia more than she wanted to admit. She didn't need Saira's approval. But she did need her cooperation. "Saira, listen, I know we've gotten off on the wrong foot with this show, but I want you to know that I am willing to listen to your suggestions. The taping schedule is just really tight, so if something will delay us, I can't do it."

Saira bit her lip.

*Shit. I know what that means.* Saira was going to say something that Mia wasn't going to like.

"I know the taping schedule is fast. My agent even tried to negotiate on it because it takes us double, triple, the time to tape for the same number of minutes in India."

"It takes double the time here too. That's what makes this schedule so aggressive. But we can do it because I know how talented you are, and I think we can do it in fewer takes."

Saira smiled. "Flattery will get you everywhere…"

*But…*

"…but getting this show right is important to me." She held out the paper script and Mia recoiled. "After the read through today, I have some additional suggestions. The script was stilted in some sections, especially if we aren't using my American accent, there are ways of saying thing in India that…"

"Saira! We're taping tomorrow. It's not fair to the other actors to change the script the night before."

Her stomach turned. Would she keep having the same argument over and over with Saira for the next three months? Mia wasn't a stranger to arguing with actors on set, but Saira wore her out. As much as she wanted to deny it, Mia couldn't ignore that there was still a physical and emotional connection between them. She hadn't forgotten Fiji and neither had Saira.

"I haven't changed anyone else's dialogue, just my own."

"Still. I have to go back to the writers, who are going to have to work well into the night. Then the script has to get approved. I need to make sure it won't require set design changes..."

"It doesn't require set design changes. You haven't even looked at my changes and you're already shutting me down. You still think of me as that naive woman you met in Fiji, but let me tell you..."

"Would you stop bringing up Fiji. What happened there was ten years ago. A lifetime. We are both different people now, and this show has nothing to do with Fiji."

Saira stepped toward her. Mia caught a whiff of Saira's perfume and her body responded immediately, her hands remembering the feel of Saira's skin, the way her nipples swelled and hardened under her touch. Her eyes dropped to Mia's lips, her own mouth remembering the kiss they shared just a few hours ago. It wouldn't take much for her to take a step and close the distance between them. Just one step and she could claim Saira's mouth, rip that stupid red top right off her breasts and feel those hard nipples in her mouth.

Saira leaned in to whisper, and Mia couldn't help the goose bumps on her arm as her warm breath caressed her .

"This show has everything to do with you and me, and we have everything to do with Fiji."

*I can't do this.*

Before she could formulate words in her head, Saira took her hand and pressed something that felt like a credit card into her palm.

"We can keep arguing or do what we want to do. You know where I'm staying. Come by after you're done with work tonight. Maybe we can finish what we started in your office."

Mia squeezed her hand shut, letting the hotel key dig into her palm. She turned away so she wouldn't watch Saira walk out. One night. That's all it would take to get Saira out of her system. Then maybe she could focus on the show instead of thinking about Saira, focus on what was between her ears instead of what was happening between her legs. Would it be so bad, to give in to temptation just this once? She and Saira never had a proper goodbye. Mia never had a last time with Saira. Maybe that's why she'd never been able to get Saira out of her system. What if she did that now? What if she had one night with Saira, knowing it would be their last time together? Could it provide the closure she needed?

"Have you seen the script changes Saira's requesting?"

Mia forced herself to look at Gail. She was holding the script that Saira had had in her hand just minutes ago.

"She mentioned them to me."

Gail sighed and fanned the pages, showing Mia a whole lot of red writing. "She's virtually rewritten every single one of her dialogues. The writers' room is going to be pissed."

They weren't the only ones. Mia pocketed the hotel room key and grabbed the pages. Saira's changes would throw the timing off. The camera crew would need to retool; the other actors would need time to adjust to the new dialogue even if their lines weren't changed. Saira had no idea how her decision rippled through everyone around her.

"Tell her no," Mia said firmly.

"Didn't you see the email from Chris O'Toole?"

Mia sighed. "Now what?"

"Apparently, they signed a new contract with Saira this morning. I thought you knew about it. She's taking a fee cut in exchange for script approval."

Mia clenched her jaw. "I asked Chris to run the changes by me before they signed. But did our financial wiz of a network executive consider the downstream costs of these script changes? Or the potential delays to our filming schedule? No, he did not."

Gail put a hand on Mia's arm. "You know as well as I do that they can't see past the ends of their noses. But that's not our biggest problem. What the hell is going on between you and Saira? Are you two sleeping together?"

Mia recoiled. "What? Why would you ask me that question?"

"Because you can't stop looking at each other, and

then there's the fact that she slipped you her hotel key card."

Mia's face heated. "There is nothing going on between us."

Gail put her hands on her hips. "Really?"

Mia's stomach knotted. She didn't want Gail to know about her and Saira, but she couldn't keep lying to her friend.

"Look, I told you we knew each other. The truth is that we were seeing each other for like a hot minute ten years ago when both of us were on vacation in Fiji."

"Ten years ago?" Gail said skeptically.

Mia nodded. "It was just a fling, over a long time ago." It was over. It had been for ten years. They hadn't spoken or been together. Still, one day back and all the old feelings were coursing through her body like a tornado on a collision course with her heart.

"Clearly not."

Mia changed the subject. "Let's go over the script changes. And how much Chinese, pizza, and espresso we're going to have to buy the writers so they don't go on strike." She couldn't talk about Saira. Not with her emotions so raw, and the feel of Saira's mouth still tingling on her lips.

She and Gail found a spot on the conference room table. Everyone else had cleared out. They worked through Saira's script changes. Mia had to grudgingly admit that Saira's changes weren't all bad. Many of them made the dialogue more punchy. She recalled Saira's accusation that she hadn't been taking her suggestions seriously. She was right. Mia had been too focused on making sure that she set the tone for their relationship, that she remained in control and didn't let her feelings for Saira resurface. She had failed on all counts.

Gail gathered the script after they'd made their notes. "I'll get this to the writers' room. They won't be happy that Saira did a better job than them, but there isn't much for them to do other than proofing."

Mia reminded Gail to also send the script to the other actors and crew. Once Gail had left, she took out the hotel key that Saira had given her. It would be so much easier to give in to what they were both obviously feeling. Maybe it would take Saira off her mind. Maybe it would make her forget about Fiji. Maybe it would clear her mind of all the noise that had prevented her from being in a meaningful relationship all these years.

Or it would destroy her. They still had chemistry—the kiss proved it. What if sex was even better? Would Mia spend the next ten years comparing every woman to Saira? Her last relationship had lasted four months, two months longer than the one before. She was finally moving on, finding a way to open her heart and her body to others. But a part of her was still stuck on Saira.

She picked up the key. *I know what I have to do.*

# Seven

"Would you please hurry up. Mia will freak if she sees you here."

"Going, going." Rahul gave his hair one last spray and set the bottle on the counter. Saira picked it up and put it in a shopping bag. She couldn't have Mia seeing Rahul's stuff all over the place. The hotel had been fully booked, so it was harder than she'd thought to get Rahul a room, let alone a room on the same floor so the paparazzi wouldn't find out that they were staying in separate rooms. Ultimately, Rahul had decided to go visit an old "friend" in Orange County, a B-list Hollywood actor. Rahul had a one-night stand with Ned Hawkins several years ago. They'd been friends since. Ned offered up his house to both Rahul and Saira, since he was leaving town the next day. Apparently, the media had made his life miserable after an announcement from his lover's wife about their affair. He'd decided to leave town and go hide in an undisclosed location.

Rahul washed his hands and dropped the towel on the floor. As much as Saira loved him, he was a slob. He was used to an army of servants in Mumbai who picked up after him. She put his things in shopping bags and handed it to the waiting bellhop. The sound bite to the media was that they were staying with Ned Hawkins. Saira was only using the hotel room provided by the studio on the nights she had an early call.

Just as she had him out the door, Rahul turned to her. "Tell her how you feel, babe. What have you got to lose?"

*My dignity.* She couldn't tell Mia how she felt. Not until she knew that Mia still felt *something* for her. There was a lot that she had to make up to Mia, and still a lot of things she needed to figure out. But the first thing to know was whether she and Mia still shared a bond. Saira couldn't give up her whole life on a chance that they could be together. She had to know for sure.

She looked at her watch. It had been two hours since she'd left the studio. She fluffed her hair, reapplied lip gloss, adjusted the silk slip she had put on. When three hours had passed, she sighed, plopped on the bed and opened her laptop to look at scripts.

She had two agents, one who worked the Bollywood circuit and the other in Los Angeles. Both had sent her new projects. Mumbai was offering her a high-budget film with an all-star cast and her as Mumtaz Mahal, the wife of Shah Jahan, the emperor who had built the Taj Mahal. The movie was about their love story and how it inspired the building of one of the wonders of the world. The script was emotive and powerful, and she'd be working with one of the best directors and producers in Mumbai. They were also offering 2 percent over her usual asking price because they wanted her exclusively in Agra for filming. Her agent was sure he could get her 10 percent over her usual fee for exclusive access. If she signed the project, that would put her in India for at least nine months after filming for *Life with Meera* ended.

Crossing her fingers, she looked at what her Hollywood agent had come up with. There was a cameo appearance as herself in an A-list movie, a best friend supporting role in a rom-com that had literally put her to sleep as she read the script and a meeting with an online streaming network to discuss a six-episode limited series. None of these were paying half of what she'd be getting from Mumbai.

She opened the latest balance sheets her accountant emailed her on a weekly basis. The rupee was weak against global currencies, including the Swiss franc. Kayra's rehab center was costing her nearly 40 percent more than it had the previous year. She closed her eyes. Kayra was so happy there. How could she ask her to move? Then there were invoices for her mother's ashram. Her mother had struggled after what had happened with Kayra. Since she'd started going to the ashram, she seemed happier. How could Saira take that away from her?

Her LA publicist had sent some positive articles and social media posts from her kissy scenes with Rahul today. Her own arrival in LA had gone unnoticed but, as usual, Rahul's presence elevated her own exposure. Rahul had invitations to some high-profile Hollywood parties and her publicist told her in no uncertain terms that she needed to go, and listed out the invited celebrities with whom she should try and get pictures.

Saira sighed. She was essentially starting over in Hollywood, building her presence. In India she was already well-known. Crowds greeted her wherever she went, but she'd have to build her reputation here, get the media to love and promote her. Was she ready to put in that work all over again?

Her watch told her that four hours had passed. It was getting late. Mia wasn't coming. She took a deep breath, then emailed her Mumbai agent.

Mia turned the hotel key over in her hand. She was standing outside Saira's hotel.

"Are you ready to come in?"

Mia smiled politely at the valet/doorman/bellhop who had turned from eyeing her with suspicion to regarding her with pity. He'd seen the room key in her hand and probably, correctly, surmised that she was debating whether or not to compromise herself.

What if she and Saira were still as red-hot as they'd always been? What if they weren't'? She'd held the idea of Saira in her heart and head for so long that she wasn't even sure what was real versus imagined. Now was a good time to find out, wasn't it?

She looked at her watch. They had an early call in the morning. Saira needed her beauty sleep. Mia needed to be clearheaded.

According to the app on her phone, a rideshare driver was one minute away. She could be home in thirty minutes. Plenty of time to get eight hours of sleep. *Or I can sleep with Saira's naked body next to me.*

She took a deep breath, then stepped into the lobby.

When she got to the room door she paused. Should she knock or just use the key? What if Saira had changed her mind? She had passed a mirror in the hallway. Retreating her steps, she considered her appearance. She never wore much makeup, but would it have killed her to swipe some mascara on her lashes and gloss on her lips? She dug through her purse and came up with ChapStick. Something was better than nothing. She tugged down her T-shirt, then squared her shoulders.

She used the little doorbell and stood with her hands behind her back. As she waited, she crossed her arms, then moved them beside her, then in front. Why the hell couldn't she figure out what to do with the damned things. She was used to always having something in her hands: a laptop, iPad, clipboard, coffee cup. Why hadn't she thought of bringing a bottle of wine or something?

How many minutes had passed? She wasn't sure but it seemed like a lot. She rang the bell again. What if Saira wasn't there? What if she'd changed her mind? Then another thought struck her. Rahul! Was he there? What if the two of them were together? What if they were making love right now?

She turned and fled down the hall.

"Mia?"

She turned so fast that she nearly tripped and fell. Saira stood at the door. *Damn that woman.* She was wearing a cream-colored knee-length silk nightgown with no bra. The straps looked like they could barely hold the piece up. Her breasts swelled against the fabric, her hard nipples on full display. Her hair was tousled, as if she'd been asleep.

Mia closed the distance between them, grabbed Saira by the hair and kissed her hard. Saira returned the kiss with equal fervor, pulling her into the room and closing the door behind them. Mia had no control left. She squeezed Saira's breasts, enjoying the moan that escaped deep from her throat. She had Saira pinned against the hotel door. She moved her hands down Saira's waist and thighs, her own body heating and zinging with need as her hands touched Saira's soft skin. Normally Mia liked to take things slowly, enjoy the initial seduction—she got off on making her partners moan and writhe under her mouth and fingers—but tonight her body seemed to be possessed with an urgency she couldn't control.

She ran her hand between Saira's thighs. Saira bit her lip, bucked her hips in clear invitation. She wasn't wearing any panties, something Mia had expected but still found intensely arousing. Her own panties were wet with need but Mia pressed her thumb to Saira's clit, enjoying the way her body tensed and vibrated; her own body responded to the sinful moan from deep within Saira's throat. She slid one finger inside Saira, as deep as it would go, then pushed even deeper. Saira broke their kiss, bent her body, tightening against Mia's finger and burying her mouth in her neck, kissing her in that spot that drove her wild. Mia slid a second, then a third finger inside Saira, her own body pulsing, vibrating and aching with desire as Saira's moans turned into cries of ecstasy, and she clenched so tightly against Mia's fingers that for a second Mia worried they might break.

Just when Saira was close, Mia used her other hand to push the flimsy nightgown off one shoulder. Saira was more than happy to help. With her fingers still inside her, Mia sucked on Saira's nipple, its firmness and sweet taste nearly throwing Mia off the edge. She sucked hard, biting ever so slightly just as she felt Saira's orgasm shudder through her body. Saira screamed, dug her fingers into Mia's shoulders and bit her lip as she threw her head back. It was a while before her body relaxed and Mia slipped her fingers out, her own body so raked with need that she wasn't sure how she was still standing.

Saira grabbed her shirt and tugged it up, then deftly took off her bra. Not waiting for permission, Saira mouthed one hard nipple and ran her thumb over the other. Mia put her hands on Saira's now naked waist, enjoying the feel of her hot, silky skin. She closed her eyes, letting the waves of pleasure course through her. Saira dragged her into the bedroom, pushing her onto the bed, and Mia complied with no resistance. She helped Saira take off her cargo pants and panties and spread her legs to let her put her mouth on her hot core. Saira's tongue teased her clit, in turn flicking across it and pushing hard on it. She slipped two fingers inside Mia, bending and curving them until Mia was writhing on the bed, trying desperately to hold on to control. She didn't want to give in quite yet. Mia wanted to enjoy the moment, drag it out, let her body burst into flames. But Saira was relentless. She put a third finger inside Mia, sucked hard on her clit, and just when Mia was on the edge, she withdrew her fingers, stuck her thumb inside, bending it just right. Mia's entire body pulsed, then convulsed and bucked so hard that she nearly threw Saira off-balance. Her orgasm was explosive, and Saira teased and caressed her with her mouth and fingers until Mia begged her to stop. When she was finally spent, Saira crawled on top of her and buried her face in Mia's chest. Their cores, still hot and eager, rubbed and melted together.

* * *

It was good to have Mia underneath her. Her body was warm and soft and solid all at the same time. She could hear Mia's heart thudding, and the sound was like a soothing balm on her chaotic soul. They were meant to be together. If she had any doubts about that, they had evaporated. Nothing had changed in the last ten years, they still had what they had in Fiji: love, passion and a future together. This time she was ready to do what was needed to make it happen. Mia was worth it. Saira would find a way to get work in Hollywood. She could move her entire family to America to keep them safe from public retribution. She would find Kayra a place that was cheaper and that she loved just as much. Maybe Kayra was even ready to come home. Saira would figure it out. For Mia, Saira would make it work.

Mia shifted beneath her and Saira lifted her head, her body moving instinctively so that their breasts crushed together, their hardened nipples rubbed against each other. Saira pushed her hips to rub against Mia. She was ready for round two, aching for it. Her body pulsed with need, her core slick and ready.

"Saira." Mia's voice was thick.

Saira put a hand between their legs and caressed Mia, enjoying the way her eyes closed. She was just as ready as Mia was. Saira lifted herself and rolled off Mia so she could reach the nightstand. She had all of Mia's favorite toys ready; there was no need for sleep tonight. Saira had spent the last ten years reliving Fiji, imagining this night. They would make love again and again, and in between they would talk about the future, but this time with the maturity to actually make it happen.

She had barely gotten the drawer open when Mia rolled off the bed. "Toilet or shower? If it's the latter, then I'll join you."

Mia wouldn't look at her. She walked around the bed and began collecting her clothes. Saira tensed, her heart racing, and not in the way that she wanted it to.

"What're you doing?"

Mia wouldn't answer, wouldn't look at her. She jerked into her underwear and cargo pants. Saira rolled off the bed. Mia slipped her shirt on top of her head and pocketed her bra.

*No, no no no. This can't be happening.* Saira placed her hands on Mia's shoulders.

"Mia, talk to me. What's going on. Why are you leaving?"

Mia still wouldn't look at her, so Saira bent her head and placed a featherlight kiss on her lips. She wrapped her arms around Mia's waist. "Babes, let's talk. Tell me what's going on. You can't just leave like this. We have the whole night ahead of us. There are so many things for us to talk about—" then, unable to resist, she wiggled her eyebrows "...—so many things still to do."

Mia reached behind her waist and unlocked Saira's arms. She took a step back and finally met her eyes.

"You wanted one night. I needed to get you out of my system. Now that's it's done, we can go back to focusing on the show."

Saira sat down on the bed. She didn't trust her legs to hold her. Tears stung her eyes. "This was just a roll in the bed for you?"

Mia nodded firmly. "We never had goodbye sex. Consider this closure on our past relationship."

*Closure. What a filthy, American term.* As if there was a way to seal closed a gaping open wound, as if mind-blowing, life-changing passion could be zipped up and put away like a winter blanket that was no longer needed in the summer.

Mia was slipping on her shoes. Saira placed a hand on her shoulder. "Mia, you can't leave like this. We need to talk. Tonight wasn't just meaningless sex."

Mia turned to her with eyes blazing. "That's exactly what it was for me, Saira. I'm not denying that we still have chemistry. Maybe now that we have it out of our system, we can move on, focus on the show. Be professional."

Saira stepped back. "That's all you care about? The show?"

Mia nodded. "That is the only thing I care about. You and I were over ten years ago. Clearly our libidos needed one last romp. Now, let's move on and stop dwelling on the past."

With that, she walked away, leaving Saira bewildered and shattered.

# Eight

Mia rubbed her eyes, hoping it would take away the dark circles and bags that betrayed the sleepless night she'd had. *Damn Saira.* Mia had hoped that once they actually gave in to their desires, it would be clear that what they had was in the past. Mia had gotten together with exes before; it was never as good as she remembered it. Mia was convinced that she'd built up a fantasy-like utopia when it came to sex with Saira and a reality check would help her move on. Except it backfired. The reality was even better than her memory.

She'd come home to her crappy apartment and spent the night reliving every moment with Saira, writhing with want and need. Her fingers and vibrator had both been useless, and now she was sleep-deprived, cranky and had the female version of blue balls.

Her watch chimed, letting her know it was time to leave. She swore, slipped on her shoes, grabbed her laptop bag and crossed her fingers that the coffee cart outside the studios was open. The damned thing opened and closed at the whim of its owner, a surfer whose schedule varied based on how good the waves were.

The way the universe was dumping on her, she wasn't surprised that the coffee cart wasn't open. She grabbed the sludge that the interns brewed in the common kitchen, then walked over to the studio where the series set had been built. She'd checked it the night before to make sure that the set design looked good. The studio was a hub of activity. The actors weren't due for another hour, but the camera crew, director and myriad other support staff had been there for a while. The director, David Rosen, was a thin, reedy man with a permanent scowl and glasses that Mia was sure were for aesthetics only. He was another source of heartburn for Mia because he was yet another control freak. But he knew how to do his job. The cameras were already positioned for the first shot, everyone knew what they needed to do and even the couch cushions were fluffed.

David strode over to her. "Script changes the night before. On this taping schedule!"

"Good morning to you too, David," Mia said

evenly. "You know as well as I do that script changes happen even after the scene is filmed. What's the big deal?"

"The big deal is that it throws off the timings for my camera crew. I had to call them in an hour early to go over things. You're going to have to pay the overtime."

*Great.*

"Thank you for making it work, David. You know the deal the network made with Saira."

David leaned forward, his tone completely changed. "What is up with that? Is she sleeping with Chris?"

Mia stiffened. "I don't think so. She reduced her fee, and as usual, they don't always comprehend what that might mean for us on the ground level."

David nodded. "On my last show, they fired the producer halfway through filming because the actors complained about him. I had to do the directing and producing."

Mia bit the inside of her cheek. She was used to men like David. "Well, then you know exactly what a tough position I'm in. Thanks for being so great, David."

Without waiting for him to respond, she walked away. She could only take so much. Gail appeared with a dry cappuccino, and she took the cup gratefully.

"Everything ready?"

Gail nodded. "Saira's already here and sitting in makeup."

Saira, the woman who claimed that Indian Standard Time was genetic and responsible for her chronic lateness, was almost an hour early?

"She said her hair takes a while, and she wanted to make sure we started on time this morning. Got off to an auspicious start and all."

"How thoughtful," Mia said sarcastically. Saira was up to something. Was she hoping to talk to Mia? Convince her to come to her dressing room for a noon romp? Mia's traitorous body pulsed at the very thought. She took a long sip of her hot cappuccino, letting it burn her mouth.

If Saira had her way, the script for their romance was written clearly in Mia's mind. They would spend three months stealing every second they could get, quickies in the dressing room, nights filled with unbridled passion, innuendo laden looks and gestures throughout the day. Saira would talk about the future, plans to move to LA, to start a new career and live with Mia out in the open. She would even go as far as to drag Mia to look at houses she would buy for them to live together. A two-bedroom house in the hills, above the smog. They would commute to the studios together—it was worth it for the view. Then as the show wrapped, Saira would get distant. The small house she was going to rent or buy would no longer be available. The contracts she was sure were coming wouldn't materialize. There was an excellent offer from Bollywood that Saira couldn't refuse. It would just be a few months, then Saira would come back. At the wrap-up party, Saira would say good-bye to everyone but Mia, promising that she would return the next weekend on a friend's private jet. It was just a few months and then Saira's Hollywood gigs would come through.

The weekend trip wouldn't materialize. The taping schedule, jet lag, a million excuses. Weeks would turn into months, and daily video calls would become emails and text messages until Saira would finally break down and admit that she couldn't make it work. She had too many responsibilities.

The truth that Saira would never admit, even to herself, was that she was afraid to leave the security of her life in India. She liked being a beloved film star where fans swooned at her every move. Directors and producers capitulated to her demands, an army of servants made sure she didn't even have to tie her own shoelaces. Why would she trade that to become a bottom list star in Hollywood where she'd have to beg or manipulate to get what she wanted and deal with the fact that her career was on the down slope?

It could never work between them. Saira wasn't suited to be an American. She would forever blame and resent Mia for making her give up a life she loved.

Mia passed by the makeup area, eyes on her iPhone, walking with purpose. She stole a glance only to see Saira's eyes on her. She gave Saira what she hoped was a nonchalant nod. Just another actress. Today was the director's show. Mia was there to make sure it all went smoothly. Saira was David's problem today, and the thought eased the knot in Mia's stomach.

The actors took their places for the first scene. It was based in the living room of the set. Saira was wearing pajamas. A set of plaid pajamas and a T-shirt that read I Love New York would've looked drab on anyone else, but it seemed to hug Saira in all the right places, giving her that girl next door combined with sexy porn star look. Mia couldn't help but stare.

The first few scenes went smoothly. The actors adjusted to the change in Saira's lines, and Mia stood mesmerized as she watched Saira act. She had seen Saira's Bollywood movies, with subtitles on. There was no doubt that Saira was a talented actress, but it was something else to watch her live. Rarely were actors able to get a scene perfect in one take. It was even rarer for directors to accept one cut. They wanted to make sure they had editing options. But Saira was magic. It was as if the rest of the world didn't exist when she got in character. Mia watched hungrily as Saira said her lines flawlessly. As much as she hated to admit it, the dialogue changes and the accent worked much better than what she'd originally approved. Saira had been right that it made the character more authentic. No, it wasn't just that—it made the character funnier, more tragic, more likable. The audiences would eat up Saira as Meera. Mia watched the director screens that showed the various camera angles. Saira wasn't the same old American sitcom star, nor was she like the South Asian actresses of previous shows; she brought her own brand of understated dramatization. It was the way she raised an eyebrow, or twitched her mouth, the way she moved her eyes and gave that look….*that look*. Mia stood mesmerized. How could one woman be so beautiful?

Mia could scarcely believe how well things were going. By lunch time they were ahead of schedule.

Saira approached David, and they seemed to talk for quite a while. When both suddenly looked up in her direction, Mia scrambled, a little embarrassed that she was caught staring. David waved her over.

"Saira has an idea that we need to run past you."

Mia sighed.

"What is it now?"

"You seem so open to hearing my idea." Saira glared at her. Mia returned her stare with blazing eyes of her own.

"We're on a tight schedule," Mia said through clenched teeth.

"Hear her out," David interjected. Mia shot him a look. If anyone should be more stressed than she was about the taping schedule, it was him.

She folded her arms. "I'm listening."

Saira narrowed her eyes and placed her hands on her hips. "I was just saying that the next scene might work better in the kitchen than the living room."

"You want to change the location of the scene on the day we're taping it?" Mia said incredulously.

"It's the same set."

Mia looked at David. How was he not freaking out about this? It impacted him more than her. He had to move his camera crews, stage crews, and on and on.

"She's right that the scene might work better in the kitchen. Plus, she had a great idea about having the mother hold a spatula as she's talking with her hands with Meera trying to dodge the thing in addition to fighting off her mother's words."

"That's a whole change in scene, even for the Devi who's playing the mother. Plus you need to move all your cameras."

David shrugged. "There are two afternoon scenes in the kitchen so we can tape those along with this one after lunch. That will give me the lunch time to get the cameras situated."

Saira blew out a breath.

"If you two have it all figured out, then who am I to stand in the way."

She turned to leave when Saira's voice arrested her. "Can I talk to you. In private."

Saira's dressing room was the most convenient. It would take them fifteen minutes each way to walk to Mia's offices. Saira had her own trailer. Inside, the outfits of the day were hanging on a rack. A dresser, couch, and small table and chair were the only other furniture. Nothing sexy at all about the dressing room. No bed, and the couch looked uncomfortable as hell.

Mia followed behind Saira but stood by the door,

one foot on the downward step. Saira took off her shoes, then began removing the pajamas that she'd been wearing for the morning scenes. Mia held up a hand. "What're you doing?"

Saira removed the pants and threw them on the couch. "I'm getting ready for the next scene. Aren't you the one that keeps reminding me what a tight schedule we're on?"

She tugged off her top and stood there in a lacy beige bra and panties that might as well not have been there. She reached behind her to take off the bra.

"Stop!" Mia hadn't mean to shout.

Saira raised a brow in that maddening way she did when she knew she'd made a point.

"I hope this is not about last night."

Once again Saira raised her brow. "I think you made it pretty clear that you didn't want more than a one-night stand."

Mia straightened. "That's right. So what do we have to talk about?"

"If you've forgotten, we are doing a show together. A show that's really important to me, and I'm tired of you rolling your eyes every time I bring up something."

"Saira, you have no idea how your little ideas create work for the rest of us. Because of your script changes, the writers were up past midnight, the camera crew and director had to be here an hour early to go over the timing changes. There are downstream repercussions that I have to worry about. Plus, there's the fact that you manipulated the network execs to get script approval into your contract ten seconds before filming was scheduled to begin. So excuse me if I don't jump for joy every time you have a bright idea."

Saira visibly flinched but Mia was not sorry for her harsh tone. Saira deserved it. She was used to everyone capitulating to her, and it was time Mia called Saira out on her manipulations.

Saira opened, then closed her mouth. She grabbed a robe off the hook and put it on. Not that it helped. Mia couldn't not notice her hard nipples or the way the lace caressed the curve of her breast.

She took a step toward Mia. "You know what your problem is?"

*Here we go again. The speech about how she's grown-up and has the experience to know better than me.*

Mia lifted her chin. "I'm sure you're about to tell me."

"Your problem is that that you hate the fact that you want me. That you love me. That you want nothing more right now than to rip off my underwear and throw me down on that table."

Mia's entire body went hot. She reached behind her and grabbed the railing leading down the steps. It would take less than five seconds for her to reach the door.

"You have quite the opinion of yourself. If I remember correctly, you're the one that gave me your hotel key."

"And you came. We had an amazing time, and then you left with some mutterings about closure. If it was just about getting your rocks off, why come?"

Mia took a breath. "What do you want from me, Saira? Come out and say it. If it's not sex, then what is it?"

"I want us to talk. Not like this, but to really talk about us. There's still something between us, and it's more than just sex. I want us to sit down and hash it out, to figure out what there is, and more importantly, what there could be."

She took a step closer, and Mia felt the railing bite into her back as she leaned against it.

"Why are you so afraid to talk about it?"

"Fine, let's talk about it. What're your plans? Tell me what's changed since Fiji. Are you ready to come out? Do you want to sit down and talk about when you're going to tell your family that you're not hetero. When are you moving to LA? Do you have a lawyer drawing up divorce papers with your husband?"

Saira's pressed her lips together.

"That's what I thought. How about you invite me to have a conversation when you have the answers to those questions."

# Nine

Saira sank down on the couch as Mia exited, slamming the trailer door behind her. Why hadn't she just said what she'd wanted to. *I'm ready to give it all up. But only if I can have you, Mia. I'll give up my career, my life in Mumba., I'll face my family, I'll face the world. But only if you're beside me.*

Before last night, she'd wondered whether she had romanticized what she and Mia had. First love was blinding, and Saira wanted to make sure that the happiness she envisioned with Mia was real. Just because none of her other relationships had made her feel Mia's magic didn't mean that Mia was the answer. But last night had proved that she hadn't imagined it all. Their connection was special and she wasn't ready to give up on them.

But Mia wasn't ready to forgive her. Saira had hoped that getting her into bed would melt her anger, make her see that they still had something, open her heart to exploring how they could make it work between them.

Her eyes stung as tears washed through her mascara and eyeliner. *What was I thinking?* She'd come to LA thinking she would focus on the show, make sure it was a success, and then, when she was sure she could make it work, she'd rekindle things with Mia. Instead, she hadn't been able to keep her hands off Mia. She'd jumped the gun thinking that if they fell back in love, Saira would find the strength to do what she needed. But Mia wasn't going to solve her problems.

She called Rahul and told him what had happened.

"Babe, I'm sorry. Maybe you're focusing on the wrong thing."

"What do you mean?"

"You're trying to convince Mia that there's still something between you two. But your decisions can't revolve around Mia. You came to LA to see if you can build a new life. A life where you can live in the open, be in a real relationship. That was your goal before Mia became this show's producer."

Saira sniffed.

Rahul continued. "If Mia rejects you, which she has, by the way, are you changing your plans?

She shook her head, then realized Rahul wasn't on video. "No, I still want to try and make it in LA. I'm tired of doing background checks on women I meet and making them sign nondisclosure agreements on our first date. I'm tired of being alone."

"Gee, thanks."

"You know what I mean."

He sighed. "I do."

She stood. Rahul was right. She'd lost sight of her objective. She couldn't get her life back on track until she made sure *Life with Meera* was a success. It was time for her to stop playing nice—her career depended on it.

As the actors took their places, Mia stiffened. Saira was dressed in the saree that costume had designed for her, but the underlying blouse that she'd taken issue with was different. Mia had expressly declined the request for a new blouse. Had Saira gone behind her back again?

She walked up to her and tapped her on the shoulder. Saira threw her luscious hair back. The same hair that had fallen on Mia's chest yesterday. The same hair she had woven her fingers through as Saira's mouth licked and sucked and drove her mad.

"Where did that blouse come from?"

"It's mine."

"Excuse me?"

"I told you the old blouse didn't work. You wouldn't

authorize a new one, so I decided to use one of my own."

"Without checking with me? We have to consider lighting and...."

"Lighting gets adjusted after all the actors are in place. I don't understand why you're making such a big deal. I'm using one of my existing blouses. It's better stitching and fit anyway, and it looks better with the saree." She stepped back and spread her arms.

Why did she always look so good? Mia hated to admit it but the blouse was much nicer. It was a modern cut with a sweetheart neckline. Saira's waist and cleavage was on full display. The saree was wrapped perfectly to show off all her curves.

"The point is not that the blouse is bad, the point is that you can't just change wardrobe. Does this work in India? Do they let you waltz onto the set with whatever you want to wear?"

"First, they know how to dress me in Mumbai. Second, they would've stitched the new blouse. Now if there's nothing else, I believe they're ready for the shot."

*What!*

Saira turned away from her. No, she didn't just turn away, she dismissed her. What had happened? Just an hour ago Saira was begging for her attention, trying to talk to her, seduce her. Now it was as if Mia was an annoyance Saira didn't want to deal with.

Mia strode over to David, who was staring intently at the bank of screens in front of him. "Did you really allow Saira to waltz onto the set wearing her own clothes?"

David didn't bother looking up. "It's one piece of the costume. What's the big deal?"

Mia blew out a breath. "The big deal is that Saira is walking all over you. Yesterday she was asking for wholesale script changes, and when I wouldn't give them to her, she made a deal with the network. Today it's costume changes. We're running a show here, David. we can't let the talent...."

David held up a hand, then turned to her. "I once had to send an intern clear across town at five in the morning so my star actor could have a particular muffin from a specific bakery. Then there was the prima donna who screamed at the makeup artists because they couldn't magically make her wrinkles disappear." He looked back onto the screens. Saira was in the picture, adjusting her saree. Mia couldn't help but notice the way that blouse dipped low on her back, exposing that piece of skin that drove Saira delirious with desire when Mia kissed it. "In the grand scheme of actor issues, Saira's are not worth our time. Her script changes are actually good—she's not trying to get more airtime. And you know as well as I do that we've got an all-white writers' room, so it's good to have someone make sure we aren't doing something that will piss off a whole bunch of South Asians."

"Sunil is also part of the writing team."

"Glad to know we have the token Indian who was

born and raised in SoCal and has to call his parents to translate any Hindi words we want in the script."

Mia wanted to rage at him, but the wind was suddenly out of her sails. David was right. She'd had the same concerns when she had first taken over the show. So much so that she'd gotten a sensitivity read on the script.

She dropped into a chair. Saira was getting to her. Mia's every decision since Saira had arrived had been based on an emotional reaction. She hadn't been thinking clearly. Once again Saira had swept Mia up in her vortex of chaos—and Mia had allowed herself to get swept up. She had slept with the star of her show! If word got out, Mia would be ruined. Not because set relationships didn't happen, but because she and Saira had been at odds, and any conflict between them would be perceived as personal rather than professional. Mia didn't need that for her first big show. *God, how clichéd—producer gets her first big break and she throws it all away for hot sex.* Producers were more easily replaced than stars.

"Mia!"

She looked up to see Gail standing with her hands on her hips. "What is wrong with you? I've been texting you for the last hour. I had to run down here to find you."

Mia looked at the phone in her hand. She had it on silent for the taping, but she usually checked her messages every few minutes. On a show like this, there was always a crisis brewing somewhere, whether it was equipment malfunction, an unexpected budget spend, or a hissy fit from a writer, actor, director. It was endless.

She stood. David was getting ready to start shooting, so Gail pulled her outside the studio doors. "They want to see you on the thirty-fourth floor."

*That can't be good.*

"What's going on?"

"I talked to Chris's assistant but she was zipped tight."

What had Saira pulled now?

Taking a breath, she made her way to the studio offices. Apparently, they wanted her to sit in the waiting room until the network kings had a second to spare for her between meetings. She waited for over an hour, texting Gail to find out how taping was going. Apparently, it was going even better than it had in the morning. They were staying ahead of schedule.

When Chris was finally ready, Mia had reached a new level of impatience. Her email was overflowing with a million little things, and she still had to do the daily wrap and go through the checklist for tomorrow. Plus, she had to go to the bathroom, but there was no way she was going to risk missing her chance—they'd probably make her wait until yet another meeting was over.

As she walked into the room, she noticed there were a number of other people there whose faces she recognized from the portraits hanging in the lobby and hallway. Half the network executives were there.

They weren't sitting on the couch drinking whiskey but were seated around the small conference room table.

Chris motioned her toward an empty chair that an assistant pulled up to the table.

"We don't have a lot of time so I'm going to just say it. We're canceling *Life with Meera*."

*Shit. Had they found out about her and Saira?* She shook the thought from her head. That would be a reason to fire her, not cancel the show.

She swallowed. "Why?"

"Not enough of the streaming services have picked it up for us to be profitable."

"Filming has begun. You'll have to pay out most of the actors. We've essentially already spent over 60 percent of the budget."

"A loss we can take. We still have to consider the remaining budget, plus marketing expenses. And with Saira renegotiating her contract, more of the budget is free."

Mia felt an unexpected anger roil deep in her belly. They had taken advantage of Saira. All along she'd thought Saira had offered up a fee reduction for script approval, but now she strongly suspected that slimy Chris had talked her into it, knowing full well they'd be canceling the show.

"We've also recently acquired the rights to a tell-all for one of the European royals, so we need to free up some cash to get that made. It's going to take the slot we had for *Life with Meera*."

Mia took a breath. She could argue, list all the reasons why the show was better than yet another royal documentary, brainstorm ways in which she could save money, even come up with marketing ideas. But one look around the table and she knew what this was about. Someone was cashing in a chit with someone else and *Life with Meera* was going to pay the price. Mia was going to pay the price, along with Saira and David and all the other actors and crew. These network weenies didn't care.

"What if I can find a way to get the streaming services interested?"

"And how would you do that?" The question came from a silver-haired man in a really nice Brioni suit.

Mia held up a finger, then pulled out her phone. With a few clicks, she pulled up Rahul Chandan's Instagram page then held up the phone. Seeing the squinting eyes, she handed the phone to Chris, who took a look and passed it around.

"Saira's husband is an international star. That one post from his Instagram account has more than a million likes. His fans posted additional photos that have hundreds of thousands. He has star power. Now imagine a few more posts like this with the hashtag *Life with Meera*. It'll create buzz."

The silver-haired man peered at the picture. "I know this guy. One of the other studios is courting him for a major movie."

Mia waited. She'd learned the hard way that in a room full of men, she needed to let them come up with the obvious plan so they thought it was their idea. Networks still worked on the GOBSAT principle. Good Old Boys Sitting Around a Table.

"Can you get him to do a cameo, do some show promos? For free?"

*Sure, and while I'm at it, why don't I ask Santa Claus for another million dollars and two months so I can do the show properly.*

"I'll talk to Saira."

"Report back tomorrow morning. We need to move fast on this."

*Sure. I've been busting my ass for the last two months working eighteen-hour days to get everything ready, but you only have a few seconds to consider whether or not to throw the whole thing out.*

"I doubt Rahul can make this decision without consulting his lawyer, publicist and agent. You can't expect an answer overnight. Plus, India is 10.5 hours ahead in time."

"Good, then it's early in the day there. Find a way to make it work."

*Yes your majesty.*

She gave a curt nod and left before she felt the urge to say something that could get her fired from the network, not just the show.

Back in the studio, filming was wrapping up for the day. They had made good progress. Mia gestured for Gail and directed her to ask Saira to come to her office once she was free. She debated telling David, then decided against it. Mia wanted David focused on filming. David was only on this show because Peter had recruited him. Someone of his talent would get scooped up in a second. If he thought the show was going to get canceled, he might bail, and Mia couldn't afford that. She crossed her fingers he wouldn't hear about it from someone else. She avoided telling Gail as well. As much as she loved her friend, Gail could be a bit of a gossip, and Mia couldn't risk this getting out.

By the time Mia got to her office, she was exhausted and her to-do list had gotten longer. She got through the smaller items, then began tackling the budget reports. She and David were scheduled to meet later in the evening to go over the dailies. He was a night owl and liked to take a break after filming. It would be another late night for her, and not quite as satisfying as last night.

Mia looked at her watch. *Why isn't Saira here yet?* She texted Gail, who replied Saira had left an hour ago. Sighing, Mia texted Saira. Why was everything so difficult with her? Maybe she shouldn't talk to her about getting Rahul to endorse the show. Maybe the show getting canceled was a good thing. Saira would go back to her fabulous Bollywood life, and Mia could move on. She'd find another show, another series, maybe she'd branch out and do a movie.

When an hour went by without Saira texting her back, Mia called her. *Voice mail.*

*She's ignoring me.*

Mia didn't bother leaving a message. She called

the hotel and asked for Saira's room. The phone rang
for a good minute before a breathless Saira answered
the phone.

Mia hung up without saying anything. She grabbed
her purse and headed to the hotel.

# Ten

Saira was more mentally exhausted than physically. She'd enjoyed her first day of filming. Her fellow actors were thoroughly professional, and David was eccentric but clearly good at his job. But she'd spent the whole day either trying to avoid Mia or find her. Despite her promise to Rahul, Saira couldn't pretend that Mia didn't exist. Or forget what had happened between them last night. When Mia asked to meet with her, Saira decided to ignore the request. She had no desire to be alone with Mia. Rahul was right—Saira had to focus on her career, on this show. Her Hollywood agent had called her before she hopped into the shower. He'd gotten her email about finding her something better, and he'd beaten the bushes, even suggested Saira read for parts, but there was nothing. Saira was not as well-known as Rahul or Priyanka Chopra. Not in America. She was still a nobody as far as Hollywood was concerned.

Rahul would help if she asked. He had contacts, and his agent had a wider reach than her own. But she'd made a promise to herself that she wouldn't exploit their relationship. Rahul wasn't just her husband, he was her best friend, and she knew he'd do anything for her. He had been taken advantage of earlier in his life by his parents and then a childhood sweetheart, both of whom ended up wanting nothing more than money from him. He viewed every relationship with a large measure of suspicion. Saira had asked for his help in getting Mia the producer's role. She had agonized over that decision. Rahul had done it for her, but the request hadn't felt right. And what had that favor resulted in? She'd wanted Mia as the producer thinking that Mia would understand the problems with the script and work with Saira to fix them. Instead, Mia was fighting her every step of the way.

Who was she kidding? Saira had seen the producer role as a way to get close to Mia again. All that had accomplished was an hour of pure pleasure that left Saira even more wanting than she had been. When Gail asked her to go meet with Mia in her office, Saira purposely ignored the request. She didn't want to be alone with Mia, didn't want to smell her, look at her, touch her. She had enough problems; she didn't need additional reminders that she was in love with a woman who wouldn't love her back.

She sighed and picked up the room service menu. She wasn't particularly hungry but she had to eat and get to bed. The makeup artist had had to put hemorrhoid cream under her eyes today to reduce the puffiness. She hadn't slept last night, tossing and turning and going over every second with Mia in her mind, feeling her touch on Saira's skin, remembering the way she'd tasted when Saira licked and sucked her, smelling the scent of Mia on her mouth and fingers. *Damn her!*

Saira ordered a Cobb salad, decaf coffee and chocolate mousse cake. After the day she'd had, she deserved a treat. She was tempted to add wine to her order, then remembered it kept her up at night. She was getting to an age when the lack of sleep showed on her face. She needed to look fabulous for this show. Flawless and beautiful, the classic Indian beauty to win the American audience. She didn't have Priyanka's lips or Rahul's charm, but she had naturally luminous skin that was the envy of her fellow actresses.

Her hair still wet from the shower, she rubbed in an Ayurvedic hair oil, then left it to air-dry while she slept. Binita, her hairdresser at home, had done wonders for her hair in the last few years by shifting Saira from chemical products to natural oils and reducing the use of hair dryers that damaged the roots and structure. She completed her skin care routine with all natural Ayurvedic creams and settled into bed to wait for room service.

At the sound of the door knock, she looked at her watch. *Boy, they are fast.* She belted her robe firmly and padded across the suite.

She opened the door and stopped short. "Mia! What are you doing here."

"I asked to meet with you."

"I was busy. You can't come barging into my hotel. How did you even get up here?" The elevators need a key card to get to the room floors.

Mia held up a white card. "Forgot to give this back to you yesterday."

Saira snatched the card and made to close the door. She could not have Mia in her hotel room. Not with her completely naked under the bathrobe, her body already itching for Mia's touch.

Mia held out her arm. "Please, this is not about us. It's about the show. I need your help."

*This is new.*

Saira waved her in. The suite had a small living area with a dining table and four chairs, a couch and TV. The bedroom was only a few steps away. When Saira did location shoots for her Bollywood movies, she got an entire apartment with multiple rooms, plus quarters for her maid. When she had FaceTimed her agent in Mumbai, he had been aghast at the "third class" place they had put her up in. But Saira knew how to pick her battles, and the hotel room was not the sword to die on.

She sat at the dining table. Best to have something solid between her and Mia.

"Please keep what I'm about to tell you between us."

Mia frowned but nodded.

"The network wants to cancel *Life with Meera*."

The words bottomed out Saira's stomach. She was counting on the show to launch her career. Her agent had pretty much told her that she needed to wait until the show released and hope it was a success if she wanted the type of offers in Hollywood that she got from Mumbai.

"What do they want?"

It didn't matter if they were network executives in LA or money laundering film producers in Mumbai, they all threatened cancellations when they were looking to get something for free.

"They want Rahul to make a cameo appearance and do some show promotions." Mia gulped, as if embarrassed to say the next part.

"And they want him to do it for free."

Mia nodded. Saira shook her head in disgust. "The industry is the same around the world." She looked Mia squarely in the eyes. "Tell them no."

Mia jolted. "What do you mean tell them no? They'll cancel the show. Can't you ask Rahul whether he'd be willing at least?"

Saira shook her head. "I will not take advantage of Rahul. And these network people are bluffing you. They want to force you and me to give them something for free. When you refuse, they'll shrug their shoulders and move on."

Mia took a breath. "Look, things might work that way in Bollywood, but shows get canceled here all the time. I don't think they're bluffing. That's probably why they so easily gave you script approval in exchange for cutting your fee. You are the most expensive actor we have on the show."

She shook her head. "Did you read my revised contract? It says that if they cancel the show or fail to air all ten episodes for any reason, then they owe me my original fee."

Mia must have missed that. She raised a brow. "That was smart."

Saira crossed her arms. "I know what I'm doing. If you think you've got snakes here in your management, I've got snake charmers in Mumbai who are so good at manipulation that you dance to their *been*—" she mimed the flute that snake charmers used "—without even knowing it."

Mia smiled and Saira's heart caught like a string on a guitar pick. Saira loved how natural Mia was. She didn't lotion and potion her face until it shone, didn't scrub and plump her lips, tweeze and thread her brows. She had that natural beauty that was effortless. Ten years had put some lines on her face, taken away some of the fat that used to be on her cheeks and given her smile and eyes a more reserved, tentative quality. Yet she was even more breathtaking than she had been in Fiji. The way Mia's hazel eyes crinkled when she smiled shot daggers through Saira's heart. *Why? Why am I so attracted to her? There are so many beautiful women in this world. Why can't they make me feel like she does?*

"They know Rahul is in town. He's created some social media stir passionately kissing his wife in our studio lobby."

*Jealous, are we?*

"I told you, our marriage is not real. It's based on friendship. He knows I'm a lesbian."

"Is that what you are now? I thought you were bi, or fluid."

Saira tilted her head. "I didn't have a supportive family and culture to help me figure out what I am. Took me a little longer than you. Give me a break."

Mia bit her lip and Saira shifted in her seat. "Why can't you ask Rahul? Even if the execs are bluffing, which for the record I don't think they are, their idea is a good one. Having a cameo from Rahul and publicity might help get interest from the streaming services. That'll be good for our show."

"First of all, wouldn't a cameo change the script, costumes, lighting, and what were the other things—" she clicked her fingers "—camera timings etc. etc. Those changes take time and effort and we're already on a tight schedule."

Mia's cheeks reddened and Saira felt a jolt of heat through her. Mia's cheeks also colored like that when she was aroused.

"Look, I want to apologize to you. I haven't been

fair in listening to your suggestions. I admit that you've been right about some things."

"Some things?"

"Seeing you again threw me off. I haven't been myself."

Saira leaned forward. "Seeing you threw me off too."

It wouldn't take much to lean over just a bit more and kiss her. From there it wouldn't be much to pull her into the bedroom.

"Do you know why it's important for me that we get this show right? That we don't perpetuate cultural stereotypes?" It was a rhetorical question. The only people who knew what had happened with Kayra were her family and Rahul. Mia knew about her sister's condition but not how she'd become that way.

Mia frowned. *That's right. You never thought to ask me.* Saira was tired of fighting with Mia on every little thing. It was only day one of filming. There were still twelve weeks to go. It was time Mia knew.

"Kayra was only fifteen when I asked her to do this show called *Ram ki Maya*. They had offered it to me but I wanted a break. I was tired of being responsible for paying the family bills. I thought if I got Kayra into the industry, it would ease the burden on me."

Mia reached out and placed a hand on top of hers.

"I didn't really take the time to look at the script or follow along as filming progressed. Turned out that the show was a satire on the classic Ramayana. But it went too far. When it aired, there was a public outcry that the show had desecrated a sacred text. Kayra's role was Seeta, who we call Seeta *maiya*, mother Seeta. The show questioned a really key principle about whether Seeta was still pure after being held captive by Ravana—the evil demon who kidnapped her. The show made light of this assumption, implying that Seeta had an affair with Ravana. It was in really bad humor and enraged a lot of people. The show went too far."

Saira swallowed against the lump in her throat. "The public wasn't just mad, they went fanatical. There were protests and burning of posters depicting the show, it was bad. They took their anger out on Kayra. We got her bodyguards because of all the threats against her. But they couldn't protect her from a particularly brutal crowd...." Her mouth soured as she thought about the image of Kayra after that attack. "A whole group of people descended on her, kicking and beating her with shoes and sticks. She was in such bad shape." Her voice cracked. "Took multiple surgeries and physical therapy."

Mia squeezed her hand. "Oh, Saira, I'm so sorry. Why didn't you tell me before?"

"It is not something I talk about." The truth was that she'd never wanted to tell Mia. Never wanted to see the disappointment Saira saw in her mother's eyes every time Kayra's name came up. *Kayra is not as strong as you. This wouldn't have happened to you.* There wasn't a day that went by when Saira didn't wish that she hadn't given that role to Kayra. She had ruined her sister's life. Kayra had healed from her physical injuries but never really recovered mentally. The center in Switzerland had been great for her anxiety.

"After what happened to Kayra, I don't just accept a script. It's my name and face out there. When the public sees something they don't like, they don't blame the producer, the director, the writers or even the studio. They blame the actor. They direct their anger, and their hatred, at the person on the screen."

"Oh, Saira, I wish I'd known. I can't believe you've been dealing with this all by yourself."

How did she tell Mia that Saira was too embarrassed. Too ashamed. Mia's hand was still on top of hers and she turned her palm and laced her fingers with Mia's. "I didn't want you to know. Fiji was an escape for me. It was the first time I was myself, the first time I'd let myself forget all my responsibilities, all my guilt."

"Guilt? Why do you feel guilty?"

"That role was mine. If I hadn't given it to Kayra just so I could sleep later in the mornings and have more free time to read books, her life wouldn't have been ruined."

Mia stood and came to kneel beside Saira. "No, no Saira. You can't blame yourself for what happened to Kayra. That is not your fault. If there is anyone to blame here, frankly, it's your parents. You were a child yourself, and you needed a break. That didn't mean that your sister had to pick up the mantle...."

"I was twenty. Hardly a child. Kayra was the child, and I am her big sister."

Mia stood and enveloped her in a hug, Saira's head resting on her belly and chest. She breathed in deeply, tears streaming down her face. After it had happened, her parents had been shattered, and it had been up to Saira to figure out how to fix it all. To get Kayra the medical attention she needed and then the ongoing rehabilitation. It had all fallen to Saira to organize and pay for.

"I am so tired, Mia. I am so, so tired. Tired of acting, tired of the responsibility, of the burden of it all."

Mia held her tight. "It's a lot for anyone to take on."

"I left you in Fiji because my parents showed up, and they reminded me of the responsibilities I had. It wasn't just about having the courage to come out to my parents. I couldn't jeopardize my career. Kayra was healing physically but she was a mess mentally. The facilities in India aren't that great, so we sent her to Europe and eventually Switzerland. All that costs money. My career isn't just supporting designer handbags...."

"Oh, Saira. Why didn't you just tell me all this. Why pretend that what we had was meaningless."

"Because I know you. If I'd told you what I'm telling you now, you would've lectured me on how Kayra isn't my responsibility and somehow convinced me to prioritize myself."

"You're right. That's exactly what I would've done. No offense, but your parents are taking advantage of you. Kayra is their responsibility. They are the ones who let her take your role because they wanted another cash cow."

Saira stiffened. She'd been afraid of this. Mia didn't share her cultural values. She didn't understand that it was the children's responsibility to take care of their parents.

"See, this is why I didn't want to tell you. You don't understand. Our culture is different. We take care of family, even if it means sacrificing ourselves. Kayra is my responsibility. She is my sister. Even if I weren't responsible for her condition…"

"You are not responsible for what happened to her…."

"She is my sister, and I need to take care of her as long as I'm physically capable."

Mia took a deep breath and Saira leaned back, pushing herself out of Mia's arms.

"I thought it would be cleaner if we just broke up. I didn't want to spend my life wondering what could have been. Remember I wasn't as big a star as I am now. Hollywood wasn't as much of an option. And we were young…"

"I've spent all this time being angry at you…"

Saira sighed. "I know. I thought you'd forget about

me, and I about you. But honestly, what we have to-gether…"

Mia nodded. Saira could see it in her eyes. She still cared about her. Still loved her. Saira felt lighter.

"I'm tired. Do you mind if I go to bed?"

Mia nodded but stood there. Saira called room service and canceled her order. The little bit of appetite she'd had was gone. She was exhausted.

"Can I stay with you tonight? Sleep with you? Just sleep?"

Saira raised her brows, then nodded in relief. She needed Mia. She offered Mia some of her pajamas and crawled into bed in her robe. She turned to her side and Mia spooned her, hugging her tightly.

Saira couldn't help the tears that streamed down her face. Years of stress, shame, anxiety, frustration and loneliness poured out of her. Mia just held her, occasionally sitting up to wipe her tears, sometimes with her bare hands, other times with the sleeve of her pajama top. They didn't talk. Saira was totally spent. Mia held on to her, occasionally rubbing her back.

Saira fell asleep eventually and slept better than she had in years. When she woke, she turned over in her bed and found it empty.

Mia was gone.

# Eleven

Mia hated sneaking out of Saira's room early in the morning, but she didn't want to wake her. Saira had had a rough night and she needed to rest. She had debated writing a note but hadn't known what to say. She would see Saira soon enough, and she still didn't know what to say.

All this time, Mia had assumed Saira didn't want to lose her lifestyle and idol status. The truth was so much more heartbreaking. *I wish she'd told me in Fiji.* They would've worked something out. Mia would've helped Saira figure out what to do, could have been there for her, helped and supported her. Even as she'd held Saira last night, Mia had ached for her, the pain she had endured, the constant stress she was under.

Good or bad, she had several fires to keep her mind occupied. David was mad that she'd blown off the review of dailies with him. She still had to report to Chris, and if he decided to move forward with canceling the show, she'd have to break the news to the crew. She'd have to tell Saira.

She had asked the front desk to wake Saira an hour before her reporting time. The hotel was only fifteen minutes from the studio; that should've given Saira enough time to get there. Makeup and hair would be in the studio, so all Saira had to do was shower, throw on a pair of jeans and sunglasses and grab a tea. Saira didn't eat breakfast.

When she hadn't shown up fifteen minutes past her call time, Mia began to pace. She texted, called, then dispatched an intern to her room. She should've woken Saira and said goodbye, made sure she was okay.

Thirty minutes past call time, Saira finally stormed in. Her hair was pulled back into a severe ponytail, her face devoid of makeup. She'd thrown on a T-shirt and jeans that curved around her in just the right ways. She searched the room then made a beeline for Mia.

*Uh-oh. Should've left a note.*

Mia held up her hands as Saira approached, her quick walk and blazing eyes clearly conveying her anger. "Sorry I left the way I did, I didn't want to…"

"Did you call Rahul and ask him to do cameo and free promo for this show?" Saira was yelling and everyone was starting to stare.

Mia grabbed her arm. "Can we talk outside?"

Saira shook her off. "No thank you, we can talk here. Did you call Rahul?"

"You didn't want to ask him, so I did. As the producer of the show."

"On my behalf."

"I made no such representations."

"C'mon Mia." She gave her a pointed look and Mia shifted on her feet. She had called Rahul after Saira fell asleep the night before. He had been surprised to hear from her but clearly knew all about her and Saira. He'd asked Mia to stay the night to make sure Saira would be okay. When Mia had explained the situation, he had readily said yes. She'd known Saira would be upset but it had to be done.

"Rahul was happy to do it."

"Rahul isn't the one who has a problem with this— I do."

"Why? I get not wanting to ask your husband for a favor but you didn't. I did."

"He did it for me."

"As he should. You've done plenty for him."

Mia gave Saira a pointed look. She'd asked Rahul whether it bothered him that Mia was spending the night. That's when he'd told her that he was gay. Rahul also confessed that he had been the one who had inadvertently ended their relationship in Fiji. When Saira called him from Fiji, he'd been going through an identity crisis of his own. He had just been blackmailed by his first sexual partner and projected his fears onto Saira when he saw the Facebook posts of her and Mia. He had mistakenly gone to her parents, thinking he was protecting her.

After the conversation with Rahul, Mia felt even more like a shit for being angry with Saira. She had been nothing but a good daughter, sister and friend, had given up her own happiness for everyone else she cared about.

"He's my husband. That was my call to make."

All eyes were on them. This was not the time to have this discussion. "I am the show's producer and I am well within my rights to ask another star to make a cameo appearance."

Saira opened her mouth, then closed it. She turned on her heels and marched to her makeup seat. She waved her hands dismissively at the gawkers. Chris had given them two weeks to see if Rahul's social media buzz would create interest from the streaming services. The world of TV had changed since Mia had been an intern. Back then, it was all about advertisers and making sure the network affiliates would pick up the show. Now shows were sold not just to the network affiliates who aired it live, but to the streaming services, some of which got the show shortly after it aired, and others got it later. The amount they paid determined when they got the show, and the more demand there was for a show, the higher its purchase price. Rahul had already posted on Instagram announcing his cameo on #LifeWithMeera. It was approaching several hundred thousand likes just an hour after posting.

Mia sighed. She would have to set things right with Saira at the lunch break. Mia had newfound admiration for her. The woman had more responsibilities than anyone she knew. Mia felt stressed about paying her rent and the payment on her car, especially when she was between projects. She couldn't imagine what it was like for Saira, having to support her whole family, including medical expenses for her sister.

Mia made herself scarce once shooting started. Now that some of the kinks had been worked out and the actors had gotten a feel for each other, shooting was going well. During a break, David approached her. "Why didn't you tell me the network was thinking of canceling the show?" He was whispering, but Mia shot him a look and pulled him into a corner, keeping an eye for eavesdroppers. "Look, I just found out yesterday and I didn't want to panic everyone until it was a done deal. Sounds like the network is having trouble selling the show to the streaming services but I got Saira's husband to do a cameo and some promos."

"Yes, thank you for telling me about that as well. He's only available tomorrow so we have to get the script, costumes…"

Mia held up a hand. "I already talked to the writers' room. We're going to integrate him into the café scene we're already filming. Costume is going to use something they already have in Rahul's size, and I'll schedule a meeting with the entire crew after we wrap up tonight so we are ready."

David crossed his arms. "You seem to have thought of everything."

"It all happened so fast. I'm sorry I didn't consult you, but you know that none of this can happen without you."

"You forget I exist sometimes."

"Of course not! You know this show was over budget. I only did it because you were the director." She gave him an appeasing smile. Stroking egos was the most hated part of her job, but one that she had become very talented at.

Gail was the next one to corner her. She had heard the news from David's assistant, who had overheard him muttering to himself after *he* heard the news from an intern in Chris's office. Gail strongly suspected that David was sleeping with that intern, who was thankfully in her twenties but at least thirty years younger than David.

Mia sighed. She'd have to address the potential cancellation with the crew in the evening. By then, even the night cleaning crew would know that the show was on the chopping block.

During lunch, Saira walked off to her dressing room. Mia assembled a plate of food from the catering table and made her way to the trailer. She knocked several times before Saira finally opened the door. She was dressed in a long silk robe that hugged her body way too tightly. She looked at Mia with narrowed eyes, then stepped inside, letting her enter. The dressing room was a mess with clothes strewn everywhere, empty bottles of water here and there, and wilting flowers that hadn't been put in a vase. Mia made a mental note to send an assistant in to clean. Saira wasn't used to keeping herself organized.

Mia pushed some clothes off the coffee table and put the plate down. "I got you some quinoa salad and a falafel sandwich."

Saira eyed the plate. "And the mini crème brûlée is for you?"

Mia smiled. "I'd be willing to share if you let me explain."

Saira sat on the little dressing room stool, grabbed the sandwich and took a bite. As Mia suspected, she hadn't had any breakfast. "You shouldn't have gone to Rahul behind my back."

"I'm sorry. Chris gave me until this morning to confirm Rahul. You were in no shape for us to argue about this. I should've waited and woken you up early this morning, but to tell you the truth, I wanted an excuse to talk to Rahul alone." She gave her a small smile.

"You still think I'm sleeping with Rahul?"

"No!" Mia reached out and grabbed Saira's hand. She struggled to find the right words to explain her sudden urge to talk to Rahul, knowing how intertwined he was in Saira's life. It was a ridiculous idea, but Mia couldn't help feeling that she needed to connect with him; there was a missing piece to the puzzle of Saira's life, and Rahul was it. "You've been with him for ten years, known him since you were a child," Mia said, her voice tinged with a hint of envy. "I can't help feeling a little jealous of the time he's had with you. I wanted to know what he was like. I don't know, I thought it would bring me closer to you."

Saira looked down, then leaned over and gave her a quick kiss on the forehead. "Rahul was a child star like me. Except he has a very different relationship with his parents than I do. They were very exploitative, and Rahul had to hire a lawyer when he was fifteen to get independence."

"He filed for emancipation?"

"Yes, except there is no such thing in India. Children are considered property and there are no laws protecting children from the financial exploitation of their parents. His case went nowhere."

*Why didn't you file for emancipation with Rahul?* Mia wisely kept her mouth shut. If there was one thing that had been clear last night, it was that Saira believed it was her responsibility to take care of her parents and sister. She didn't feel taken advantage of.

"Finally at the age of eighteen, he had to give up all of the money he made as a child, including ongoing royalties for old films, and start new." Saira took another bite of her sandwich, and Mia handed her a bottle of water to wash it down. "It didn't end there. His parents sued him for ongoing support. That went on for like ten years, and they were going to lose but then they blackmailed him."

Mia's heart lurched as it suddenly became clear. "Rahul told me he's gay. His parents used that against him, didn't they?"

Saira stared at her. "He told you?"

When Mia nodded, she raised her brows. "You must've had a really good conversation. That's not something he shares. His parents threatened to out him and ruin his career. So he pays them hush money. It's supposed to be a monthly sum but it never ends. Every few months they have an urgent cash need. You know, his mother sees a diamond necklace she must have, or his father wants to buy the new MG SUV."

"That must be awful for him."

"I try to be the one person in his life that isn't exploiting him, that isn't always asking for things. I already asked him for help getting this role, and then getting you as producer...."

*You don't want to treat him the way your parents treat you.* Mia almost said the words out loud but managed to restrain herself.

"I'm sorry I went behind your back. But, if it makes you feel any better, Rahul was happy to do it."

"He also hands over the checks to his parents with a smile and some dialogue about how it's important to have a parent's blessing and good wishes for a successful life."

Mia slumped into the couch, not bothering to move

the saree that was underneath her. Saira stood and pulled her off the couch. "Don't sit there, you'll crush the saree. As it is, your costume people did a horrible job of pressing it."

"Pressing it?"

Saira rolled her eyes. "Ironing."

Mia stood and helped Saira redrape the saree on the couch. "Shit, this is for today?"

Saira nodded. "That's why I was late this morning. They delivered this to me and it had so many wrinkles, I had to get them to send me an iron and board."

"You ironed this?"

"You think I don't know how to iron?"

"Honestly, no. Have you ever ironed before?"

Saira smiled. "Actually no. I had to video call my assistant in India. It was like the middle of the night there. She talked me through it."

They both laughed.

"You know what, you shouldn't have to be figuring out how to iron a saree. I'll talk to costume about getting someone who knows Indian clothes."

"Thank you! I had to tie the saree myself yesterday."

"Why didn't you say something?"

Saira raised her brow. "And have you bite off my head? I've been picking my battles."

Mia sighed. "You're right. I've been so wound up about you, about us, that I haven't been really listening to you about the changes to the show."

Saira picked up the mini crème brûlée. "You can make it up to me by letting me eat this whole thing."

Mia grabbed a fork and popped a small bite in her mouth. "Not a chance. You know how I feel about sharing dessert."

Saira set down the small ramekin after gobbling the rest of the crème brûlée in three bites. "As I recall, you are perfectly willing to share your dessert, as long as I'm licking it off your body." She pulled Mia by the shirt and kissed her. Mia expected the kiss to be hard, but it was gentle, maddeningly so. Saira cupped her cheek and touched her lips to Mia's, gently kissing, tugging and tasting her. Their breasts brushed against each other, and Mia placed her hand on Saira's waist to tug her closer. She moved her hand to Saira's hips, longing to touch her through the silky robe, but Saira pulled back.

Mia's body was hot, her core wet. She needed Saira. She wanted Saira, naked and lying on that couch.

"If you're worried about the saree, I'll reiron it."

Saira smiled. "I don't want it to be like last time between us. Quick and dirty, as you Americans say." She touched Mia's cheek. "If you're ready to be with me, come spend the night. We can order room service, stay up late, wake up slowly in the morning. Tomorrow's not a workday."

It wasn't a workday for Saira—Sunday wasn't a shooting day—but Mia still had things she needed to do.

"On one condition."

Saira raised an eyebrow and Mia took a breath to try and cool her body. The idea of a night with Saira was enough to send her pulsing with need. "Wait up for me."

# Twelve

Rahul showed up for his cameo appearance with his usual swagger, dressed in jeans and a deceptively bedraggled T-shirt. Apparently, he had a fan base among the crew. They were all used to dealing with stars, so were reserved in asking for selfies, but the excitement was infectious. Saira remembered a time when people just asked for autographs; now she had to look selfie perfect everywhere she went.

She sneaked a look at Mia, who was standing back. They'd spent the night together, talking, making love, then talking some more. It was different than it had been in Fiji. There was more raw honesty between them. Mia had told her all about how hard it had been for her as a female producer in a male dominated industry, how she still wished for a reconciliation with her parents, even though they still didn't accept her sexuality. She'd never seen Mia so vulnerable and it made her feel even closer to her. Mia had opened up about how hurt she'd been when her parents kicked her out of the house, how she'd missed their presence in her life all these years. Saira better understood why she was so insistent on living her life openly. Mia had given up everything she valued, her home and the love she shared with her mother, so she didn't feel the crushing vice of her secret every day. It inspired Saira, made her want the same for herself, and for Rahul. While he was smiling for his fans now, he'd been stressed all morning. The story with Hosiang was catching steam on social media. They both lived in fear that a picture, an overhead comment could ruin their lives in a hot minute. It was no way to live, and she was done with it.

Saira introduced Rahul to Mia. They hugged as if they were old friends, and Saira felt a rush of warmth and irritation. "Now, now, you two better not be scheming behind my back." She'd meant to sound teasing, but the words came out accusatory.

Rahul kissed her on the cheek. "We are absolutely scheming. Somebody has to take care of you, and now I have a partner in crime."

"I understand you have a party to get to, so I'll see you both tomorrow." Mia raised her hand to wave goodbye but Rahul touched her shoulder.

"Why don't you come with us?"

Saira raised a brow. "Isn't it invitation only?" Her own agent had called her twice this morning to make sure she could go to this exclusive party with Rahul. She needed the exposure.

Rahul shrugged. "I'm invited. I don't think they'll mind if I bring plus two rather than plus one."

"This isn't India, Rahul. This type of thing isn't so casual here."

Rahul pulled out his phone. "I'm texting my agent now. He'll take care of it."

"Your agent is coming?" Her agent couldn't even get her a ticket let alone get himself invited.

"I told you that agent of yours is a dud. I don't understand why you don't sign with mine."

Saira sighed. "Because your agent would only take me because I'm your wife."

Rahul shrugged. "So?"

Mia turned to her. "Rahul's agent has a much bigger agency. He can probably do better for you."

Anger bubbled in her veins. She wagged a finger at both of them. "See, this is why I don't want you two scheming."

Rahul put an arm around her and kissed her head. "*Aare yaar*, we love you, and we want what's best for you."

Saira looked at Mia, who was studiously looking at her shoes. Had she said something to Rahul about loving her?

"Thank you for the party invitation, but I'm afraid I can't go. I have a lot of work to do and nothing to wear."

Rahul put both hands on her shoulders. Mia startled and Saira smiled. Rahul's friendliness took getting used to. "Work can wait, and Saira has plenty of clothes. I think you two are roughly the same size. If you don't like what she has, I'm sure your costume shop can come up with something."

Mia began shaking her head, but Rahul wasn't to be deterred. "We are not leaving without you. Go get your purse and whatever else you need. We'll stop by the hotel, pick up what you and Saira need, then go to my friend's house in the Hills to get dressed. My assistant will arrange for a hairdresser and makeup artist to meet us there."

"I really don't need all that I can do my own…" Mia's protests were completely drowned by Rahul's continued chatter. Saira smiled. It would be nice to see Mia all dressed up. She had just the dress in mind as well. It was one she hadn't yet worn and would look perfect on Mia.

When they got to the hotel, Mia seemed too overwhelmed with the clothes crammed into the small hotel closets, so Saira picked the dress.

Ned Hawkins's bungalow was a cute two-bedroom, three-bath modern house with a fantastic view of downtown LA. It had a step-down living room, open kitchen, and sliding French doors that led to a lap pool and hot tub. The living room walls were decorated with framed movie posters of Ned. Rahul had mentioned that this was Ned's "poor house," the one that he'd bought after he had to sell his mansion.

Apparently, he'd never accounted for the fact that leading roles in movies decreased as age increased. To Saira, the house was perfect. Spacious enough for parties but cozy enough for a family. She and Mia could have a house like this, one bedroom for the kids, and one for them.

"How is Ned?" Saira asked. She'd heard rumors on set that he was being hounded by the media as a home-wrecker.

Rahul shook his head. "I talked to him yesterday. The poor guy thought that after George came out, they could finally be together, but it's actually harder for them to even see each other with the tabloid reporters following them everywhere. Plus, George is in a messy divorce, and his lawyer told him to keep away from Ned for now."

They only had a half hour before the hair and makeup people showed up. and Saira did not want to waste a minute of alone time. She pulled Mia into Ned's bedroom. Rahul was using the guest room.

"I feel bad for the guy but he's a little vain, isn't he?" The bedroom walls were littered with headshots of Ned through the years. Saira found a hook at the back of the door and hung up the dresses she had brought for Mia, who was furiously texting on her phone.

She grabbed the phone from Mia's hand.

"How about we focus on having fun tonight."

Mia sighed. "I have a lot of work to do."

Saira pulled Mia into her arms and kissed the spot

between her neck and ear that drove Mia crazy. Sure enough, goose bumps filled her skin, and Saira ran her hands down her arms as she whispered in her ear, letting her lips brush against Mia's skin. "We won't stay long at the party, and afterwards, we'll go to my hotel and order room service for dessert. How about it?"

Mia wrapped her arms around Saira and pulled her close. Her mouth found Saira's lips, her hands slid beneath the tank top she'd thrown on after the shoot. She was wearing a bandeau bra and it didn't take long for Mia to push it over her breasts and find her nipples, rolling them between her thumbs. Saira deepened the kiss, her body eager for Mia's touch. Her own hands worked the belt on Mia's cargo pants, pushing them down along with her panties. Mia was so slick that Saira slid two fingers inside her, her own body responding to her lover's moans. Saira knew what Mia wanted. She broke the kiss and stepped back, then put the fingers she'd just had inside Mia in her mouth, tasting Mia's juices. Mia's eyes darkened.

She pulled down her jeans, chucked off her top and bra. Saira followed with her clothes. They came together at the same time, mouths hungry, breasts crushing against each other, hands exploring with fervor. Saira pushed Mia onto the bed, then grabbed her purse, pulling out Mia's favorite sex toy.

"Is that…" Mia's eyes went wide.

Saira nodded. "You left it in my hotel room in Fiji."

"I hope you've gotten good use out of it."

"It's a little hard to enjoy without you." She inserted one side of the double-headed penis inside her, then put the other side inside Mia, watching with pleasure as her head rolled back and she bit her lip. Saira moved on top of her, changing positions ever so slightly, her hand on Mia's stomach to balance herself. She tried but failed to control her own orgasm as Mia squeezed her breasts, rolled her nipples between her fingers and pressed and teased her core with her thumb.

She didn't count the times Mia orgasmed. It was hard enough to keep track of her own as years of pent-up desire and sexual frustration exploded out of her. It wasn't as if she hadn't had sex, not as if she hadn't used the toy, not as if she hadn't orgasmed with her other partners. But it was different with Mia, always had been. There was a freedom in her release, a connection with Mia that she'd tried to achieve with others and never had. It was as if there was an invisible string that connected their hearts and souls and the physical part of their relationship just allowed them to pull that string taut until they were joined together.

Afterward they lay there spent, entwined in each other's arms, kissing and touching, making up for years of missing each other's touch.

Rahul eventually knocked on the door. "I don't hear any moaning and screaming, so hoping you guys are done. The makeup and hair people have been waiting for an hour."

"Be out in a minute," Saira yelled. They both looked at each other and laughed. Saira glanced at her wristwatch and gasped. "Oh, my God, we've been in here for an hour." They'd lost track of time talking and holding each other.

They decided to take a shower separately, knowing that if they did it together, it would be another two hours before they emerged. When Saira emerged from the bathroom, Mia had already put on the dress that she'd brought for her. It was a silky, royal blue, one-shoulder dress that ended just above her knees. The hairdresser was busy getting Mia's short locks pinned so they framed her face in curls. She looked stunning. If Rahul hadn't gone through all this trouble to make the night special for them, she would've begged off, dragged Mia back into the bedroom.

Saira wore a shimmering silver dress in a twenties flapper style that ended midthigh. They were short on time so she settled for her hair in a quick updo and minimal makeup. Rahul looked stylish in designer jeans, an open collar shirt and a Balenciaga jacket. By the end, even Mia was excited about the night.

A limo took them the twenty minutes up the hills to the mansion where the party was being held. Mia stepped out in the heels that Saira had lent her and pulled down her dress. Luckily the paparazzi were not allowed past the gates. Saira and Rahul had waved to them from the window of the limo, while Mia did her best to slink as far down in her seat as possible. After being checked in by the security guard up front, they entered the foyer where they were greeted with hundreds of LED balloons floating in the ceiling, which created a mesmerizing starry night effect. Rahul's agent found them immediately. Saira turned to Mia. "Do you mind if I make the rounds with Rahul real quick? I need to get some selfies onto insta."

Mia nodded. She needed a few minutes to adjust to the party, and there were several emails that she needed to respond to. The bar was packed, so she picked up a pink cocktail that a waiter was passing on a tray and found a table on the terrace overlooking the pool. It was a cool night and most of the guests were inside, networking, socializing, gossiping. It wasn't her scene. Every now and then, she caught sight of Rahul and Saira, arm in arm, laughing, smiling, posing for photos. They were both so natural at it. Could she ever fit into Saira's world? It felt nice to dress up for a night, pretend she was going to the prom, but it wasn't something that felt natural.

When they were alone, everything seemed so easy, like they belonged together. But every time she stepped outside their cocoon, Mia was hit with the reality that Saira lived in a different world than she did. Saira was used to having hairdressers and makeup artists come to her house to get her ready for a party. Wearing designer clothes, air-kissing people, nibbling on little toasts with dribbles of sauce on them and calling it food—it wasn't something Mia could get used to. The dress she was wearing itched her skin, the pins in her hair hurt, the heels pinched her feet and she was starving. She'd taken five of the last set of cute square thingies that the waiter had passed. It took stuffing two of them in her mouth at one time to figure out it was something with crab in it. She'd drunk four screwdrivers just for the orange juice.

How would they ever make it work? Saira wouldn't be happy going to these parties alone, and Mia wasn't sure she could bring herself to do this on a daily basis. She stared as Rahul and Saira posed with the party hosts, a celebrity couple who would definitely bring some attention to their social media posts. Would Saira ever want to give up the fame and adoration? She was doing it to support her family but she also enjoyed the attention; it was clear in the way her face lit up every time someone asked to take a selfie with her.

"You in love with him or her?"

She turned to find herself staring into the brown eyes of Rahul's agent. Steve Machelan was wearing a funky plaid green suit that made him look like a dressed-up leprechaun. He gestured to the empty chair beside her, and she felt rude not nodding even though she had no desire to make small talk.

"I'm Steve by the way." He held out his hand and she took it, returning his warm smile.

"I know. I'm Mia." Despite his tragic sense of dress, Steve had a nice smile. He had a Southern California tan, well-styled sandy brown hair and perfectly white teeth.

"So, you in love with him or her?"

"I'm not in love with either of them. I'm producing her show."

"I know. *Life with Meera.* Rahul had me call in quite a number of favors to get you the gig."

She looked at him. "I didn't ask her to do that."

He quirked a brow. "Then why did she do it?"

Mia shrugged. "We were friends a long time ago. She had some issues with the show and knew I'd do a good job."

*Why am I even talking to this guy. It's none of his business.*

As if he'd read her mind, he leaned forward. "Rahul loves his wife. I suspect he loves her in the way one best friend loves another."

Mia stayed silent. She had no idea what Rahul's agent did or didn't know, and she was not in the habit of accidentally outing people.

"He wants me to take Saira on as a client, and I'd be happy to. She's talented and has a lot of potential. If *Life with Meera* is a hit, she'll have a lot of options. But…." He paused, as if waiting for her to fill in the blanks. Mia stared at him expectantly. She wasn't going to give him anything. He wanted to talk to her, he could keep up the conversation.

"But, I worry that their personal lives are about to implode."

Mia kept her face impassive but her pulse raced. What was Steve talking about?

He slid his phone toward her, and Mia gasped. On his screen was a photo of her and Saira from a few hours ago. They were both naked, their entire bodies on full display, Saira's hand between her legs, Mia's hand on her breast, their mouths devouring each other. The picture wasn't grainy; someone had taken it from fairly close range. Neither Mia nor Saira had paid attention to the windows in that room.

"I make it a point to have a full-time staff member who has just one task—to keep an eye on all the websites where freelance photographers—I refuse to call them journalists—put up pictures for sale. Know the sale price for these?"

Mia's stomach churned.

"It's five thousand dollars."

*What?*

"You're a nobody and the photographer didn't recognize Saira. He was after Ned Hawkins, hoping to get a picture of him and George. I was able to negotiate him down to two thousand."

Mia breathed a sigh of relief.

"But that doesn't mean that he, or someone else, won't be back. Two thousand for a couple hours' worth of work is good enough for most of these guys."

Mia's throat was dry. She took a gulp of the pink

cocktail and coughed as the sickly-sweet liquid went down her throat.

"So tell me, Mia, was this just a one-night stand, or do I need to worry that my client's marriage is about to end?"

Mia took another sip of the horrible drink, looking away from the picture on the phone.

Steve leaned forward. "I'm only looking out for their best interest."

She very much doubted that. He was looking out for his best interest, to get ahead of any issue that would affect his ability to get top dollar for his client, and therefore himself.

"What do you want me to say or do?"

He took his phone back. "I want you to tell me whether Rahul knows you're having an affair with his wife."

She nodded. There was no harm in acknowledging that.

"Is he gay?"

She looked up in surprise.

"Oh, don't give me that wide-eyed look. They won't be the first closeted celebrity couple."

"I'm done talking with you."

She pushed her chair back but he placed his hand on top of hers. "You don't have to talk to me. But hear me out. Rahul is at the top of his career right now. So is Saira. I understand she wants to work in LA. She can do that, bright future ahead and all that. But, not if she comes out. Not right now. I'm negotiating a major contract for Rahul, a part in an upcoming superhero movie. No matter how woke we all are, he won't get the part if he comes out right now. If Rahul makes it, Saira's career will follow. They are as lovable as Harry and Megan. Don't ruin it for them."

# Thirteen

Saira tried to keep an eye on Mia. Why wouldn't she come join them? She'd been sitting by herself on the lawn, nursing the same drink for the last hour. As she posed for a picture, she was glad to see Steve approach her. Maybe he would convince her to join the party. Despite how she hadn't wanted to come to this party, Saira was enjoying herself. The crowd was very different from Mumbai. People talked about art, literature, the industry. Gossip and fashion were staples in LA as well as Mumbai, but Saira found herself enjoying being a new face on the social circuit. People wanted to talk to her, get to know her. At least one director and two producers had asked for her agent's name.

As much as she hated to admit it, she liked the

adoration. When she was with her family, the conversation revolved around Kayra. Even before Kayra's illness, dinner talks were filled with questions about whether she had memorized her lines, what offers had come her way, which movies were currently casting and how best to position her to get the parts. Her publicist, agent and staff were always focused on what was wrong with her—is that a pimple starting on your face? Did you eat dessert last night, because there's an extra centimeter on your waistline. It was only when she was with her fans when she felt that somebody appreciated how hard she worked. It took her hours to memorize her lines for every day of shooting. If the scene was complicated, she practiced with her assistants. She prided herself on showing up to every shoot prepared to act well enough for one take.

Mia was still sitting at the same outside table she'd seen her at almost an hour ago. Why wasn't she enjoying this? Mia loved to talk art, literature, politics, pretty much any topic you threw at her. Why was she sitting in the corner sulking like someone had given her a sour Popsicle?

Once they were done taking pictures, she turned to Rahul. "I'm going to go see if Mia is okay."

He nodded absently as he continued his conversation with a director about some superhero role they were negotiating. Maybe Rahul was right, perhaps she should take advantage of his offer and sign with Steve. It had been Rahul introducing her to Peter Denton at a party that had gotten her the part for *Life with Meera*. Her agent had just negotiated the deal, he hadn't found it for her. Steve, on the other hand, was constantly bringing offers to Rahul. It was Rahul who turned them down. Always because of a man. Hosiang was in Tibet, which was much closer to India than California. Before Hosiang there had been London-based Norris. What if Rahul hadn't turned down the offers from LA? What if he had become a Hollywood A-lister rather than a Bollywood one? He could have come out, lived his life openly.

By the time she wove through the crowd, Mia was no longer there. She approached Steve, who was still sitting at the table.

"Where did Mia go?"

He shrugged. "Saira, can we talk for a second? There's something I need to show you."

The picture stopped her cold. How could she have been so stupid? The first thing she did when she entered a room was drop the curtains. She closed her eyes, not wanting the beautiful memory of being with Mia to be tainted by the sleazy-looking picture.

"I've taken care of this picture. But you need to be more careful."

Saira nodded. There was nothing else she could say. She had been stupid and careless.

"Thank you, Steve. I'll pay you back…"

He waved her off. "It was a minor expense. Trust me, it could've been worse. Pictures like these go for tens of thousands of dollars, in the hundreds of thousands if you're an A-lister. That's why these guys spend so much time stalking all of the houses in the Hills."

She turned to Steve. "Can I ask you for some career advice?"

"Don't come out now."

"Are you telling me this as Rahul's agent?"

"I'm advising you based on twenty years of experience as an agent in LA." He put a hand on her arm. "LA is not Mumbai. You're not going to be vilified for being a lesbian. Most people will celebrate your courage in coming out. You will get some backlash from some members of the LGBTQ community for being ashamed of your identity and perpetuating the belief that you need to be straight in order to succeed in life. But that can be countered with a narrative about how you are now standing up against the heteronormative culture in India and showing your courage in coming out." Now that he had her attention, he picked up his drink, a whiskey on the rocks from the look and smell, and took a sip before continuing.

"You're at the top of your career but from here, the slope is downhill. You've got a few more big movies, maybe a couple of TV series. After that, you'll be limited to roles specifically written for you, and those are rare. If you come out now, you'll get a lot of media attention, but it won't be good for your prospects. That saying—there is no such thing as bad press—is totally wrong. Movie financiers want a sure thing. They don't want a potentially controversial figure who the public can't buy in the role that she's portraying. I can't sell you for a lead part in a male-female rom-com if you are constantly in the press as the poster child for gay rights. I can't even sell you as the girl next door if the boy is going to be interested in her."

Saira took a breath. "So much for LA being more tolerant."

"It is better than most parts of the world. You're not going to get stoned to death for being a lesbian. You can live openly and freely. But yeah, we're a lot less liberal than we claim to be. It's one of those things no one talks about. We pretend we're above the rest of the world, that we promote gay rights. If you look at the well-known actors and actresses who're out, they are front and center at parties, talk shows and award ceremonies—but not in leading roles on the big screen. Movies have to appeal to a broad audience, and that includes parts of America where being gay is considered a sin."

Saira's legs were so weak, she didn't know if she could stand on them. This whole time, she had counted on the fact that LA was a way out for her, that she could build a new life. But if she couldn't support her family, then how could she leave Mumbai? How could she make a life with Mia?

# Fourteen

Could she call an Uber from a celebrity mansion? Mia stood at the doorstep debating how to get out to the front gate when Saira caught up to her. "I've been looking everywhere for you."

"I need to go home."

"Is everything okay?"

Mia looked around. There were so many people milling about, taking pictures, cell phones at the ready. "I think that pink cocktail doesn't agree with me. I feel a little sick."

Saira pressed her lips, then pulled out her phone. "I'm calling Rahul to send the driver for us."

"No, you should stay, enjoy the party. You need to

network. I think I saw Steven Spielberg and Kevin Blum earlier."

Saira hesitated. It was just for a second, but enough for Mia to see the want in Saira's eyes. She squeezed her arm. "I'll take the car. Text me when the party's over."

Saira shook her head. "I'd rather spend the time with you."

The odd tone of Saira's voice rang a little alarm for Mia, but she couldn't pay attention to it with Saira looking at her like she was her entire world.

They rode in silence to the hotel. Once there, they spent the night making love, both of them hungry and eager and making up for lost years. They slept naked under the sheets, and this time when Mia held Saira, there was nothing platonic or comforting about it. It was late morning when they woke up to the hotel doorbell. Mia glanced at her wristwatch and startled at how late it was. She was used to waking up before dawn.

As Saira put on a robe to open the door, Mia checked her emails. Several from David with a bunch of tedious things she needed to take care of, one from Chris, asking her to prepare a pitch for the streaming services by tomorrow. At least the social media campaign was working. #LifeWithMeera wasn't big nationally but it was trending locally, which meant a lot in LA.

The sound of a metal trolley and the popping of a champagne bottle got Mia out of bed. She threw on the hotel robe and walked into the living room to see a room service trolley with a scrumptious-looking breakfast, a bottle of Cristal champagne and chocolate-covered strawberries laid out on the table.

"Where did all this come from?"

Saira waved to a note that the waiter had placed on the coffee table, picking up a chocolate-covered strawberry. "Rahul must have sent it. He does stuff like this all the time. Especially after he makes me pose for a million photos."

Mia wanted to say something but kept her mouth shut. Rahul was a genuinely nice person, but Saira couldn't see that he too was using her, like everyone else in her life.

Saira held out a strawberry. "I'll share."

Mia smiled and took a bite as Saira held out the strawberry, letting her mouth suck and lick Saira's fingers. She pulled Saira into a hug. "We were young in Fiji, unsettled in our lives, unsure of ourselves. We're not those people anymore. We can figure this out, Saira. We can figure out how to be together."

Saira nodded, then pulled out of her arms. "I am starving, and even the five-star hotels in India haven't quite figured out how to make pancakes, so I'm going to enjoy these while I'm here."

She sat at the table and added two pancakes to her plate from the stack. Mia picked up the card on the table and opened it. Her stomach turned. "Breakfast isn't from Rahul," she said dryly.

Saira raised her brows. "Well, are you going to tell me or keep me in suspense?"

"Steve sent this."

Saira stopped midchew, then recovered. She set down her fork. "I meant to tell you last night but we... um...got caught up with other things. I've decided to fire my agent and sign with Steve."

Mia's stomach turned even more.

"What made you change your mind?"

"I bumped into him at the party and he gave me some advice. I found it useful and realized that he knows Hollywood a lot better than my agent. He'll be better able to navigate it for me."

Mia's mouth was dry. She picked up a glass of orange juice and nearly downed half of it. She herself had suggested that Saira sign with Steve. But that was before her conversation with him at the party. "Did he show you the pictures?"

Saira stared at her for what seemed like forever. "He showed the pictures to you too?"

Mia nodded. "With a warning to stay away from you and not ruin your career. And Rahul's too."

Saira sighed. "He said something similar to me." She reached out her arm and grabbed Mia's hand. "Look, I'm not blindly following his advice. Unlike my agent, he's got a better network of contacts to help me land roles, and he's got a whole staff that does public relations. Not all agents offer that type of full service."

"I'm not arguing that he's a good agent. What

I'm wondering is why you selected him, knowing he won't support you living your life openly. He made it pretty clear that he thought you and Rahul should stay firmly in the closet."

"That doesn't mean we're going to listen to him. Rahul and I are on the same page that we're tired of living our life in secret, constantly afraid of being outed, considering each partner with suspicion. We're just trying to be smart about how we manage our careers so we don't end up like those stars who get invited to every party but don't have the money to buy a dress."

Mia pushed her plate of eggs away, her appetite gone. Those last words were not Saira's, but Steve's.

Saira moved and knelt next to her. She took both of Mia's hands in her own. "I'm going to find a way for us to be together, openly. But it's going to take time. I have to see what roles Steve can get me, develop a financial plan, talk to my family… There's a lot I have to do. I need you to be patient with me…. please."

It all made perfect sense. It hadn't even been a week since that day in the costume room when she first saw Saira. So much had happened that neither of them had had time to sit back and think or reflect.

She nodded and kissed Saira lightly on the lips. But the alarm bells in her head were loudly clanging.

Weeks later, *Life with Meera* wasn't completely off the chopping block but the knives had been set down. One of the streaming giants agreed to pick it up after seeing a clip from the first day of filming. As Mia suspected, Saira's charm and talent shone through the screen. But they were still on the hook to get filming finished in six weeks, and they were currently running two days behind schedule.

Mia slung her messenger bag across her shoulder; she needed to hurry to make it to the studio. She'd spent all morning stuck in meetings, and now it was almost lunch time and she and Saira had a routine. Six weeks had gone by since she and Saira had taken up together, but they still couldn't get enough of each other. Mia didn't spend every night with Saira, especially not after her makeup artist and David had complained about the puffiness under her eyes, but they did eat lunch and dinner together when they could. Mia had cooked for Saira a couple of times, and then there was room service. Mia barely slept five hours each night but she didn't care. She had waited for ten years to be with Saira and was going to savor every second.

As soon as she entered the studio, she knew something was wrong. According to the schedule, they should be in the middle of taping but everyone looked to be on break. The actors were nowhere to be seen, the camera crew and staff were scattered about, many at the catering table, which hadn't yet been set up for lunch.

David found Mia just as she began searching for him. "We have a problem."

"Clearly. What's going on?"

"You need to rein Saira in. She requested more script changes..." Mia nodded. She had started to go over those with Saira yesterday, but it had been in Mia's bedroom and they'd gotten distracted before finishing the full review.

"The other actors are getting frustrated. They get changes the night before, they don't have enough time to relearn their lines. We were on the sixth take for the last scene when I sent everyone to their trailers to go learn the lines."

Mia sighed. She'd been afraid of this. "Saira has script approval."

"I know. But at the end of today, we're going to be three days behind. It's not just the script changes. Saira isn't coming prepared. She needs constant reminding of her lines. We've been running late for the last week and everyone is tired. Saturday was supposed to be a half day but I need to extend it to catch up."

"I'll talk to her."

David shook his head. "I've already talked to her." He leaned in conspiratorially. "I heard that she's having an affair, and that's why she's so distracted."

Mia went cold. After the pictures that Steve had bought, she and Saira had been so careful. They never entered her hotel together. Mia had even figured out an entrance through the parking lot that was less public. For their afternoon romps, Mia always knocked loudly on her door and announced that she needed to go over script changes, or went to her dressing room before Saira and left after. The window shades were always drawn and white noise turned up high.

"David, you know better than to listen to set gossip."

He shook his head. "It's not just the gossip about the affair. I think she's busy preparing for another project. I was at a dinner last night and—" he looked around to make sure no one was in listening range "—one of my fellow directors… I can't name names…he said that he was casting for a movie and Saira's name came up. But her agent said that she wasn't available to read for the part because she was busy preparing for some big Bollywood project."

Her mouth soured. She had to admit that they didn't seem to have much time to talk between Saira's filming schedule and Mia's meetings, but Saira would have told her if she signed on to some big Bollywood project. Wouldn't she? How many times had she mentioned the various roles that Steve had found for her? She had even read for a supporting actress role in a major film. Saira hadn't gotten the part.

David was looking at her expectantly. Mia sighed. "It's really none of our business what Saira is doing. But her performance on our show is something we should address, and I will."

"You do that. We need to right this ship now."

Mia made her way to Saira's dressing room. Saira greeted her like she aways did, with a kiss that made

Mia forget why she'd come in the first place. She pulled away.

"We need to talk."

"Uh-oh."

"David's upset."

Saira nodded. "I know. And he's right. I've been messing up my lines, and today I forgot half my actions too. I sat down when I was supposed to be pacing and clapped by hands when I was supposed to slap my forehead."

"That's not like you."

Saira nodded. "Just been so stressed lately. I'm reading a ton of scripts, plus there's all this social stuff."

"Something's got to give. You've been going out three or four times a night. Can you skip the parties?" She kept her voice neutral. She didn't want to come across as the nagging girlfriend.

Saira sighed. "Steve thinks it's important I network in LA." She reached over and ran a finger down Mia's arm. "Then there's making sure I keep you happy." Her tone was teasing but Mia caught the stress between the words.

"We don't have to spend so much time together. I've been falling behind on my work too. I had to stay up until 3:00 a.m. last night just to get through my emails and invoice approvals."

Saira shook her head and pulled Mia into her arms. "No. That's the one thing we can't compromise on. You and I have waited so long to be together. We can't let the pressures of daily life keep us away from each other."

Mia nodded but her stomach was in a thousand knots as she looked at Saira. How had she not noticed the bags under her eyes, the paleness of her skin under the cream-colored foundation.

"Why don't I leave you to go over the lines for the afternoon taping."

"It's almost lunch. Are you sure you don't want to stay?" Saira ran a hand up her thigh and Mia's body responded immediately. She could spare some time, couldn't she? They could be quick.

She placed a hand on top of Saira's. "You need to practice your lines, and I need to go smooth things over with David."

Saira did that thing with her lips that was somewhere between a pout and a smirk, and it took every ounce of Mia's self-control to leave.

By week ten, they were six days behind on their taping schedule. David was ready to quit; one of the writers had already thrown a fit and walked off. The crew was upset because they had been working overtime, and everyone's temper was on the last string.

"No more script changes!" David screamed at her. They were in Mia's office, having just met with the editing staff. She and David had both missed an inconsistency between episode one and five.

"To be fair, David, neither one of us, or the writers caught that we had to change the episode five script."

"A problem we wouldn't have to deal with if we weren't wholesale rewriting the script as we tape."

"You were in love with the script changes. I'm the one who had a problem with it."

"For about thirty seconds, then you started sleeping with Saira and lost all control over the show."

Mia froze. *How does he know?* "That's a rude accusation."

David crossed his arms. "It's not an accusation— it's a statement of fact. You think no one notices that you two hole up in her trailer at lunch, and both of you come out looking all flushed and smelling of sex?"

Her face heated. Did everyone on set know? How could she have been so careless? Her reputation would be ruined. It was one thing to have an affair on set, it was another when their relationship was being blamed for the star's performance.

"Don't worry. The only people who know are Gail, my assistant, and me. We've done our best to quash the talk. Gail even went as far as to tell people that you're dating someone else."

Mia sank into a chair. There was no point in denying it. David pulled out the guest chair and sat opposite her. "Why are you protecting me?" It would've been so much easier for David to let the rumors take hold and have the network fire her. He'd been wanting to call Saira's agent and threaten nonperformance on the contract if she didn't improve. Mia had stopped him. Then he'd wanted to call a meeting with the network executives and change the schedule. Production delays happened on every show and film—it wasn't that unusual a request. But Mia had dug her heels in. She was still afraid the network would cancel the show.

David rolled his eyes. "Believe me, I'd like nothing more than to throw you to the wolves. But you're one of the best producers I've worked with. You're not a network ass-kisser, you care about the quality of the show and you don't try to blow smoke up my ass when something isn't working."

Mia smiled. It was actually quite a compliment coming from David.

"What do I need to do?"

He put up four fingers. "First, you need to tell Saira that she gets one last go at script changes. All of them need to be turned in in a day or two. That'll give us some time to review the changes and make sure we don't have more mistakes that require reshooting." Mia nodded. It was a reasonable request, and if she hadn't been so busy with her head between Saira's thighs, she would have insisted on that a long time ago.

"Second, you need to get us more time with the network. I need two extra weeks. We can make up the time in editing."

Mia bit her lip. "It'll be tough getting time on the actor's calendars."

"We can work around that. There are a number of solo scenes with Saira. As long as we have her, I can make the schedule work."

"The bigger issue is the budget for the crew's time."

David nodded. "That's an issue you're going to have to solve. I'll do my best to go with a skeleton crew, but you're still going to have to convince the network weenies to open their wallets."

Mia nodded. She had already calculated a week of extra budget and had a proposal ready, but that was if they had no further delays, which was wishful thinking.

"Third, you're going to give the crew the entire weekend plus Friday afternoon off."

Mia opened her mouth but David shook his head. "Don't protest. Everyone is exhausted and making stupid mistakes. They need a break. I've baked that into the time extension."

Again, Mia nodded. These were all things she'd been thinking about anyway.

"Last, you're going to break it off with Saira."

Mia froze.

"I'm not saying forever. Just until we finish filming. You are a distraction and we're at a critical point now. We can't afford to waste time. Plus, it's only a matter of time before everyone finds out. Unless she's ready to come out of the closet, it's not fair for you to keep at it."

As much as she hated to admit it, David was right.

# Fifteen

Saira rubbed her temples, closing her eyes with the hope that her headache would disappear. She had too much work to do. Mia had asked for all remaining script changes by tomorrow. On top of that, Mia hadn't had lunch or dinner with her, begging off with some excuse about meetings. She was a horrible liar. There was something going on. Had she found out about the Mumtaz Mahal role? Saira had been in discussions with the movie producers; they were offering 8 percent above her regular fee. It wasn't just the money. The role was amazing. She'd get to play a tragic historical character who inspired an iconic monument of love. The movie had international blockbuster written all over it. Even Steve was encouraging her to do it.

Saira had been hoping Steve would come up with a better option for her in LA. He had done better than her last agent but also given her the same advice that she needed to wait for *Life with Meera* to come out. There was some nice buzz about the show, but because Saira was still untested with American audiences, the offers coming in were limited to supporting roles that didn't pay even a quarter of what Bollywood was offering.

She had to discuss the Mumtaz Mahal role with Mia, but every time she tried to bring it up, the thought of how Mia would react stopped her. Their entire relationship felt as though it was held together by cello tape. Any day now, one piece would get ripped off and the whole thing would collapse. Mia said she was trying to give her the time she needed to figure things out, but not a day went by when Mia didn't ask whether she'd heard from Steve, or when she planned to talk to her family. How did she make Mia understand all the pressures that were on her? On top of everything, Kayra wanted Saira to come see her. Even if she used Rahul's private jet subscription, it was twelve hours each way. They were already behind schedule on filming, a fact that was stressing Mia out. Saira couldn't ask for extra days to go visit her sister.

She grabbed her purse and shook out two paracetamol tablets, washing them down with the can of soda sitting on her bedside table.

She looked at the WhatsApp message from Kayra.

I really need to see you, di. There's something important I want to discuss with the family. I can't do it without you.

What could it be? The last time Kayra had a request, it was to permanently stay at the Swiss center. Had she found another place, or did she want to come home? She had tried calling Kayra, but all she would say over video is that she wanted to talk to Saira in person. Her mother had no idea what was going on; all she said was that Saira had to find a way to go visit Kayra.

In the meantime, she had an impossible deadline for script changes, and she still had to learn her lines for the next day. Maybe it was a good thing that Mia hadn't come over. No matter how hard Saira tried, it was difficult to focus on anything when she was with Mia. She had fallen behind on so many important tasks: reviewing her accountant's reports, reading the new scripts from both her agents, learning her lines. All Saira wanted to do was be with Mia, spend time with her, suck up every last ounce of her. But that didn't leave much time for anything else.

Her phone buzzed with a call from Rahul. He was filming in Greece. She put the phone on Speaker.

"Isn't it the middle of the night there?" she said when she answered.

"Yes, but I miss my wife. I had to talk to her."

"You do know there is no one listening on this line."

"It's the truth, *yaar*. I do miss you. What happened with Jay is really troubling me."

She sat up. "What happened with Jay?"

"You didn't hear?"

She shook her head, then realized they were on a voice call. "No. I haven't been looking at the news back home. Too busy."

He sighed. "I hope you're sitting down."

She was, but she pulled a pillow closer and hugged it tight. Jay Goshal was a prominent director, and a really nice guy. Saira had worked with him on six projects. "He was leaving his apartment complex in Bandra, just getting ready to meet his driver in the garage, when a worker—I think it was a gardener or something—approached him and threw acid in his face."

"Oh, my God! No! Is he okay?" Bile rose in the back of her throat and her stomach heaved. She clutched the pillow to her stomach and doubled over it.

"Half his face, neck and the top of his shoulder are badly burned. He's still in the ICU. For security reasons, they won't disclose what hospital he's in. Last I heard, he'll make it, but it's going to be a long road to recovery."

"Give me a second."

She rushed to the bathroom and made it just in time as the meager contents of her stomach came up her throat. She could hear Rahul calling out to her from the speaker.

She returned to the bed.

"Are you okay?"

"What the hell, Rahul? How did this happen?"

"The guy who did it was a nutjob. Apparently, his only son just told him he was gay and Jay was his idol or something. He wanted to be a director. The father snapped, got a job in the apartment complex. You know how these guys are—they blame the celebrity for their problems, thinking by hurting us, they're somehow solving their own problems."

"No, they're punishing us. They think we're the ones to blame for whatever is affecting their personal lives. I mean, if Jay isn't safe in his own home, what hope do we have?"

"India's not ready yet, Saira. It's getting there, but not yet."

"How long, Rahul? Are we going to have to wait for our children's generation to be able to live openly?"

"I don't know. Look, it's not all bad. I mean, there was *Chandigarh di Aashiqui*—that movie where Vaani Kapoor played the transgender woman...."

"Yeah, a nice movie, except that Abhishek didn't cast a trans woman to play the role. Instead, he chose Vaani, who did a nice job, but she's not trans." Saira had been approached about that role but had declined it because she'd felt that a trans woman should play the role.

"See, that's what I mean. It's changing but not fully there. Next time, they'll cast a trans woman. Look, Sonam Kapoor played a lesbian in *Ek Ladki*

*Ko Dekha.* There's hope. Hey, imagine if you had taken that role?"

Saira wished she had. The movie was about a woman who had to come out to her traditional family in order to marry the woman she loved. It was only four years ago, but her parents had talked her out of taking the role. Kayra had finally been settled and happy and they didn't want her affected by any backlash.

"I wish I had. It would make it so much easier to come out."

"You're not still thinking of doing that, are you? Not after what happened with Jay?"

"How long are we going to wait, Rahul? It's never going to end, is it? There will always be someone dangerous out there." But even as she said the words, her stomach heaved. It was one thing to put herself at risk, but what if they came after her family? Kayra was safe in Switzerland and Mia was in America, but what about her parents?

They were both silent for a while, then Rahul spoke, "Hosiang said he's decided to leave the monastery. Being with me has made him realize that he has unresolved issues and he needs to figure them out."

"Are you getting back together with him?"

"He didn't betray me on purpose."

"It's not fair to him. He's trying to confront his truth and you're telling him to hide and lie for you."

"It's not by choice."

"Isn't it?" That's what Mia kept telling her. It was

a choice. Not an easy one but it was a choice. Mia had lost her parents. It hadn't been easy for her to live openly—it wasn't as if she'd gotten the acceptance she wanted—but she hadn't taken the easy path.

As if reading her mind, Rahul sighed deeply. "If you're thinking about Mia, she had more of a choice than we do. Yes, she had to fight against her parents, but you and I both know that if it was just about standing up to our parents, we would do it. Mia doesn't get thrown out of her job for being a lesbian. She doesn't risk her livelihood, she doesn't worry every time she leaves her house that a seemingly innocent servant will throw acid in her face. I mean look at Ned—he had to stay away from his own house for months because he was being called a home wrecker."

Tears stung her eyes. "How are we ever going to be happy?"

"*Yaar,* I called you 'cause I was feeling low, and now we're both even lower."

"That's life, Rahul."

She hung up with him and closed her eyes, her stomach still heaving. How was she ever going to keep her family safe if she came out? How was she going to be with Mia? Her head hurt. She needed time to figure it all out. Was Rahul right? Was this just something she couldn't have in her lifetime and should just hope that her children could have it in the future?

Her laptop pinged with another email. It was daytime in India and people were waiting on answers.

A little time. That's all she needed. Some space to catch up with everything she had to do so she could think clearly, figure out how she was going to sort out her life.

It was early morning by the time she finished with the script changes. She was tired and had to be on set in four hours. She had to get some sleep if she was going to be functional.

The next day just got worse. Saira had such a headache that she couldn't remember her lines. David sent her home. Mia was nowhere to be seen, supposedly in meetings with the network.

Saira had several emails from her Bollywood agent. She needed to make a commitment to the Mumtaz Mahal role. He'd managed to convince them to give her 8.5 percent above her normal asking fee. Nine months wasn't that long of a time to be away from Mia. *Maybe we can find a way to make it work. I can fly here once a month and Mia can come visit.* It was a nice thought, but Saira knew what filming schedules were like. Any free time she had would go toward any number of social events or endorsement deals. Mia would get busy with another project and she wouldn't be able to come. They would grow apart. Could their relationship withstand the distance? Mia understood what Saira was dealing with. She would understand, wouldn't she? If they hadn't moved on from each other in ten years, what was nine months of being apart? Steve had assured her that after *Life with Meera* came out, he'd have better offers for her.

Her accountant sent her a red envelope email. She opened it to find that an unexpected bill had come in from the ashram her mother frequented, and Kayra's facility bill was again higher than normal. He was asking permission to break one of her fixed deposits to cover the payments. Saira rubbed her temples. The fixed deposits were her savings, and she lost money if she broke the deposit before the due date. She looked at the invoice from the ashram but the numbers swam before her eyes. She slammed the laptop lid shut. There weren't enough hours in the day.

A WhatsApp message pinged on her phone. It was Kayra asking whether they could talk. Normally Saira tried to talk to her sister a few times a week, but calls with Kayra took at least an hour and she still had to memorize her lines for tomorrow. She couldn't have another bad day on set. A second later another text came in, this one from Mia, saying she was on her way to the hotel. Saira rubbed her temples. For the first time since she'd come to LA, she was not looking forward to seeing Mia. With Mia there, Saira wouldn't be able to focus on her lines, plus she couldn't keep putting off telling her about the Mumtaz role.

She washed her face and changed her clothes. Mia keyed into the hotel room. Saira knew something was wrong the moment she walked in. It was in the way her smile didn't reach her eyes, in the stiff way she walked and sat down on the couch with her legs crossed. She was wearing a black business suit. Mia hated business suits. She only wore them when she had to. Things must be really bad with the network.

"I'm sorry I didn't get my lines right today. I stayed up all night working on the script changes and didn't get enough sleep."

"So it's my fault?"

"I never said that." Saira went and sat beside Mia. She put a hand on her knee. "What is going on?"

"We need two more weeks to finish the show. The network isn't happy about it, but thankfully it's too late to pull the plug. They *are* going to torture me by giving me a ridiculously small budget in which there is no way I can have all the staff I need to finish filming. I'm going to have to fire Gail."

Saira squeezed her hand. She knew how much Mia valued Gail's friendship. "I am so sorry. But filming was scheduled to end anyway, right, so it's not like you're really firing Gail."

Mia squeezed the bridge of her nose. "Actually, she was supposed to be my assistant through the end of production. But the only way I can make the budget work is to let her go now. Which means more work for me, by the way."

"I am sorry." She didn't know what else to say. Mia seemed miserable, but Saira didn't have a way to make her feel better.

Mia opened her mouth, then closed it.

"You blame me, don't you? This wouldn't have happened if I hadn't screwed up my lines all those times."

Mia shook her head. "This happens on all shows. There are always production delays, the bosses are never happy, and at this point, I'm usually questioning my career choice."

"Then what is it?"

"A few people know about us on the show."

Saira's throat closed. "Who? How?" she choked out.

"It's just David, his assistant and Gail."

Saira's pulse raced. "Gail is a huge gossip. By now the whole crew probably knows."

Once again Mia shook her head. "We can trust David and Gail."

That was easy for Mia to say. She hadn't been betrayed over and over again, nor did she have to worry about what would happen if someone did leak their relationship.

She stood and paced the length of the small living room. "We can't meet in my trailer anymore. And you can't come to the hotel."

Mia was silent. Saira paced some more. How much did Gail and David know? Had they taken any pictures? She turned to Mia. "We should take a break. Just for a little while. Until filming is over."

"That's exactly what David asked me to do."

Saira stopped. "Okay, then we're in agreement."

Mia stood. "Actually, I told him no. I promised that we wouldn't get together while on set, but that our relationship is not up for negotiation." She gave Saira a hard look. "Glad to know where I stand with you."

Saira stepped back, her chest and throat so tight that she wasn't sure if she was even getting enough air. "That's not fair. I can't have our relationship go public now. We've talked about this. You know how much I have at stake."

Mia placed her hands on her hips and Saira stiffened. She knew this posture. "We've talked a lot about what you have at stake, but have you considered that I'm affected too? David has already implied that our relationship is affecting the show, that I've been too soft with you, that I've been distracted. This is a big show for me. I mess this up and I'm going to be stuck doing projects no one else wants. I don't want our relationship getting out any more than you do. But, unlike you, I'm not willing to throw away our relationship every time there's a bump in the road."

*She still doesn't understand.* They'd been having the same argument since Fiji. Mia saw everything as black and white; either Saira was willing to come out or she wasn't, either she was willing to give up her life in Mumbai or she wasn't; either she loved Mia or she didn't. How many times did she need to ask Mia for more time? Mia knew the position she was in, the stress she was under. Why couldn't she be more understanding?

Saira rubbed her temples. "That's not fair. I didn't say we should break up, I just think that a break might not be a bad idea—to protect us both."

As soon as the words were out of her mouth, Saira

knew it was the wrong thing to say. The look on Mia's face sent daggers through her heart.

"Have you ever taken a break from being a daughter or sister?" Mia grabbed her purse and wrenched the door open. "You don't take breaks from the people you love."

# Sixteen

The fact that things improved on set only made it harder for Mia. Saira had sent her an apology text and begged her to come back to the hotel room so they could talk. Mia suggested that they take the night to think on it. Saira had appeared on set looking fresh and bright. She'd delivered her lines flawlessly, and David had beamed. Had he been right? Was their relationship affecting Saira's performance? Maybe they had been spending too much time together. She had to admit that having the evening to herself yesterday gave her the time she needed to rework the budget that Chris had requested. She'd figured out a way to pay for two more weeks of the crew's time.

Maybe a break wasn't such a bad idea. Things had

been so intense for the last two and a half months, neither of them had any breathing room.

"Can I talk to you?"

How did Saira always manage to sneak up on her? Mia had just finished pouring herself a cup of coffee from the catering table.

They found a quiet corner in the studio. The crew was setting up for the next shot and Saira could get called any second.

"Look, I'm sorry about yesterday. I was stressed about messing up my lines, and I had just been thinking about how there is so much to do and so little time and...."

"And spending less time with me felt like a good way to make space in your day."

"Yes... I mean no. Wait.... just give me a second."

She put a hand through her hair and Mia instinctively reached out to stop her. "Don't ruin your do."

Saira leaned forward. "I love you. I've loved you since the day we met."

David called for the actors. Saira sighed. "Please try and understand where I'm coming from."

Mia stood rooted as Saira walked away. Saira loved her. They'd said it to each other in Fiji, but that was different. Mia had spent a sleepless night wondering whether Saira was tired of her. Whether Mia had misconstrued really amazing sex for love. Whether she was once again in a one-sided relationship and destined to be left alone.

The day couldn't end soon enough for her. She

kept herself busy in her office, afraid that if she were in the studio with Saira, she wouldn't be able to resist pulling her into a dark corner or her dressing room. She'd promised David that she would not be distracted during working hours and would leave Saira alone to focus on her lines. He hadn't been happy that Mia wouldn't break it off, but she reminded him of the countless relationships that happened on set, including one that he notoriously had with a previous actress. After being pinned in his glass house, he resisted the urge to throw any more stones at her. But that didn't mean he wouldn't go low and spread rumors if he felt she wasn't keeping up her side of the bargain.

Gail stuck her head in just as Mia was getting ready to leave. "Can I talk to you for a second?"

Mia nodded guiltily. She had yet to break the news to Gail that she wouldn't have a job. She was trying to find a way to keep her, but it wasn't looking good. Mia had put out feelers for other positions. It would be easier to break the news if she had options to give Gail.

Gail sat in the guest chair across from Mia. She clasped her hands. "You can't fire me."

"Excuse me?" It took a second for Mia to process what Gail had said.

"I know you're working the budget, and there's no way you're going to make it work unless you get rid of some people. Naturally I'd be at the top of the list."

While it was true, it still irritated Mia that Gail

had come to that conclusion. "Why would you make that assumption?"

She folded her arms. "Am I wrong?"

Mia couldn't lie to her. She shook her head. "I'm not done with the budget yet. I'm trying to find options. That's why I haven't mentioned it to you."

Gail leaned forward. "You're a horrible liar, Mia, always have been. You've been avoiding me the last two days, and you've stopped cc'ing me on the budget emails to Chris. I see the writing on the wall, but I'm here to ask you not to do it."

Mia sighed. "I'm sorry, Gail. I will do my best to try and find you something good."

"Oh, I'll find another job in a minute. My old show has been begging me to come back. I'm not worried about me, I'm worried about you."

"Excuse me?"

"Saira. I've been worried about you since you started seeing her."

"That's not fair." Mia and Gail were close but she'd been limited in how much she shared. She didn't need Gail to tell her all that was wrong about her relationship with Saira—her inner critic did a pretty good job of that.

"I've worked with you before. When the show is filming, you are hyperfocused. On this show, you've been distracted. You haven't been yourself."

"It's the biggest show I've done. There's a lot to do…it has nothing to do with Saira."

Gail pinned her with a hard look. "Tell me something, Mia—are you happy living your life in the closet?"

"What're you talking about?" Mia said wearily.

"You talk about how important it is to live openly, and here you are, sneaking around with a married woman. Tell me, are you enjoying hiding out in hotel rooms? Getting good at looking away when someone catches you staring at her? Having your friends lie for you?"

"Gail... I'm grateful you covered for me and Saira. Our relationship is complicated, I don't deny it. She needs some time to sort things out. She's got a lot of responsibilities. As soon as she finds a good project in LA, she'll come out and our relationship can be more open."

"I hope you're right but are you sure you can trust her? I hear she's signing some big period film for Bollywood."

"What? When did you hear this?"

"There has been chitchat about it for weeks now. Didn't Saira tell you?"

Gail had to be mistaken. There were always rumors and gossip about movie contracts.

"I'm sorry about the budget, Gail..."

Gail stood and gave her a hug. "Take care of yourself. Try and remember why you have your principles."

Mia put her forehead on her desk once Gail left. Her friend's comments had poured salt on the gaping wound that was her relationship with Saira. Hiding, sneaking away was wearing on both of them, but Saira had asked her for time and understanding and Mia had agreed to be patient. But, was Gail right about the effect it was having on Mia's job? Had she been so focused on protecting Saira that she'd jeopardized her show and career? David had accused her of the same thing, of losing control over the star of her show and letting it run over schedule and over budget. She took a breath. If the show got a second season, she would resign as producer. It wasn't fair to the crew if she couldn't handle Saira. She could get another job as producer, but she couldn't replace Saira as the love of her life.

The last month of shooting went smoothly. After Saira's declaration of love, they'd made up, but Mia saw less and less of Saira as their working days got longer and Mia got busier with editing. As much as she hated to admit it, Saira was better at remembering her lines when Mia didn't spend the night at her hotel.

The wrap party to celebrate the end of filming arrived way too soon. Saira was scheduled to leave the next day to see her sister in Geneva. Saira had promised to return to LA in a few days. Though filming had wrapped up, there was always something that came up in the editing process, and sometimes they needed actors to come back in to redub lines in the sound studio.

Mia had a bad feeling about Saira leaving. She

couldn't explain what it was, but there was a gnawing ache deep in her belly about saying goodbye to Saira. They were spending the night together, and Saira kept saying it was only a few days that she'd be gone but there was no real reason for Saira to be in LA. She didn't have another project lined up, and Mia was going to be very busy getting the show ready to air.

Mia made it to the hotel before Saira, who had texted to say that she was meeting with Steve and would be late. Mia hoped that Steve had come up with something good for Saira. They'd discussed the offers he'd brought her to date, and Mia hadn't been impressed. As much as she wanted Saira to pick up a project in LA as soon as possible, she knew the offers he'd brought Saira were not right for her.

The smell of flowers greeted her as she opened the hotel room door. A beautiful bouquet of pink and white peonies sat on the dining room table. Mia set down her messenger bag. The envelope with the card was open. Was it wrong to see who the bouquet was from?

Mia picked up the envelope. Saira was a star; plenty of people knew peonies were her favorite. Plus, any number of agents, studio execs, directors, producers, even costars sent flowers to each other, especially on wrap day. But something about the flowers called to her.

She opened the envelope, read the note, then placed it back on the table.

*Congrats to the new Mumtaz Mahal. See you in Mumbai soon.*

It was from her Bollywood agent. This was the movie David and Gail had told her about. She had asked around about it. There was a big project being financed out of Dubai, a period piece about the wife of the guy who built the Taj Mahal for her. The role was huge, but there was no way Saira would take it. The shooting schedule would be months in India. Saira hadn't even mentioned it to her. They had talked about all the other offers that Saira had received. Mia assumed Saira hadn't brought it up because she wasn't considering it. *She lied to me.* Was she even going to Geneva or was she headed to Mumbai?

Mia sat on the couch and buried her face in her hands. She had written this script from the beginning. Saira was never going to stay. Mia didn't doubt that she wanted to, that Saira loved her. But it took more than love and wanting to do what Saira needed to do, and Mia knew her well enough to know that she wasn't ready. Saira was used to being the heroine—of her family, of her country. She liked taking care of her family, being the provider. She enjoyed being the darling of a country. It was a lot to give up to come live with Mia in a crappy one-bedroom condo.

Saira had asked if Mia would be willing to give up her own life to come be with her. The truth was that Mia didn't have the courage either. Sure, she made excuses: she didn't speak Hindi, or any of the Indian languages; she had no job prospects in India. There wasn't exactly a demand for American TV producers with mediocre titles behind their name. The real issue was that she wasn't ready to go live in hiding, pretending to be Saira's friend or whatever, watching her lover go to parties with her husband and carry on with a fake marriage. This whole time, Mia had assumed she was on the moral high ground, wanting them to live openly. But wasn't she asking Saira for a sacrifice when she wasn't willing to do the same? When Gail had asked her whether she was willing to live in secret, Mia had recoiled. She wanted Saira to give up her whole life and come out, but if Saira seriously asked her to do the same, Mia couldn't.

Saira breezed in late at night. "So sorry I couldn't break away earlier. Steve and I had a lot to talk about, so we went and had dinner and drinks."

"Good meeting?"

Saira nodded. "He's in discussions to get me a small walk-on role in a really cool espionage thriller movie."

Mia let her go on telling her about the project. Her stomach was in knots, her mouth completely dry. "You got flowers."

Saira hadn't noticed. "Oh...who are they from?"

"Your Mumbai agent. Congratulating you on that role you just took."

Saira froze. "Listen, I was going to talk to you about that."

Mia narrowed her eyes. "When were you going to tell me? After you got to Mumbai, when you wouldn't have to face me?"

"After I got back from Geneva. I'm meeting with the film financiers there. The deal isn't final."

"I thought you were going to Geneva to sort out whatever is going on with Kayra."

"I am. Look, I haven't signed the final papers and the movie financiers want to meet with me. I think they're going to offer me more money. The financiers are from Dubai, and since I was going to be in Geneva, my agent got them to meet me there."

Mia didn't trust herself to speak.

As if reading her mind, Saira took Mia's hands in her own. "I am going to Switzerland to see Kayra. That was always the plan. This meeting only happened yesterday. This role, Mia, it's huge. It has international appeal. Even Steve thinks I should take the role because it'll help me land better in LA. I am only considering this project because it helps me ultimately get to LA."

She was looking at Mia so earnestly it cut through her heart. Saira really believed she was doing the right thing. "How long is the project?"

"Nine to ten months. But that doesn't mean I'll be gone the entire time. I'll come here, and maybe you can visit me."

"Visit you on set? Where you'll introduce me to everyone as what? Your ex-producer? Your friend? Your former lover? Or your secret girlfriend?"

Saira let go of Mia's hands. "I haven't figured it all out yet."

"Why didn't you tell me you were considering this movie?"

Saira looked away and Mia had her answer.

Mia swallowed against her tight throat. "You and I both know what's going to happen. You're going to go back to India and resume your life as a beloved and happily married star. You'll leave me waiting here for years before finally admitting that you can't give up your life there."

Saira was shaking her head as she spoke. "That's not fair Mia. You haven't even given me a chance. I can't topple my whole life in a day. I have to start with my family, prepare for what's coming. It's about their safety too. You know what happened to Kayra. I can't risk something like that happening to them." Her eyes were wet and Mia's chest burned. Saira would keep getting sucked into her responsibilities. Until she admitted to herself that she couldn't do it all, she would keep sacrificing her happiness, and Mia's.

Mia sank down on the couch and buried her face in her hands, unable to look at Saira. *I'm tired of waiting for you.*

Saira clicked on her phone and turned it toward Mia. She recoiled. "What is that?"

"That's a picture from a news story about a director I worked with in India. He's openly gay. Some guy threw acid in his face because he thinks Jay is responsible for his son being gay. That's a picture of him in the hospital. He's looking at months of plastic surgery and even then he's never going to look right. This happened just a few days ago."

"That's horrible." Mia sat on the couch and grabbed Saira's hand. "I'm so sorry that happened to your friend."

Saira squeezed her hand. "I know there's a certain risk involved in being a public figure. You get threats and stalkers no matter what. But you have to understand that India is where America was fifty years ago with gay rights—most of them still think the way your parents do. They think that when celebrities come out, they are corrupting their children, Westernizing them. Things are changing, but slowly. It was only 2018 when our Supreme court struck down the penal code that made homosexuality illegal. Until then, police threw people in jail and beat them for no other reason than a neighbor or family member's complaint."

"We've had this conversation so many times, Saira. I understand the risks in India are different than they are here. I thought you were ready to leave, to start a life here with me."

Saira sighed. "I am. I just need more time. We've waited ten years, what's a few more? It's just until my career takes off. Then I can move my family, and we can live together openly."

"That was your plan ten years ago."

It was her fault. Mia knew this was where it was

headed from the very beginning, but she'd let herself get sucked into a fantasy.

She cupped Saira's face. "I know you love me. I don't doubt it for a second. But you can't have it all. You can't have your fame, your lucrative movie contracts, keep your sister in that expensive facility, take care of your parents and live your life openly with me. You want things to be perfect for everyone, but that's just not possible. You have to decide, Saira. What are you willing to sacrifice for your happiness? For us?"

Tears streamed down Saira's face. Her own eyes were wet. She'd known they were headed toward this. Had avoided it, tried to tell herself there was a way they could work it out. It was too much to ask of Saira. She wasn't ready yet. Maybe she'd get there, but Mia couldn't spend her life waiting, hoping, living in the shadows.

"Can't you wait, just for a little while?"

The plea in Saira's voice shook her resolve. She could wait for Saira, couldn't she? What was a few years for the love of her life? It's not as if she'd had luck finding a life partner in the last ten years. Except she hadn't been looking for a life partner. Now Mia was ready for permanence. If anything, the time spent with Saira talking about the future, a home, children, date nights—it had helped Mia realized she was ready for all that. She wanted to come home to someone each night, have that special person she could take to the insufferable parties; she wanted to plan a future, including children.

"It's not fair to you or to me to put our lives on hold, waiting, hoping that things will change."

Mia pulled Saira into a hug, closing her eyes and breathing in her scent. Saira kissed the corner of her neck, then her check, and her mouth found Mia's. They kissed with all the pent-up passion of the past ten years, and the future they each knew they wouldn't have. They held each other for a long time, their bodies melded together. Mia finally broke free before she lost the last of her crumbling nerve. "At least we get to say goodbye this time."

She picked up her messenger bag and walked out of Saira's hotel room, and her life.

# Seventeen

Saira waited in the family lounge of the Clinique Lake Geneva. The glass wall overlooked snowcapped mountains and a landscaped garden that could've inspired a Monet. She sat on a lemon-yellow sofa that was hard on the back but too stylish not to like anyway. Mia would've hated this place. It was pretentiously beautiful and uncomfortably luxurious. Saira had spent the entire plane trip alternatively crying and arguing with herself. Finally after eight hours, she'd realized that she couldn't give Mia what she wanted. Saira couldn't choose between her own happiness and that of her family. She'd thought about begging Mia to give her more time. Mia was right, it wasn't fair to her.

Kayra came breezing in and gave her a warm hug, which Saira returned. Like last time, Kayra looked happy and healthy and Saira instantly relaxed. Whatever Kayra wanted to talk about, it wasn't bad news.

"Saira, I want you to meet someone." It was only then that Saira noticed a tall man, athletic, with sandy brown hair. He was wearing a stylish khaki jacket, jeans and a black T-shirt.

"This is Paul."

Saira stuck out her hand and Paul leaned in and hugged her. "It is so nice to meet you. Kayra talks about you all the time." He had a European accent that Saira couldn't quite place.

"Well, I must admit that she has kept me totally in the dark about you."

Kayra grinned and pulled Saira back down to the couch. Paul pulled up a chair across from them. "I wanted to tell you in person, after you met Paul. We're in love. Paul wants me to marry him."

Saira looked at Paul, who smiled back at her. He leaned forward. "I'm in love with your sister, and it's important to both of us that you approve."

"This all sounds wonderful, but how about you start from the beginning. How did you two meet? How did you fall in love? I want to hear it all." Paul and Kayra were only too happy to tell her the whole story. Paul was the son of a Swiss banker. He had come to Clinique Lake Geneva six months ago for a one-month stay. He didn't elaborate on why, just that he was stressed and needed to figure some things out. They fell in love. Initially Paul extended his stay but then his father refused to pay for it, so he'd been visiting every weekend.

"How does your family feel about Kayra?" Saira asked carefully. She was happy for her sister but Paul had yet to mention what he did for a living.

"They think she's been good for me. They've been on me to finish my degree and I've been making really good progress since Kayra's been helping me."

Saira smiled at Kayra. Her sister had managed to do her schooling online and even finish an international bachelor's degree. Saira herself hadn't studied further than the Indian equivalent of high school. It was hard enough to get tutoring on set and find time to study to pass her exams; there had been no time for college, especially once she'd had to start paying for Kayra's medical care. Saira had hoped that eventually Kayra would find a job and become independent.

"So what're your plans after you get married?"

Kayra leaned forward. "That's what we want to talk to you about. Paul needs a year to complete his studies but we don't want to wait to get married. I want him to live here with me."

Saira was sure she'd misheard. "Why would he live here? Don't you have a home of your own?"

He nodded. "I live with my parents, but they're not willing to support us until I finish my degree."

Saira shifted in her seat. She didn't want to rain on Kayra's happiness.

"*Di*, please, Paul makes me so happy. It's only a matter of a year, two tops. Plus, if we're living together, you're just paying a little more for him."

"Kayra, you know I'd do anything for you but… I am not sure I can afford to keep *you* here, let alone Paul too. This place is really expensive, and they just raised their rates."

The look on Kayra's face pierced her heart. Saira grabbed her sister's hand. "I can't afford to pay for you to stay here, but we can work something else out. Maybe you can get an apartment. I'll pay for everything until Paul gets on his feet."

"You want me to leave here?" Kayra's eyes got big. "*Di*, I can't. I feel safe here, I can't go somewhere else."

Saira sighed. She'd had this conversation with Kayra many times. "You have to at some point, Kayra. You can't live here forever. It's a hotel, not a home." She looked at Paul with some hope. "You two will want to start a real life together, in your own home."

Paul nodded at first. "Of course, but we just need a few years, to figure it out, you know. This place, it's so peaceful, so healthful, I can focus on my studies."

It didn't escape her notice that they started with a year, then two years, and now it was a few years. She rubbed her temples. She could barely afford to pay Kayra's way with the new rates at the facility. There was no way she could pay for Paul too. "Kayra, I'm getting on in age, I have maybe a few more years of being able to earn what I do now. I can't keep paying for you here." She looked at Paul. "I want to help you guys, I really do, but you're going to have to ask your parents for support if you want to live here."

Kayra stood. "So what, you're abandoning me? After everything I've been through because of you."

Saira's mouth soured. "Because of me? If I recall correctly, you wanted to do that movie. You were always jealous that I was the star. You begged me to get you a role."

Kayra's eyes blazed. "And you gave me the one role you didn't want."

"I gave you the only role they'd take you for. Do you think I didn't try? You think Ma didn't try? She sent your photo for every role that came my way. She hounded my agent. I didn't deliberately give you that show. It was bad luck you ended up with that show."

"Luck!" Kayra scoffed. "What luck I have, spending half my life in hospitals and treatment facilities while you get to enjoy the luxuries of being a big star."

Maybe it was the view of the snowcapped mountains, or the appearance of a waitress with three tall glasses of lemonade served in cut glass crystal. Everything that Mia and Rahul had been saying came crashing down. "Luxuries? I've had luxuries? I work eighteen hours a day, nonstop. If I'm lucky, I get Sunday off, and in that time, I think about more ways in which I can make enough money to support the family. Here you are living in the lap of luxury, going to the spa every day, taking nature walks, all charged to my account with no consideration as to what it takes to pay for all this."

"I didn't ask to be here, what happened to me…"

"Was not my fault."

"You're saying it was mine?"

Saira shook her head. "It was bad luck, fate, call it what you want. It was my duty as your sister to get you the best medical care possible, which I did. But now you're asking me not only to pay for you to live in this palace, but also support your fiancé?"

"You know I'm still getting therapy."

Saira tapped on her phone and pulled up the latest report from the center. "Your psychiatrist discharged you two years ago. The therapist you see is a wellness specialist. He's not a medical doctor. There is nothing you're getting here that you can't get at home." Then it hit her. She held up a finger and pulled up the invoice her accountant had sent her when he asked to break one of her fixed deposits to pay for the latest bill from the facility. He'd said the bill was much higher than usual. "Has Paul been living here with you? Have you been putting his expenses on my account?"

Kayra lifted her chin. "It's not that much….and we had no choice….I couldn't just see him on the weekends…"

"Do you have any idea how much this place costs? Do you know how much I've been stressing about money. How I'm making decisions based solely on how much money I'll earn? I just broke up with the love of my life because…."

"*Di*, I don't want to hear anything. I love Paul and you'll have to find a way to support us."

How had she never noticed how petulant Kayra was? How spoiled her sister had become? Saira had been so focused on protecting her, shielding her, giving her everything she wanted to make up for what she'd had to go through that she'd never noticed how entitled her sister was. Rahul had been telling her for years that Kayra was like an only child who was given everything she ever asked for.

Saira stood. "I am leaving, Kayra. You can finish out the month here, after that I'll let you know what arrangements I've made. I'm not paying for you to stay here anymore."

Kayra stared at her wide-eyed. "Ma is going to want to talk to you."

So Kayra had already discussed this with her parents. Of course she had. How had Saira missed it? Her parents and Kayra were always on the same page. Against her.

"I'm headed to Mumbai now." It was time for her to have a serious talk with her parents.

She breathed out when she stepped onto the tarmac at Mumbai airport. It was hot, sticky, and the air smelled of salt, fish and jet fuel.

Her regular car and driver were there to pick her up. She was greeted at her apartment complex by a crowd of fans. Someone had posted her arrival at the airport on social media and despite the early morning hour, a crowd had gathered. She told the driver to stop right before the building gates. She lowered her window and grasped the hands that came forward, blowing kisses at the gathered crowd. A little girl was hoisted on shoulders until she made her way to the car and handed Saira a bouquet of flowers.

Saira asked the girl her name, accepted a kiss on her cheek and took a picture with her. These were the moments she loved.

As she entered the building, the security guards lined up to greet her. There was a new person there she didn't know. He'd been hired a few days ago, and when he stepped forward to introduce himself, she thought about Jay and the acid in his face. Like her, he would've felt perfectly safe walking into his own home, wouldn't think twice about a new face. All that would change if she came out. She would have to live in a bubble, unable to interact with her fans, fearful of anyone she didn't know. Her life would be very different.

Her parents were waiting for her when she arrived. Their two-level, five-bedroom condo smelled as it always did, like sandalwood incense from the morning prayers. The living room was marble white floors, glass coffee and accent tables, and comfortable black leather couches. Her parents greeted her with warm hugs. Her favorite cutting chai, a strongly brewed cup with ginger and cardamom, appeared as soon as she sat down on the couch. She took a sip. "I've missed chai. Americans have no idea how to make a good cup of tea."

Her mother smiled. Parvati Sethi had been a beautiful and talented actress. She claimed her career had been derailed by the arrival of Saira first, then Kayra. Saira never knew what her father really did for a living. He had some family money, which he'd lost early in life, then was involved in several failed businesses. For a while he'd managed her mother's career and then Saira's, until she realized that he couldn't resist starting more businesses than he could manage. As soon as she turned eighteen, Rahul had made her hire a proper accountant. It hadn't been easy to take the power away from her father, but she'd had to do it—at the time, the family was close to losing their home. She took a deep breath as she sipped her chai. If eighteen-year-old Saira had the courage to tell her father he couldn't manage her money anymore, then she could do this now.

"You look tired dear, why don't you go rest for a little while." Her father patted her hand.

"Tell me what you want to have for lunch. I'll have the cook make it," Parvati added.

Saira was exhausted. She hadn't slept on the plane from Geneva. Her head hurt and nothing sounded better than some sleep and the cook's rajma chawal. Their cook had been with them since Saira was a child and old Lata *didi*'s red beans and rice were her comfort food.

She looked at her watch and shook her head. Due to the fog in Mumbai, the plane had had to delay departure from Geneva. She had a meeting with the movie producers in a couple of hours. The meeting with the financiers in Geneva had gone really well. They'd agreed to 13 percent above her usual fee. The casting wasn't even complete, and *Mumtaz*, as the movie had been named, was already creating buzz.

"I wish I had time to rest but I have a meeting in two hours."

"You sound so tired, *jaan*." Her mother put an arm around her. "Is everything okay?"

Saira smiled and leaned into her mother, taking some comfort in the way she squeezed her tight.

"I have to talk to you about a few things." She took another fortifying sip of the tea, letting the hot liquid strengthen her.

"Is this about Kayra?" her father asked. "Sweetheart, I know how much pressure you're under trying to launch your Hollywood career, but God willing, your show will be great and then you'll be earning in dollars."

Saira pressed her lips. "Dad, don't you think it's a bit much to have to pay for Kayra's fiancé, who is perfectly healthy, to stay in that really expensive place?"

"Don't think that way. You're supporting your sister. You know how hard it's been for her to be in a relationship. Paul is a nice guy."

"How would you know?"

"He came to the ashram last month to ask us if he could ask Kayra to marry him. So wonderfully old-fashioned."

*The extra charges from the ashram.*

"And you paid for him to stay at the ashram."

Her mother frowned. "So what, he was our guest."

"Ma, I had to break one of my fixed deposits to pay last month's ashram and clinic bills. Do you understand what that means? The money coming in couldn't cover the expenses, I had to dip into my savings. I'm getting old now, the leading roles are going to stop coming. We'll have to live off our savings, and then what? How long can that last?"

Her mother pulled her arm away, clearly upset. How could she not understand? Her mother had gone through the very same thing; when she'd tried going back to acting after taking a break, she'd been told she was too old for leading roles.

"Maybe after the next role it's time for you to start thinking about having children. The next generation."

*She can't be serious?*

"You want me to have children so I can work them the way I've worked all my life?" She must be misunderstanding her mother.

"What's so bad about the life you had?"

Saira stared at her mother. Rahul and Mia's voices were playing in her head. All her life, she'd vilified Rahul's parents and been grateful for her own family, assumed that they were letting her take care of them because they had no other choice.

"My entire childhood was spent on a set. I can't even remember what's real and what was a scene in a movie. I didn't go to school, play with friends or do anything other than work. I wouldn't wish that life on my children."

Her mother looked away. "If you were that unhappy, why didn't you tell us?"

"What choice did I have? We needed the money and you made it very clear that we'd lose our home if it weren't for the money I was bringing in."

Her parents were silent and Saira downed the rest of the tea. "But there's an even bigger reason why Rahul and I will never have children."

She had their attention now. Saira took a deep breath. This is what she'd come to do, and she had put it off long enough. "I don't love him, not in the way a wife should love her husband. In fact, I never have and never will love a man. I've been a lesbian all my life."

She met her parents' gazes, expecting shock and anger, but they just stared passively back at her.

"Is this about that girl in Fiji?"

She nodded."

Her parents looked at each other and her mother sighed. "When you were a teenager, you were only obsessed with the female actresses. Girls your age had posters of Salman Khan on their walls, but you had Madhuri Dixit. Then there was Fiji. At first, I thought you were just experimenting, but you were so depressed when we brought you back, it was clear what had happened there."

Saira could scarcely believe what she was hearing. Her parents had known all along. After Fiji, they made it seem as though it had been a one-time thing, that she'd lost her way, that she was experimenting. Saira had spent years agonizing over the decision to tell them that Fiji wasn't just her experimenting, cried buckets of tears over the guilt of how she'd treated Mia. It had all been for nothing. Her parents had known!

"If you knew, why did you push me to marry Rahul?"

"Saira, you're a grown woman now. I thought you understood when I explained it to you back then. You can't live your life like that. You heard what happened to Jay? Forget Jay, you've lived through what happened to Kayra, and that was because she misrepresented a religious figure. It would be one thing if you were a nobody. Maybe you could live your life quietly. But people look up to you. The public will blame you for every young girl that tells her parents she's a lesbian, and they'll take their anger out on you."

It was Saira's turn to look away from her mother. She couldn't argue with anything Parvati said. They were the same concerns and fears she had.

"I can't keep living a lie. I want to come out with the truth, go live in America where I can live openly."

Her mother shot her father a look. "Let me talk to my daughter alone."

Narayan didn't argue; he was more than happy to escape to the upstairs terrace.

Her mother turned to her after he'd left. "Saira, do you think I've spent my life in love with your father?"

It wasn't really a question Saira had thought about. Her parents weren't always lovey-dovey but they seemed to get along.

"Your father has been like my best friend. The same way Rahul is yours. Do you think I don't know about him? I've known both of you since you were children. Do you think any Indian mother would allow her *jawan* daughter to be alone in her bedroom for hours with a boy?"

Saira's eyes widened. "Then why did you want us to marry?"

"Because you are good friends, you understand each other and will keep each other happy. Marriage is not about love and romance. Sex and passion fade, especially when your arthritis kicks in—" she gave Saira a small smile. "—but what endures is when you have an understanding with your partner. When you are willing to share in their successes and their failures. That's what a lifelong marriage is. I knew Rahul would take care of you, treat you well, give you comfort. What can you hope to have with a woman? You will be shunned from India. All those fans that give you flowers and balloons when you walk through the door will throw rotten tomatoes and eggs at you. You want to leave your home and go live in America? Then what? You think you'll live happily ever after as a nobody?"

"I can be an actress in LA. The woman from Fiji, Mia, she's the love of my life. I can be with her there."

"What about us? You think that public, those people that are sitting outside our building right now will leave us alone? Kayra hasn't come to Mumbai because just the sight of the crowds stresses her. How do you think she'll handle the media attention?"

Saira looked away. Her mother grabbed her hand, pulling Saira's attention back to her.

"There was a time when I thought that I could have everything in my life. But I've learned that life is all about compromises. No matter what people say, women really can't have it all. We are mothers, daughter, sisters, and because we are stronger than the fathers, sons and brothers in our lives, we are the ones who make the sacrifices, who hold the family together."

Saira's stomach turned. Wasn't that exactly what Mia had said to her? That she had to choose—between her family's happiness and her own.

Parvati grasped her hands. "We need you to hold this family together. You don't want to pay for Paul, fine. You want us to reduce our expenses, fine. Whatever you say. But don't give up your life on the hope that you'll find happiness with that Mia woman. How long have you known her? Is she willing to give up her life for you?"

Saira bit her lip. Her mother squeezed her hands.

"What if it doesn't work out with her? You'll have destroyed your life, and all of our lives—for nothing."

Saira closed her eyes, letting the tears flow down her cheeks. She knew what she had to do.

# Eighteen

"Earth to Mia!"

Mia looked at David, who was frowning at her. "I've asked you the same question three times and you are off in space."

"I'm sorry, David. Just a lot on my mind right now."

They were in the screening room reviewing the first episode. The network wanted to release it as soon as possible, even before the other episodes were ready, to garner more interest in the show.

"I know what's on your mind. It's that announcement that Saira's going to star in the Mumtaz movie. She's not coming back and giving you your happily ever after, is she?"

Mia sucked in a breath. "No, she is not." David

had become a friend in the last few weeks. Turned out that he was a romantic and a fair share of heart-breaks had inspired his empathy.

He put a hand on her shoulder. "It's for the best. Trust me, actresses are a pain in the ass to deal with. They are so full of themselves, always wanting the spotlight."

*That's what I used to think too.* "I knew she was going to sign that movie. That's why I broke up with her."

"Still hurts to see it in print. I will say I notice a few more wrinkles on her forehead. I predict she won't age well."

Mia smiled and punched David playfully in the arm. "I appreciate what you're trying to do but it's not necessary."

"She's coming to the release party next month."

Mia sucked in a breath. That, she hadn't heard. "I can handle it." It had been two months since she'd last seen Saira. The last message she'd received from her had been a text—*I love you*—a few hours after Mia had left the hotel room, probably before she left for Geneva. That's it. Nothing since then. No "I've reached Mumbai safely." Or "I miss you." Mia hadn't really expected it, but that didn't stop her from want-ing it. She had avoided Saira's social media, but her days had been filled with images of Saira. Even now, her face was paused on the big screen, frozen in a half smile, half smirk. Mia closed her eyes. They had another month of editing before she could take a break. Except, how was she going to get Saira out of her heart and soul?

"You need to get out, meet people."

"I've lost count of how many women Gail has swiped right for me."

"Meet anyone?"

"About five someones." They had all been intelligent, beautiful women. The type of women who were ready to settle down and were perfect matches for Mia. She'd had five great dates, and none of them came close to making her heart beat the way Saira's image on screen did.

"You have to move on."

"Easier said than done."

"So you're going to spend the rest of your life pining for her?"

"Pretty much."

"If the show gets a season two, she'll be back here for several months."

"And will be another producer's problem."

David raised his brows.

"It would be too tempting to fall into her bed again. I can't do that to myself and to her. I won't produce another season."

"So I've been nice to you for no reason?"

Mia smiled. "Total loss for you."

"You wouldn't take up with her, even if you're single?"

Mia shook her head. "It's not the way I want to live my life, sneaking around, pretending... I'm trying to respect that Saira isn't in the same place in her life. But I'm not going to torture myself with stolen moments." She turned away from David. It was so much easier to say than to do. She'd spent every night away from Saira longing for her, crying for her, barely holding on to the last vestiges of control she had left to keep from texting or calling her. She pulled out her phone. "Do you mind if we take a break?"

David shrugged. "I could use a coffee." As he left, she opened up her Facebook account. Her birthday was two days ago. Her mother had sent the usual message wishing her a happy birthday and asking if she was "normal" yet. It was the only communication she ever received from her parents. The same message every year on her birthday. Mia never responded. She hadn't talked to her parents since she graduated from high school. They hadn't even come to her graduation, just signed the final school forms before she turned eighteen. She had lectured Saira about courage, but there was one thing she hadn't gotten the nerve to do, and it was about time she did.

*Mom, I am normal. I always have been and always will be. It's time you accepted it. If you can't, please don't contact me again.*

A part of her had been waiting for her parents to come around. She'd never said goodbye to them. It was time to do that. She hit Send on the message.

A text message popped up from Jessica, the woman she had gone out with two nights ago, one of the dating app matches from Gail's online swiping spree.

Jessica was a lawyer, had nothing to do with the entertainment industry and was classically beautiful.

Saira's face was still on screen.

She texted Jessica, inviting her to dinner. It was time to move on.


"You're wearing that to the premiere party?"

Saira twirled in front of the mirror. "What's wrong with it?"

Rahul clicked his tongue. "A little risky, isn't it? Too much on the nose?"

"Are you sure you want to come with me?" she asked.

"I wouldn't miss it for the world. Don't worry, my publicity machine is ready."

Saira took a deep breath. "Are we ready to do this?"

Rahul rolled his shoulders. "We will never be ready. But, it's time."

"I will miss your money. This hotel suite is far better than where the network puts me up." The hotel room was indeed splendid. A top floor suite, it had two bedrooms, a spacious living and dining room and closets that fit all the clothes she'd brought, as well as Rahul's.

Rahul laughed. "You know you get a settlement, whether you want it or not. It's in our prenup."

She shook her head. "I'm not taking it." She applied a last coat of lipstick, checked her makeup one last time in the mirror, then turned to him. "I don't want to be one more person who takes from you, Rahul.

I'm fine, really I am. I got a great deal on Mumtaz. They're paying me 1 percent above my usual fee."

"I thought they were giving you a lot more."

"They were, but I negotiated alternative terms."

Rahul offered her his arm. "Shall we?"

The party was being held in the rooftop ballroom of their hotel. Networks didn't always throw lavish premiere parties, but this one was doubling as a PR event. Selected press outlets had invitations. When Rahul and Saira stepped out of the elevators, they were directed to walk down the red carpet so the media could snap pictures.

Saira's eyes searched for Mia but she was nowhere to be found. *What if she doesn't come?* She took a breath as they made their way to the gathered media. It didn't matter whether Mia was here or not. Saira wasn't doing this for Mia. She was doing it for herself.

"Saira, love the dress. Can you tell us what you're wearing?"

Saira smiled. She'd had the dress custom designed. It was a strapless gown that fell to the floor with a front middle slit. It was a beautiful silk in rainbow colors.

"I'm wearing this dress to show my pride, and announce that Rahul and I are getting a divorce."

There were murmurs in the crowd, some in surprise, most in confusion.

"Why are you getting a divorce?" someone shouted.

Rahul put an arm around her. "We're getting a divorce because she's found the woman of her dreams, and I've found the man of mine."

There was a momentary pause before the gathered journalists all began hurling questions at once. Rahul and Saira spent thirty minutes explaining it all before an assistant finally moved them off the carpet. They were immediately accosted by actors and crew who wanted their own scoop of the announcement. It took a while before Saira was able to break free of the crowd and find some quiet on an outside terrace. The night was still warm. She took a deep breath, feeling amazingly free.

"Never a dull moment with you." Saira turned to find Mia, looking gorgeous. She was wearing a strappy emerald green dress that wrapped around her in a way that caught Saira's breath. Mia hated dressing up. Had she done it for Saira's benefit? *I hope she did it for me.*

Saira smiled. "I told you to give me some time and I'd figure it out."

Mia was still standing several steps away, looking wary. "What made you do this now?"

Saira wasn't going to wait for Mia to come running into her arms. She stepped toward her. "I finally realized what you and Rahul were telling me all along—my family has been taking advantage of me. All my life, my parents have made decisions based on what was best for them. I decided it's time for me to choose my happiness over theirs."

Mia stood there, maddeningly still. Saira took

small steps toward her. She looked like a deer caught in the headlights, ready to flee any second.

"I know you, Saira. You won't be happy abandoning your family."

She was only a few steps away from Mia, close enough to see the tears in her eyes. "You know me so well. I'm still going to take care of them. Just not in the style they've become accustomed to. I'm giving them the money I'm getting from Mumtaz, plus the apartment we own in Mumbai. They can live a comfortable life with that money if they spend it well. If they don't, then they have to figure out a way to earn some of their own. That includes Kayra. She's an educated woman, who is perfectly healthy and capable. I'm done being their ATM. If there are security concerns, I'll have to figure out a way to pay for that, but I have some ideas."

"What about your career? What about that big movie you just signed?"

Saira could hear the fear in Mia's voice. She couldn't believe it was really happening. Saira could barely believe it herself. She and Rahul had spent the last month planning their announcement. Both of them had lost at least five kilos because they were too anxious to eat. Now that it was done, Saira finally felt like a weight had been lifted off her shoulders, a lifetime of weight. It almost felt surreal, like a dream that she might wake up from.

"Mumtaz might be the last film I do, but I made a deal with them that they'd support my announcement. Turns out the main financier has a son who's trans. He's all about bringing social change."

Saira was close enough to see the tears on Mia's cheeks. She reached out, cupped Mia's face and wiped the tears with her thumbs.

"You shouldn't have done this for me," Mia said softly.

"I didn't do it for you. I did it for me. I knew my family had been been taking advantage of me, but I truly believed that they wanted my happiness. That's why theirs mattered so much to me. But when it came to it, what they wanted was for me to sacrifice my needs and wants for theirs. I am done living my life for them, and in hiding. I don't want to be without you."

She touched her forehead to Mia's. "I love you. I've loved you for more than ten years. If you'll have me, I want us to be together. I want a life with you. I want you to marry me."

Mia closed her eyes, and for a second, Saira thought her knees would give out waiting for Mia to answer. Then Mia lifted her chin, found her mouth and kissed her hard. When she finally pulled away, her eyes were shining. "I love you so much. Do you know how hard I tried to get over you? For more than ten years?"

Saira nodded. "I know exactly how hard. That's why I don't want to live another second without you. So will you stop torturing me? Will you or won't you marry me?"

Mia smiled. "Yes Saira Sethi, I will marry you."

She wrapped her arms around Saira's waist. "I will marry you, have your babies, I'll even produce your show if I must. I'll do whatever it takes to make you happy for the rest of my life."

This time when they kissed, it was with the sweetness of their past and the future to come.

\* \* \* \* \*

### UNDER THE SAME ROOF & KEEPING A LITTLE SECRET
### UNDER THE SAME ROOF
*Texas Cattleman's Club: Diamonds and Dating Apps*
by Niobia Bryant

Investigator Tremaine Knowles was hired to find stolen jewels—not seduce the prime suspect. But Alisha Winters is captivating...and hiding a secret that could change the case *and* the ongoing Winters-Del Rio family feud...

### KEEPING A LITTLE SECRET
*Texas Cattleman's Club: Diamonds and Dating Apps*
by Cynthia St. Aubin

Nothing will derail Preston Del Rio's plan to take over his family's oil empire—except a tryst with Tiffany Winters, daughter of his father's bitter rival. And now there's a baby on the way...

### RANCHER UNDER THE MISTLETOE &
### ONE NIGHT WITH A COWBOY
### RANCHER UNDER THE MISTLETOE
*Kingsland Ranch* • by Joanne Rock

Outcast Clayton Reynolds is back in Montana for Christmas, and all he wants is local veterinarian Hope Alvarez. But she wants no part of the man who ghosted her three years ago, until a heated kiss tempts her to play with fire!

### ONE NIGHT WITH A COWBOY
by Tanya Michaels

Workaholic Dr. Mia Zane decides the perfect cure for stress is one wild night with a sexy cowboy. Mia never expected that ranch hand Jace Malone would turn out to be a billionaire...or that she would be expecting his baby!

### BREAKING THE BAD BOY'S RULES &
### THEIR WHITE-HOT CHRISTMAS
### BREAKING THE BAD BOY'S RULES
*Dynasties: Willowvale* • by Reese Ryan

When former rock star drummer Vaughn Reed inherits a run-down ranch, he hires his best friend's sister to fix it up. But annoying little Allie Price is now all grown up—and too dang tempting...

### THEIR WHITE-HOT CHRISTMAS
*Dynasties: Willowvale* • by Jules Bennett

Ruthless businessman Paxton Hart says he always chooses money over love. So life coach Kira Lee vows to show the town's resident Scrooge that Christmas miracles can happen—and their fiery kisses are just the first step!

You can find more information on upcoming Harlequin titles,
free excerpts and more at Harlequin.com.

HD2in1CNM1023

# HARLEQUIN
## PLUS

Try the best multimedia subscription service for romance readers like you!

---

## Read, Watch and Play.

Experience the easiest way to get the romance content you crave.

Start your **FREE TRIAL** at
<u>www.harlequinplus.com/freetrial</u>.